The Remarkable Adventures of
TOM SCATTERHORN

THE HIDDEN
WORLD

The Remarkable Adventures of
TOM SCATTERHORN

THE HIDDEN WORLD

Henry Chancellor

OXFORD
UNIVERSITY PRESS

OXFORD
UNIVERSITY PRESS

Great Clarendon Street, Oxford OX2 6DP
Oxford University Press is a department of the University of Oxford.
It furthers the University's objective of excellence in research, scholarship,
and education by publishing worldwide in

Oxford   New York

Auckland   Cape Town   Dar es Salaam   Hong Kong   Karachi
Kuala Lumpur   Madrid   Melbourne   Mexico City   Nairobi
New Delhi   Shanghai   Taipei   Toronto

With offices in

Argentina   Austria   Brazil   Chile   Czech Republic   France   Greece
Guatemala   Hungary   Italy   Japan   Poland   Portugal   Singapore
South Korea   Switzerland   Thailand   Turkey   Ukraine   Vietnam

Oxford is a registered trade mark of Oxford University Press
in the UK and in certain other countries

British Library Cataloguing in Publication Data

Data available

ISBN: 978-0-19-272086-3

1 3 5 7 9 10 8 6 4 2

Printed in Great Britain

Paper used in the production of this book is a natural,
recyclable product made from wood grown in sustainable forests.
The manufacturing process conforms to the environmental
regulations of the country of origin.

COMHAIRLE CHONTAE ÁTHA CLIATH THEAS
SOUTH DUBLIN COUNTY LIBRARIES

STEWARTS HOSPITAL BRANCH
TO RENEW ANY ITEM TEL:

Items should be returned on or before the last date below. Fines, as displayed in the Library, will be charged on overdue items.

1|9|(1)		

CONTENTS

CHAPTER 1

LISTENING FOR FUN

At six o'clock the last yellow flash of sunlight dipped behind the mountain and night came up fast. The banks of cloud, which had been building slowly along the horizon all afternoon, now advanced in from the ocean, turning from white and orange to purple and black. And the wind was rising, too. It was not going to be a pleasant night. 'Too damn hot,' muttered the heavy, grizzled man as he stood in the doorway of the shack and squinted up at the black tentacles of cloud, silhouetted against the purple sky. Arlo Smoot could almost smell the storm coming. Reluctantly he made his way up the steep jungle path to the base of a tree where a set of steps was lashed. Shoving the torch he was carrying into his back pocket, he laboriously climbed up to a long narrow hut perched precariously in the crook of a giant tree. This was his office. From here he could see out over the jungle to the dark sea and the islands in the distance, now bathed in the strange purple light. Lightning flashed in the distance. Yes, there would be a storm tonight all right: a big one. Leaning out of the open window, Arlo Smoot shook the long aerial attached to the hut—it was secure—then he glanced back to the top of the hill to where his weather balloons were tethered in a cage. He could just see one large orange helium balloon dancing on the end of its rope. Still there. Good. He had lost all of them in the last storm.

Flopping down into an old swivel chair, Arlo Smoot rubbed his unshaven face violently, trying to wake himself up. It was too hot to work, and he had no enthusiasm for the night's task. Listening to hours and hours of radio reports, decoding the movement of aeroplanes, the patterns of ships out in the ocean, submarine communications . . . sometimes this job was very boring indeed. Idly he flipped on the banks of switches in front of him, and listened to the crackle of static as the radios warmed up. Maybe he could permit himself an hour or two of fun first. Yes, why not. After all, it beat working for a living. Wheeling himself across to the other side of the room, Smoot lifted aside some files on a shelf and, stretching his hand inside, pulled out a thick old textbook. He opened it precisely in the middle, to reveal a dog-eared red notebook hidden inside. 'For Smoot's Eyes Only' was scrawled on the cover.

'Yes sir-ree,' Smoot murmured, brushing the dust away. 'Known only to the Smootster.'

This little notebook contained all the strangest secrets Arlo Smoot had ever heard over the airwaves. They were shocking, bizarre, and downright unbelievable, and if Smoot ever found himself in serious trouble, he reckoned these little facts might just be worth a whole lot of money. His fingers brushed through the pages passing chapters headed *American Presidents*, *Chinese experiments*, *alien landings*, *UFOs*, *parallel universes*, *time holes*, until he reached the very end, and the page he was looking for.

'Mr Zumsteen, my main man,' murmured Smoot, staring at the mass of figures and dates. Why not go after the big cheese? After all this Zumsteen guy was turning out to be the missing piece in this whole jigsaw, and by now Smoot had become quite intrigued.

'Let's do it,' he said, and paddled himself back to the radio. Checking the date in the notebook, he punched some numbers into the computer, and listened as waves of white noise hissed across the room. It was all working; good. Standing up, Smoot turned and stretched, and noticed the figures of two children in the window of the shack down below. They looked up at him and he waved, and the tall girl and the young boy waved back. Knowing they couldn't hear him, he mimed putting on his headphones and pretending to be very bored, scribbling in the air. The girl shrugged her shoulders. Then he made a sign that the girl should put the boy to bed, and the small boy made a thumbs up in return. Then the girl blew him a kiss. Smoot blew one back.

Smoot smiled, then walked over to the door and closed it. They knew he was working now: there would be no disturbances. Perfect, as what he was about to do required intense concentration. Smoot sat down in the swivel chair and, putting on his headphones, began to work the machines with a practised hand. Arlo Smoot was a radio spy, and eavesdropping on other people's secrets was his profession. Through a web of satellite connections he could access the most advanced listening stations in the world, and then direct the microphones to pick up any sound, made anywhere on earth. Though many universities had begged for his skills, the military organizations of some very large countries paid him better . . . so this is what he did: he found out military secrets—for a price, of course—and he undertook some private work too, if he felt like it. But this was not all: for Arlo Smoot had a secret, a very big secret indeed, that in his humble estimation, made him probably the best radio spy in the business . . .

Slowly Smoot began to scan the airwaves, both his hands on the dials, adjusting his frequencies, setting and resetting the coordinates of his microphones. The constant, hissing roar of white noise filled his headphones. Smoot knew that sometimes it could be like this for hours, days even; he must be patient. And Arlo Smoot could be very, very patient. What was he searching for? Not the bleeps and tweets of battleships and submarines talking to each other: it was something much more interesting than that. For Arlo Smoot was directing his microphones to find forgotten sounds, obscure sounds, conversations from the past, still resonating through the upper atmosphere, and the sounds of the future, too . . .

Tonight, for some reason, Smoot felt lucky. He did not know why: perhaps it was the approaching storm; sometimes adverse weather conditions actually helped him find things. Slowly his fingers moved the dials, back and forward, his ears attuned to the smallest fluctuations in the hiss. To anyone else, Arlo Smoot was listening to nothing, just a badly tuned radio, crackling and fizzing. But Smoot was concentrating intensely, and already he was somewhere else, flying through the black ocean of noise, shining his torch into the darkness, hunting for something very specific . . . again he changed frequency, and again. The numbers spun. And then he heard them: distant at first in his headphones, barely distinguishable from the hiss and static, but to his well-trained ear they were there, buried beneath. Voices . . . human voices. Smoot's heart quickened a little, and he licked his lips. Even though he had done this thousands of times before, this moment was always like the first time. Voices coming in across the airwaves, ghosts from the past, the future, he couldn't tell yet, but people, emerging out of the fizzing fog towards him, strangers about to tell him their secrets . . . Smoot worked quickly now, focusing his microphones, making a series of minute adjustments to sharpen the sound. The machines blinked and flickered before him, trying to keep up.

'Smoot, you beaut,' he muttered to himself, smiling as he carefully peeled away the layers and layers of hum and static, filtering and refiltering the sound. Could this be him?

A minute later Arlo Smoot had got a clear signal. Instantly he knew he was in a jungle somewhere, as the noise of the insects was deafening. There was a jabber of voices—in a language he did not understand—a huddle of men, squatting in the dust. A village on the edge of the jungle maybe, a few piglets running around, the splashing of puddles . . . the vivid sound picture appeared before his eyes. Then a nervous English voice. It was him! He knew that man. He knew that voice.

'Smootie toot-toot,' he purred, turning up the volume. 'Did anyone tell you you're a genius?' This was exactly what he wanted.

'Where did you say he found it?'

'In a cave. Way, way down, masta. Very dark. He saw the belly shining.'

'When was this?'

'Oh—long time back. My grandfatha is old man now. He was just a boy then, like me.'

'And it was definitely a beetle, you say?'

'Oh yes, masta. Head, legs, big jaws like this. They all gone. Dust now. Just belly left, masta.'

'The belly?' said another voice. 'Well, well. Curiouser and curiouser.'

'And you painted it—I mean decorated it. These patterns . . . '

'Spirit patterns masta, yes. It's an ancestor. You understand?'

'I do. It's very beautiful. How much do you want for it?'

'You wan' buy?'

'Yes. I like it very much.'

'Oh.' The boy muttered something in another language. 'Is rare. I never seen before, ever.'

'Neither have I,' said another, commanding voice. 'Extraordinary, it feels rather like rubber, but it isn't. Makes you want to squeeze it, somehow. What on earth is it made of, August?'

'No idea. Some kind of fungus, perhaps. Definitely not man made. Not out here, at any rate. You buy it, Nicholas old bean. It's not a forgery.'

'Forgery? No forgery, masta. No no no. Is real ting. Beetle ancestor, masta.'

'I'd believe him if I were you, old chap. Give the lad what he wants.'

The negotiations continued, Smoot noting them down word for word. For him the excitement was always in the chase, hunting down the voices, what they said was not always that interesting. But this object, whatever it was, sounded intriguing; and Smoot found himself doodling what it might look like in his notebook. Egg-shaped, covered in dark patterns, made of a kind of clear plastic material, which the boy claimed was actually a beetle's abdomen. Could this be true? Smoot knew nothing about beetles but he thought it sounded pretty far-fetched. Eventually he stopped listening and made a note of the frequencies, then slid his chair across to a map, flicked open a page and made a calculation. Satisfied that he was correct, he drew three lines on the map in pencil with a ruler.

'No wonder no one knows where you are . . . ' he muttered to himself, as the lines intersected on a small cluster of islands out in the middle of the Pacific. They were so small he could barely see them. Smoot squinted hard at the map, then returned to his little red notebook, and recorded the following entry: 'Nicholas Zumsteen, August Catcher, Sir Henry Scatterhorn, purchasing strange "beetle" object on the Tithona Archipelago, November 28th 1961.'

Smoot leant back and rubbed his eyes, feeling very pleased with himself. This was something indeed. The strange story that he had been piecing together over the last year had taken a new and important twist. It was like a movie without pictures that was happening out there over the airwaves. First there was some kind of an elixir of life, which a guy named August Catcher had invented and some kid named Tom Scatterhorn had stolen. Then this strange, crazy guy named Don Gervase Askary had gotten hold of it. Now Askary wanted to find this Nick Zumsteen guy, lord knows why, and he was searching heaven and earth to find him.

'Betcha don't know what I know, Askary,' he smiled, absently flicking to another frequency and watching as the numbers settled onto a familiar wavelength that he happened to know came from the future. Through the static he heard familiar voices. Flicking several switches he brought the sounds nearer.

'The elixir is, I believe, performing very well, your grace,' announced a high nasal whine.

'Good. Excellent. Now, what about Nicholas Zumsteen?'

The deep voice boomed around a large space that Smoot always imagined to be some kind of cathedral. There was an awkward silence.

'Erm . . . he is . . . yet to be found, Don Gervase—I mean, your grace, but I guarantee we *will* find him. We just need more time . . . '

'More time,' replied Don Gervase, with a trace of anger. 'Does anyone even have the faintest clue where he is?'

There was no reply. Smoot imagined rows and rows of elderly men staring blankly at their master. He put up his hand.

'Please sir, I do. But I'm not going to tell you . . . ' he giggled.

'Hmm. What about his friend, August Catcher?'

The silence deepened. A chair creaked.

'Sir Henry Scatterhorn?'

'Nada,' Smoot cut in, out loud.

'How very tedious you all are.'

'There is . . . there is *Tom* Scatterhorn,' suggested a thinner, weasely voice from somewhere near the back. 'If your grace so desired, we could . . . err . . . quite easily—'

'Please, spare me. Do you really think I need your advice regarding a twelve-year-old boy?'

The silence was deafening now. Arlo Smoot could almost feel the fear seeping through his headphones.

'Does it not strike you as odd, that after many months, and much effort, none of you have discovered *anything* at all?'

There was a pause, and a couple of nervous coughs.

'Or perhaps you are not telling me the truth. Perhaps you *do* know where Zumsteen is. Perhaps you are helping him.'

'Your grace, we . . . we are doing our best. It just so happens that—'

'Your best is not good enough? Are you aware of the gravity of the situation?'

'Indeed,' added Smoot, in mock seriousness. 'How useless *are* you people?'

'We really are trying—'

'Are you? Really, are you? Lotus, would you mind?'

There was a sound of soft footsteps echoing on stone, and then the creak of a mighty door opening. Suddenly a ripple of anxious murmuring filled the hall. Smoot bent his head and listened closer. What was that which had just been brought in?

'I don't believe you have met one of these before?'

'My lord,' continued the pinched voice, clearly terrified now, 'this is the Council Chamber, I really must insist—'

'Lotus,' barked Don Gervase, 'unleash it.' A sharp click of fingers echoed around the room. 'You will be pleased to know, gentlemen, that they show no mercy and are always hungry. Goodbye; and good luck.'

There was a strange clattering, rushing sound, followed by a scream and a burst of static as the frequency was momentarily lost.

'Whoops-a-daisy,' murmured Smoot, impatiently scanning the airwaves for that booming voice once more. He had heard these scenes before, many times in fact, and he found them strangely compelling. Who were all these old guys that kept meeting their grisly ends, and what was that scratching thing that killed them? Arlo Smoot was so busy chasing the frequencies that he did not hear the dull thud of a car engine in the jungle far below. Then suddenly Don Gervase Askary was back on a quite different wavelength.

'Is it this way?'

'Indeed, my lord.'

'What is his name?'

'Arlo Smoot, my lord.'

'What?' said Smoot out loud. The voices seemed to be getting louder in his headphones. His fingers flew across the dials . . .

'No doubt he is listening to all this anyway. He calls himself the ears of the universe, does he not?'

'That is correct,' replied the thin, nasal voice. 'Umbrella, sir?'

'No. This won't take long. Up here?'

'Yes sir.'

'Ah! Good evening, Dr Smoot.'

The voice boomed so loudly that Smoot ripped off his headphones and stared at his machines in bewilderment. How did the voice become so loud? It wasn't as if he—

'I said, good evening, Dr Smoot.'

Smoot spun round to see a tall, narrow man in a black linen

safari suit sitting in a chair behind him. He had a large domed head, oiled hair streaked with silver, and peculiarly small feet. His skin was pale yellow and his eyes were a strange, milky green. He looked both elegant and hideous at the same time. The man smiled, dangerously.

'I confess I am somewhat perplexed to find you still here.'

Smoot shifted uncomfortably in his chair, his mind still spinning. How had *that* just happened?

'You know who I am, of course, so I shan't introduce myself. And you must have known I would be coming,' continued the tall man, evenly. 'After all, a radio spy of your calibre can hear anything and everything. The past, present, even the future. Am I right?'

Smoot smiled weakly.

'Any sound that has ever been made, you alone can hear. Sound travels for ever, I believe; it never stops. There are no secrets.'

'You have to know where to listen.'

'Indeed you do, Dr Smoot. And you do. Which is why I am confused.'

'Confused?'

'Very. You see, we have something in common.'

'Oh?' Smoot tried to look as innocent as possible.

'Yes. Odd, isn't it? You see, I am looking for someone. A man named Nicholas Zumsteen. He took part in an air race across the Pacific Ocean and it is rumoured that he crash-landed somewhere in Micronesia. Apparently he found a remote volcanic archipelago and made some remarkable discoveries there. Need I say more?'

Smoot considered his position. Of course he knew all this and much, much more besides . . . but should he let the cat out of the bag? Not for nothing, definitely not. Hey, beggars can't be choosers, and Smootie-toot's got to live, hasn't he? He knew this Askary guy was nuts, but he clearly had a large organization and almost certainly played for big bucks . . . string him along a bit.

'I'm not sure what you're talking about,' said Smoot, clearing his throat.

Don Gervase regarded him quizzically.

'No? That is a shame. How disappointing. And then we have Mr Zumsteen's friends, August Catcher and Sir Henry Scatterhorn. They too have mysteriously vanished. Have you heard of them, perhaps?'

'Never. Sorry.'

Don Gervase took a deep breath and frowned at the floor.

'But I could try to find them, if you like,' suggested Smoot helpfully. 'It may take time, of course. Six months, maybe more. And the costs, well, you know,' Smoot exhaled loudly. 'Getting a fix on individuals is never easy. No sir. Could be past, present, future, even. We're talking serious spondoolicks, señor. Muchas wongas.' Don Gervase fixed him with his large green eyes. He was marvelling at the gall of the man. Arlo Smoot shifted in his seat uncomfortably.

'You seriously want me to find these guys for you? Because you know if you do—'

'Don't make a fool out of me, Dr Smoot.'

Don Gervase twirled his long fingers into a knot. Where to begin . . .

'What if I were to tell you, Arlo Smoot, that you are lying through your teeth. You know all about Nicholas Zumsteen.'

Smoot did his best to look surprised.

'And August Catcher,' Don Gervase continued, 'and Sir Henry Scatterhorn too. And what if I were to tell you that you have been spying on me for months. You have listened in to my organization. You have heard of my little triumphs and my . . . setbacks.' Don Gervase eyed his prey carefully. 'You have been deliberately building up a picture of everything about me. What do you say to that?'

Smoot shrugged his shoulders.

'Very well then. I'll get to the point. Who are you working for, Smoot?'

'What do you mean?'

'You cannot be alone. Who are they?'

'Who are who?'

'Are they paying you to find it before I do?'

'No one is paying me anything,' said Smoot, and cursed himself that they weren't.

'Then why do you seek what I seek?'

'I don't "seek what you seek", man. Hey look, it's . . . OK!' Smoot threw up his hands. 'You're right—it's me, whatever. Sure, I'm listening in. For fun, right? Just goofing around. It's cool. "Let's go get the Zumsteen guy!" So what? It doesn't mean anything . . . does it?'

'That is for me to know, and you to decide, Dr Smoot.'

'Excuse me?'

'Enough,' growled Don Gervase, silencing him with a sweep of his hand. Arlo Smoot could see that the strange looking man was boiling with rage now; his head seemed to be visibly pulsing. There was an awkward silence, and in it Smoot spotted his small red notebook lying open on the desk . . . holy schmoley, he hadn't hidden it away! How could he be so darned careless?

'What to do, what to do . . . ' murmured Don Gervase, staring out of the window at the oncoming storm. 'I suppose you wouldn't have been so foolish as to keep any evidence of your treachery?'

'Treachery?' snorted Smoot, casually resting his fingers over the small red notebook. 'What is this, the Spanish Inquisition?'

'What is in that notebook?'

'Notebook? What notebook?'

'The one you have just put in your pocket, Dr Smoot.'

Don Gervase turned to look at him. Arlo Smoot smiled nervously.

'I . . . it's . . . just a diary, that's all. My diary.'

'May I?'

Don Gervase held out his hand. His large green eyes held Smoot's like a magnet, and Smoot felt his courage start to waver. There was no way this guy was getting his notebook. No smokin' way.

'Look, Mr Askary, I'm sorry for listening. I didn't know it was such a big deal, for Chrissakes.'

'Invoking the Almighty cuts no mustard with me, Smoot.'

Don Gervase stared at him hard, his brow furrowing. Then he smiled.

'Give it.'

Smoot shook his head.

'No can do, amigo. All kinds of stuff in there. Classified and all that.'

Don Gervase sighed and listened to the wind whipping through the trees outside. The sound concealed the soft footsteps of Smoot's daughter climbing up to the tree house with a phone in her hand.

'OK,' she said quietly, 'that's great . . . would you like to speak to him? Hold on I'll get him . . . hold on.'

The girl climbed up the steps and heard the strange low tones of a voice she did not recognize. A visitor? Reaching the top step, she peered in through the door to see the outline of a tall, narrow man sitting with his back to the door. Her father sat facing him, with a fixed, awkward expression on his face. She was about to walk in but something about the visitor's demeanour made her hesitate: something serious was happening here. She checked herself on the dark threshold and listened.

'So it seems we are at an impasse,' said the man in the dark safari suit. 'Which I predicted, of course. You see, Dr Smoot, I really *do* need to know where Nicholas Zumsteen is, and one way or another, I shall find out. I'm not sure you appreciate that.'

There was a heavy scratching sound on the roof—a branch perhaps. Don Gervase smiled hideously, revealing a set of blackened teeth.

'Oh, the suspense. It is killing.'

Smoot smiled nervously and wiped the sweat off his brow. This guy was seriously weird. Maybe they could strike a deal, to hell with the money . . .

'Listen,' he began, 'the problem is my notebook has—'

15

'Did you know that three hundred million years ago, the largest insect on the planet was a centipede?' droned Don Gervase, ignoring him.

'Is that so?'

'*Estraordinario*—no? An unruly beast, about four metres long, with no teeth. No teeth! Like a little old lady!'

'Really?' replied Smoot, trying to humour the tall man who was now chuckling to himself. 'Incredible.'

'Really incredible, Dr Smoot. It strikes its victims with its poisonous fangs, swallows them whole then dissolves them into a soup in its mouth. Bones and all. Ingenious, no? I like soup. Gazpacho. Do you like gazpacho, Dr Smoot?'

Smoot shrugged in confusion. Centipedes? Soup? This guy was even more insane than he looked . . . and creepy too, alien, somehow . . .

'Give me that book, Smoot, or I shan't spare you, or your children.' Don Gervase's large green eyes narrowed to slits and his voice dropped to a whisper, barely audible above the wind. 'My men have your daughter down below, right now. One shout from me, and she is dead.' Don Gervase uncurled his long, powerful fingers and waited.

'Give.'

Smoot glanced towards the dark doorway, and saw Pearl, his twelve-year-old daughter, standing there. Well, *that* was a lie. But Pearl looked terrified. Again there was a loud scuffling on the roof: what *was* that? Smoot was sweating freely now, desperately trying to think . . . something told him this guy was not going to pay for anything . . . there must be some way out of this . . .

'Well, Dr Smoot?'

Smoot struggled to hold Don Gervase's gaze. He felt the wind cooling the sweat on the back of his neck. The wind . . . that meant the window in front of the desk was open . . . suddenly a dangerous idea formed in his mind. Come on, Smootie-toot . . . He needed a distraction, just a moment, that's all. Perhaps Pearl . . . he stole another glance over to the dark doorway. Pearl was no longer staring at him. Her attention had been caught by something silhouetted in the open skylight, there was something up there . . . and in that fraction of a second, Don Gervase caught the flicker of Smoot's eyes.

'Tell me, Dr Smoot, why do I have this feeling that there is someone behind my back?' he muttered with a trace of irritation. With one deft move Don Gervase shook a small knife out of his cuff and flicked it open. There was a sudden clatter behind him, and Don Gervase whipped round rapidly to see an empty doorway. Pearl had fled. The second his back turned Arlo Smoot leapt to his feet and dived through the open window behind him, somersaulting down into the jungle. In the same instant the head of a vast orange centipede dropped in through the skylight and watched him go . . .

'That was very unwise, Smoot,' boomed Don Gervase, but Arlo Smoot did not hear him. Landing heavily in the undergrowth, he tore down the slope towards his shack, but as soon as he saw it he checked: there were the silhouettes of men, standing in the window. Moving around he saw the shape of a woman's feet lying motionless in the doorway. The housekeeper . . . his children . . . he must find his children.

'Pearl!' he shouted, his voice carrying away in the wind. 'Rudy!

Pearl!' Smoot flailed through the jungle, desperately shouting his children's names. The men in the house looked up from their search and pointed in his direction. He'd been spotted, but Smoot did not care.

'Dad!'

Smoot stopped.

'Pearl?'

'Dad!'

Somewhere behind him. Where . . . ?

'Pearl?'

The sounds of the men crashing through the jungle were getting louder now . . . Smoot doubled back and threw himself down a narrow path skirting the side of the hill until he tripped over a large tree stump.

'Careful . . . '

Smoot pulled himself up out of the undergrowth to see Pearl and Rudy huddled together in the tree root hollow.

'Oh my God,' panted Smoot, falling to his knees and grabbing them, 'you're safe . . . I thought . . . I mean, I never—'

'What is going on, Daddy?' asked Rudy, in a small frightened voice. 'What were those things going up the hill? I saw—'

'I-I don't know,' stammered Smoot, 'looks like the crazy gang have arrived.'

'Why do they want to kill *you*, Dad?' asked Pearl. 'What have you done?'

'Nothing!' replied Smoot vehemently. 'Nothing at all. Listening, you know, just—'

'Will they kill us too?' Rudy stared at his father with large, questioning eyes. 'Will they?'

Smoot looked down at his six-year-old son and thought desperately.

'No one is going to kill anyone, Rudy. There's just been some kind of serious misunderstanding. You kids just stay right here, and don't make a sound. Promise? I'll lead them round the mountain and when it's all over I'll come back and get you. Just stay right inside this hole. Will you do that for me? Pearl? Will you?'

Pearl looked into her father's grizzled face and saw a fear that she did not recognize. Her dad was always so confident, always joking. He was deadly serious now.

'OK. But—'

'Not a sound.'

Seconds later Arlo Smoot crashed off into the jungle. The two children burrowed themselves into the tree root and huddled together. Confused shouts rang out above the howling wind.

'What if Daddy doesn't come back?' whispered Rudy. Pearl said nothing. 'Pearl?'

'Sssh, they'll hear us.'

There was silence.

'I want to go with him.'

'Rudy—'

'I'm going to find him.'

'No you're not. Stay here. Come on Rudy.'

'It's not up to you. He didn't make you in charge, it's—' Rudy never finished his sentence, because Pearl had clamped her hand firmly over his mouth.

'Listen,' she whispered, very quietly.

There was an odd clicking sound to the left, from the direction of the tree house. It appeared to be coming closer. Very definitely, getting louder. The children burrowed deeper into their hole and covered their heads. The clicking seemed to be passing down the path right in front of them. Pearl dared to open one eye, and could scarcely believe what she saw. There right before her was a vast centipede, as high as a donkey and as wide as a car, making its way down the path. Its brownish scales glittered and bent in the moonlight, its pale legs clicking as it went. The creature was so close that Pearl could almost touch it. Stifling a gasp, she covered Rudy's eyes with her hand.

'Don't look,' she breathed.

'What is it?'

'Rudy—'

'I'm not looking,' he said out loud. And then Rudy saw it too.

'Wow.'

Rudy gasped as the long rear spikes of the centipede trundled past, then before Pearl could stop him he slithered out of the hiding place to watch it go.

'It's a centipede,' he whispered loudly, stepping onto the path. 'A massive centipede.'

'Has it gone?'

'Yep.'

'Well come back in here.'

'OK OK,' replied Rudy. 'Don't keep hassling m—'

He stopped mid-sentence and looked up. There, directly behind him, was another one. For a moment the small boy and the vast insect stared at each other in the moonlight.

'Rudy, what are you doing?'

There was no answer.

'Rudy, what did Dad say? Rudy!'

Angrily Pearl leapt out of the hiding place towards her brother.

'Rudy, you've got to list—' And then she saw what he saw, silhouetted against the purple sky. Her mouth opened to make a sound, but nothing came. The centipede's antennae twitched slightly, and its head arched forward. A blob of saliva dribbled out of the long wide jaw and hit the damp earth. It seemed to be raising itself higher, preparing to strike. Pearl's fingers groped for Rudy's and grasped them tight.

'When . . . I . . . say . . . go . . . run . . . up . . . the . . . hill . . . ' she whispered, concentrating so hard on standing still that her teeth chattered. 'Ready . . . '

Higher and higher climbed the creature, like a living escalator, till it was almost directly above them. Its orange brown claws opened . . .

'Steady . . . '

The creature's front legs waved uselessly in the air as two glistening black antennae uncurled from the top of its head and extended towards their faces, almost touching their skin . . .

'GO!' she screamed.

WHUMP!

Mud and leaves flew up into the air as the colossal creature hurled itself at the ground, but it was too late. Already Pearl and Rudy were tearing through the jungle, creepers slashing their faces and arms.

'Keep going!' shouted Pearl, as they sprinted up the hill. 'To the weather station! We can hide in there!'

'I can't do it! I can't go as fast as you!' screamed Rudy.

The enraged creature tore up through the jungle behind them, twisting over rocks and smashing through the bushes. It was getting louder every second . . . Pearl grabbed Rudy's hand and they ran together.

'Come on Rudy!'

'I can't,' whimpered Rudy as Pearl's strong grip dragged him along, 'it's faster than me.'

'Rubbish!' shouted Pearl. But glancing back she saw he was right, she could see its dull red eyes, hear its clattering armour . . .

'Nearly there,' she breathed, her heart hammering as they burst out of the undergrowth at the top of the hill and sprinted across the stretch of flat open ground towards the hut. All around the wind was howling through the trees and the sky was purple and black. Pearl glanced back to see, first one, then two more centipedes explode like orange missiles out of the undergrowth and hurtle towards them. They must catch them now, surely . . . Ignoring the clattering of legs behind her, Pearl picked up Rudy with a strength she did not know she had and ran with him in her arms. Her legs were burning now . . .

'They're catching up!' screamed Rudy, his eyes widening as the creatures approached. The hut was getting closer, closer, and beyond it there was nothing but the rough rocky promontory and the cage of weather balloons. If they could just hide in there . . .

'Get back!' shouted a voice.

'Daddy!' screamed Rudy as they raced around the side of the hut.

'The weather balloons!' shouted Arlo Smoot, glancing back desperately at his children. 'Get to the balloons . . .'

Arlo was slashing at an enormous centipede with a long rusty section of radio aerial as it darted at him this way and that, trying to skewer him with its claws . . .

'Daddy!' screamed Rudy one more time. 'There's more than one!'

And on the creatures came, converging now, as Smoot cut and slashed at the line of terrifying tangling spikes before him. The four centipedes were all abreast, forcing them back towards the rocky promontory. In moments they were all three together, cornered. The children huddled behind the cage of weather balloons, and Arlo Smoot stood before them, panting, his aerial raised aloft. This was the last stand. He had done his best, but it was not enough. The wind lashed at their faces, and great balls of rain began to hammer down. This was it.

'Well well, Dr Smoot,' came a low booming voice above the wind. Two weasel-faced gentlemen and a girl with a long black ponytail marched forward, forcing the snarling centipedes apart, and Don Gervase strode between them.

'Snick, snack! Snick, snack!'

Don Gervase fenced with an imaginary beast in mid air. '*Bravissimo!* I like this very much. He's good, yes?' Don Gervase laughed. 'Touché Smoot!'

Pearl and Rudy stared back at the tall man in contempt.

'He's a lot braver than you!' shouted Pearl, her heart bursting. 'Leave him alone.'

'I regret to say, young lady, that is not possible.'

Arlo Smoot stood motionless, his long aerial still raised in both hands, ready to strike. He was not quite sure what to do next.

'Yes, yes,' said Don Gervase, motioning Smoot to put his weapon down. 'Please, Dr Smoot, please, we are not cave-men . . . '

Slowly Arlo Smoot lowered his weapon.

'That's better. Now, where were we? Ah yes, I asked you for some information. I wonder whether you have reconsidered your position.'

Smoot said nothing, but his mind was whirring. This guy and his hideous creatures were going to kill them anyway, whatever happened . . .

'Surely you were not so naive as to think you could really *escape*, were you? And take the children too? Really, Dr Smoot. Now please, hand it over.'

Smoot threw down his stick and, still facing Don Gervase, took a step back till he was standing next to Pearl and Rudy. Don Gervase watched them impatiently.

'Is that a yes, or a no?'

Arlo Smoot did not reply, but he knew exactly what he was going to do. It was a crazy idea, but so crazy that it might just work . . .

'The balloon rope . . . ' he whispered out of the corner of his mouth. It was so quiet that Pearl could hardly hear it.

'Grab the balloon rope, Pearl,' he whispered again.

Pearl stared ahead at Don Gervase, and her fingers closed around the thick cord attached to the orange helium balloon, secured to the bolt at the bottom of the cage. Smoot glanced back at Don Gervase and smiled.

'I'll give you what you want, Askary!' he called out. 'But you must promise me something first.'

'Promise? *Promise?*' Don Gervase shook his head, clearly enjoying the irony of the situation. 'I really don't understand. What must I promise?'

'Rudy too,' whispered Smoot. Pearl's other hand gripped her brother's tightly.

'Dad,' whispered Pearl between her teeth. 'What about you . . . '

'Just hold on tight,' he hissed. Then he turned back to Don Gervase. 'Let the kids go!'

'Ahh,' exhaled Don Gervase. 'Always the children. Les kiddi-winks! Please don't sacrifice my family, la-di-da. I knew it! Very well, Smoot,' he said, looking at the two bedraggled children cowering beside the cage. 'They are nothing to me.'

'Good,' smiled Smoot, and he withdrew the small red note-book from his back pocket. 'It's all in here!' he shouted.

'All?'

'Zumsteen, Scatterhorn, Catcher. Everything you need to know.'

Don Gervase's eyes glittered keenly, but then he checked himself.

'How can I believe you?'

'You can't. That's for me to know and you to find out, isn't it?'

Don Gervase smiled thinly.

'Touché, Smoot. Now hand it over.'

Smoot turned to face Rudy and Pearl.

'Come, children,' he said in a loud voice, 'I don't think

Mr Askary here is going to hurt us.' He stood beside Pearl, slipping his arm around her waist, and his notebook into the large side pocket of her skirt.

'For God's sake don't let go . . . ' he whispered as loudly as he dared. 'I'll catch the end.'

Pearl's face was white with fear, and she gripped the rope tighter.

'Daddy?' Rudy looked up questioningly at his father. He still didn't know what was going on.

'What is it, Rudy?' said Smoot as calmly as he could. 'Just hold your sister's hand now.'

'We . . . but we can't go with him,' gasped the small boy, looking at Don Gervase in terror. 'He'll kill us, won't he?'

'Don't be so silly, Rudy. Watch me.'

Smoot stepped forward towards Don Gervase.

'All we've got to do is stick together . . . '

Suddenly Smoot lashed out with all his force at a steel lever on the side of the cage, and the back door crashed open. The next instant the orange weather balloon bobbled against the wire mesh roof, then the rope pulled clean off its fastening, dragging Pearl and Rudy away with it. It was much too fast for Arlo Smoot.

'Hold on to me, Rudy! Hold me!' screamed Pearl, taking huge leaps to keep up with the accelerating balloon. The young boy clung to his sister's waist as both their feet left the ground.

'Daddy!' shouted Rudy desperately. 'Daddy help!'

Smoot sprinted after them, lunging desperately at the trailing rope as the balloon began to rise, flying towards the edge of the cliff.

'He's slipping!' screamed Pearl, one hand around her brother, the other wound around the rope. 'We'll both fall . . . Dad! We can't do it!'

Smoot was running flat out now. He could see what was going to happen.

'Rudy jump!' he shouted at the top of his voice. 'Jump!'

The edge of the cliff was rapidly approaching and the balloon picked up speed. In seconds they would be over . . .

'Jump Rudy—please!' screamed Pearl.

'Daddy!'

In the next instant Rudy let go and tumbled down into his father's arms, sending them both sprawling to the ground. The balloon lurched high into the air and was buffeted over the edge of the cliff, taking Pearl with it.

'Whatever happens I'll find you!' shouted Smoot. 'I promise!'

Smoot's words were torn away by the wind as Pearl twisted desperately to watch them go.

'Dad!' she screamed helplessly, but it was too late. Pearl was on her own. She glanced down at the inky sea boiling far below her, and the waves thundering against the cliffs. If she let go now— she would fall down there. She couldn't do it. It was too far. She must hold on. Pearl gritted her teeth and ignoring the pain in her fingers she wound the trailing rope around her feet. She was being blown higher and higher now, straight out to sea. Maybe she would reach the distant islands, maybe not. She couldn't look. Pearl buried her face in her shoulder and sobbed.

'The notebook, Dr Smoot, if you please.'

Arlo Smoot hauled himself to his feet, cradling Rudy in his arms. He stared in disgust at the hideous man before him.

'The notebook.'

Smoot nodded towards the ocean and spat roughly.

'She's got it.'

Don Gervase's eyes narrowed in silent fury.

'Well it looks like you'll just have to tell me all about it instead,' he growled, and an unpleasant smile spread over his face. 'Unless of course, you'd like to have *another* attempt at escaping. Though I don't believe that you will get very far.'

Smoot glared savagely at the wall of giant centipedes, barely under control.

'I thought not. Remove them.'

Don Gervase watched as Arlo Smoot and Rudy were shackled and led away, then he took one last look at the small orange balloon disappearing fast across the ocean. The girl had very little chance of survival . . . and then he noticed something rather unusual. Out at sea a dark column of water was rising, whipped up by the howling wind. The column was growing taller and taller, lurching this way and that like a giant black cobra, till it connected to the low cloud above.

'A waterspout?' said the girl in white beside him, with a wicked grin.

'So it seems, Lotus,' murmured Don Gervase, 'how convenient. Dr Smoot!' he boomed merrily. 'Dr Smoot, you mustn't miss this.'

Arlo Smoot, holding Rudy's hand, sullenly turned back to face the sea. Before him, a huge waterspout connecting the black sea with the black clouds above danced across the waves . . . and there, blowing directly into its path, was the tiny orange helium balloon with Pearl hanging from it. Any moment now she would be sucked in . . .

'Oh my God . . . ' he whispered. It was almost too painful to watch.

'Pearl, watch out!' shouted Rudy, in the vain hope that his sister could hear him.

Pearl had seen it, but there was nothing that she or anyone else could do. A moment later she felt the valiant little balloon being sucked up and into the watery, spinning air. She began to rise, swinging round and round, her legs lifting so that she was almost horizontal, rotating faster and faster around the thick dark column of water rising up from the sea.

'Please,' she whispered, 'please stop . . . '

The force was so great now it felt as if her arms were wrenching out of their sockets . . . higher and higher the balloon climbed up the wall of grey water, whipping her eyes, stinging her face . . . it hurt so much she could hardly breathe . . . she opened her mouth in a silent scream . . .

Don Gervase watched in genuine fascination as the balloon and the girl accelerated into a dizzying blur, a small orange shape sucked up towards the vortex in the cloud . . .

'Sweet dreams, young lady,' he growled. 'I think you may be the first person ever to—'

But Don Gervase never finished his sentence, as the next instant there was a sudden hollow boom, like thunder, and in that second both the balloon and the girl disappeared. The waterspout lurched on drunkenly across the waves. She had gone . . .

BANG!

Tom Scatterhorn opened his eyes and sat bolt upright in bed, sweating. He had just been having the strangest dream, but even as he tried to remember it, he forgot what it was. What was that noise? Turning to the window, he saw shadows flaring against the curtains, and pulling them to one side he saw the moonlit harbour of Dragonport spread before him, erupting in a massive firework display. Red skyrockets, blue bombs, purple screamers, cascades of white sparks . . . the whole river was exploding. Tom groggily pushed his thick tangle of blond hair aside and then he remembered—it was the opening of the Dragonport festival. Of course it was. Uncle Jos had promised it would be a great show: fireworks, acrobats, street entertainers and—what was that? There was a great cheer and suddenly he saw, high above the river, a small orange balloon drifting down through the smoky air. It seemed to have appeared from the clouds. Tom rubbed his eyes violently and looked again. Was that real? It looked real. And as the fireworks exploded all around he could just make out the figure of a girl, hanging on to a rope beneath.

'What did I tell you, Tom?'

Tom looked down and there in the street below was Uncle Jos just pulling up on a bright red motorbike. He pointed up at the girl on the balloon drifting over the streetlights towards the marsh beyond.

'Dragonport crazees!'

'Daft as brushes,' said the thin figure in the sidecar, pushing up her goggles and smiling. It was Aunt Melba.

'Hello, Tom dear. Glad you found your way in. How was your trip?'

'Fine,' mumbled Tom. 'The train was very late.'

'Excellent excellent. Great to have you back, lad,' rasped Jos, 'so much to tell you—'

'But not now,' interrupted Melba firmly, 'the boy must be exhausted. Tomorrow, Tom. And don't get up too early.'

'Right.'

'Night then.'

'Goodnight.'

Uncle Jos waved cheerily, then shambled after Melba to the front door of the cottage. With a loud yawn, Tom flopped back down onto the bed and saw his mobile phone buzzing. Lazily he picked it up and read the message.

Tom darling. Arrived safely. Just in time as raining hard now. Dad v excited to be here. Hoping to go up river in the next few days. Love you, M xxx.

So they had arrived, that was good. Tom smiled, and closed his eyes, vaguely wondering who would be so brave, or so foolish, as to float on a balloon through a firework display. But before he found the answer, he was already fast asleep.

CHAPTER 2

THE SAME: BUT SOMEHOW DIFFERENT

'Just like the bad old days, eh Tom?'

Tom smiled and blew on his scalding hot tea.

'Almost.'

The summer sun was pouring in through the small windows of the fuggy little kitchen, and Tom was just polishing off a particularly large plate of eggs, bacon, and toast. Uncle Jos, a small, round, entirely bald man with eyebrows as thick as hedges, which met in the middle, beamed at him across the table.

'Good lad. Hungry as a hawk, but thin as a whippet, as ever. He gets more like his old dad every day. What say you, Melba?'

The tall, rather severe looking lady with black hair cut like a medieval king turned back from the sink and watched the blond boy eating hungrily.

'I don't think he's changed one little bit. Longer in the limb, certainly, and his hair you could thatch a barn with. Other than that—he's still our Tom. Unmistakable. And here for a whole month this time you say? What a lovely luxury.'

'That's right,' smiled Tom, finishing his plate. This was a luxury indeed. Usually Tom spent his summer holidays squashed into the back of a camper van driving around the hot roads of Europe helping his parents collect rare insects. Tom was quite good at prising scorpions out of rocks, and catching mayflies on rivers, but the problem was, it was all they ever did. This summer, however, it was different. His parents had gone to the Andes in search of rare butterflies, leaving Tom with his distant relations Jos and Melba.

'Oh, they've arrived safely, by the way. Mum texted me last night.'

'Mum "texted" you? Did she indeed?' Uncle Jos eyed Tom's new mobile phone sitting on the sideboard mistrustfully. 'Well, I suppose it has its uses. Your dad never stops these days, does he? Gallivanting from one side of the world to the other, dragging poor Poppy through swamps and up mountains. Tell me Tom, does your mum actually *enjoy* chasin' all them creepy crawlies about?'

'I think so,' replied Tom thoughtfully, knowing full well that living his father's obsession was not easy. 'She never complains about it anyway.'

'Won't let him out of her sight, more like,' chipped in Melba as she finished the drying up. 'Not after *last* year's little adventure.' She flashed Tom a knowing smile. 'That's all sorted out now, is it, Tom?'

'It is.'

'Excellent,' said Jos, folding his arms across his chest. 'Well the more time you spend out this way the better, as far as I'm concerned. Now I'm retired I'm finding the old record needs changing now and again,' he whispered, nodding at Melba and winking at Tom. '*If* you get my drift.'

'What was that?' said Melba.

'You are tremendous, my dear!' roared Jos. 'But young Tom here has saved me buyin' a dog. Get myself some decent conversation.'

'A dog? For conversation?' repeated Melba absently. 'So it's a circus dog you want now, is it?'

Jos's eyes screwed up like bullets and his shoulders started to shake.

'See what I mean?'

Tom smiled politely and glanced from Melba to Jos and back again. One was thin as a twig, the other was round as an orange, and he had forgotten quite how eccentric they were.

'You will notice, Tom, that though we have formally retired, nothing's changed around here,' remarked Melba curtly.

'Oh Melba my peach, how can you say such a thing?' protested Jos, standing up and flinging the newspaper across to Tom. 'Have a squint at that, lad.'

Tom picked up the *Dragonport Mercury* and studied the page. In the middle was a picture of a large derelict house surrounded by ancient cedars. He recognized it immediately.

'Catcher Hall Nursing Home plans finally approved?' he read.

'No no, lad,' snorted Jos, 'but hey, *that's* not bad is it?' he added mischievously. 'We finally saw off the old enemy in the end, didn't we? The three hundred year long battle between the Catchers and the Scatterhorns has finally come to an end methinks, and it's Scatterhorns ten, Catchers nil. No, look further down in "What's On".'

Tom scanned down through the speedway reports and small ads until he found a small heading that read

'NEW COLLECTIONS OPENING TODAY.'

'Scatterhorn Museum, 10 a.m. till 5 p.m. Restored permanent exhibits now joined by the Hellkiss Collection. Exciting new tableaux, including rhinoceros, crocodiles and cheetahs, created by August Catcher for Nicholas Zumsteen of Hellkiss Hall, never seen in public before. Also, new exhibition of local specimens and other curiosities, donated by Dragonport folk.'

'How about that?' beamed Uncle Jos. 'New exhibits, never seen before: I reckon it's about time we went to have a gander at it all, don't you? Are you ready, lad?'

'I certainly am,' said Tom eagerly. This is what he had been looking forward to.

'Well done, lad. Well done. Now allow me to escort you to the chariot.'

Minutes later Tom found himself sitting in the sidecar of Jos's ancient motorbike as they raced noisily down the sunlit streets. As he watched the neat rows of Dragonport's terraced houses flashing by, Tom found himself smiling. He couldn't wait to see the museum, which he had last visited the previous year. How different his life seemed now: and yet, in reality, he knew it wasn't that different. He still lived in the scruffiest house in Middlesuch Close, an unremarkable grey street in an unremarkable grey town on the other side of the country. He still went to school, where he wasn't particularly good, or bad, at anything, except he did happen to know a lot about insects, and he found himself getting into a lot more trouble than he used to.

Somehow he just couldn't stop himself from doing dangerous things; it was like a magnetic attraction. 'That's those reckless Scatterhorns for you,' sighed his mother, despairingly, 'chancy chancers the lot of them.'

She was still a teacher, and his dad . . . well, he was the same tall, spare, shaggy blond man he had ever been, with smiling eyes and few words. He worked full time as an entomologist now, but deep down, he was a chancy chancer, too . . .

In the normal world, Tom Scatterhorn was just another normal boy, but when he came up here to Dragonport, everything was somehow different. The sun shone brighter, the wind blew harder, the rain fell more heavily, and most importantly, Tom *felt* different. And he was different: for in Dragonport, Tom Scatterhorn was not just another normal boy. Here he was special—very special indeed.

'And here we are,' roared Jos as the bike clattered to a halt outside the large red-brick building at the top of Museum Street. 'What do you think?'

Tom climbed out of the sidecar and squinted up at the familiar façade, its towers and pinnacles gleaming against the deep blue sky. Everything seemed cleaner and sharper.

'Buffed up a treat, hasn't it?' said Jos, standing on the steps and leaning back to admire the brickwork. 'They've even fixed the roof, you'll be pleased to hear.'

'It looks almost new,' said Tom in admiration.

'Well some of it is. Have you read that?'

Jos pointed at the crumbling plaque held between the two angry dragons above the door. It read:

THE SCATTERHORN MUSEUM
FOUNDED 1906 BY SIR HENRY SCATTERHORN
BEQUEATHED TO THE PEOPLE OF DRAGONPORT
GOD SAVE THE KING

Underneath these old words was inscribed:
Renovated 2009 with funds provided by Mr Tom Scatterhorn
'There you are, Tom, immortalized for ever now,' said Jos with a sweep of his hand. Tom stared up at the plaque with embarrassment.

'You never told me you were going to do that.'

'I certainly did not,' grinned Jos, 'because I knew what you'd say. But we couldn't let your generosity go unremarked, lad. After all, if the sapphire of Champawander, one of the largest uncut sapphires in the world, had mysteriously come into *my* possession, I am not at all sure I would have sold it to buy this old place; *and* pay for its restoration. But that's where you and I is different. Now,' he said, ceremoniously taking a large key out of his pocket. 'Would the new owner be so good as to open the door?'

Tom smiled, and taking the key he thrust it into the old lock. He felt nervous, excited, and somehow he still could not quite believe this was true. After all, how many twelve-year-old boys actually owned a museum?

The door creaked heavily then swung open, and it took a moment for Tom's eyes to adjust to the darkness. All around were the looming shapes of cases, stuffed with animals that he knew well. Wandering into the central hall he saw the mammoth beside the stairs, his long shaggy hair glistening in the half-light, the dodo on its podium, the gorilla relaxing in the cleft of its tree. There was the proboscis monkey, leaning nonchalantly against the side of its case, the gang of pangolins, the lines of white sturgeon, the anteaters, the porcupines, and the hummingbird tree inside its glass dome. All around the walls were dioramas stuffed with animals from every continent . . . there was the Arctic fox and rabbit and wolf, lost in the gleaming snow, the Brazilian rainforest, whose large green leaves concealed snakes and monkeys and tapirs, and stretching along the far wall were the great African plains, alive with gazelles and lions and meerkats. It was all just as Tom remembered. Every animal collected by his distant relation, the legendary hunter Sir Henry Scatterhorn, then stuffed by August Catcher, the equally legendary taxidermist, who happened to be Sir Henry's greatest friend.

'Nicely done, don't you think?' said Jos wandering over to where Tom stood in a pool of light. 'It took two old boys the best part of a year to restore them.'

'It's fantastic,' agreed Tom, looking around. The animals may have been well over a hundred years old, but they seemed livelier than ever.

'I'll take that as the owner's approval then,' wheezed Jos, walking over to the corner where a large model of ice-bound Dragonport stood. Tom followed and peered down at the town spread out before him, just as it had been a hundred years ago. Like everything else, this was just the same, but somehow different. 'Come up a treat hasn't it?' said Jos, fumbling with the light switch that turned the scene from day to night. 'Cleared those damn beetles out, gave it a good clean and a repaint, and hey presto—just like new. Well, almost,' he added, rattling the switch in vain. Tom stared down at the busy streets blanketed with snow and the ice fair out on the frozen river, and memories of his last visit to the museum came flooding back . . . to think he had actually *been* there . . . it all seemed clearer than ever before . . .

'Anyhow,' Jos continued, 'this is all old hat, isn't it, lad? I reckon what you really want to see is the new crowd, and who wouldn't?'

Tom looked up at Jos and he winked.

'Step right this way,' he grinned, and shuffled off towards the stairs. 'Now I know you're busy at school and haven't been kept entirely up to speed with the refit,' he said, forging ahead into the gloom, 'but rest assured, Tom, it's all in keeping. This place is a time capsule in its way, and long may it remain so. There's none of your fancy computers and interactive falderals in here. Just good old-fashioned taxidermy of the first order.'

Uncle Jos paused for breath on the landing, and surveyed the jumble of dark shapes below.

'And if I'm honest, Tom, though I've spent the best part of my life in here, what we have recently acquired puts this lot in the shade.'

'The Hellkiss Collection?' said Tom expectantly.

'Correctamundo.'

Jos cleared his throat loudly and turned to face the man-eating tiger, still crouching in her alcove at the top of the stairs ready to spring. 'Why I'm not sure even Tigger here quite matches up now.'

Tom smiled in anticipation; he had heard small titbits about this from his mum and dad while he was at school.

'Where is it?'

'Patience patience,' rasped Jos, enjoying the suspense, and he led the way up around the bird gallery to a large wooden door. 'Now you won't remember this because last time you were here it didn't exist. Well it *did*, but it was bricked up. See, when Sir Henry Scatterhorn built this place way back when, he had an East Wing to match the West Wing. Which was a logical thing to do, because if the museum ever expanded, this is where it would go. But as you and I know well, lad, there was never any cause to do that—and absolutely no funds either. In fact I do believe we had all almost forgotten it existed. Until now.'

With a flourish Jos flung open the door to reveal a long, high room with tiny windows up near the rafters. At first sight it looked like every other room in the museum, with dark cases around the walls stuffed with creatures. But in the centre it was different. Three large tableaux dominated the room, a jumble of shapes and bodies that were unlike anything Tom had ever seen before. Jos turned to Tom expectantly.

'What do you reckon to *that*?'

To begin with, Tom was not sure what they were. He walked forward to the first exhibit, which he recognized as a pair of cheetahs, chasing a large gazelle. Nothing remarkable about that, except that all three animals were running at full speed, and set at an acute angle, twisting and turning through the grassland. They looked as if they would take off at any moment, and Tom wondered how August Catcher had managed to capture such a scene, let alone make them stand up. Walking further into the gloom he saw another extraordinary tableaux, larger than the first. It was of a muddy waterhole, busy with drinking wildebeest. Out of the centre of the pool a huge crocodile exploded through the air like a flying tree trunk, its tail thrashing in the muddy swirl of water, its great jaws clamped around the nose of a very surprised wildebeest. Again August Catcher had chosen the moment precisely: the herd were all just about to gallop away, the crocodile had just begun to twist its jaws downwards, and the quivering wildebeest wore an expression of shock mixed with pure terror.

'Almost like a still from a movie, isn't it?' said Jos appreciatively. 'Suspended animation caught in three-D.'

Tom reached forward and brushed his fingers against the vertical cascades of water that August had made from melted glass.

'How did he do it?'

'How indeed,' winked Jos. 'But if you like that one, Tom—then spare a little awe for this beauty.'

Shambling over to the far wall he switched on a spotlight.

'Wow.'

Tom's eyes shone with excitement. What had appeared to be a collection of boulders flying through the air against the back wall suddenly took form. At the base was a large black rhinoceros, plunging head-first off a cliff. Following it down into the darkness was a collection of wild-eyed animals, set in terrified flying poses. There were lions, warthogs, a giraffe, two small bears, an old white tiger, lemurs and vultures, monkeys and pythons—it was like the contents of a zoo tipping into a ravine. And behind them rose a steep wall of glistening dark water foaming white at the top.

'Its called "The Deluge",' said Jos proudly. 'Biblical, ain't it? The Great Flood.'

Tom shook his head in astonishment. It was spectacular, but what made it even more remarkable was that all of these creatures were apparently suspended in mid-air, set in the act of plunging off a cliff. But how could they stay up, what supported them? Tom looked closer; there were no wires or steel bars, and then he noticed that each creature was touching another in some way; a tail casually brushing against a wing, a claw glancing against a back, every single animal in this vast flying tableaux was joined together through an intricate series of connections, and they all led down to the great rhinoceros itself. But even that rhinoceros wasn't touching the ground . . . or was it? Tom walked around the side and saw that only the back toe of the rhino's left foot was connected to the cliff-face behind it. Everything else was hanging in the air.

'But how,' Tom began, not wanting to appear stupid, 'I mean—'

'How the blinkin' blazes does it stand up?' grinned Jos. 'I've been wonderin' that myself, Tom,' he said, 'rackin' me brains. I reckon it's all cantilevers.'

'Cantilevers?'

'You know, weights and balances and all that. Like a see-saw. I reckon most of those animals up there is stuffed with nothing more than papier mâché or plastic, so they weigh next to nothing. Whereas that rhino's foot is actually solid steel inside, strong enough to bear the weight of all this lot, and that cliff is heavy enough to balance it out. Dead clever, isn't it?'

Tom's mind whirred; he never concentrated much in physics

at school, but this was quite amazing. It was almost like magic—but of course, it wasn't. No wonder Jos was so pleased.

'In my biased opinion I consider this to be August Catcher's finest achievement,' rasped Jos grandly, 'and very probably the showiest piece of taxidermy in the world. It's pure invention of course, a wild flight of fancy, but I for one have never seen anything like it, and I doubt anyone else has either.'

Jos turned to Tom, his small black eyes shining with excitement. 'And to think that here it is, lad, in the Scatterhorn Museum!'

And that was another mystery that Tom could not quite understand.

'So . . . so Nicholas Zumsteen has *given* all this to us?'

'In a manner of speaking, yes. He's long gone see, but his widow's still alive. It's been all her doing, really.'

'Why?'

'I think she liked the sound of you.'

'Me?'

'You, Tom. Let me give you a little of the history. The Zumsteens are a funny bunch. Rich as kings once upon a time, diamond dealers I think, and very, very secretive, with houses all over the shop. Monaco, South Africa, Mexico, and even Hellkiss Hall, right up the river from here. It's a weird old place, surrounded by miles and miles of forest—I wouldn't live there if you paid me. And neither by all accounts would Nicholas Zumsteen, the youngest son. He was a harum-scarum fellow, mad about aeroplanes and animals, no interest in the diamond trade whatsoever. Somehow he bumped into August Catcher on his travels and commissioned him to do these tableaux—no expense spared. Drove his father half-mad I believe.'

'Why, didn't he like them?'

'Couldn't stand them,' said Jos. 'Which is why all this lot have been mothballed in the great hall of Hellkiss Hall for nigh on fifty years. The old man almost pretended they weren't there. Probably because they reminded him of Nicholas.'

'What happened to him?' asked Tom. 'You said he died?'

'Well, disappeared more like,' said Jos, knowingly. 'Out in the Pacific somewhere. Some story to it, I think. One of them "mysteries", you know.'

'And his widow? You said—'

'Oscarine?' Jos chuckled to himself. 'Oscarine Zumsteen. The bride of Dragonport.'

'The bride of Dragonport?'

'In her day there was no one that could touch Oscarine. Beautiful she was. Legendary. But ever since Nick disappeared she's become a bit of a recluse. Of course the Zumsteens wouldn't have her living in the main house, so they gave her one of the estate cottages, down on the edge of the marshes. And she's been there ever since, going slowly round the bend by all accounts.' Jos paused, his eyes twinkling beneath the huge hedges of his eyebrows.

'That is, until she read this curious story in the paper about a young lad who sold a sapphire to do up the Scatterhorn Museum. Must have pressed a button somewhere. So she came down and had a look.'

'Did you meet her?'

'Indeedy. Gave her a tour. She wanted to know all about it—

and you, of course. Then the next thing you know, she's persuading the Zumsteens that all these unloved beauties should come here, to be with the rest of August's stuff. And amazingly they said yes. I think they couldn't wait to get rid of them, to be honest. But one man's meat is another man's poison, ain't it?'

Tom and Jos stared for a moment at the three tableaux in silence.

'If only my old dad could have seen this little lot,' murmured Jos; 'this should have them lining up in the street. Which reminds me, I think it's about time we opened the doors, don't you?'

At ten o'clock precisely, Tom pushed open the heavy front door and stood for a moment, blinking in the sunlight.

'Are you opening up, or what?'

The beaky lady peered at him over the top of her spectacles.

'Sorry?' said Tom. 'Are you—'

'Waiting for a bus? What do you think?' interrupted her companion. 'Just cos we's grannies doesn't mean we've got all day, y'know.'

Tom stood to one side as the small group of old ladies filed in, chattering excitedly. This was amazing, there *were* people actually queuing to come into the Scatterhorn Museum. No one ever did that before. Scratching his head, Tom wandered back inside. Things had most definitely changed . . .

And as the morning went on the stream of visitors continued. Groups of tourists, mostly, intrigued by what a genuine old English taxidermy museum looked like, and a steady flow of locals too, many of whom seemed to be as interested in the new owner as the Hellkiss Collection.

'Are you the real Tom Scatterhorn?'

A small boy with large eyes stood staring up at Tom in wonder.

'Erm . . . that's right,' mumbled Tom, a little embarrassed.

The small boy shook his head: this was amazing.

'And you own the biggest sapphire in the world?'

'Not any more, I've sold it now. And it wasn't quite the biggest.'

'So was it like, this big?' said the boy, holding his arms out to make the size of a football.

'No,' smiled Tom, 'more like this big,' he said, making the shape of a plum with his hand. 'But it was worth a lot of money.'

The boy thought about this for a moment, not quite sure if it was true.

'Like how much?'

'Erm . . . '

'Like a hundred million?'

'No.'

'Like ten million, billion, trillion?'

'Well—'

'A squillion?'

'Nearly,' laughed Tom, and he noticed that a couple of girls across the hallway were pointing at him and smiling. Tom felt the colour in his cheeks start to rise. The boy shook his head in disbelief.

'Wow.'

'More than you'll ever know, Bradley,' interrupted his mother.

'I'm sorry, love,' she smiled at Tom, 'he's been looking forward to meeting you for ever such a long time. Wants to own a museum when he grows up, you see. We've been doing a bit of collecting ourselves, haven't we, Bradders? Go on, show him what you've got.'

Bradley nodded, and with a very serious expression reached into his bag and pulled out a box of small green, red, and blue beetles set in plastic. 'I've been collecting these from Mr Chan the birthday man. He gives them out at parties.' Bradley began laying out the beetles in an elaborate pattern on the table in front of him. The girls came closer to have a look.

'Nice one Bradley,' said one. 'Like 'em.'

'Them red ones's well good,' said the other, giggling.

'So do you want them then, for the museum?'

Tom was not quite sure what to say.

'He's spent ever such a long time collectin' them things,' crooned his mother expectantly, 'he'd be so pleased.'

'I'd have to start again, but I don't mind,' said Bradley, staring at Tom with his large eyes. 'Much.'

'Erm . . .'

'Well, well, what have we here?' wheezed Jos, shambling over to the rescue. 'More exhibits for the Dragonport's finest exhibition?'

He squinted down at the motley collection of beetles young Bradley had carefully laid out on the table.

'What an excellent collection, young man. Truly excellent.'

Bradley swelled with pride, and then he leant forward to let Tom into a secret. 'I am collecting—by *colour*. Look: red, green, blue,' he said very seriously. 'Do you understand?'

'I think I do,' said Tom, still somewhat mystified.

'Well Mr Director,' said Jos, turning to Tom with a wink. 'After all, it's your museum. Can we take Bradley's beetle collection?'

Tom saw a mischievous look in Jos's eye.

'Erm . . . yes. Why not,' he said, hoping this was the right thing to say.

'Good lad,' wheezed Jos, 'I know just the spot for them. Come on, Mr Director.'

The girls giggled as Jos picked up the beetles and led Tom across the hall and up the stairs.

'Sorry to land you in it there, lad,' grinned Jos, 'got a bit of a wheeze going for the Dragonport festival. I took the liberty of putting an advert in the paper, asking for local collectors to donate stuff for a little exhibition. All manner of stuff has turned up. Most of it's junk, of course, but quite a bit of Mr Catcher's handiwork has come out of the woodwork too.'

Jos made his way through the bird galleries into a small room in the new East Wing, where he placed Bradley's beetles in a cabinet marked 'newer collections'. Tom looked around and saw that the rest of the exhibition was mainly rather tatty stuffed pets that looked as if they had all been found in an attic. There was 'Poor Polly the parrot', who had witnessed the battle of Waterloo and lived till the age of ninety-three; 'Badger', a very cross-eyed Jack Russell with one ear missing; and a cage of dirty blue and yellow budgerigars that once belonged to one Miss Snowdrop Scott. In amongst these exhibits were collections of stones, eggs, foreign currency, and old glass milk bottles all lent by Dragonport folk.

'What's that?' asked Tom, walking towards a large model in a glass case that occupied the centre of the room.

'That is the surprise find of the exhibition,' wheezed Jos, shambling forward to join him. 'Only turned up yesterday. It's the "Tithona archipelago", apparently. Out in the Pacific some-where—I'd never heard of it. Made by none other than August Catcher.'

'Made by August Catcher?' repeated Tom, peering down at the collection of hundreds of islands, moulded into weird shapes. He could see villages on stilts stretching out towards the reefs, fish-ing boats basking in the crystal blue waters, jungles clinging on to the steep slopes of the mountains and huts hidden in the trees. It was another world, as detailed and complete as the model of Dragonport downstairs.

'Who did he make it for?'

'Lord knows. It came from Hellkiss House. Oscarine Zumsteen found it in a stable somewhere. Thought we should keep it.'

'Really?'

'So she says. August must have been there once upon a time, I reckon. How could you make something like that if you hadn't? But why he made it, and who for . . . ' Jos shrugged his shoul-ders.

Tom peered through the glass at the weird volcanic shapes of the islands rising out of the crystal blue sea. What secrets might it contain? he wondered to himself.

'Is this the boy we've heard so much about then?'

Tom turned round to see a short, wiry man wringing Jos's hand. He was wearing a light blue beret that was so greasy it looked as if it had been polished onto his head, and a brown caretaker's coat.

'Ern!' roared Jos. 'I wondered where you'd got to.'

'Here I am, reporting for duty, sir.'

'Tom,' wheezed Jos, 'allow me to introduce you to my new first mate, who runs the show now. Ern Rainbird, Tom Scatterhorn.'

'Nice to meet yer, boss,' said Ern, stepping forward and taking Tom's hand between his powerful, knobbly fingers.

'Hi,' said Tom, wincing slightly as Ern Rainbird squeezed his hand mercilessly, and he stared back into Ern's wizened, freckled face: there was something distinctly odd about Ern Rainbird, and for the moment Tom could not decide what it was.

'Ern is in charge of the day-to-day maintenance of HMS Scatterhorn now that Melba and I have formally entered middle age,' explained Jos. 'An old pal of mine from the merchant navy.'

'That's right,' grunted Ern, scrutinizing Tom with his sandy-coloured eyes. 'Any cleaning, brassing, tatting-about to be done, boy—I'm on to it, lickety-split.'

'That's old Ern. You've got a new regime going here, haven't you?'

'Indeed I have, son,' growled Ern. 'Got a bit of order in the place. Proper locks on doors, labels on cupboards, you know the drill. Can't run a ship like this without order. As I always say to Mr Scatterhorn: if the system breaks down—'

'We break down,' interrupted Uncle Jos, who had obviously heard this refrain many times before. 'Well done, Ern. Carry on then, number one,' he blustered, and gave Ern Rainbird a mock salute.

'Aye-aye, skip,' grunted Ern, touching his beret, and his sandy eyes swivelled back to Tom. 'Nice to meet you, lad.'

Tom watched the bow-legged Ern Rainbird turn on his heel and march off into the gloom, wondering how Uncle Jos could have hired someone so different from himself.

'I know what you're thinking, Tom,' said Jos quietly. 'He's a bit . . . military, but that's what we need. Melba and me don't want to be chasin' around after some layabout. Ern's got his rules, rotas, charts, even his own poky little scullery in the boiler room with a kettle and a tin of biscuits. All he needs is a hammock and he's back in the navy. Don't you fret about Ern.'

Tom was not so sure, but he decided to keep his doubts to himself. And he had little time to worry about it anyway, because the rest of the day he spent smiling and shaking hands with strangers. Everywhere he went people stared and pointed, and Tom lost count of the times he had been asked, 'Are you *really* Tom Scatterhorn?' Tom began to wonder why people ever wanted to be famous. It was exhausting.

'Good-jab, good-jab, good-jab,' murmured a herd of elderly Americans as they went out of the door, followed by Leaky Logan, the new mayor, who was, as always, pleased to be the last to leave.

'Well done, Scatterhorn junior,' said Leaky, clapping Tom on the back so hard he almost knocked him over. 'Dragonport needs young chaps like you with initiative to put it right back on the map.'

'If we weren't on the map there'd be no one here,' said Melba, who had arrived to help close up the museum.

'Agreed, Mrs Scatterhorn, but I want Dragonport to embrace the business leaders of tomorrow. Celebrate excellence in tomorrow's world today. I regard that as mission critical.'

'That'll do, Leaky,' said Melba, pushing him out of the door and closing it.

'Dear oh dear,' wheezed Jos, rubbing his head, 'mission critical? Lordy lord, and to think he just used to be a plumber.'

For a moment all three of them stood in the cool gloom and said nothing, listening to the last voices echoing away down the street.

'Silence is golden,' whispered Melba, her voice echoing around the hall. 'Never thought I'd say that again.'

'Good though,' smiled Jos wearily.

'Very,' said Melba, locking the takings from the till in the safe. 'If we're not very careful the Scatterhorn Museum will start paying for itself.'

'What a disaster that would be,' winked Jos, as he shambled over to Tom, who was sitting exhausted on the stairs. 'Now lad,' he said, ceremoniously taking a set of keys out of his pocket. 'Seeing as you are the owner and quite clearly a business leader of tomorrow, I think you deserve a set of these,' he said, dropping the keys into Tom's lap. 'Well it's yours, isn't it? Why shouldn't you come and go as you please?'

Tom did not know what to say. The whole day had been so overwhelming.

'Thanks. Really. Thanks a lot.'

'Think nothing of it, lad,' smiled Jos. 'We'll see you later.'

Tom waved as Jos and Melba went out of the door. Only now, at last, was he finally alone. Tom took a deep breath and looked around. Jos was right, things had certainly changed around here, but how much had they *really* changed? There was the mammoth, the gorilla, the dodo, the tiger, crouched in the darkness, waiting. Tom walked out into the centre of the hall and looked up. The sky through the skylight had turned from blue to purple: evening was approaching. Good. Darkness was better. Tom nervously cleared his throat: should he? Go on. Try. Won't know till you try. OK, thought Tom. I will.

'Hello?' he said.

His voice echoed away into the darkness.

'Hello?'

CHAPTER 3

Arsenic

The silence was deafening. The only sound Tom could hear was a slight humming in his ears.

'Hello?' he said again, louder this time.

Somewhere in the distance a car alarm went off. Tom looked around at the inky black shadows growing deeper in the gloom. Maybe silence was all there was now. Just silence. Idly, Tom glanced over towards the mammoth beside the stairs, and noticed something glinting next to the wall. It was a padlock, fixed to the small door to the cupboard under the stairs. Ern Rainbird's new regime, thought Tom to himself, probably got the whole place locked and barred and bolted up now. Maybe that's why they were so quiet. Maybe Ern Rainbird was given to prowling around here after the visitors had gone. Maybe that's it.

'Rainbird's gone, if you want to know,' said Tom out loud. 'I saw him leave myself.'

Silence. Perhaps he *was* talking to himself. Just as well no one was listening, they might think he was crazy. The shadows were so deep now that all he could see were eyes and fangs and claws. Everything was a deep, velvety brown. Suddenly Tom felt worried, perhaps the restoration had really changed everything . . .

'Well, that's a shame,' he said, his voice echoing into the heavy silence. 'I'd been looking forward to this for a long time. But obviously this is how it is going—'

'To be.'

Tom stopped. His ears strained. Was that—

'Or not, to be.'

'Indeed.'

'That is the question.'

There was a pause.

'But is he really worth it?'

'I'm not so sure any more.'

Tom's heart was beating faster now. He felt hundreds of eyes watching him out of the gloom. Was that all? It couldn't be.

'Ahem!'

Tom whipped round and stared hard at the small mammals' case. Something flickered in front of it—a tail. Tom followed it up, and there sitting on the ledge above was the pale shadow of the proboscis monkey.

'Long time no see,' it said, scratching its head. 'We'd almost given up on you.'

Tom breathed a sigh of relief.

'Hi.'

'Hi indeed.'

Tom started. A sharp Welsh voice sounded very close. Tom looked down to see the dodo staring up at him angrily.

'High and dry more like,' said the bird. 'Right up to our necks in it we was. No thanks to you. What were you thinking of, boyo?'

'I—' Tom began, 'what do you mean?'

'I mean being taken apart and put back together again! I mean being buffed and fluffed! I mean havin' me eyes taken out, polished, and put back in upside down! I mean Tweedle-dum and Tweedle-dee stitching me a brand new khyber, that's what I mean!'

The dodo was so angry now she was chasing her own shadow with rage.

'Restored is what she *actually* means,' boomed a low, rumbling voice that seemed to come from far away but was actually very close, whereupon one whole side of the museum appeared to move forward. It was the mammoth.

'I'm afraid my lady-friend the dodo has been saving that up for rather a long time,' he rumbled, curling his trunk into Tom's hand and shaking it. 'Very good to see you again, old chap. *Entre-nous*, I think she looks rather splendid—if a little cross-eyed.'

'A little? A *little*? I will have you know my eyesight is absolutely perfect, sir,' screeched the bird. 'I can see everything that is wrong with *you*.'

'Indeed, madam.'

'And this museum.' The dodo clattered up to Tom and fixed him with one large yellow eye. 'You may have had us restored, Tom Scatterhorn, and some may be grateful to you for that—'

'Here, here!' said the sturgeon. 'I've got my barbels back.'

'And my scales,' added the pangolin.

'And my lovely long tongue,' crooned the anteater.

'And why precisely do you need a tongue?' trilled the

porcupine. 'To eat more ants? This is a museum you know—not the African bush.'

'Be that as it may,' continued the dodo, 'in my considerable opinion, your changes have ripped the very character out of this place. Ripped it.'

Tom looked at the dodo. He did not understand what she was talking about.

'It's the new arrivals,' explained the gorilla, climbing down from the cleft in his tree and rolling onto the floor on his back. 'Not our sort, old boy.'

'Do you mean the Hellkiss Collection?' said Tom.

'That is *precisely* what I mean,' nodded the dodo. 'The flying Fratelli brothers upstairs, balancing on their finger tips and what have you.'

'What's wrong with that?'

'Lowers the tone,' sniffed the gorilla. 'What do they think this is—a circus?'

'They're all bigger and better than us,' hissed the anaconda. 'What am I supposed to do now—tie myself in knots?'

'Well, no . . . ' mumbled Tom, 'that is—'

'Do you not like me?' squawked the dodo, fixing him with an angry yellow stare. 'Am I not good enough for you?'

'I—'

'I am a *dodo*, Tom, a *talking* dodo. *Extinct*. Is that not sufficient, boyo?'

It was clear that the well of resentment was very deep. There was now a general murmur of unhappy voices as the proboscis monkey leapt from case to case, sliding them open and allowing the animals to escape.

'I just didn't realize quite how boring I was,' moaned the sloth. 'I mean I hang upside down in a tree. I never move. And I'm brown. What's the point in that?'

'Just because you're brown doesn't mean you're boring, old boy,' rumbled the mammoth. 'Brown is a fine colour. If one has age and class one is generally brown. It's a byword for distinction.'

'Extinction, more like,' muttered the wombat.

'Brothers and sisters, please!' trilled a high squeaky voice. Tom looked up to see a black shrew sitting on the edge of a large case.

'Is this not the land of milk and honey?' it said, stretching one bony claw into the air. 'Have we *all* not passed through the valley of death, brothers and sisters?'

'Yes, indeed, we have!' shrieked a congregation of smaller shrews lined up on the ledge below.

'Then unfurl your minds, unleash the love in your hearts.'

'Funny how they've always got the answers to everything,' grumbled the gorilla, 'and something tells me they are about to start singing.'

'Music, just what we need,' hissed the dodo.

'When the Hellkiss Collection reached the gates of heaven,' sang the preacher shrew.

'What did they see, boys?' responded the shrews eagerly. 'What did they see?'

'They saw the good lord Jesus talkin' to you and me.'

'What did they say, boys, what did they say?'

'They said, "Please Mr Jesus sir, may we come in?"'

'And what did he do, boys, what did he do?'

'He said have you folks been honest and faithful and true?'

'Have you done to others what would be done to you?'

'Have you eaten the bread? Drunk the wine?'

'Have you banished Satan from your minds?'

The congregation of shrews began to squeal and shout with excitement.

'And what did they say, boys, what did they say?'

'Hallelujah Hallelujah Lord, e-ver-ree day!'

The shrews screamed and punched the air in joy.

'Hallelujah brothers and sisters, hallelujah!' shouted the preacher shrew. 'The Hellkiss Collection are chosen ones, same as you and me. The good Lord he makes no distinctions. Man, mammoth, moth or mouse, all is welcome here.'

'Some is more welcome than others,' muttered the dodo.

'You see, Tom?' murmured the mammoth above the din. 'There may be something rotten in the house of Scatterhorn, but those little fellows will always be in heaven.'

The mammoth winked and Tom grinned; he had almost forgotten that when August Catcher had stuffed all the mice and shrews he had filled their brain cavities with shavings from the Bible. Like every other creature in the museum, they drew their characters from whatever happened to be inside their heads, and through August's extraordinary elixir which he had used to preserve them, they were all still alive—in a way—as Edwardians. Were the animals in the Hellkiss Collection just the same? Perhaps they had been stuffed with something different, or maybe Jos was right, and they were entirely hollow.

'So, you haven't spoken to them?' asked Tom as he slowly wandered up the stairs.

'Who, the new crowd?' replied the proboscis monkey, assisting the ancient pangolins out of their case.

'Yes,' continued Tom. 'The new crowd. Who else?'

There was silence for a moment, and Tom sensed this was a burning question.

'The thing is,' began the aardvark, 'really, I mean, there are just so many of them—'

'Where to begin?' chimed the skunk.

'And they're all connected together,' sniffed the anaconda, 'hand over foot—'

'Engage one in conversation the rest will fall over—'

'Nothing can persuade me to converse with a crocodile,' announced the turtle gloomily.

'It's the principle of the thing,' agreed the gazelle.

'Dry as dust,' droned the moose. 'Like talking to a pair of shoes—'

'In other words, little boy, no, they haven't.'

The voice rumbled through the darkness ahead of him and Tom stopped precisely where he stood. There in the shadows of the alcove lay the long, yellowy shape of the man-eating tiger, stretched lazily across her rock.

'But that's men for you,' she yawned. 'Prevaricators. Why do something today that you can put off until tomorrow?'

The tigress fixed him with her flame coloured eyes, and Tom shuddered, despite himself. He knew this cat of old, and experience had taught him to be very, very wary of this creature.

'So here you are, Tom Scatterhorn,' said the great cat slowly, 'back to haunt us, I see.'

There was a gasp of astonishment from below.

'It's that suffragette—'

'She'll eat him—'

'Don't give her ideas—'

'Ssshhh.'

There was silence.

'Hello,' said Tom nervously.

The tiger scrutinized him in the gloom.

'Don't be afraid Tom. We may not be quite friends, but we are no longer enemies, remember?'

Tom stared into the dark recess of the alcove, trying to make out her expression. He knew this to be true, but could he trust her? The great cat yawned loudly.

'It seems that those nitwits down below are correct,' she said in a bored tone, 'the country club has been restored, but we do appear to have been upstaged somewhat. And despite their rather extraordinary appearance, the new additions have no conversation whatsoever. Which is a shame. I was rather hoping for someone intelligent to turn up.'

Tom heard a rumble of dissent down below, but the great tiger ignored it.

'One wonders if they really *are* filled with nothing but fluff and air. Or failing that, they are keeping their own counsel. Either way, their silence is rather intriguing, don't you think?'

'Erm . . . yes, I mean, probably,' mumbled Tom.

'I think so,' she growled. 'But you have more important things to worry about. Or you will do, shortly. Run along, young Tom, run along.'

The tiger stretched lazily and dropped her head on the rock.

'Bye,' said Tom, relieved that the most dangerous animal in the museum was no longer trying to eat him.

The tiger did not reply; it just flicked its tail in irritation. It was time to go. Tom walked gingerly around the gallery to the West Wing and opened the door to the Hellkiss Collection. There before him was the dark tumble of animals, plunging off the edge of the cliff. Perhaps they *were* right, it would be incredible if these new tableaux could somehow take themselves apart, run around the museum whenever they felt like it, and then reassemble themselves at a moment's notice. But he was also quite sure that their hostility had nothing to do with rhinoceroses, or crocodiles or warthogs. The simple fact was that they were new and different, and that was bad enough.

'Arsenic!'

The sharp hiss interrupted Tom's thoughts. Arsenic . . . wasn't that the watchword for danger? Tom heard a rapid scurrying and the click of cabinet doors closing down below, and looking back, he just spotted the dodo stepping up onto her podium and resuming the same pose she had held for a hundred years. Arsenic . . . someone, or something, was here, who could it be? Ern Rainbird, making some kind of nocturnal visit? Uncle Jos, perhaps? Tom's ears strained to hear anything in the thick blanket of silence. There was nothing. Gingerly he tiptoed around the gallery and stood at the top of the stairs. There was no one down there . . . or—what was that? Something was swaying behind the gorilla. Something like a dress. Tom took a few quick steps down the stairs and then he stopped. Out of the shadows stepped a girl, strangely dressed in a ragged skirt and a jumper.

She hadn't seen Tom; she was looking intently into the cases of animals, murmuring to herself. Tom watched her for a moment. Who was she, a thief? She was about his age, and wild looking, and Tom noticed she wasn't wearing any shoes.

'Can I help you?'

Tom's words shattered the heavy silence. The girl whipped round and stared up at him. She looked both dangerous and scared at the same time.

'Can you help me,' she repeated. 'Can *you* help *me*?'

She peered at the wiry blond boy with dark eyes standing halfway up the stairs in front of her. 'Maybe you can. But then again, maybe not.'

'Who are you?'

The girl did not answer. Even in the near darkness Tom could see that her skin was coffee-coloured, and her accent was unusual.

'You're Tom Scatterhorn,' she said suddenly. 'I know all about you.'

'You do?'

The girl nodded. She peered up at him curiously.

'But you're not at all like I expected. You're the one who gave them the little blue bottle.'

Tom felt himself start to bristle, and with great effort held himself in check. He had no idea who this person was, but somehow she seemed to know about the guilty secret that he had hidden from the world.

'What do you want?' he said harshly.

'I'm Pearl,' said the girl, somewhat puzzled by Tom's reaction. 'Pearl Smoot. Odd name, isn't it? Still, there you go.'

Tom came down the stairs and stood facing her across the dark hall. There was an awkward silence.

'I'm looking . . . actually I'm looking for someone who can help me.'

'So what are you doing in here?'

'It's complicated,' she began. 'Erm . . . where to begin? Right. You see, we are similar, you and I. We know about them.'

'Them?'

'You know. They're everywhere. "*Them*".'

Tom said nothing. He wondered whether she meant what he thought she meant.

'The "*thems*",' continued Pearl, by way of explanation. 'The "you-know-whats".'

Again Tom had a suspicion of what she was talking about. Who was Pearl Smoot? He racked his brains; he was sure he had seen her somewhere before, but where?

'So you have broken into my museum just to tell me that?'

'Well, almost . . . there's a lot more, you see,' smiled Pearl. 'My museum—I like that though, Tom, it's cool. Actually I didn't break in. I was in here earlier and I kind of sneaked myself away and then fell asleep. Whoops.' Pearl laughed at herself nervously. 'No . . . erm . . . but seriously, I don't suppose you have any scones?'

'Scones?' repeated Tom.

'Or maybe they're called biscuits here? Or is it toast? Or cookies? Really, anything will do. You see I am insanely hungry, and I don't have any money. In fact I have nothing at all.'

Tom looked at Pearl Smoot, shifting uneasily in the darkness. She certainly did seem genuinely desperate. But how did she know about the bottle? The only way to find out was to trust her, and that is exactly what he decided to do.

'So you want a biscuit?' repeated Tom, putting on a friendly smile.

'Or two. Yup. I'm just famished.'

'OK. Let's err . . . let's have a look. Follow me,' he said, and led the way down the stairs to the boiler room. Uncle Jos had said that Ern Rainbird had made a den down here somewhere, and sure enough after a little hunting around amongst the tangle of pipes Tom discovered Ern's secret biscuit supply, along with a kettle and an orderly line of jam jars containing tea, sugar, and milk. Five minutes later, Pearl and Tom were sitting opposite each other beneath a single light bulb at Ern's tiny table and the tartan tin was completely empty. Pearl had finished the lot.

'Thanks for that,' she said wiping the crumbs off her mouth. 'I confess I haven't eaten for a bit.'

Tom had been watching her eat in silence, and he had decided that she wasn't a burglar. And what's more, she wasn't from anywhere around here, either. Pearl's face was brown because she had a deep suntan, almost the colour of a nut, and she was covered in freckles. Her light blue eyes shone like lanterns out of her dark face and her black hair was flecked with gold. Tom noticed that on one of her toes she wore a gold ring. All this, coupled with her strange old-fashioned skirt printed with large flowers and a baggy blue jumper, made her look very exotic indeed. She had either come back from a long holiday in the sun, or she was from somewhere else entirely.

'You're not from Dragonport, then?' asked Tom politely, knowing full well what the answer would be.

'Uh-huh,' said Pearl, taking a sip of hot sweet tea. 'I . . . it's kind of an accident that I'm here. I don't really know much about this place, you know. I travelled here, last night. During the fireworks,' she said, glancing up at Tom over the steaming cup.

The fireworks, was that where he had seen her before? Then Tom remembered the girl hanging from the balloon . . . that was it! That was Pearl Smoot, she was wearing the same clothes. Gradually it was making sense: Pearl must belong to some circus troupe—Jos had said there were a few of them about for the festival.

'I think I saw your trick last night,' began Tom, tentatively. 'It was really good.'

'My trick?'

'Yeah. With the balloon,' continued Tom, less convincingly. 'That looked dangerous.'

Pearl eyed Tom carefully.

'That wasn't no trick, it was an accident, and it scared the bejesus out of me. And I happen to know that how I got here is what happens to you too. I *travelled* here, you see.'

Tom said nothing, and Pearl gave him a hard look.

'Your dad is called Sam Scatterhorn, right? And your mother is Poppy?'

'They are,' replied Tom warily. 'How do you know?'

Pearl took another sip of her tea and continued to look at him. She seemed to be weighing up something in her mind.

'Where are they?'

'In Chile. They arrived last night.'

'Are you sure?'

'Yes, definitely,' said Tom impatiently, 'why, what are you saying?'

Again Pearl did not reply, and her silence made Tom nervous.

'Do you know where they take them? You know, the "you-know-whats"? Do you know where they take people once they've captured them?'

Tom did not understand. This conversation was just too weird to make any sense.

'Look I'm really sorry, but *who* has taken *them* where? Who are the "*thems*"? The "you-know-whats"?'

'I don't know!'

Pearl was exasperated.

'This is it, I just don't know!'

She stared at Tom, her eyes blazing, and then suddenly her expression changed. It was as if she was suddenly looking at someone else entirely.

'Oh my god,' she gasped, 'maybe that's it, you're . . . '

Suddenly she reached into her dress and pulled out a battered red notebook. Flicking fast through the pages, she suddenly stopped.

'Don Gervase Askary,' she said, pronouncing each word very clearly. 'Do you know him?'

Tom felt his throat tighten. It had been a year and a half since he had heard that name, and he had successfully managed to banish all thoughts of him to the back of his mind. But those words instantly brought him right back.

'A tall guy. Big green eyes, weird looking.'

'I know.'

'You do?'

Pearl swallowed hard. This seemed to have made her even more nervous.

'Is he your leader?'

'Of course not!' snorted Tom.

'Is he your friend?'

'No—'

'But you do know him?'

'Yes, but—'

'And you gave him the elixir? The one made by August Catcher. The liquid that gives off a gas that makes things immortal, that he discovered by accident. The same liquid that he used to preserve all the animals in this museum?'

Tom could feel himself begin to boil. Why was Pearl interrogating him?

'I had no choice,' he began, 'it just happened that . . . look, how was I supposed to know that he was a—'

'What?'

Pearl stared at him. She seemed very frightened now. 'That he was a what? Tell me.'

Tom shifted uncomfortably. She obviously didn't know, and he certainly wasn't going to tell her and make it worse.

'Just . . . just a seriously bad guy,' he protested. 'How do you *know* all this?'

'Because he bust into our house last night.'

'Oh.'

'On the cliff top. We were cornered, by these . . . creature things, lord knows what they were. My brother Rudy and me were going to get away on the weather balloon and my dad was going to grab after it but . . . ' Pearl stopped, her pale blue eyes were shining with tears. 'I couldn't . . . it didn't work. Rudy fell, and I got sucked into some kind of hole in the air, on the rim of a twister.'

Tom sat in silence, taking it all in. All kinds of thoughts and memories were flooding back. He had heard such things were possible, and he had seen her at the fireworks. He believed every word.

'So they've gone. Don Gervase Askary has taken them off somewhere,' said Pearl, sadly. 'I'm sorry, I thought maybe you might know more, seeing as he seems to have got your parents too.'

Tom looked up at her, not sure if he had heard correctly.

'What did you say?'

Pearl pushed the battered red notebook she had been holding across the table.

'It's all in there if you want to know.'

Tom picked up the notebook and glanced at the front cover on which was written: 'For Smoot's Eyes Only'.

'Whose is this?'

'My dad's,' replied Pearl, 'he's a radio spy. He listens to stuff, you know, then sells it to people. It's all a bit of a secret.'

'A radio spy,' murmured Tom turning through the closely written pages on UFOs, military secrets, alien experiments, time holes, along with a mass of dates and map references. 'He actually *hears* all this?'

'Yup.'

'Then how come he gave it to you?'

'This book is what Askary wanted—I don't know why, I didn't even know my dad had it. You're right at the end.'

Tom flipped through the pages with an increasing sense of dread: what had this man heard? Soon he recognized the familiar names of Sir Henry Scatterhorn, August Catcher, and several long sections on Nicholas Zumsteen. And there, at the end, were several pages on himself. 'T.S. is born, T.S. fifth birthday party, T.S. father in Mongolia, T.S. meets August Catcher, T.S. and the elixir, T.S. in the museum, T.S. in India, T.S. and Don Gervase Askary.' Section after section recording snippets of conversations, events he couldn't even remember . . .

'But why has your dad been spying on *me*?' demanded Tom angrily. 'What's so interesting about me?'

Pearl shrugged her shoulders. She seemed calmer now.

'It's just what he does. He spies on anyone in the world. Because he can, I suppose. I know it's not, well, very nice exactly, but if you don't know it doesn't matter, does it?'

Tom stared at the pages and bit his lip. The last thing he wanted was to be considered important enough to be spied on. During the last year he had returned to his normal life, his school, his scruffy old house, his slightly crazy mum and dad, just doing normal things. Yes he owned a museum, and yes, he had sold a sapphire to have it restored, but so what? Tom's eyes scanned down the chapters of his life until he reached the bottom. 'Curious end?' it read. 'Sam and Poppy Scatterhorn—taken by DG. TS betrays?' Tom stared at the words without understanding their meaning. He read the line again, and his heart began to beat a wild rhythm in his temples. He could barely bring himself to read on.

Hissing sound. Jungle. River in background. Large creature appears?

'Oh my . . . good god . . . what's that?'

Another crash. Scream. (Is that an <u>animal</u>?)

'Who are you?'

Pause. Scratching. Digging?

'What do you want from us?'

DG laughter. Vicious.

'You really don't know who I am, do you?'

'No.'

A rustling pocket.

'Are you the parents of this boy?'

Deafening silence.

'I'll take that as a yes.'

'He's got nothing to do with this! Nothing at all!'

(Brave speech, Sam.)

'You really never guessed, did you?'

'What?'

Poppy uncertain. Nervous.

'Guessed what?'

'Young Tom is the reason why you are here. And he is the reason why we are here, too.'

Silence.

'He has set you up. He has betrayed you.'

'What? What are you talking about?' Sam shouts.

'Oh I know, it's hard to take. Why would he do a thing like that?' DG sniggers. 'So trusting. So foolish. It's tragic.'

Click of fingers. Screams—a fight. Heavy thump. Silence. Sam and Poppy Scatterhorn <u>dead</u>? Hard to know. Much insect noise.

'Remove them. Destroy the evidence. See that they are taken down to join the rest of the riff-raff.'

Tom stared at the lines helplessly. Then with great effort he read them again.

'Scary, huh?' said Pearl noticing that all the colour had drained from Tom's face. 'That's what I thought too.'

'But . . . this has got to be a mistake,' blustered Tom, 'your dad must have got it wrong. It doesn't make sense.'

Pearl raised her eyebrows.

'My dad is pretty good at this. He doesn't normally make mistakes. If he wrote it down, it's true. But you're right, there's the question marks, and no date, so . . . ' She shrugged her shoulders.

'But . . . but *why*?' stumbled Tom, staring at the words. 'Why would I . . . and why would he take them?'

'I don't know. Why would he take anyone? And *where* would he take them?' Tom sat in silence; it was still almost too much to contemplate. In one brief moment, the bottom had fallen out of his world.

'Sorry,' said Pearl apologetically, 'I thought maybe you knew, which is kind of why I came here. I thought maybe we could help each other. And also, I wondered if I could ask you something.'

Tom looked up at her in a daze.

'What is it?'

'I wondered if you would mind if I slept here tonight?'

Tom considered this for a moment. His heart was still racing.

'It's just that I . . . I've nowhere else to go, if truth be told. And there are these guys . . . I think they are following me.'

'Following you? Which guys?'

'I . . . I'm not entirely sure. Just get that feeling. Maybe because of this,' she sighed, picking up the notebook. 'I don't know. Sorry.'

There was silence for a moment.

'There's a small room at the back,' said Tom, 'I used to sleep there last time I was here. You could have it if you like.'

'Really?'

Pearl smiled: she seemed extremely relieved.

'That would be so nice of you, Tom.'

'No problem,' he muttered, his head still spinning. 'It's down here.'

Tom led the way down the long corridor to the back of the museum, entering the small sliver of a house where Jos and Melba had once lived. None of the lights worked back here, but Tom knew his way in the darkness and found the rickety stairs at the end without difficulty. Climbing the narrow, twisting steps he pushed the small door hard. There before him was the small attic room, the walls sloping in under the eaves and boxes strewn across the floor. In the corner was the narrow bed that he had slept on, still with a faded print bedspread thrown across it. It was all exactly the same. Even the window was still slightly ajar.

'Would this be OK?' said Tom, picking his way through the boxes and leaning against the window frame to try and shut it, without success. 'I'm sorry it's a bit cold. Maybe I—'

'Oh no, it's fine. Really. It's inside—which is much better than outside, believe me.' Pearl smiled. 'Thank you.'

'It's nothing,' he mumbled. 'So . . . so what do you think you're going to do now?'

Pearl thought for a moment.

'Maybe tomorrow I'll look for someone else in Dragonport who can help me. I don't know. This notebook's full of strange information. What are you going to do?'

Tom looked at the floor in confusion.

'Ring my mum and dad I suppose. To make sure, in case, you know . . . '

'Sounds like a good idea. You should do that.'

Tom smiled weakly.

'Yeah.'

There was a moment of uneasy silence, as neither of them knew quite what to say.

'Bye then,' said Tom.

'Bye.'

'See you tomorrow maybe.'

Tom closed the door, and made his way back down the corridors and dark galleries to the foyer, and stepped out into the street. The sun had set long ago, but there was still a pale purple light in the sky. Suddenly he felt angry, blindingly angry. He wanted to scream, but instead he started to run. And he ran and he ran, sprinting back down the hill to Flood Street. What had happened to his parents? He imagined some dark jungle hillside, with a tent pitched in a clearing beneath some great trees. He saw horsemen approaching the tent, galloping up a track towards it, with Don Gervase in the lead . . . it couldn't be, could it?

Tom raced through the back door and straight up to his room without disturbing Jos and Melba in the kitchen. Breathlessly he sat down on the edge of the bed, and with his phone quivering in his hand he typed out a message.

Are u ok? Need to know. Urgent. Tom xxx

Tom pressed the send key, and watched as the words disappeared. He wanted to send another straight away, but knew it made no sense. He could do nothing more. Taking a deep breath he flung himself back on his bed and stared at the ceiling. It didn't make any sense at all. How had he betrayed them? Betray . . . the word bounced round and round his head like a ricocheting bullet . . . Angrily Tom wiped away the tears welling up in his eyes and tried his best to think straight. Whatever may or may not be true, one thing was certain. Arlo Smoot may have listened to many secrets, but he missed one fundamental detail. He did not know that Don Gervase Askary, and all his many thousands of workers and accomplices, were not exactly real people. They were in fact beetles: from the future. Askary had obtained the elixir of life and now, quite clearly, he was after something else. And Tom knew that he would stop at nothing to find it.

CHAPTER 4

SKEET MARSH

Tom got up early the next morning, and pulling on his clothes in any old order he scrambled down the stairs.

'You're in a hurry lad,' shouted Jos blearily out of the window, as he spotted Tom rushing down the garden to the gate. 'Is everything OK?'

'Fine!' shouted Tom, pausing to do up his shoelace. 'Just want to open up in time.'

'Right you are,' said Jos, not entirely sure why Tom wanted to get to the museum so early. After all, it was only just gone seven o'clock in the morning.

'Keen as mustard and mad as a wet hen,' he muttered to himself. Mind you, his dad was quite crazy too. Once these Scatterhorns got the bit between their teeth there was no stopping them.

Tom hurried up through the empty, sunlit streets, thinking hard. He had slept badly, checking his phone every two hours for messages but there were none. And now he had suddenly remembered that he had forgotten to warn Pearl about Ern Rainbird, the military caretaker. Ern was probably in the museum at first light on one of his cleaning routines, and in

Tom's mind he had pictured the scene of Ern finding Pearl asleep in the attic room and using some old commando tactic to knock her out before calling the police. And then there was the small matter of his secret supply of biscuits . . .

Either way, Ern Rainbird was not going to be happy when he arrived for work, and sure enough, he wasn't.

'Ah. It's you,' growled Ern Rainbird as he strode out of the darkness, somewhat surprised to see Tom slip in through the side door this early in the morning. 'Lookin' for someone, are we?'

'No,' said Tom as innocently as he could. 'Is there a problem?'

Ern grimaced.

'Could call it that. It seems we had a visitor last night.'

'A visitor?'

'Indeed. An 'ungry one an' all. Snaffled all me blinkin' biscuits.'

'Oh. Dear. That's erm . . . bad. Is she still here?'

Ern raised an eyebrow and stared at him suspiciously.

'She?'

'I mean, or he,' added Tom quickly. 'Have they gone?'

Ern did not reply immediately. He was still studying Tom with his sandy coloured eyes, and rolling a matchstick from one side of his mouth to the other. Tom could almost hear the cogs in Ern's brain whirring. He was looking for a culprit.

'Reckon,' he said at last. 'Winda at the back's bust open. Must have shimmied down the drainpipe. I've been sweepin' for clues.'

Ern uncoiled a long strand of black hair and held it up to the light.

'See this?' he rasped. 'Vagrant, I reckon. Dog on a string. Bone through the nose. Bottle of cider, they's all over Dragonport like a rash. You know the sort, don'tcha?'

'Oh,' said Tom, inwardly relieved that Pearl had got away. 'Shall I go and have a look?'

'If you like, son,' grimaced Ern, 'it's technically a crime scene, but this is your gaff, innit?'

Tom felt Ern Rainbird's stare follow him as he made his way across the hall and through the door to the small house at the back of the museum. Climbing the rickety stairs at the end of the corridor he opened the door to find that it was all just as Ern had described. So Pearl had gone, as Tom suspected she might. But where to? Tom sat down on the bed and idly looked around the room. The wind was already blowing in through the broken pane and Tom noticed something swaying gently in the breeze behind the door. It was the corner of a piece of newspaper. Getting up, Tom pushed the door shut and found a note scribbled in pencil pinned to the back. Ern must have missed it. Tearing it down, Tom sat on a box and began to read.

'Dear Tom,' it began,

'Sorry about the window, it was a bit stiff. Sorry about the biscuits, (found another pack behind the pipes I'm afraid). And sorry I'm not here. Discovered the names of a few folks in Dragonport scribbled in my dad's notebook. Maybe they can help . . . see you later—hopefully,

Pearl

PS There were some old sneakers under the bed that kind of fit. I hope you don't mind.'

Tom stared at the scribbled note, and then out at the rooftops of Dragonport and the river in the distance. Could there *really* be someone who might know something out here? It sounded unlikely, but in truth Tom was almost as much of a stranger in

Dragonport as she was. He had only been here once before, during the school holidays, and half of that time he wasn't actually 'here' at all . . .

Tom pulled out his phone and fiddled with it impatiently—still no messages from his parents. He was trying to tell himself that it didn't matter, that it was probably the middle of the night, and they were almost certainly out of range, as they almost always were; deep in a jungle or up a mountain, but still . . . those words in the notebook were still smouldering at the back of his brain, he couldn't let them go . . . supposing they *had* been taken, where had they been taken to? It was almost certainly the future, wasn't it? Tom had often tried to imagine this, the place from where Don Gervase and Lotus and possibly a good deal of the others had mysteriously arrived, and he always pictured a vast, dusty, desert landscape, dotted with the last relics of human civilization. There was nothing much there, except millions and millions of beetles. Tom looked down at the note once more and shook his head. Maybe he should have told Pearl the truth about Don Gervase . . . no—she'd never believe him, who would? He'd never really told anyone about it, and sometimes he wondered whether it was even true himself. But it was.

'So we've had a little break in, have we?'

Jos shambled across the hall leaving Ern Rainbird still muttering in the gloom.

'Dear oh dear,' he wheezed, sidling up to Tom. 'And nothing's been taken—'cept Ern's beloved biscuits, and lordy-lord, is he miffed about that. Not to worry,' he whispered. 'Actually, Tom, this is rather good news.'

'Why is that?'

'Lets us off the hook, doesn't it?' said Jos, his eyes narrowing to the size of bullets beneath his enormous eyebrows. 'Ern loves nothing more than a bit of argy bargy, and someone half-inching his secret supply of Jaffa cakes is perfect. Gives him something to moan about.'

Tom wasn't quite sure that he understood the logic of this, but Jos seemed quite happy.

'And I have another piece of good news for you, lad. Just after you left this morning I took a call from Oscarine Zumsteen.'

'Oscarine Zumsteen?'

'Exactly. Most unexpected. And what's more, she wants to meet you.'

'Me?'

'You. The *owner*,' said Jos grandly. 'She's invited you to tea this morning.'

'Oh.' Tom was not sure what to say. 'Did she say why?'

'No.' Jos shrugged. 'Not precisely. So I said you'd be there in about an hour.'

'You did?' replied Tom, slightly taken aback.

'If that's all right with you, that is,' he added casually, 'only, I wasn't sure whether you had anything else planned for this morning, and I wouldn't want you getting bored.'

'Bored?' Tom snorted indignantly. 'Why should I be bored?'

'I ain't sayin' that you is, lad,' replied Jos, clapping him on the shoulder. 'But this is like an invitation from the queen. It's peculiar enough even to see Oscarine—let alone get invited out to her cottage. *I* never have. So, just have a cup of tea and smile: charm her, lad. And between ourselves, I got the feeling she had something to tell you,' he said with a wink.

'Really?'

'Really. Oscarine's a rare old bird, well known for playing her cards very close to her chest indeed, so she wouldn't tell me of course. Just . . . *implied* that might be the case,' he said mysteriously.

Tom could see that there was no backing out of this one. And however much he did not feel like going to tea with an eccentric old lady, her late husband, Nicholas Zumsteen, intrigued him. Perhaps he too was connected to all of this . . .

'OK then,' said Tom. 'How do I get there?'

'Easy,' smiled Jos. 'You can take the boneshaker.'

Several minutes later Tom found himself wobbling uncertainly down the road on a very old and rusty black bicycle with a small front wheel and a long basket strapped on top.

'You'll get used to it!' shouted Jos cheerily. 'Just keep pedalling and remember: don't use the back brake, it will lock dead and send you flying!'

'The front brake,' corrected Melba, standing beside him watching Tom go. 'It's the front brake that does that, Jos.'

'Is it? I thought you said—'

'I didn't say anything at all. Don't tell me you set him on his way without testing them? Did you, Jos?'

'Erm . . . ' Jos scratched his head. 'Well, I wouldn't exactly call it—'

'It's the front brake that jams, Tom!' she shouted. 'Use the back!'

Tom was already moving swiftly down the hill of Museum Street towards the river. Which brake worked: the front, the back, both—neither? It was hard enough to keep the heavy boneshaker upright as it wobbled strangely and began to let out an alarming sound as it picked up speed.

'Oh lordy,' muttered Jos, putting a hand over his eyes.

Tom's feet came off the pedals and he leaned into the bend at the bottom of the hill and swung round it without using any brakes at all. But somehow the crash Jos was expecting never came, as Tom suddenly found himself up on the pavement, narrowly missing a bench, shooting between two bollards then thumping back down onto the road again, hitting it so hard that his teeth rattled. No wonder it was called the boneshaker. But riding this ancient machine without brakes was quite fun, and Tom wondered if he could make it all the way to Oscarine's cottage without having to use them.

Jos had explained that the best way to get there was to follow the river north out of Dragonport, till the houses gave way to fields and reed beds that marked the edge of the Hellkiss estate.

'There's a new path will take you round the edge of Skeet marsh,' he had said, 'it's a bit longer that way, but you'll get there. There is an old smugglers' path through the reeds too, a shortcut, but I don't know whether it still exists. I'd go round, lad, if I were you.'

Tom kept repeating these instructions to himself as he bicycled down the sleepy terraced streets, which eventually turned into lines of garages and a few burnt out cars. The river glittered brilliant blue in the sunlight and there was no one about, though at the end of the last street before the marshes he did notice a car with a couple of men in dark suits sitting inside it. They appeared to be waiting for something. Perhaps it's a stakeout, thought Tom, undercover policemen, spying on a fugitive. The men watched Tom suspiciously as he pushed the boneshaker through the narrow gate and set off down the marsh track. Definitely a stakeout, thought Tom, and he spent the next few minutes lost in an imaginary scenario that involved a bloody shootout and ended very badly for the policemen. By the time he looked up again from his daydream Tom could see a narrow, tumbledown cottage, standing on its own at the far side of the marsh. Beyond it was a great army of dark pine trees stretching on up the river. That must be Oscarine's cottage, thought Tom, and it was nothing like he was expecting: somehow he had it in his head that it would be something much grander, given the wealth of the Zumsteens and the fabulous tableaux. But maybe Oscarine had become a recluse for a reason . . .

Tom's uneasiness grew as he turned onto the sandy track leading down to the cottage, as there at the end of the long, straight ride up through the forest was another parked car. It also appeared to be waiting . . . Tom ignored it, and turned down past an old wooden boat overgrown with nettles and a mouldy caravan on bricks and several other bits of rusting machinery lurking in the long grass. It was like a messy old farmyard, and he half expected some huge dog to suddenly bound out of the undergrowth and chase him away. But there was no sound here except the hiss of the wind in the pine trees. Tom dug his toes into the red sand and brought himself to a slow stop, climbing off the boneshaker and leaning it against the gatepost. Turning round, he looked up at the two dark windows peeking out of the thatch like eyes. He was sure he caught a flicker of movement behind the curtain. Was that Oscarine? Tom hitched up his trousers and pushed the hair out of his eyes; he wasn't sure why he was suddenly feeling so nervous. There was something spooky about this isolated place: maybe it was those cars, maybe it was the silence . . . Taking a deep breath, he walked up the path and determinedly rapped on the door. There was no answer. Tom waited, and he was about to knock again when he noticed that the door was ajar. Pushing it open he peered into the dark interior, and noticed half-filled cardboard boxes strewn across the floor.

'Hello?'

'Hello,' came a high, singsong voice from somewhere at the back. 'Who is it?'

'It's Tom Scatterhorn.'

'Oh? Oh yes! Wait a minute, wait a minute wait a minute.'

Tom stood anxiously in the doorway. Jos had described Oscarine as a rare old bird, which could mean anything at all, but when the small silhouette appeared from somewhere round the back and scurried towards the front door, Tom saw that it was remarkably accurate.

'Hello hello,' she said, poking her head around the door.

'Hi,' said Tom, looking at the small lady with bright red hair and narrow shoulders, wearing a long embroidered dress. On the end of her beaky nose balanced a pair of half-moon glasses that magnified the bottom half of her pale blue eyes to an enormous size.

'It's . . . erm . . . You—'

'Tea?' said Oscarine, cocking her head like a pigeon. 'Will you have tea?'

'Yes,' mumbled Tom, 'great.'

'Come come come,' she said briskly, and led the way through the boxes to a couple of old chintz wing-back chairs beside the fire that was blazing in the grate despite the summer's day.

'You sit there, you sit there, so I can see you properly,' said Oscarine, indicating the chair by the window. Tom did as he was told, and waited as Oscarine bustled off into the kitchen. Oscarine may have looked a little strange, but she certainly knew what she wanted. Tom sat fidgeting, and as he took in his surroundings he realized that this room was also half packed up. Along one wall stretched a pattern of square yellow patches on the wallpaper where pictures once had hung, while along the other a jumble of fisheye mirrors reflected the heaps of books and old magazines that dotted the Persian carpet. In the corner a grey Siamese cat sat snoring on a cushion, and on the mantel-piece Tom noticed some black and white photographs of a dark-haired, dashing man smiling in front of a gleaming silver biplane.

'Sorry about the mess,' said Oscarine as she returned with her tray. 'It's all happening today and I don't know whether I'm coming or going.'

'Are you moving?' asked Tom politely.

'Evicted evicted evicted, my boy,' said Oscarine quickly, stir-ring the tea. 'Quite a different kettle of fish. It's all change on the Hellkiss estate, you see, and I've been given my marching orders.

All change, all change. How do you take it, strong?' she said, handing Tom a fine blue cup and saucer decorated with birds. 'Of course I should have seen it coming. Should have seen it, should have seen it,' she went on, addressing the teapot. 'It was inevitable. They need the money. Can you blame them? Ginger thin?'

Tom leant forward and took one.

'Thanks.'

'All this lot has got to go to auction. This afternoon. Which is very trying indeed. Particularly as . . . ' her large eyes glanced up at the clock, 'they'll be here in a minute. What a kerfuffle. Well well well.'

For the first time since he had arrived Oscarine stopped talking and looked at Tom in silence. Tom smiled nervously, listening to the clock ticking in the corner.

'Err . . . thank you for the tableaux,' he said. 'They are amazing. The deluge . . . it's incredible.'

Oscarine cocked her head and nibbled at the corner of a biscuit.

'So they say, so they say.'

'And the model too,' continued Tom, 'I was wondering why August Catcher made it? Had he been to the Tithona archipelago?'

'Well it was a present,' replied Oscarine. 'A birthday present. To me, as it happens.'

'Oh?'

'Yes. Nick commissioned it when he was out there. Have you heard of my husband, Nicholas Zumsteen?'

Tom nodded.

'Used to fly aeroplanes,' continued Oscarine. 'Jolly good at it he was too. That's him up there,' she said pointing to the black and white photographs on the mantelpiece. 'Dashing, don't you think? My, was he dashing. He could charm the birds from the trees. God-like, almost.'

Tom looked up at the photographs of the dark-haired man, leaning casually against the wing of the silver aeroplane. So that was him, the famous Nicholas Zumsteen. He looked every inch the headstrong, rebellious young man Jos had told him about.

'Was he famous?' asked Tom.

'No no, my boy, infamous perhaps.' She grinned. 'Certainly amongst his family. He was a thorn in their side right up until . . . ' Oscarine's birdlike voice trailed away. 'That is, until he vanished, many years ago. Somewhere near the Tithona archipelago. Rather ironic really, given what happened.'

Tom smiled politely, not quite following what she meant.

'Well they've gone too, haven't they?' she said peering up at him in surprise.

'They have?'

'Tithona is volcanic, my boy. Volcanic volcanic volcanic. They had an eruption there, my gosh—about thirty years ago. Most of the islands went up in smoke. Written right off the map. So they'll never find old Nick now. Not that it matters anyway, because he's . . . ' Again Oscarine stopped mid-sentence to nibble the corner of a biscuit. She seemed to be holding herself back.

'Odd, isn't it?'

Odd it certainly was, and Tom wondered how much longer it

would take Oscarine to get to the point. Had Jos been imagining things when he said he thought she wanted to tell him something? The silence continued, and Oscarine continued to stare at him, her fingers playing restlessly with an exotic silver bangle around her wrist.

'Do you mind if I ask you a question?' she said suddenly.

'No.'

'Do you lose things?'

'Lose things?' repeated Tom, rather taken aback. 'I . . . well . . . sometimes I suppose.'

'You see the problem is I do. Frequently. That's the problem. I hide things, then I lose them. Lose them. Can't find them. Gone. So I have summoned you here under false pretences. Which is a problem,' she said, scratching her head and staring at the mess all around. 'Apologies.'

'So, you had something to . . . give me?' asked Tom.

'Correct.'

'Well, maybe I can help you find it,' suggested Tom helpfully.

Oscarine looked at Tom blankly, and then suddenly a smile lit up her face.

'Yes!' she exclaimed. 'Yes yes yes. Maybe *you* could find it. You could, you could. Could you?'

'Maybe. What is it?'

'Well, I'll explain. It belongs with that model of Tithona, and can't be parted from it. Very important that, I remember, which is why it's so annoying, and if it wasn't for these blasted auction people . . . ' She looked at him, exasperated. 'Because that's the other thing. They know, and what's more, I *know* they know.' Oscarine nodded her head and leant forward conspiratorially.

'They have been waiting for me to dig it out for months. Waiting. It's obvious, I've seen them lurking up the track. Because they know it's hidden somewhere, but where? In the house, in the forest, in the well, in the river?' Oscarine shrugged her shoulders. 'They don't know. So let me find it, because it could be anywhere—couldn't it?'

'Could it?' said Tom.

Oscarine looked at him desperately.

'I can't remember! That is the problem.' She began to wring her hands together. 'And of course you won't find it either, unless you can put two and two together to make five. Think laterally . . .'

The sound of a van clattering to a halt on the track outside interrupted Oscarine's ramblings, and Tom glanced through the window to see a gang of men walking up the path to the front door.

'You see?' Oscarine glanced up nervously. 'Is this a coincidence? Is it? Gosh gosh gosh. What are we going to do?'

The doorbell rang.

'Mrs Zumsteen?' shouted a rough voice. 'Anyone at home?'

Oscarine stared at the door in agitation.

'Coming!' she shouted cheerily.

'When you say it goes with the model,' said Tom, 'is it like a letter, or a key that opens it up?'

'No, no no it's . . . it's much larger than that,' whispered Oscarine, 'it has a key itself.'

Tom racked his brains: what could have a key and go with the model?

'My mum keeps loads of stuff in teapots,' he said, looking

down at the tray. 'Teapots and socks. Those are her hiding places.'

'Not teapots. Not socks,' replied Oscarine, briskly dismissing the suggestion. 'But of course, you must see it,' she said, and jumping up, she plucked one of the black and white photographs of Nicholas Zumsteen off the mantelpiece. Holding it out before Tom, her thin jewelled fingers pointed at the narrow wooden box at his feet that was covered in airline stickers and bound up with cord. Tom recognized it immediately: his father took one with him wherever he went.

'An expedition box?'

Oscarine nodded quickly.

'Precisely. Exactly.' Her large blue eyes bulged, and she shot a meaningful look at Tom. 'That, I believe, is it. But you mustn't say a word. Nothing. You see what I mean now?'

Tom didn't, try as he might. Why would 'they' want an expedition box? If it was anything like his father's it would be full of glass trays and killing jars and pins and paper, all the paraphernalia for collecting insects in the wild . . .

'I will have to do this some other way,' she whispered, thrusting the photograph into her pocket, 'a brain wave, that's what I need, my boy. *Un wave de brain.*'

Oscarine hustled him out of the door, past the gang of burly men in blue overalls who were already lifting boxes into the back of the van.

'All to go, is it, love?' said the foreman, eyeing Tom suspiciously as he walked down to the gate.

'That's right. All to go,' said Oscarine, with an air of mock cheeriness, 'take it all.'

'Don't worry, Mrs Zumsteen, we will,' joked the foreman. 'You want us to put the bike in the van an' all?'

'Erm . . . actually, that's mine,' said Tom, walking over to the boneshaker leaning against the fence. The foreman looked at Tom doubtfully.

'You havin' a laugh, son?'

'No,' said Tom defensively, 'it does work. Once you get going.'

A couple of the other removal men sniggered as they came out with more boxes.

'If you say so, mate,' cackled the foreman. ''Ere Tel, look at this, the Tour de France is about to start!'

Tom ignored the audience gathering behind him as he pushed the boneshaker up onto the track.

'Hope you solve your puzzle, Mrs Zumsteen,' he said, looking back at the narrow, birdlike figure of Oscarine, her bright red hair glowing in the sunlight.

'Indeed,' she said, attempting to smile, but there was a curious, tortured expression on her face. Tom turned and jumped on, pedalling furiously, and a gale of laughter erupted behind him as the boneshaker wobbled and lurched drunkenly across the red sand ruts. Tom just had time to notice that the black car was still waiting at the end of the track in the woods before he gratefully slid back down onto Skeet marsh once more, the laughter still ringing in his ears.

'What did you say that lad's name was?' asked the foreman as he watched Tom wobble away towards the river.

'I didn't,' replied Oscarine Zumsteen cocking her head. 'But it's Tom Scatterhorn, if want to know. From the museum.'

The foreman grunted suspiciously, his eyes following the

blob of blond hair bobbing away through the tall green reeds.

'Helping you solve a puzzle, was he?'

'Something like that.'

'Only Tel here's a black belt at Sudoku, incha Tel? He's obsessed. Stick a bomb under him when he's on one of them puzzles an 'e wouldn't notice!'

The foreman laughed, his keen eyes still on Oscarine. Tel grunted as he hefted a box up onto the van, and Oscarine stood in the doorway thinking hard. Puzzle, belt, bomb . . . the odd combination of words had opened a door in her mind and it was starting to come back, yes indeed it was . . . Nicholas's strange request . . . that was it! The puzzle, the belt and the—she had remembered. She glanced nervously across at the reeds but there was no sign of Tom. Rats! He had gone . . . too bad. Then she looked up the track to where the car lurked in the shadows of the pine trees. This was obviously the day, she knew it. Right-ho. Well, she was not going to make it easy for them. Absolutely not. She must give these nitwits the slip and find that boy, pronto.

'Scatterhorn, you say?' muttered the foreman, pulling out a telephone and punching in a number.

'That's right. From the museum,' said Oscarine gleefully, and scurried back into the cottage.

A couple of minutes later Tom had found his rhythm and the boneshaker was travelling along very nicely. All he could think of now was Oscarine's box: what was so special about it that it had to be protected, and were 'they' who he thought they were?

Not knowing any of the answers was very frustrating and confusing, but Tom had a nagging suspicion that Oscarine was not nearly as mad as she seemed . . .

Halfway round Skeet marsh Tom stopped for a rest. The wind, which had been blowing hard earlier, had stopped now, and the air was heavy and still. Tom's face itched with thunderflies, and wiping the sweat out of his eyes he noticed that large black rain clouds were piling up over the estuary. Straight ahead he could just make out the cranes of Dragonport, shining like silver spikes above the reeds, and Tom doubted he would get back before the heavens opened. Cursing to himself, he was just about to climb up onto the boneshaker when he remembered the smugglers' path that ran straight across the reed beds. Maybe he could find it. From where he stood there was no sign of an obvious entrance into the wall of green, but a little further along he noticed a post standing on the other side of the track. Could that be it?

Wheeling the boneshaker on he saw that he was right; it had been a signpost, but the sign had long since disappeared, though it seemed to line up with a small opening in the reeds opposite. Pushing the green curtain aside, Tom peered in and saw a long narrow path running into the reed beds. It looked like a shortcut, as it led directly towards Dragonport: should he take it? A distant rumble of thunder behind him made up his mind. If it was wrong he could always turn round and come back. Pushing the boneshaker through the entrance Tom jumped into the saddle and began pedalling, and soon the ancient bicycle was bouncing along under its own momentum. Tom was so busy concentrating on keeping the boneshaker on the narrow sandy trail that he barely noticed anything but the high green walls of

reeds on either side, and the occasional flash of a path or clearing beyond. There was no sound in here, just the whispering of
the reeds, and no life either, and the deeper Tom bicycled into
that strangely alien place the more he felt that if he really did
get lost it was quite likely he would never find his way out again.

After five more minutes of concentrating hard Tom was thoroughly hot and covered in thunderflies once more, and the path
he had been following divided. Which way next? He couldn't
see over the top of the reeds towards Dragonport, but his
instinct told him to go left. Looking down, he noticed that the
sand had been turned by footprints on that side—someone else
had been there recently. That must be the way to go. OK. It
couldn't be that much further now.

Tom wiped his eyes and he was just about to get back into the
saddle when he heard something above the hissing grasses. He
stopped and listened. What was that?

'Zis is the place, no?'

'For sure. Zey said zey saw her zis morning.'

'You believe them?'

'Who knows? I am only believing what you are believing.'

Tom stood still. The voices seemed to be in front of him.
Should he go on and try to catch them up? They might be
able to point him in the right direction. Yes, that is what he
should do. Stepping up onto the boneshaker once more Tom had
just begun to pedal when he heard the voices again.

'Sssh!'

'What is it?'

'Zomeone is coming, zomeone is coming!'

'I hear zem, I hear zem!'

Tom slowed himself to a halt and strained to catch the sounds. The voices were coming from the right of the path now, somewhere beyond the wall of green reeds.

'Is it her?'

'Maybe so. Are you ready?'

'Ja for sure. Both barrels loaded.'

'Vait for my signal.'

Tom felt his heart begin to quicken. On second thoughts, maybe he shouldn't ask these people the way. Whoever they were they were obviously lying in wait for someone and their intentions did not sound friendly. Carefully Tom got off the boneshaker and set it down beside the track.

'Zer it was again! I heard it!'

'Sssh. Vait vait. Silence please. Any moment now.'

Tom stood up as quietly as he could and looked about him. It was quite clear that these people were very close . . . were they about to shoot him—or someone else? Maybe he should shout out and let them know he was there . . . that would be the sensible thing to do. But at this moment Tom was not feeling very sensible, because somewhere at the back of his mind he had a terrible suspicion that he knew who these people were waiting for . . .

Tom quietly padded further down the track until he came to a small opening in the reeds on the right-hand side. Peeking through the narrow gap he could just make out a small path. Should he take it? Yes, he should. Taking great care to disturb the reeds as little as possible, Tom slithered through and crept silently forward. A little way in front of him the path disappeared into another impenetrable wall of reeds. To the left it was the same, but to the right . . . Tom hooked a reed stalk around his finger and gently bent it aside.

It was just as he had suspected. There, just beyond, was a clearing, a small patch of yellow surrounded by thick green walls. In one corner was the half-deflated orange weather balloon, and beside it, a blanket. This must have been where Pearl had landed on the night of the fireworks. But who were those two crouching men clutching shotguns on the far side? Tom pushed himself forward as far as he dared to get a better look. At first glance they appeared identical. They were both small and wiry, with long, bony faces, and they were dressed as if to go duck shooting. They looked faintly ridiculous.

'Can you hear anyzing?'

The other shook his head.

'Maybe it was animal. I don't know. My ears are kaput.'

'You zink really the girl is here for sure?'

'Ja maybe. Vy not? Zer balloon is here, zo zer girl is here also.'

The man on the left sniggered.

'Boom!' he said. 'Boom boom boom.'

'Ssshh. Zis is serious.'

'Sorry. I was zinking. Zey will be very surprised.'

'For sure. You and me hero men.'

'Hero men!'

They grinned identically and turned their attention back to the entrance. Tom watched the curious little men in silence, knowing that he had met these types before . . . in their thousands. The memory of it sent a shiver down his spine, and at that moment Tom felt heavy drops of rain begin to fall on his back.

'You and me very wet,' he muttered to himself, and moments later the rain that had been threatening came pouring down. It was time to go. Leaving the hunters staring silently at the entrance, Tom carefully retraced his steps to his bicycle. The noise of the rain hammering down on the path was more than enough to conceal his exit, and jumping up onto the ancient boneshaker he slithered away as fast as he could down the track.

Ten minutes' hard pedalling brought him to a gap in the reeds and he emerged to find himself almost in Dragonport once more. Wiping the tangle of wet hair out of his eyes, Tom dismounted and heaved the heavy bicycle through the narrow gate and out onto the road. He was relieved to be back, but those ratty-faced men had set his nerves jangling. Pearl obviously had some sort of price on her head, and he must find her—somehow—before they did. And he must also tell her the truth about Don Gervase Askary. Who were these people in Dragonport she had gone to find? Tom didn't know, but it worried him.

He pedalled on grimly, sweeping past the burnt out cars and garages, standing forlorn in the rain. The two undercover agents he had seen earlier had gone. Maybe they were somehow involved too, maybe the removal men as well, and that car on the track, maybe they were all in it together . . .

A small knot of fear tightened around Tom's heart; and in his mind he pictured a sprawling, many-tentacled organization, staffed by thousands of grey workers, who had infested every part of the world he knew. And at its very centre sat Don Gervase Askary himself, like a monstrous spider, pulling all the strings, listening to every quiver of the web. Tom knew that he and his legions would never stop until he had got exactly what he wanted. The question was, what was it?

CHAPTER 5

DEATH BY CHOCOLATE

'We'll be late Melba, we'll be late.'

'But we can't leave him like this. He looks like a drowned rat.'

'So what if he does?'

'But what if he gets a chill or something?'

Uncle Jos and Aunt Melba stood in the doorway of their cottage in Flood Street, dressed from head to foot in black shining waterproofs and wearing their motorcycle helmets, staring at Tom standing shivering and soaked before them. The rain was still hammering down.

'I suppose you're right,' muttered Jos, reluctantly. 'But it's about to start. There won't be much left.'

'I don't care, Joshua,' trilled Melba. 'We're not all built like walruses, you know.'

Jos harrumphed loudly. They stared at Tom standing in the garden.

'C-c-can I come in?' said Tom, his teeth chattering.

'In?' repeated Jos. 'I thought you liked swimming, lad?'

Tom could just make out Jos's eyes twinkling through his thick glass goggles. 'Oh if you must. Get in here, you crazy fool,' and he dragged Tom's skinny frame through the door and out of the rain.

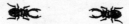

Five minutes later, Tom was sitting in the fuggy kitchen wearing a collection of brightly striped towels and looking doubtfully at the cup of milk Melba insisted he should drink.

'Now if you feel in the slightest bit peaky, there's all manner of pick-me-ups in the medicine cabinet in the bathroom,' said Melba, staring at Tom with some concern.

'I'm fine, honestly. Just got a bit wet that's all,' said Tom.

'Exactly Melba, what's a bit of rain?' wheezed Jos. He was still dressed in his waterproofs and motorbike helmet, and he was pacing about impatiently.

'You never know what can happen,' replied Melba, unconvinced. 'Look at him, he's still shaking like a dog. Now Tom, there's the number of a doctor by the phone—'

'Oh for goodness' sake, stop faffing!' exploded Jos from inside his helmet. 'Can we go now?'

'I'll be fine,' said Tom, managing a smile. 'Really, I'm fine.'

Melba looked at him hard.

'You don't look fine. You look like death. I don't want any deaths in this house.'

'Deaths? Christ on a bike,' rasped Jos, banging his helmet against the wall. 'Melba, sweetheart, if we don't go now—there will be no point going at all. Now. Off—we—go,' and he calmly manhandled Melba out of the door. 'Just do as your aunt says,' he said, winking at Tom, 'there's a good lad.'

The door slammed, and Tom heard the sound of the motor-bike firing up, and they were gone.

Tom sat in damp silence, feeling the occasional drip on the back of his neck. The rain was still thundering down on the windowpanes. The reason Jos had been so impatient to get going was that he was determined to pick up a bargain or two at the auction house, where all Oscarine Zumsteen's furniture and pictures and other bits and pieces had been taken. The fact that Oscarine hadn't given Tom anything had not put him off. If anything, it had only encouraged him. Jos was convinced that Oscarine was quite as absent-minded as he was, and this was precisely the sort of auction where the unexpected could be snapped up for nothing. Tom wondered about that . . . and his mind kept returning to that small patch of flattened grass in the middle of the marshes, and those two narrow-faced men crouching in the rain. Had Pearl come back yet? Had they killed her? A shiver ran down Tom's spine. If only he knew what this was all about. Why did they want to kill her so much?

The soft burr of the telephone ringing broke across Tom's thoughts. Tom shuffled across to the hall and rubbing a towel violently across his face he picked it up.

'Hello?'

'Yes hello. Is that you, Jos?'

'No. It's Tom.'

'Tom? Tom who?'

'Tom Scatterhorn.'

'Ah.' The quick, high voice paused for a moment. 'Right right right. Well that's actually quite good. Very good in fact.'

There was a silence.

'You see it's Oscarine here. Oscarine Zumsteen. Do you remember?'

Given that Tom had only just got back from her house about ten minutes ago there was only one answer to that question, and Tom resisted a strong temptation to say something sarcastic.

'Yes I do. Hello.'

'Good. Marvellous. Well, I . . . erm—are you busy at the moment?'

'No.'

'You see I've given them the slip. I'm now in Noah's Café, at the end of your street. Flood Street.'

'Oh. OK.'

'Not much time, so can I expect you in about five minutes, then. Yes?'

Tom was perplexed.

'Erm . . . but why—'

'Can't talk. But you should know I've found the blasted thing. That's right. Found it found it found it. Noah's Café.'

The line went dead.

Oscarine Zumsteen was in the café at the end of the street. She had given them the slip, and she had found it. At any other time, Tom might have thought that Oscarine was just a strange and slightly mad old lady who was suffering from delusions, but right now, for some reason, he didn't. There *was* something going on here. Tom began pulling on the driest clothes he could find, but then a shadow of doubt crossed his mind. If she was right, did he really want to take possession of something Don

Gervase wanted? Did he *really* want that? But he knew that it was already too late. He had to take whatever Oscarine wanted to give him, as he was already part of this great jigsaw, just as Pearl was, and even his parents, too . . . but Tom kicked that thought firmly to the back of his mind. Grabbing one of Melba's wide brimmed hats that looked vaguely waterproof he ran out into the rain.

The neon sign blinked 'No Caf' uncertainly as Tom opened the door. Had he been paying more attention, he would have also noticed a car with two men in it lurking on the far side of the road. Inside, the place was fuggy and bustling with soaked customers grumbling about the storm. Tom threaded his way past the hassled waitress down the line of faded green formica tables until he reached the booth at the far end, where a shape in a large yellow sou'wester sat with her back to him. Was that her? It must be. There were wisps of red hair peeking out from under the brim.

'Hi.'

Oscarine glanced up from her fidgeting as Tom slipped down onto the bench opposite. She looked like a small, strange animal dwarfed by her plastic coat, and she seemed nervous, a little frightened, even.

'Ah.' She half-smiled. 'Thank you. I thought you'd come.'

'Yes. Well here I am again.'

'Indeed. Here you are again. Here we all are again. Gosh.'

Oscarine took a deep breath and played with her teaspoon once more, running it round and round the rim of the cup. Tom stared at the spoon, and felt a rising sense of frustration as silence descended on the table.

'So you found it,' he began, 'where—'

'I did, yes indeed I did,' interrupted Oscarine quickly. 'And now I have to be sure. Absolutely certain.'

'About what?'

Oscarine looked uncomfortable.

'Think think think,' she muttered to herself under her breath. She seemed agitated, and glanced up at the wall.

'Promise me something, Tom,' she said suddenly, her large, china-blue eyes holding his. 'If I give you this to keep, on no account must you lose it, or tell anyone about it. Not even your uncle. Can you do that?'

'Sure,' said Tom, not quite sure what he was committing himself to.

'*Are* you quite sure?' Oscarine studied him nervously. 'You see, I know I'm a gonner. They'll get nothing out of me, you can be damn sure about that. But you—'

The waitress came forward and wiped the table.

'You finished with that, love?' she said, running a dirty cloth around Oscarine's cup.

'Yes. I have. I mean—I mean no. No, no no. Sorry, no. Still on the go.'

The waitress raised her eyebrows and turned to Tom.

'And what can I get you, love, tea, coffee, cake—what?'

'Hot chocolate, thanks.'

'One 'ot choc!' shouted the waitress and bustled away. Tom watched her go, and noticed that two large men in overcoats had come in out of the rain and were standing by the door.

When they turned round Tom recognized one of them immediately: he was the undercover policeman in the car Tom had seen earlier that day. The man's eyes swivelled across the tables briefly, then he sat down next to the flickering sign in the window. What were *they* doing in here? A creeping sense of panic began to gather inside him as the waitress went over to them, took their order, and then marched back to the counter. Tom caught her eye, and tried to read her blank, bored expression as she hurried back into the kitchen . . . surely she had looked at him for just a fraction of a second too long? Something was going to happen in here, this wasn't just a coincidence. Tom pressed himself further into the booth so that he could not be seen.

'All going horribly wrong, isn't it?' muttered Oscarine to herself. 'They tailed me, of course they did. Nicholas was dead right. We'll all end up in Scarazand in the end. Oh yes. Horribly, horribly wrong.'

'What?'

Oscarine was still fiddling with her spoon. She appeared not to hear him.

'Where did you say we are going to end up?'

'Scarazand my boy. Oh yes oh yes oh yes. The central place,' she whispered, peering up at him through her half-moon spectacles. Tom held her gaze uncomfortably.

'Where's . . . Scarazand?'

'Beyond. Elsewhere. Betwixt and between,' she hissed. 'But then I don't precisely know do I? Does anyone? How does one get into the future?'

Oscarine nodded violently. Anyone might assume that this

strange, bedraggled old lady dwarfed inside her large yellow mackintosh was crazy, but Tom had a strong instinct that she wasn't. Quite the opposite, in fact.

'I know what's coming,' she continued defiantly, 'indeed, I've been expecting it. Don't think I'm not ready.' Oscarine leant forward and whispered very carefully. 'I can see everything, you know.'

With a flicker of her eyes Oscarine glanced up to Tom's right, and, following her gaze, he saw a fish-eye mirror reflecting the whole café. In it, Tom saw the shadows of the two men talking, then one of them stood up and positioned himself squarely in front of the door.

'But what *is* going on?' replied Tom, who found that he was whispering too. 'Are you in trouble?'

Oscarine continued to play with her teacup.

'Trouble of a kind,' she murmured. 'They think they are so very clever. Following me here, backing me into a corner, forcing me to give it up. But then of course I remembered, didn't I? I don't have it, do I? Not in *ma maison. Non non non.*'

Tom watched Oscarine chittering to herself in confusion.

'So, you *don't* have it?'

'No I don't. Not at all.' She looked up at him with a knowing smile. 'You do.'

Tom was astonished.

'Me? What, the expedition box?'

Oscarine nodded.

'Where is it?'

'Inside,' she whispered, her eyes enormous through her

half-moon spectacles. 'Inside the model. Hidden within. Nicholas was very precise about it. Very, very precise. It's a marvellous puzzle, you see, but rather dangerous too. And on no account must you try to remove it. That is absolutely *verboten*. Never do that because—'

Oscarine glanced up at the mirror and suddenly her expression changed. The larger of the two men was threading his way through the tables towards them.

'What is it?' asked Tom.

Oscarine shook her head violently.

'Too late. Found out. No time. Rattlesnakes rattlesnakes,' growled Oscarine between her teeth. Then suddenly she had an idea, and pulling out a pen she scribbled a series of odd-looking letters on the paper mat.

'Always shake hands with the jerboa,' whispered Oscarine breathlessly, 'it will let you in. Remember that.'

'The what?'

'The jerboa. The jer—'

'Mrs Zumsteen?'

The large, pasty-faced man stood staring down at them. Oscarine shot a glance up at him, full of venom and spite.

'If you would just come with us, madam.'

Tom stared at Oscarine: what had she done?

'Are you asking me or ordering me?' she said curtly.

'It would be for the best, madam,' breathed the heavy man, glancing over at his colleague by the door.

'Very well,' she said, 'I've been expecting this. I'm ready.'

'Wait, wait a minute,' blurted Tom. 'Where are you taking her? What has she done?'

The man stared down at Tom with lazy, stupid eyes. Tom felt that he was looking at him, but at the same time, he wasn't.

'Best stay out of this, son,' he growled. 'It's a private matter.'

'But—but you can't just take her away,' protested Tom, his voice rising, 'what are you, the police or something?'

The man ignored Tom and stepped back.

'Mrs Zumsteen?'

Oscarine had a steely expression on her face, and made something of a fuss of zipping up her coat.

'Oscarine,' hissed Tom, desperately trying to catch her eye. 'You don't have to do this. Don't go with them.'

Oscarine made a point of ignoring Tom until she was absolutely ready, then she casually picked the teaspoon off the table to replace it on the saucer.

'Goodbye, young man,' she said to Tom, with such a strange formality it was as if they had never met before. Tom stared back at her blankly.

'Given the dangers we all face, I hope that you will *reflect* on what I said,' she continued, articulating the words very carefully, and with a flicker of her eyes glanced down at the spoon in her hand. Tom looked down, and saw that she was holding it directly above the mat. He could just make out words reflected in its dull surface . . . mirror writing, was this some kind of signal? Tom glanced up at her narrow, bird-like face, and she winked. It was! With great difficulty Tom stifled a grin.

'I'll . . . I'll do just that,' he said, and with the merest nod he showed her that he understood. The heavy-eyed man in the raincoat shifted impatiently on his feet, unaware of what had passed between them.

'Good good good,' continued Oscarine, 'I knew you would. And don't worry about me, my lips are sealed.' With a small, satisfied smile, Oscarine got up, and she was escorted to the door by the large man, whose colleague opened it for them. Together all three stepped out into the rain, and disappeared.

The instant they had gone, Tom grabbed the spoon and held it just above the mat to be sure he understood what Oscarine had written backwards. 'In the tea cup', it read.

'One 'ot choc!'

Tom glanced up to see the waitress walking towards him with his hot chocolate. Without thinking he thrust his fingers into the cold tea and felt a small metal object hidden below the surface.

'Watch out it's hot, love,' she said, setting the mug down, and he snatched his hand away guiltily just as she whisked the tea cup away. The waitress shot him a disapproving glance and bustled off. She probably thought this was some kind of sting and he was some kind of informer, but right now Tom didn't care what anyone thought. As soon as he dared he glanced down at his lap. It was a very ordinary looking key, made of dark polished metal. Obviously it belonged to Nicholas Zumsteen's expedition box that was somehow hidden inside the model of Tithona. But finding the box involved solving a puzzle, and shaking hands with a jerboa . . . where was the jerboa? And where, for that matter, was the place Oscarine called Scarazand?

Tom finished his hot chocolate in silence, paid and walked out into the street. The wind and rain had died away now, and everywhere large white puddles reflected the pale sky. Taking out his mobile phone he checked the screen: still no messages from his mum and dad. That was nothing for two days now. Did it mean anything? No it didn't, he told himself, no messages was normal, this is how it always was, this was how it always would be . . . wouldn't it? Tom took a deep breath and looked up the street. What should he do now? Find Pearl, if he could, warn her about those people in the marsh. Tell her about the model, too, see if she had any ideas. And tell her about Oscarine, and this place called Scarazand . . .

Turning up into Museum Street, Tom saw a steady stream of visitors making their way down the steps. There was the distinctive shape of Ern Rainbird in his beret and caretaker's coat, ushering the visitors out. Had Pearl come back already? He didn't know. But as Tom drew closer he noticed a woman and a man hovering in the shadows inside. There was something familiar about these two, with their ill-fitting grey suits and briefcases and their pale, yellowy complexions . . . Tom crossed the road and trotted up the steps into the gloom. At first Ern didn't notice him, he was in deep conversation with the two sallow-faced people, who were now lurking behind the mammoth with their clipboards, but as soon as he spotted Tom on the far side of the hall he marched over.

'Closin' up for the night, boss,' said Ern, his face cracking into an apparently cheery grin.

Tom nodded; he wasn't in the mood for Ern's false attempts at friendliness.

'Who are they?' he said watching the inspectors climb the stairs.

'Them? Oh, they's from some National Museum board,

conducting some sort of survey, not sure about what. You know the drill. Officials, eh, always got some sort of form to fill in, haven't they?'

Ern was plainly doing his best to distance himself from these two, and Tom did not believe a word he said. 'Oh by the way, someone was asking after you earlier. A girl.'

'Oh really?' said Tom, trying not to sound too interested.

'Funny-looking. Raggle-taggle, if you know what I mean. With long black hair. Ring any bells?'

Tom said nothing. He knew exactly what Ern was implying, and he wasn't going to give anything away.

'What did she want?'

'She wanted to go down to the docks to some meeting. Wondered if you wanted to come along.'

'A meeting?' said Tom. 'What kind of meeting?'

Ern pulled a rolled up copy of the evening paper out of his back pocket and opening it up, squinted down at the small ads. 'Legion of the White Ant. Upstairs Room, The Golden Duck, Whelk Street. 8.30p.m. onwards,' he said.

Tom scanned down to where Ern's knurled finger thumped the page.

'The Legion of the White Ant?' read Tom. The name sounded ridiculous. 'What's that?'

'Pikey central, that's what it is,' grimaced Ern Rainbird. 'All the flotsam and jetsam of Dragonport. Now why would she come in here and ask you to go down there, I wonder?' Ern moved a match from one side of his mouth to the other and Tom avoided his lizard-like eyes.

'I have no idea,' said Tom flatly.

'Me neither,' replied Ern. 'Anyways, I told her where Whelk Street was, gave her all the directions and that. Course she had no idea where it was. A total stranger. But very polite—y'know, for a gyppo, like.'

'Is it far?'

Ern's yellow eyes narrowed and his mouth cracked open into a grin.

'What, *you* goin' down there an' all?'

'I might.'

Ern's face split into a hearty laugh.

'Best of luck, mate,' he chortled.

Tom wandered back out onto the museum steps and thought hard. Obviously Ern Rainbird was up to something, and his first instinct was to bicycle down to Whelk Street—wherever that was—and find Pearl, but something held him back. Ern had seemed so pleased when he said he was going too . . . this was some sort of trap, wasn't it? Maybe Pearl had sensed it too— maybe she had seen through Ern Rainbird's false kindness . . . Tom shook his head; *maybe*, but it was unlikely. Pearl was a stranger here, and Ern Rainbird was just a peculiar old caretaker trying to be helpful . . . Tom stared down the street and felt a spark of anger ignite inside him. Jos had been completely wrong ever to hire the shifty Ern Rainbird; what could he have been thinking of?

But he should make sure, just in case. Trotting down the side alley, Tom levered himself over the wall and dropped down into the small garden at the back of the museum, where Jos and

Melba used to live. What had once been a neat well-tended garden was now entirely overgrown with brambles and decorated with slimy plastic bags blown in from the street. The museum annex, or 'go-down', as Jos was in the habit of calling it, ran along the back wall, and when Tom peered inside he was surprised to find it untouched. There were the piles of tea chests brimming over with mouldy photographs, half-stuffed animals and bits of machinery gathering dust. Nothing had happened in here since his last visit to the museum two years ago. Why hadn't Jos got round to sorting all this out? After all, that's why he had sold the sapphire, wasn't it?

Tom kicked a tea chest angrily: he was annoyed now, and what's more, he was annoyed that he was annoyed. He was still only twelve, yet somehow he felt as if he had been thrust into a position of responsibility that he didn't particularly want. He felt like a teacher at school, cross that things hadn't been done as he had wanted them to be done. Maybe Jos was just too lazy; maybe now he didn't have to keep the museum running himself he didn't really care. Glancing through the filthy window at the back of the museum he could see Ern Rainbird making his way up the back stairs with a flashlight, and the two dark shapes behind him. When he reached the narrow landing Rainbird paused and stared out into the garden, his grim face lit up like a gargoyle. What were they after? It looked as if Rainbird was leading the unlikely inspectors up to Tom's old bedroom . . .

Just then there was a scrambling sound and the next second someone slithered over the wall and landed lightly behind the brambles. The figure tensed for a moment, like a cat, then stood up and began to creep silently towards the back of the museum. Rainbird and his cronies had already disappeared off into the darkness as the red hood moved quietly and deliberately towards the broken drainpipe hanging off the side of the house then glanced back furtively, and Tom saw a flash of thick dark hair—

'Pearl!' hissed Tom as loudly as he dared.

The red hood paused: it was her! Pearl was still alive! But for some reason she hadn't seen him, and she hadn't seen who was inside, either. Tom moved out of the doorway of the old annex as Ern Rainbird's flashlight suddenly appeared in the bedroom window above. The two silhouettes stood beside him now, their thin shadows stretching high up the wall. Ern Rainbird was obviously explaining the crime scene, and Tom was so distracted by Ern's wild gesticulations that by the time he glanced back down to the side of the house Pearl had already shimmied halfway up the drainpipe. She was obviously intending to climb back in . . .

'Pearl!' he shouted, louder this time, and then without a second thought Tom bolted out of the annex across the garden up to the museum wall.

'And this was the point of entry,' came Ern's rasping voice from above. 'She's even bust the glass, see.'

Tom just managed to scrabble up onto the water butt and with one hand he grabbed at Pearl's leg.

'What the bejesus—'

Pearl swore and kicked viciously, and was about to kick again when she glanced down to see Tom's face staring up at her. He waved wildly up at the window and pressed his finger to his lips, and at that moment the window shuddered as it was forced open.

'Are you quite certain, Rainbird?' trilled a nasal voice from inside the room.

'Definitely, ma'am. There's a drainpipe somewhere hereabouts. If you would care to—'

'I'm quite capable of looking out of a window, Rainbird. Get back.'

Tom pressed his face against the wall as the torch beam hunted around above him. One foot was slithering around on the greasy top of the water butt, the other was braced against the wall, and his hand was holding on to Pearl's leg. It was very, very hard to keep still. He was hidden in the shadow of the overhang, but Pearl was almost in touching distance of the window. How could they not see her?

Suddenly the beam stopped.

'Mr Rainbird?'

'Ma'am?'

'You claim to know everything that is going on in this museum, do you not?'

'That is correct.'

'Then may I ask you a question?'

'Fire away.'

'Why is there a girl in a red raincoat, matching our description, hanging off this drainpipe?'

There was a silence. Tom felt the leg he was hanging on to begin to slip. His feet slithered dangerously on the lid of the water butt.

'I never bin good at brainteasers, ma'am.'

'I said, "WHY IS A GIRL IN A RED—"' But the woman's shrill voice got no further, as at that moment Pearl dropped and Tom slipped and there was a muffled splash as the water butt thudded over on its side.

'That's the one! That's her!' shouted Rainbird as Pearl jumped to her feet and sprinted for the wall.

'Get the little minx!'

The voices disappeared; they were obviously running down the stairs and trying to head off her exit.

'Pearl!' shouted Tom. 'Pearl, stop!' And the next moment he too was over the wall and sprinting away down the alley. Pearl was fast, but Tom was faster, and running hard across the street he managed to catch her and push her behind a hedge.

'What are you doing!' she shouted breathlessly as they tumbled into a garden. 'You're nu—'

'Sssh!'

Tom pressed his finger to his lips and pointed towards the footsteps clattering out into the street just beyond.

'Which way?' panted Rainbird.

'Down to that meeting I suspect,' the woman replied breathlessly.

'Lock the doors,' instructed the man to Ern. 'Then call us.'

'Right you are,' rasped Rainbird.

The footsteps ran away down the road, and Rainbird marched purposefully back into the museum.

'Sorry,' whispered Tom, 'I saw you from the annex, and then I saw them and I—'

'Sure you did,' said Pearl crossly, and looking at the long graze on her arm sucked it hard. 'Well, I suppose thanks are in order,' she said at last. 'Actually, I was looking for you, too.'

'I know. Ern Rainbird told me.'

'He did? What, the janitor guy?'

'Sending you off down to the docks to some crazy sounding society. The Legion of the—'

'White Ant. The name was in my dad's notebook, I know. I've been looking them up in the library. They're some descendants of some strange expedition and they're into weird insect stuff . . . I thought we should . . . that is, I was *wondering* if you'd like to come with me. Seeing as we are, like, kind of in the same boat now.' Tom knew what she meant, but he still did not want to believe it.

'I'm not sure if that's such a good idea.'

'Really?'

'Not after what's just happened. I think it's a trap. Ern Rainbird was trying to lure you down there.'

Pearl seemed genuinely surprised.

'But why would he do that? He seemed so helpful.'

'I think . . . I think he's with them. They're all trying to find you, Pearl, they're everywhere. They—' Tom checked himself; he was aware that Pearl was studying him closely. 'I was bicycling through the marshes and I came across your balloon. There were some guys there, too, waiting for you to come back.'

'And I suppose they were going to kill me as well?'

Tom shrugged his shoulders.

'They had guns. I think they might have done.'

Pearl was exasperated.

'You see, it's all real! I wasn't making it up.'

Tom nodded and looked down at the puddles. He couldn't pretend he wasn't relieved to see Pearl alive again.

'So what should I do now?'

Tom thought hard. There were very few places left.

'Well you could come back to Flood Street with me. Jos and Melba wouldn't mind if you slept on the floor. In fact they probably wouldn't notice.'

'Could I?'

Tom shrugged his shoulders.

'It would be the safest. And they certainly won't find you down there.'

Pearl beamed. It was the first time Tom had ever seen her really smile, and even in the darkness he could see that she had dazzling white teeth.

'You're a real brick, Tom, you know that?'

'A brick?'

'Yeah,' she laughed. 'A brick. You know.'

CHAPTER 6

CLOSING THE TRAP

Tom woke up early the next morning to find the sun streaming in through the small window. The whole room was glowing. He rubbed his face and looked across to the corner of the room to where Pearl lay sleeping on the floor, rolled up in a couple of blankets. Her face was almost obscured by a cloud of black hair, but she looked so peaceful Tom decided he didn't want to wake her up. They had talked long into the night, and Tom had told Pearl all about strange Oscarine Zumsteen, the puzzle, and shown her the metal key, but neither of them could make much sense of it. It was just another strand in the great web that had enveloped them both. They had agreed that Pearl should lie low then come up to the museum around closing time and they should try and solve the problem together.

Tom looked up at the ceiling and yawned. He had slept lightly, his dreams a tangled mess of memories and one recurring nightmare that he knew was not a dream at all. Picking up his telephone, he could barely bring himself to turn it on, as he knew what the answer would be. No messages. Nothing. That was normal. That was how it always was. But Tom felt a gnawing emptiness in the pit of his stomach that was becoming harder to ignore. Taking a deep breath, he pulled on his clothes and shambling down to the kitchen he was relieved to find that Jos and Melba were not there.

'*Gone up to the deck of HMS Scatterhorn,*' read a roughly scrawled note on the corner of the *Dragonport Mercury*. '*Help yourself to whatever and come and join us.*' Tom glanced across the page and saw the headline: 'ZUMSTEEN SALE BREAKS ALL RECORDS.' Intrigued, he read on.

What was to have been a routine house clearance sale at Tantrum's Auction House yesterday afternoon saw scenes of mayhem rarely witnessed in Dragonport. 'It's been totally amazing,' said auctioneer Tony Skillett, 'anyone would have thought the furniture was made of gold dust.' Mirrors, chairs, even spoons went for as much as twenty times their estimated value, netting the owner Mrs Oscarine Zumsteen a fortune. Highlight of the afternoon was lot no. 176, entitled 'small wooden box, 1960s, possibly used as a travelling case'. 'It's a normal sort of a thing, made of plain wood with a handle on one side, and completely empty,' explained Mr Skillett. But to one telephone bidder there must have been more to this plain little object than met the eye, as it went under the hammer for almost half a million pounds. 'I'm still sweating just thinking about it,' said Mr Skillett. 'It's a plain wooden box. Nothing more, nothing less.' Miss Oscarine Zumsteen was not present at Tantrums, and has not been seen since yesterday's record breaking afternoon.

'So you saw the paper?'

'I did,' smiled Tom, ambling up the steps in the morning sun-light. 'I didn't know you collected boxes.'

'Don't you be so cheeky!' wheezed Jos, his eyes twinkling beneath his thick eyebrows. 'That was insanity. Sheer bare-faced lunacy. I never knew there were quite so many people with more money than sense.'

'So did you get anything at all?'

'Not a noggin,' he said, thrusting his hands deep into his pock-ets and shuffling inside. 'See Oscarine and I were school-buddies once, before she was married to Nicholas, of course. And she was always collecting odd native stuff, you know, like masks and beads and amulets—all that jazz. And I just wondered, what with her eviction, if she'd be sellin' some of them curios off. Obviously not.' Jos turned and surveyed the jumble of cases all around. 'Problem is lad, when you've spent your entire life in a place like this you become a magpie. You can never have enough "clag" as my father called it. Clag, clag, clag everywhere,' he said, waving an arm around the room. 'It's an addiction, as I'm sure Melba will tell you.'

Tom smiled in agreement, and felt in his pocket for the key Oscarine had given him: it was still there—good. Perhaps Jos knew far more than he thought . . .

'Looks like it's going to be another busy day,' he said, eyeing the large party of men wearing identical blue tracksuits that had just come in. They looked as if they were part of a sports team.

'Wouldn't have thought they'd have much interest in this old place,' wheezed Jos. 'Still, it's all money, ain't it?'

Tom watched the party snake through the entrance hall: there must have been about sixty of them. Jos was right; the men

didn't look as if they belonged in here. They were all short, pow-
erfully built, with hard, bony faces, and strangely expressionless
eyes . . . Tom swallowed nervously, he knew what they were all
right. A cold shiver ran up his spine.

'I'll see you later,' he murmured, and made his way up the
stairs and through the bird hall to the new galleries. The Hellkiss
Collection was busy as ever, with groups of people already marvelling at the crocodile catching the wildebeest and the stampede of animals plunging down the cliff. Tom avoided catching
anyone's eye as he passed into the small side room which housed
Dragonport's finest exhibition, and he was pleased to find that
apart from a couple of old men discussing the merits of 'Badger
the one-eared dog', the place was deserted. Tom walked across
to the large glass case in the centre of the room and peered
inside at the Tithona archipelago, its green jumble of islands rising up out of the iridescent lagoon. Carefully, he pulled out the
small dull metal key and felt its jagged edges. There must be
some secret compartment somewhere, but where?

'Remember to shake hands with the jerboa,' whispered Tom to
himself as he walked around the model, running his fingers
along the dark mahogany base. But there was no jerboa here . . .
Tom felt a curious tickling sensation in his back. He was being
watched.

'Well, well, who would have thought it?'

The voice cut through Tom's thoughts like an icicle, and he
thrust the key back in his pocket.

'We meet again.'

Tom turned round to see a girl with pale skin and long black
hair standing poised like a dancer in the doorway. She walked

forward, catlike, and Tom could feel her large green eyes boring into him. Lotus Askary: older, taller, slightly awkward in a long white dress—but unmistakably her. A tumble of thoughts rushed through Tom's brain . . . and before he could consider any of them her long cold fingers had entwined in his.

'I must congratulate you on your museum, Tom,' she said smoothly, shaking his hand. 'After all the trials and tribulations I never thought it could look so good.'

'What . . . erm . . . what are *you* doing here?' muttered Tom, rapidly recovering himself.

'Oh, you know, odds and ends, sorting a few things out,' she replied airily. 'Dragonport is hardly my preferred destination but I'm always on the look out for the next big thing.'

'The next big thing,' Tom snorted harshly. 'And what's that, I wonder?'

Lotus's eyes sparkled with excitement.

'Tut-tut Tom: my, how aggressive you have become. I always thought you were a such a sweet boy.'

She smiled and Tom could feel himself begin to boil inside. The last thing he wanted was to be patronized by Lotus Askary.

'So does the next big thing have anything to do with Oscarine Zumsteen?'

Lotus laughed. 'Oscarine Zumsteen? That mad old bat. What do you know about Oscarine Zumsteen?'

'Not much,' replied Tom nonchalantly. 'Except that she's just auctioned all her possessions, and some idiot paid almost half a million pounds for a small wooden box that had nothing inside it.'

Lotus's expression hardened. 'Who told you that?'

'I read about it in the paper,' replied Tom, enjoying her discomfort. 'Looks like that person has probably got a lot of explaining to do.'

Lotus's milky-green eyes narrowed. 'I'd be very careful if I were you, Tom Scatterhorn. Very, very, careful indeed. That you are still alive to have this conversation is a miracle. If I had had my way—'

'There you are.'

Aunt Melba came up cheerfully through the crowd.

'Tom? Tom there's someone . . . oh—' Her face froze as Lotus spun and smiled winningly.

'Mrs Scatterhorn. We meet again. What a wonderful surprise.'

Melba looked as if she had seen a ghost.

'You do remember me, don't you? Lotus Askary. We almost bought this tatty old place.'

'How could I forget,' she said, staring with disbelief at the tall, willowy girl.

'I was congratulating Tom on the refurbishment,' explained Lotus. 'I never believed it could look so good.'

'It must be a very pleasant surprise,' said Melba frostily.

'Particularly The Deluge,' she smiled, staring through the doorway at the vast, tumbling tableau. 'I saw them restore it, you know. It's a remarkable construction inside.'

'Oh really?' grunted Tom. 'How very interesting.'

'It might be, one day,' she said with a half-smile.

Tom did not know what she meant, and he didn't care.

'And did I not read somewhere that you were going to build a new wing dedicated exclusively to beetles?' Lotus continued. 'I think you should, you know. It would be lovely.'

Melba was mystified.

'Actually we don't much care for insects. We've had a few infestations in the past.'

'Filthy, disgusting, revolting creatures most of them,' added Tom forcefully. 'Why would we want any beetles in here?'

Melba was rather taken aback by Tom's vehemence, but Lotus merely shrugged.

'Maybe they don't care for you much either.'

'Maybe,' replied Tom. 'Does it matter?'

'Not especially,' said Lotus, haughtily. 'I'm sure if you choose to stay out of their way they won't bother you.'

'Is that so?'

Tom glowered at her angrily, but Lotus seemed entirely unconcerned. Melba looked from one to the other and was more confused than ever. Suddenly Lotus remembered something and glanced down at her watch.

'My, my, Mrs Scatterhorn, didn't realize how late it was. I must gather the troops and leave right now.'

'Oh?'

'Yes, I am afraid the roads will be completely jammed. There's been a fire you see. Down near the docks.'

'A fire?' said Tom. 'What fire?'

'Oh, on some of the houseboats,' replied Lotus airily. 'There's a gang of riff-raff that live down there, apparently. Call themselves "the Legion of the White Ant" or some such ridiculous name. I can't remember.'

Tom stared at Lotus open-mouthed. There was an unmistakable hint of triumph in her eyes.

'So sad. But I suppose they must have had an accident. Who knows why. But they've all gone up in smoke.'

'How do you know this?'

Lotus turned to Tom with a bored, condescending expression.

'Do you really believe I don't know *exactly* what is going on, Tom? Please, a little respect. Goodbye, Mrs Scatterhorn.'

Lotus turned on her heel and strode away through the busy crowd, her plait of sleek black hair writhing like a snake.

'I never dreamed I'd see her again,' muttered Melba to herself. 'I must say, I'm rather shocked.' Tom said nothing. There was nothing to say. He walked over to the balcony and watched Lotus march out of the door as if she owned the place, followed by the large gang of athletes in blue tracksuits. And there was Ern Rainbird, bowing deferentially as she swept past. Of course he would, thought Tom angrily. Lotus Askary was quite clearly some kind of superior creature, and what exactly was Ern Rainbird? What indeed . . .

Hurrying down the stairs Tom slipped through the heavy door into the small house behind the museum and up the rickety stairs to his old bedroom. Pushing open the door, he made his way through the jumble of boxes to the narrow window and looked out across the roofs of Dragonport down to the docks. Of course, Lotus was right. There, hanging over the estuary, was a large pall of black smoke, and Tom could just hear the scream of ambulances and fire engines in the distance. So this is what Lotus meant by sorting out a few odds and ends. Who were all those people down in the houseboats? And was this all about

Pearl, or something else, like Nicholas Zumsteen's expedition box, perhaps? Tom did not know. Suddenly he felt very unsure of himself. It seemed that overnight Dragonport had become a battleground.

'Looking for someone?'

Tom turned round to see Ern Rainbird standing at the door. He had a padlock and a screwdriver in his hand.

'Only I'm gonna put a lock on this, just in case we get another break in.'

'Right,' grunted Tom. 'I was just looking at the fire.'

Ern glanced out of the window briefly at the black smoke: he didn't seem very interested.

'The people on those houseboats had something to do with that meeting last night, didn't they?'

'So I've been told. I take it you didn't go then?'

'No,' replied Tom. 'Should I have done?'

Ern sniggered.

'What about your friend. Did she go, do you know?'

'I have no idea,' said Tom tersely. 'I haven't seen her.'

Ern glanced up from his screwdriver.

'Well that's good then, isn't it?'

'It is.'

Tom brushed past him and clattered back down the stairs. This was insane, now he felt he was being hounded in his own museum. What kind of stunt were they going to pull next, burn the museum down?

Tom spent the rest of the afternoon studiously avoiding Ern

Rainbird, and decided to help Jos and Melba hang a long line of photographs along the corridor on the first floor.

'Found these in the old office out the back,' announced Jos, his mouth full of nails, 'part of Sir Henry's collection. Thought they deserved a bit of an airing.'

Tom studied the photographs as they hung them in a long line along the wall. They were taken on a lake somewhere, surrounded by high mountains, and showed some kind of extraordinary carnival taking place. There was an elephant on waterskis, a bear on stilts, a biplane flying low through a flaming house, and an Indian man standing beside a vertical rope, at the end of which a small monkey sat. It was all wild and strange, and at the end of it all there was a group portrait of Sir Henry, August Catcher, a small Indian man whom Tom immediately recognized as the Maharajah of Champawander, and various other people, including a tall, cropped-haired young woman in jodhpurs and a flying jacket.

'Strange crowd, aren't they?' said Jos, standing back and admiring the line of photographs. 'Recognize any of them?'

Tom nodded noncommittally.

'Who's that?' he said, pointing at the tall young woman standing with August.

Jos pushed his glasses up onto his forehead and squinted forward.

'If I'm not mistaken, that's Trixie Dukakis—August's niece. Well known stunt pilot in her day. Inventor of the famous Dukakis double-flip.'

'The Dukakis double-flip?'

Jos raised his eyebrows.

'Well, it's aeronautical. It's . . . it's a flip—doubled. You flip one way, then you sort of flap back again—'

'Oh stop talking nonsense,' smiled Melba. 'But it sounds interesting, doesn't it? Trixie became August's nurse, later on, I believe.'

'That she did Melba,' agreed Jos.

Tom looked at Trixie's wide, easy face. He wondered why he hadn't heard of her before.

It was starting to get dark now and the last of the visitors were making their way out. Picking up their tools they made their way back through the galleries, past the Hellkiss Collection towards the stairs.

'Well I never,' said Melba, as they walked past the small side room containing Dragonport's finest collection. Standing in front of the model of Tithona stood a visitor in a sweeping red and grey patterned dress. 'I've got a dress just like that,' she said. 'I wore it at the school hop, gosh, must have been forty years ago now.' Jos squinted into the gloom.

'You know I think remember it, Melba. And that's something, because that hat is a dead ringer for my old fedora.'

Tom could have added that she was wearing his old green trainers, but he didn't.

'Oh look, there's Ern, just when we want him,' he blustered, hustling them across to the stairs, at the bottom of which stood Ern Rainbird in deep conversation with a small sweaty man in a dark suit. 'Hello Ern!'

The moment Ern Rainbird saw them he straightened up guiltily and marched forward, leaving the hot little man to retreat into the shadows.

'Need a hand with that, skip?' said Ern, with a mock smile, man-handling the ladder off Jos and taking the toolbox from Melba.

'Thank you, Ern,' said Melba pleasantly. Tom waited until Ern had stomped off into the shadows with his load, then dashed back up the stairs into the gallery, aware that the sweaty man was watching him beadily.

'That's not the best disguise in the world, you know,' he whispered, quickly walking round to where Pearl stood.

'Oh hi,' said Pearl, evidently deep in thought. She looked up at him, distractedly. 'Sorry, they were the only things that fitted. And I kind of liked them anyway. Is that OK?'

'I suppose so,' said Tom. With her hair tucked up under her hat and the brightly patterned dress Pearl looked quite eccentric, but it suited her in a strange way. 'What are you doing?'

'Working things out,' she said calmly, feeling along the base of the model, with her fingers. 'The puzzle of how to get into this thing.'

'Any ideas?'

Pearl nodded.

'A few. My dad loves brainteasers. Obsessed by them. It's kind of rubbed off.'

'Well just don't do anything till after closing time,' whispered Tom. 'Rainbird's prowling about, not to mention everything else.'

Pearl looked up at him questioningly.

'What do you mean?'

Tom was going to tell her about the fire down in the docks,

then thought better of it. Pearl didn't need reminding just how much danger she was in already.

'I think . . . maybe if you came down to the office and hid in the cupboard for twenty minutes while Ern does his rounds might be a good idea.'

'Hide in a cupboard?'

Tom looked embarrassed.

'I just . . . believe me, it's a good idea right now. Twenty minutes, that's all.'

Pearl shrugged. 'OK. Whatever you say.'

Pearl obediently followed Tom down the corridor to the small spiral staircase at the back of the museum, and reaching the ground floor, he peered round the corner into the main hall. It was almost empty now, and he could hear Ern Rainbird stomping around in the small mammals collection.

'Let's go,' Tom whispered, and crept across to the office. A minute later Pearl was sitting in a cupboard opposite the desk.

'Are you sure this is really necessary?' she said. 'No one knows who I am.'

Tom nodded. 'I know. Trust me. Sorry.'

He closed the door, and hearing Ern's footsteps marching across the marble hall he just managed to slip round the back of the desk and into the chair before there was a sharp knock on the door.

'I'll be lockin' up now, Master Scatterhorn, if it's all the same to you.'

Tom looked up to see Ern Rainbird standing in the doorway, glancing around furtively.

'Oh. OK.'

'Five minutes, then?' he said, scratching his freckled head and flicking the front door keys in his hand.

Tom attempted a smile. 'Don't wait for me, Ern. You go home. I can let myself out later.'

'Later?' repeated Ern Rainbird, still flicking his keys from side to side.

'That's right. I've got my own key so I'll let myself out later.'

Ern Rainbird paused a moment, his brain whirring. Obviously this was not what he had expected.

'Very well, lad,' said Ern, staring at Tom with his large sand-coloured eyes. 'Will you be . . . err . . . long?'

'I don't think so,' replied Tom, his voice hardening. 'Is that OK with you?'

'Course it is, mate,' said Ern, his face cracking into what he obviously thought was a cheery grin. 'I'm sorry. I have to keep reminding meself that this is your gaff.'

Tom did not bother to reply.

'No worries. I'll . . . I'll just be lockin' up then. Goodnight.'

Ern glanced around the office once more, then closed the door. Tom did his best to ignore whatever it was that Ern Rainbird had been planning to do later, and pulling the dull-looking key from his pocket he examined it closely.

'Shake hands with the jerboa,' he murmured, feeling the rough grooves along the circular end. 'The jerboa?'

The great front door creaked on its hinges and slammed shut, and the scrape of the lock turning echoed across the dark hall. Ern Rainbird had gone, for the moment. Tom waited until it was completely silent, then stood up.

'You can come out now,' he said.

There was nothing.

'He's gone.'

Silence. Pearl was still there wasn't she? She must have fallen asleep. Tom got up and walked over to the cupboard.

'Look there's no point hiding any more. We've got to—'

Tom was just about to open the cupboard door when he sensed something moving to his left. His eyes darted across to the small dark cabinet under the window, and its brass doorknob, gleaming against the dark wood. The doorknob was moving . . . but surely Pearl was . . . instantly Tom's astonishment turned to fear. Glancing down at the desk his fingers closed silently around a large grey eagle's foot paperweight. That should do it. The cabinet door was opening outwards . . . slowly . . . slowly—

Bang!

The cabinet flew open.

'Oh!' came a muffled gasp.

Tom was astonished to see a small sweaty man climb out of the corner cupboard. He was wearing a thick woollen suit and looked extremely hot.

'Who are you?'

The small man stood up and looked at him with as much composure as he could manage through his steamed up glasses.

'This is . . . an inspection.'

His voice was so high it might have best been heard by bats. Tom blinked, then he recognized the man: he had seen him talking to Ern Rainbird earlier.

'A what?'

'I am part of an inspection team and we are making an inspection.'

Tom glared at the man menacingly. He was a good deal shorter than him.

'But you will be pleased to hear that your museum has passed with flying colours. Full marks. Congratulations,' said the man, lowering his dull, yellowy eyes and edging towards the door. Tom clenched his fists around the eagle's foot. This was just about the last straw, and the little man sensed it.

'What did you say?'

'My inspection team can find no fault here, so without further ado I will bid you a goodnight, young man.'

The small man turned on his heel and thrusting his clipboard into his briefcase snapped it shut and marched quickly across the dark hall.

'Wait!'

Tom approached the man and stared at him. He was so small he was almost not real.

'I need to let you out.'

'Oh yes, if you could I'd be very much obliged. Most kind.'

Tom led the way to the front door and unlocked it.

'So you are a one man inspection team?'

'Oh yes Mr Scatterhorn, I am always the first man in and the last man out.'

Tom stared at him quizzically.

'Really?'

The man glanced down at the eagle's foot, still clenched between Tom's fingers.

'That is correct.'

'It had better be.'

Tom pushed the door open and the small man skipped down the steps and out into the street. Tom slammed the door hard shut and locked it. Another one: how many more of these dead-eyed people were there? This was becoming ridiculous.

'Who was that?'

Pearl had appeared in the doorway of the office and walked out across the hall.

'Someone from an inspection team. Inspecting the inside of a cupboard.'

Pearl laughed. 'Seriously?'

'He was waiting for you, obviously.'

'That's insane. What's going on in this place?'

'I really don't know,' said Tom shaking his head. It would be funny if he didn't suspect there was some dark purpose behind it all. 'Come on, why don't you show me how to get into that model.'

CHAPTER 7

THEY HAVE THEIR EXITS

A minute later Tom and Pearl were staring at the large wooden case with the model of Tithona archipelago in the upstairs gallery.

'So she didn't say anything else about it?' asked Pearl, peering in at the dark pattern of islands rising up out of the sea.

'No,' said Tom, feeling under the lip of the base for anything like a keyhole. 'I reckon there must be a sliding panel somewhere, hiding it.'

'What is a jerboa?' asked Pearl.

'It's like a large mouse. It has long back legs and it lives in a desert,' said Tom, lying down on his back and peering underneath the case. 'It's nocturnal, I think.' Tom switched on his torch and ran the beam across the tangle of spider's webs and screws on the bottom. There was nothing there that he could see.

'You're certain she's called Oscarine?' said Pearl, examining the wooden edge of the model, along which there was a regular pattern of dark wooden circles inlaid in light squares.

'As far as I know. Why, is it written somewhere?'

'Oscarine,' muttered Pearl to herself, her fingers busy counting the circles of dark wood. 'Yes that makes sense.'

'What does?' huffed Tom as he pulled himself to his feet. 'There's nothing down there at all.'

'These,' said Pearl crouching down and examining the dark circles. 'I noticed them earlier. They look like buttons, don't they? Make you want to press them.'

Tom had to admit that the dark circles of wood did indeed look like buttons, and the inlaid pattern was repeated on all four sides of the case.

'And guess how many there are on each side?'

Tom shook his head. 'About thirty?'

'Twenty-six. I counted. The same number of letters as there are in the alphabet.'

'Isn't that just a coincidence?'

Pearl looked at Tom and smiled. 'Not if you like puzzles. This is a clue. It's a code. This was made for Oscarine Zumsteen, right? So therefore we should start with O, which is the . . . ' Pearl made a quick calculation, 'fifteenth letter of the alphabet.' Quickly she counted down to the fifteenth button and pressed it as hard as she could. Nothing happened.

'Maybe that's the wrong side,' suggested Tom, watching Pearl struggle. 'That's south. We should probably start with the north.'

'Why north?'

'You know, north, east, south, west, the compass. It always goes like that, doesn't it?'

Pearl's face lit up.

'Genius,' she smiled, moving round to the far side. 'I knew there'd be something. OK, here goes.'

Counting along to the fifteenth button she pressed it hard. There was a low scraping sound of wood sliding against wood, then suddenly the button shot into the base.

'Wow!' whispered Tom.

'S,' said Pearl excitedly, 'which is—'

'Number nineteen,' replied Tom, rapidly counting on his fingers.

Pearl moved on four buttons from where she was and pressed the dark wooden button hard. Nothing happened. She tried again with all her might, but still it didn't move.

'Wait,' she said to herself. 'Wait wait. That's right, we move round. Move round each letter . . . ' Walking to the east side, she counted up to the nineteenth circle and pressed it with her thumb. Sure enough there was a hollow scrape, and the button shot inside.

'I think it's going to work,' she smiled. And so on they went, running round the model pressing all the right buttons until they reached the letter Z.

'Kind of makes sense if it was the last one, wouldn't it?' said Pearl as the button shot away inside, but this time another sound followed swiftly afterwards, like the spinning of a wooden cog. Then, quite unexpectedly, the whole west side of the base dropped forward, revealing a deep drawer.

'Is that it?' wondered Pearl.

Carefully they pulled the drawer open and marvelled at an elaborate procession of wire figures inlaid on a patchwork of different coloured wood. There were lines of elephants, groups of turbaned men playing instruments, the giraffes on leads, the cheetahs, mongooses, and ostriches.

'Must be some kind of ceremony,' suggested Pearl. 'But where's the jerboa?'

Tom avidly searched the scene but he couldn't find anything like a small desert mouse.

'Maybe it's not here. Maybe there's another level underneath.'

'Wait a minute,' said Pearl suddenly, 'didn't you say it was nocturnal?'

'I think so.'

'Well then it won't be here. Look, the sun's shining,' she said, pointing to the large golden ball in the top right hand corner. 'I just wonder . . . '

Pearl flattened her palms and ran her fingers across the flat surface until they bumped against a small steel nut, barely visible against the dark wood.

'There.'

'What is it?' asked Tom.

'Feels like a lever,' she replied. 'Maybe I should push it, or pull it even. What do you think?'

Tom shrugged his shoulders.

'Might as well.'

Pearl gingerly pulled the small lever towards her, then back, and a strange thing happened: the disc of the sun dropped down and slid away, revealing a crescent underneath. And as it did so, Tom caught a movement out of the corner of his eye. It came from a tree to the left. Something had changed in it.

'The moon has moved something,' whispered Tom, searching the branches of the tree. 'Look,' he said suddenly. 'There it is! The jerboa!'

Pearl pressed her face down close to his to see a small circle of wood had dropped out of the centre of the tree, revealing a spindly wire animal underneath.

'But how did that happen?'

'It must have been connected to the moon somehow,' reasoned Tom. 'You know, like those books you used to have where you pull a tab and something appears in a hole in the page.'

'It's just so elaborate,' said Pearl, who was still marvelling at the mechanism. 'Why do you think August Catcher went to all this trouble?'

'He likes tricks,' said Tom, 'the more unexpected the better. And he's a genius, of course.'

'Have you met him, then?' asked Pearl, curiously.

'I have. It was a while ago now.'

Pearl seemed puzzled.

'But if he stuffed all the animals in this museum over a hundred years ago, isn't he seriously old?'

'Kind of,' said Tom, with a wry smile on his face, 'you could say that. But let's shake hands with this jerboa.'

Tom ignored Pearl's confusion and, reaching forward into the small hole, his fingers brushed against a thin steel lever attached to the jerboa's spindly left hand. Carefully he began to move it up and down in its wooden groove, and somewhere underneath he heard a clicking noise, like a spring being wound up . . .

'Shaking hands with the jerboa,' smiled Pearl.

There was a soft click, and the panel of dark wood on which were the tree, the moon, and a couple of elephants lifted slightly. Tom felt along the edge with his fingers, and pulling it found the whole panel was hinged on one side. Lifting it up, he saw a shallow chamber beneath, in the centre of which was a plain wooden box with airline tags all over it. It looked a bit like a medicine chest.

'Is that . . . it?' said Pearl, surprised to see such an ordinary looking object, battered and scratched by many years of travel.

'I think so,' said Tom excitedly. 'This is the expedition box of Nicholas Zumsteen that he sent back to his wife Oscarine just before he disappeared on the Tithona archipelago, many years ago.'

'How can you be sure?'

'Oscarine Zumsteen showed it to me in a photograph.'

Pearl was confused.

'And so did she tell you what was inside it?'

Tom shook his head.

'Nothing. Except that I should keep it a complete secret. But she did give me this,' he said, taking the roughly made key and placing it in the lock. 'So she must have trusted me a little.'

Tom turned the key twice, and then opened both of the small doors. Inside was a series of compartments and drawers in which lay a collection of bottles, glass jars and other curious implements that might have belonged to a doctor. Tom recognized them immediately.

'What is all this stuff?' asked Pearl.

'Nicholas Zumsteen was a scientist,' explained Tom, 'and he was very interested in insects. That's a killing bottle,' he said, pointing at the small funnel shaped object, 'where you kill what you catch. And there's the chloroform, the pins and swabs and dissecting tools. My dad takes all this stuff with him on field trips when he's collecting.'

Pearl was impressed. Her eye drifted down across the paraphernalia to a series of small drawers at the bottom.

'KB?' she said, reading the faintly scrawled label. '"Handle with extreme care." Do you know what that is?'

Tom gave the drawer a small shake and found it was locked. But he heard the distinct chiming of glass knocking against glass inside. 'It sounds like specimen tubes.'

'Could that be what they want?'

'Maybe,' muttered Tom, trying the other narrow drawers. Curiously, they were all locked too.

'Shall we try and smash it open?'

Tom thought for a moment.

'I don't know whether that would be a good idea,' he said, inspecting some pink cowrie shell amulets and feathered bracelets on the shelf above. Nestling in the corner was what looked like a dark plastic ball the size of an egg. He picked it up.

'Zumsteen must have locked those drawers for a reason,' continued Tom. 'Maybe they contain something we don't want to let out. Something very dangerous, perhaps.'

'Do you think so?' Pearl's eyes widened and she cautiously ran her hands over the narrow drawers. Tom looked down at the ball in his hand: it was decorated with dark patterns across its surface and it felt curiously warm to touch. There was something tactile about it that made him want to keep squeezing its surface.

'You know what we should do, don't you?' said Pearl, staring down at the expedition box. 'We should take this thing away.'

Tom was roused from the ball and he looked at her.

'Take it? Why?'

'To use as a ransom. A bargaining chip.'

Tom did not understand.

'Look,' Pearl went on, 'Don Gervase wants this box, right? More than anything in the world. Who knows why, and frankly, who cares. But he has got my dad and Rudy, and almost certainly your parents too. So, maybe we could do a swap.'

Tom smiled and shook his head.

'I don't think you quite realize who these people are. They don't do swaps.'

'Why not? Everyone's got a price, haven't they?'

'Not Don Gervase Askary. Really Pearl, he's different.'

Pearl looked at Tom with a peculiarly determined expression on her face.

'I don't believe you,' she said. 'If he wants this box so very much then he can bargain for it. I'm going to take it away. Now.'

Pearl began putting all the objects back into the box. Tom could see that she was serious.

'I'm really not sure this is a good idea, you know,' said Tom uneasily. Pearl ignored him and closed the doors. 'Look how close they came to killing you only this afternoon? It would be much safer in here.'

'Maybe it would,' agreed Pearl. 'But that's not the point, is it? Don't you see it could be our only chance?'

Tom shook his head in exasperation. In a way he knew that Pearl was right, but what would be the consequences? Should they really give Don Gervase what he wanted?

'This is a big, big mistake.'

'Maybe,' said Pearl, reaching into the drawer with both hands and gripping the sides of the box tightly. She tugged hard, and there was a strange scraping sound below.

'It's stuck,' said Pearl crossly, feeling beneath the box. 'It seems to be attached to something underneath.'

Absently pushing the ball into his back pocket, Tom reached his hand inside and his fingers brushed against something hard and cold and circular beneath the box. It was a bit like a can. What could that be?

'I'm not sure we should force it,' he said, vaguely remembering something that Oscarine had said. 'There's probably some kind of mechanism to stop someone taking it away. Makes sense if—' Out of the corner of his eye Tom saw something silver lurking just beneath the surface of the wood. A thin line of steel. It glinted. Was that a—

'Knife!' shouted Tom, and at the same moment knocked Pearl away as a steel disc flashed across the surface of the wooden box and juddered to a halt on the other side.

'Wow!' gasped Pearl. 'That was . . . was . . . '

'Very close indeed,' breathed Tom, watching as a leather belt slowly wound the guillotine blade back across the surface of the box and the mechanism reset itself, hidden beneath the surface of the drawer. 'It must have been attached to a spring and primed when you tried to lift it.'

'But . . . but why would August Catcher make something like that?' asked Pearl in a small, shaken voice.

'I don't know,' replied Tom, thinking hard. This certainly did not fit in with everything he knew about August Catcher, who he remembered as being gentle, if a little eccentric. 'Maybe he didn't. Maybe it was put in later, by someone else.'

'Who?'

'Maybe Oscarine, maybe even Nicholas Zumsteen himself. Someone who knew its value and wanted to protect it.'

Pearl said nothing. She stared at the expedition box, the one object that she had thought might help them. It was close enough to touch but it might as well have been a million miles away.

'So what do we do now?' she said sadly.

Tom took a deep breath. He was secretly very relieved that this plan hadn't worked.

'Think of something else,' he said. 'I don't know about you, but I don't fancy putting my hand in there again.'

Pearl was forced to agree, but Tom could see that she was very disappointed.

'Maybe there is another way to do this. Maybe instead of bargaining or waiting for someone else to help us we could find a way to Scarazand.'

'That would be nice,' said Pearl sarcastically. 'Sure, why don't we just ask a policeman. Or perhaps we could take a train.'

'That's not what I meant.'

'I know,' said Pearl sulkily. 'Sorry. It's just really difficult that's all.'

Tom said nothing. They stood looking at the drawer in the darkness.

'Actually, what did you mean?'

'Let's close this first,' said Tom.

Folding the wooden panel back over the box, he slid the sun back into position. Then he pushed the heavy drawer back until it locked into the base.

'Must be resetting itself,' said Tom, listening to the distant knocking of wood and steel. There was a series of pops as all the dark wooden buttons around the rim slid back out again, and in seconds the cabinet looked exactly as it had done before.

'No one's going to find that easily,' he said.

'Well?'

Pearl was looking at him expectantly. 'What's the idea?'

'You know how you travelled here on the rim of a twister?'

'I do.'

'And you know that I once travelled too. To the past, to Dragonport a hundred years ago.'

'I do. I read about it in here,' she said, pulling out her father's battered notebook. 'My dad listened to August and Sir Henry talking about it years after they met you. They thought that is what had happened.'

'Right,' said Tom, uneasy at how much Pearl already seemed to know about him. 'And did they also guess how I got there?'

'No. That they didn't know. How did you do it?'

Despite everything, Tom suddenly felt awkward, as he had never spoken about this with anyone before. For nearly two years he had been keeping it secret.

'There was this wicker basket in the cupboard under the stairs,' he began. 'It was full of rags and old bits of paper. I was hiding in it, when suddenly I fell out of a hole in the bottom, through black space, and then I found myself inside a trunk in the past. It was like some sort of portal, I suppose, an opening between one time and another. And I have been told that there are other places dotted around, too. Nooks and crannies where you can slip between times . . . '

'I'm sure there are,' said Pearl, not in the least bit surprised. 'So what are you saying?'

'The cupboard's locked up now. Ern Rainbird's got a padlock on it. But I have always wondered if there might be *other* places in the museum like it, where you can travel into the past.' Tom looked at Pearl sheepishly. 'Or maybe even into the future. Does that sound . . . possible?'

Pearl stared out into the darkness at the shadows of the tableaux.

'So, you think this museum might be like some kind of junction? A place where different times collide together?'

'Something like that.'

Pearl thought hard. 'But if it is, how do you know where you are going?'

'You don't, necessarily. But for me, I went back to a place that I had seen. It was that snow-covered model of Dragonport downstairs. That was the portal. I wasn't literally in it, it was just the way through. So maybe there are other portals here, too, hidden in pictures, photographs, anything,' he said, looking round the walls. 'You just have to find the right entrance.'

Pearl stared at the Tithona archipelago through the glass.

'I don't suppose you have a picture of Scarazand?'

Tom smiled and shook his head.

'If only. Plenty of other places, though.'

Just as Tom finished speaking there was the sound of a large truck pulling up outside. He glanced down at his watch, it was almost eleven thirty. He heard the truck door slam and the scrape of footsteps up the steps outside.

'Who's that?' said Pearl, who heard the footsteps too.

There was a distant rattling of keys, and then the sound of the lock turning.

'I've got a pretty good idea,' murmured Tom, remembering Ern Rainbird's furtive behaviour. 'Let's go.'

But barely had they tiptoed out into the gallery than the sound of voices echoed up from below.

'Are you sure?'

'Absolutely, ma'am. I saw her climb into the cupboard in the office myself.'

'Bring them in then,' snapped the high voice. 'And be quick about it.'

Tom slid his head out as much as he dared and tried to identify the three people. One was Ern Rainbird, of that he had no doubt. The other was a small bent man, fatter than Rainbird and wearing a wide-brimmed hat. The third was tall and moved gracefully . . . more like a cat.

'That's . . . that's . . . her,' stammered Pearl, 'I've seen her before!'

Lotus took off her hat and stared into the gloom. She seemed both bored and irritated.

'She was with those guys that took my dad, she was—'

'Ssh!' whispered Tom, as four men came in carrying a pair of long wooden boxes between them, and set them down in the centre of the hall.

'Ready ma'am,' said the fat man, nodding at Lotus excitedly. Lotus glowered at the boxes with revulsion.

'Can you guarantee they will find her?'

'Of course, my lady. The mordant maybe utterly blind, but its sense of smell is far superior to a bloodhound.'

'Very well then,' she snapped. 'Get on with it.'

The short fat man motioned to the men standing beside the boxes, who undid the latches in unison. Instantly six oily shapes scuttled out, moving so fast that Tom could barely see what they were.

'Oh no,' murmured Pearl, watching the creatures wagging their tails excitedly like dogs trying to pick up a scent. They looked like long grey worms, with thousands of sharp little feet, and their heads were dominated by two large black holes.

'What are they?' gasped Tom, craning forward to see the hideous creatures barge into the office, their tiny feet scraping on the stone. 'Some kind of centipede?'

'Something like that,' breathed Pearl, in a low worried voice. 'I have met larger. We must get out of here.'

Before Tom had time to answer the four men ran up the stairs towards them and began to whistle.

'Quick,' he whispered, and they scampered along the gallery to the far end and hid behind a fire extinguisher.

'You're certain she was here?' barked Lotus irritably.

'Absolutely ma'am,' faltered Ern Rainbird, wringing his hands together nervously. 'We have kept watch as instructed. She hasn't left yet. And nor has the boy, neither.'

The mordants burst out of the office, hissing excitedly, and rampaged straight up the stairs into the small annex, clambering up all over the model.

'They've picked her up now ma'am,' tittered the small fat man, wiping his brow with relief. 'Won't be long now.' Lotus frowned: this was precisely what they had told her down at the docks.

'What can we do?' whispered Pearl, her voice shaking. Tom tried to ignore the thumping of his heart in his temples and racked his brains. The front door was cut off. The back door was cut off. Every cupboard was a possibility, but these creatures would sniff them out . . . what they needed was a place impervious to smell, somewhere with its own air . . . suddenly he felt something hairy tugging at his leg insistently. Glancing down he was about to kick it away when he saw that it was the mammoth's trunk.

'What's that?' gasped Pearl, shrinking back in terror.

The trunk pulled at Tom's ankle insistently. The mammoth: it was trying to help them . . . trusting his instinct Tom broke cover and tiptoed over to the railing. There was Lotus down below, pacing about impatiently, and the fat man and Ern Rainbird too.

'One at a time,' came a low, rumbling whisper, from somewhere far below. 'Hold on.'

'But—'

The next moment the trunk curled up around Pearl's waist and swung her out over the main hall behind Lotus and passed her to the anaconda, which lowered her swiftly into the outstretched paws of the standing Kodiak bear, which set her down in the shadows. It all happened so fast that barely seconds later Tom had followed suit and found himself held in the massive black paws of the bear.

'Rainforest,' it growled, a fraction too loud. 'The monk—'

Lotus whipped around and shone her torch suspiciously into the black eyes of the bear as it stood upright, its arms aloft, just as it had done for a hundred years. What was that sound?

She was sure she had heard something. Tom clung on to the bear's back for as long as he could, then the instant Lotus's beam moved off he slithered down to where Pearl crouched, waiting.

'I think we may have a result ma'am,' chortled the small fat man, watching the mordants tumbling over each other towards the fire extinguishers at the far end of the balcony, hissing excitedly.

'Will they kill her?' asked Lotus, distractedly hunting around the hall with her torch.

'Quite possibly,' he said in an oily voice, 'if that is appropriate.'

Pearl looked at Tom, quite terrified. It was clear that she did not know what to fear more, these strange talking stuffed animals that seemed to be helping them or the squirming creatures hunting her down. But there was no time to explain. Tom felt a cold hard hand press into his, and looking down he saw the yellow shadow of the proboscis monkey put its fingers to its lips. Swiftly and silently the monkey led them both through the jumble of cases to the side of the rainforest panorama where the side panel stood fractionally ajar.

'Mum's the word,' it whispered, rubbing its long pink nose. 'We're not going to stand by and watch you two be done in by those frightful creatures.'

The proboscis monkey pushed them quickly through the small gap then pulled the glass case shut behind them, and Tom and Pearl barely had time to look back and see it leap high up into the antlers of a moose and disappear into the thick blackness.

'Tell me Rainbird, do you get the impression something is

moving around?' said Lotus, her torch arching across the moose and down to the cabinets.

'I was thinkin' the very same thing meself, ma'am,' replied Ern Rainbird obsequiously. 'But then it's always a bit like that in 'ere, innit?'

Lotus scowled and walked towards the rainforest diorama, hunting through each case as she went.

'Where now?' hissed Pearl, crouching behind a tapir that stood towards the back of the display. Tom tried to ignore Lotus's flashing torch and peered into the jumble of black leaves, past the boa constrictor and the flying squirrels to the large base of a tree against the back wall. Its roots stretched out like tentacles across the forest floor.

'It's hollow, in case you're wondering,' croaked the red tree frog on the leaf beside Tom's ear. The amphibian had a surprisingly deep voice for one so small.

'What?' whispered Tom in amazement, looking at the tiny creature.

'Oh yes, 's all front,' said the tree frog wisely. 'You see this isn't *actually* a rainforest. It just appears to be one. This leaf, for instance, it's not a leaf at all. In point of fact it is made of paper. Decidedly odd that, don't you think?'

'Thanks,' said Tom, and with a nod to Pearl he crawled over to the base of the great tree and hid behind the root.

'We can get inside this tree,' he hissed. 'It's hollow.'

'How?'

Tom pointed to the cleft near the top. If they could just climb up there and slip inside . . .

'Rainbird, this cabinet is open!'

Lotus was standing at the side of the case, furiously pointing her torch at the catch.

'O-o-open, my lady?' repeated Ern Rainbird, marching uncertainly towards where she stood. 'Erm . . .'

'Follow me,' breathed Tom, and he rapidly shimmied up the dark side of the tree, using the branches to support himself, and clambered up into the cleft. As he reached the top there was an angry squawk, and two large parrots clattered off their perch and flew noisily out into the display.

'What is going on in there?' Lotus demanded furiously, fixing the birds in her torch beam. Ern Rainbird scratched his head in bewilderment as the large parrots fluttered this way and that, blinded by the torchlight.

'It's . . . It's a phenomenon, certainly, oh yes, miss, no mistake about it.'

Lotus stared at him as if he was insane.

'Can you hear the mordant music ma'am?' simpered the fat man, holding his finger up to indicate the excited squeaking upstairs. 'Is it not the sweetest sound?'

'Get your musical mordants down here this instant!' exploded Lotus. 'Now!'

Tom ignored the commotion outside and glancing down he saw that the tree frog was right; the inside of the tree was entirely hollow. With a quick nod to Pearl he dropped down and landed in a pile of rags.

The next moment he heard a creak above him and then Pearl dropped down into the tree hollow. They crouched in the darkness, breathless and terrified.

'What are we going to do?' whispered Pearl.

'I don't know,' Tom replied, feeling around the web of steel and plaster and canvas for an opening. The case of the cabinet creaked open.

'Shall I . . . send them straight in, my lady?' enquired the small fat man.

'If you value your life,' she snarled.

A shrill whistle split the gloom and the mordants bayed excitedly, and their needle-like feet rattled across the hall. Tom thought desperately: there was no way out of this, and there was nothing here except a mess of rags and newspapers covering the floor. It was almost like a large waste-paper basket.

'Bury yourself,' he whispered suddenly, as loud as he dared. 'Burrow down as far as you can.'

Pearl didn't ask why, just did as she was told.

'They won't destroy anything, will they, my lady?' asked Ern tentatively, 'only, if we let them mordants into the display, then—'

'Then what?' barked Lotus. 'You will have some explaining to do. Won't you?'

Ern Rainbird winced away from the furnace of Lotus's temper. Tom heard the mordants climb into the display, and buried himself deeper, until he felt his fingers brushing against rough canvas beneath him. It was old and rotten, and even as he touched it he began to feel it tear.

'Is this the bottom?' whispered Pearl, who had burrowed down beside him and felt it too.

'I think so,' said Tom breathlessly. Twisting through the rags he pushed his hand into the gap to feel nothing underneath. 'Feels like . . . we are suspended above something.'

'The cellar?' whispered Pearl as the canvas began to creak alarmingly.

'I . . . I don't think so,' said Tom, feeling the canvas beneath him start to give. He did not know whether to hold on or let go, but he had a suspicion what was going to happen . . .

All around the outside of the tree the mordant's tiny feet scratched excitedly, trying to climb up.

'Run to ground,' announced the little fat man, gleefully. 'Shall we go in for the kill?'

'Do it.'

'It can't hold our weight,' whispered Pearl as the canvas began to stretch and tear beneath her, 'we should—'

Suddenly there was a loud rip and the ancient canvas on which they were suspended gave way. Before they could even think Tom and Pearl tumbled forward into black space beyond . . . plummeting through the howling air Tom felt himself spin and accelerate through streaks of colour, until he was suddenly shooting upwards, towards a shimmering net of gold and green . . .

CHAPTER 8

Not Even on the Map

'Oh!'

Tom felt himself shoot up through a skin of water into the air—then he slammed down flat onto something grainy and soft. All the breath was knocked out of him, and a strange smell filled his nostrils. Like fish . . . Dizzily, he dug his fingers hard into the coils of ropes swaying beneath.

'Help!'

Tom opened his eyes to see a shadow flying up through the white air and felt a thump behind him. The surface rocked once more. There was silence.

'Pearl?'

There was a muffled grunt somewhere beside him.

'You OK?'

'Just about.'

Tom raised his head as much as he dared and looked around. They were lying in the bottom of a long boat on a pile of nets. The air was sharp and cold and there was a thick blanket of mist all around. Shadows of steep grey mountains loomed in the distance, and he could just make out a rim of dark forest lining the edge of the water. A torrent of thoughts rushed through Tom's mind . . . this was not Dragonport in the past, but it was not unfamiliar, either.

'Wow,' said Pearl, hauling herself up. 'So that's what you meant about travelling, huh?'

Tom nodded.

'Something like that,' he said, looking across at her, and suddenly found he couldn't stop smiling. Pearl looked as if she was wearing a huge silver wig.

'What?' she asked, embarrassed. 'What's so funny?'

'Your hair.'

Pearl pulled at a strand and found it was covered in tiny silver flakes. Fish scales. Then she looked down at the nets. They were full of them.

'What about yours,' she said, glancing at Tom. 'You look like an alien.'

Tom shook his head, sending tiny silver flakes spraying everywhere.

'Call that shaking?' smiled Pearl, and began whirling her silver mane around, covering Tom and the deck.

'Stop it,' he laughed, as the narrow boat began to wobble, 'we'll tip over.'

'All right,' said Pearl. 'But don't you forget, Tom, that anything you can do, I can do better.'

'If you say so.'

'You bet I do,' she winked.

They both stopped for a moment and smiled. Neither of them could hide their relief at having escaped.

'OK,' said Tom, staring out into the mist. 'Where do you think we are then?' Pearl looked around. A thin sun had started to burn the mist away and forms were beginning to appear all around them: grey shadows of punts paddled by figures wrapped in thick hats and blankets. Beyond she could just make out the shapes of houses and thin columns of smoke drifting up over the lake.

'Looks like some kind of water market,' said Pearl, watching the dark-skinned men paddling their loads. 'The Himalayas, maybe? Kashmir? I don't know. It has got to be connected to the museum somehow, hasn't it?'

Tom racked his brains, there *was* something familiar about this lake surrounded by mountains—and the word Kashmir.

'Maybe there is something here that can help us, and we don't know it yet,' he said, as every moment the busy market came more clearly into focus. 'Maybe we arrived here because we wanted to.'

'What do you mean?' said Pearl. 'Why did we want to come to *this* place?'

Tom was trying hard to think.

'Maybe what we wanted . . . directed us somehow. I don't know. There has to be a reason.'

'There does.'

Tom could tell that despite her bravado, Pearl was as apprehensive about suddenly arriving on this misty lake as he was. There *had* to be a point to all this. It couldn't just be an accident, could it?

'OK,' said Tom, sounding a lot more determined than he felt. Looking up to the bows of the fishing boat he spotted a small punt with two paddles nudging alongside.

'Can you paddle?'

'Sure I can paddle.'

'Let's go and find out, then.'

Untying the narrow punt Tom and Pearl carefully stepped inside and set off towards the market, and soon found themselves in amongst the throng.

'Definitely India somewhere,' whispered Pearl, watching the farmers hawking their apples and apricots, and children in thin dugouts carrying stacks of flat bread. 'Do you understand what they are saying?'

Tom shook his head. Looking at the faces of the men and the women, he couldn't even tell what time they were in. Everyone was wearing woollen hats and blankets, and there was nothing made of plastic that he could see.

'Hello,' said Pearl to a young girl and her mother in a canoe who caught her eye. 'Hi.'

They smiled and she smiled back.

'Do you speak English?' she began.

The girl looked at her shyly and drew up the edge of her shawl over her mouth.

'No? You see, we're lost.'

'Postcard! Postcard postcard postcard!'

A young man had seen them and paddled up fast through the crowd. Around his neck hung lines of postcards on a string.

'Postcard,' he said, thrusting the cards at them.

'You speak English?' asked Tom.

'English ya. Postcard!' he smiled, revealing several missing teeth.

Tom took the card and studied it. The black and white photograph had been roughly coloured in, and it showed the lake in summer. In the centre was a speedboat, towing a small elephant on water-skis. And riding the unfortunate creature was a plump little man in a green turban, looking very serious.

'Champawander lake. Maharajah pleasure sports parade. Specialist postcard. Best price me give you.'

'Champawander lake?' Suddenly Tom knew where he had seen this place before: it was on the wall of the museum corridor, the long line of strange photographs he had been hanging with Jos and Melba only the day before. And that was the maharajah himself, the previous owner of the sapphire.

'Listen,' said Pearl suddenly and looked up into the sky. Somewhere underneath all the noise of the market there was the familiar, distant drone of an engine.

'Is that a plane?'

Tom scanned the sides of the mountains hopefully.

'Sounds like one, doesn't it?'

'There it is!' said Pearl, pointing to the small silver object arcing towards them from the far side of the lake. The engine noise grew louder, and several of the market traders turned round to watch.

'It's coming in to land,' she said excitedly.

The silver plane dropped lower and lower, hesitated for a moment in mid-air, then its long white skis broke the golden-mirrored surface of the water and it slowed rapidly and taxied over to a small, steep island out in the centre of the lake. As it did so the glint of a window flashed open somewhere high up in the trees, and the silhouette of a man leaned out.

'Strange place to live,' said Pearl, watching the plane draw alongside a small wooden jetty. 'Who do you think they are?'

Tom's mind was spinning as the plane door opened and a tall figure in a flying jacket stepped out, followed by another, who took her hat off to reveal her bobbed auburn hair. The couple looked very glamorous as they tied up the plane, then disappeared up some stone steps into the trees.

'Do you think they can help us?' asked Pearl.

'I think they might be the only people who can help us,' replied Tom thoughtfully. Could that really be them?

The woman grabbed Pearl's arm and said something to her in her own language, pointing at the island.

'Engleesh, engleesh,' translated her daughter.

'They're English?'

'Engleesh, engleesh. Scatterhorn sahib.'

'Excuse me?' said Pearl, not sure she had heard correctly.

'Scatterhorn. Yes yes,' said the young man with the postcards, waving his arm in the direction of the island. 'He coming now. Mr Catcher upside.'

Pearl looked back at Tom and saw that he could barely contain his excitement.

'There's the connection,' he grinned. 'It's the reason why we are here, isn't it?'

Various boats had already started paddling across the lake towards the small jetty, and Tom and Pearl quickly joined in the procession. The mist had burnt away now, and by the time they reached the island the sky was a brilliant blue and the trees that lined the steep hillsides burned red and orange in the sun. Tying their boat alongside all the others gathered there Tom and Pearl stepped up onto the jetty, and threading their way through the baskets of apricots, peppers, and nuts they made their way to the path that meandered up through the woods.

'I can't believe I'm going to see them again,' said Tom excitedly as they hurried up through the shadows.

'If it is them. When was the last time you saw August Catcher?'

'About a hundred years ago.'

Pearl laughed. 'Well in that case he may have changed a bit.'

'I'm not so sure,' replied Tom breathlessly, 'the animals in the museum are still pretty lively, aren't they?'

Pearl smiled to herself. 'So August Catcher used the elixir he invented on himself as well? Made himself immortal?'

'They both did,' replied Tom. 'And I don't think they are actually immortal. Just very, very old. About a hundred and fifty, I suppose.'

Tom and Pearl reached the top of the path and there, just beyond the trees, the ground flattened out onto a sunlit lawn and a small white bungalow beyond, surrounded by brilliant red roses. Tom boldly led the way out of the shadows onto a sunlit terrace, which was ringed by a low parapet wall. Beyond it the ground fell away into the trees that stood motionless in the golden autumn sunshine, and far below lay the silver surface of the lake.

'What if it isn't them?' murmured Pearl, looking doubtfully at the small wooden bungalow before them. Suddenly she felt very conscious that they were in some way trespassing.

'It will be,' said Tom, peering in through the windows.

Somehow he felt very certain about this even though he couldn't see any movement inside.

'I think we should be honest. Explain that we—you know—found an opening and, well, here we are. August Catcher and Sir Henry Scatterhorn have been watching the beetles for years. I bet they know all about Don Gervase Askary. And Scarazand.'

'Do you think so?'

'We could ask, couldn't we?'

He tried the front door and found it was open.

'Hello?' he said, walking into the sparse hallway. There was no answer. Beside the door stood a narrow table, a hat stand, and a mirror.

'Anyone at home?'

Tom noticed a button by the door and pulled it, whereupon a bell rang somewhere off in the hall.

'Hold it right there.'

Instantly Tom turned round. On the other side of the hall there was a bench, and beside it there was another mirror on the wall. Perched in front of the mirror was a large, blue-black crow. Its eyes stared at his reflection beadily.

'Just like the man says, hold it right there.'

Pearl whipped round and saw a second crow perched on the hat stand, also staring at her reflection in the mirror.

'Right there.' A third voice squawked from the ceiling.

Tom looked up to see a fish-eye mirror suspended above them, with another crow peering into it.

'Erm . . . we've come to see—'

'Seat,' rasped the crow on the hat stand, and indicated the bench beside the door.

'Got it,' growled the bird on the ceiling.

'Check that,' added the third. Tom and Pearl looked apprehensively at the three menacing black crows staring into their mirrors without blinking.

'We should probably do as they say,' whispered Tom, and they edged across to the bench. The birds followed them in their mirrors.

'Nice and gentle, folks,' instructed the bird on the ceiling. 'If nobody does nothing to nobody then we might be able to work this thing out.'

'Right. There's enough blood on the street already.'

'What?' mouthed Pearl.

'Check that,' agreed the crow in the corner, watching them sit down meekly. 'Triggers to safe and wait on my signal.'

Tom and Pearl looked at each other and then back at the three strange crows glued to their mirrors. This was really very bizarre.

Silence resumed: but not for long.

'I must be losing my marbles, unless they've gone already,' came a familiar muffled voice, whereupon the front door banged open and a man dressed in a beekeeper's suit walked swiftly through the hall into the house beyond.

'Was that him?' whispered Pearl.

Tom shrugged. 'I . . . I . . . I don't know. Maybe.'

'If only people didn't keep tidying up,' muttered the beekeeper reappearing at the door. 'Then I might have the first idea—'

'Windowsill, one o'clock, sir,' said one crow.

'Affirmative. Have in sights now,' rasped the bird on the ceiling.

The beekeeper stopped and saw the glasses case on the windowsill.

'Recovered from the garden. Yesterday p.m., sir.'

The beekeeper paused. 'Right. Thank you, Inspector Kinski,' he said, picking them up. 'Now—'

'Visitors, sir. Holding in position.'

'What?'

The bird on the hat stand shifted its weight and pecked the mirror with its beak in the direction of Tom and Pearl.

'Just arrived. Seem to know you.'

The beekeeper turned round and stared at the bench upon which Pearl and Tom sat. There was a moment of silence.

'*Do* you know me?' he said, squinting down through his mesh visor at the two children sitting before him. One was thin and rangy, with piercing dark eyes beneath a mop of blond hair. He looked somehow familiar . . . but the other one didn't. She was very suntanned and wearing a curious grey and red dress and old green shoes.

'Who are you?'

'Mr August,' said Tom nervously as he stood up. Pearl followed suit. 'Do you remember me? It's Tom. Tom Scatterhorn.'

August Catcher suddenly took off his hat and put his glasses on. A smile of recognition burst across his face.

'Hell's bells! I don't believe it. Tom Scatterhorn?'

Tom smiled as August rushed forward and grabbed him by the shoulders. 'It's really you?'

'It is,' said Tom, smiling into the old man's face. He was thinner than he remembered, and with a shock of white hair and a white moustache August looked a little like an ancient hermit, and his skin was entirely covered in tiny creases. But even so Tom recognized him, and his eyes sparkled with life.

'Well I'm rarely, rarely lost for words, but—' August burst out laughing. 'So you . . . I mean . . . it's just . . . and who's this?' he said, beaming at Pearl.

'Hello,' said Pearl, holding out her hand. 'My name is Pearl Smoot.'

'Very pleased to meet you, Pearl,' said August, shaking her hand warmly. 'So may I ask, how on earth you managed to find me?'

Tom and Pearl looked at each other.

'Well,' began Tom, 'we found an opening. A place where you can travel through . . . I think you know what I mean . . . which led from the museum to the lake down there.'

'We came up through the water,' added Pearl.

August looked at them both quizzically.

'Up through the water?' he repeated. 'But . . . are you quite sure?'

'Definitely,' said Tom, knowing that as a scientist August would find this incredible. 'We were . . . well, sort of blasted out, in fact. Into a fishing boat full of nets.'

August could do nothing more than stare at them in bewildered amazement.

'I'm flabbergasted. Well Tom, you always did manage to surprise me, and I have to admit you have done it again. This place is not even on the map, did you know that?' He looked at them both, his eyes sparkling. 'But this is extraordinarily serendipitous as I have a surprise for you,' he said excitedly, holding open the door, and ushering them out. 'Good day, gentlemen. Stand easy.'

'Right you are, boss.'

'Stand easy, murder three.'

'That's what the man said.'

The crows all shifted position in unison and Tom and Pearl smiled as they followed August out into the sunlight.

'Don't mind them,' grinned August as he strode out across the lawn. 'I thought I'd better have some protection and made the mistake of stuffing their heads with a crime novel. Of course now they're living in a shootout.'

Pearl giggled, and August smiled too.

'Still, I suppose it works after a fashion.'

'When did you find out about them being able to, well . . . talking?' asked Tom.

'Oh many years ago now, Tom. I suspected as much from the start, and frankly my memory is so bad nowadays I don't know where I'd be without them all.'

'So you have more?'

'Good lord yes, but first things first,' said August, trotting up some stone steps to a terrace under a large oak tree. 'Hello!' he called out. 'Coo-ee!'

'Over here!' said a woman's voice.

'Come come,' said August to Tom and Pearl excitedly. 'They are not going to believe this, simply not going to believe it.'

'August,' said a familiar voice. 'Why don't you—'

A tall figure in a checked shirt and linen suit stepped out from behind the tree. He had a streak of white hair and the sharp, quick eyes of an eagle.

'Good lord.'

The man stood staring at Tom in amazement.

'It's you.'

Tom smiled nervously.

'Hi.'

'Henry, may I present Tom Scatterhorn and Pearl Smoot, who have arrived from Dragonport, *via the lake*, only this morning.'

'Via the lake?' snorted the tall man. 'But how on earth—'

'There's a hole in it,' added August. 'A time slip.'

'Is there indeed,' beamed Sir Henry, fixing Tom with his quick eye. 'Well I knew you had gumption, lad, but really, do you realize quite how secret August's island is? It's not even supposed to exist!'

'Oh,' smiled Tom, 'sorry.'

'Why apologize?' laughed Sir Henry. 'We'd rather you found it than anyone else. But more of that later.'

Then the tall young woman in khaki slacks stepped forward.

'Say August,' she drawled in a strong American accent, 'aren't you going to introduce me too?'

'Of course, my dear,' replied August, 'Tom, Pearl, this is Miss Trixie Dukakis, my boss.'

'Oh please,' she smiled. 'I'm not *that* bad, am I?'

'Of course not my dear. Trixie just happens to be the daughter of a very good friend of mine, and she looks in on us occasionally, now that we are entering middle age. She's a fine doctor, superb pilot, and fellow traveller to boot,' he added pointedly.

'I do what I can,' she grinned, somewhat embarrassed by the glowing introduction. 'Enchanted to meet you,' she said, shaking their hands formally.

'Hi,' said Tom.

'Pearl Smoot,' said Pearl.

Trixie looked at Pearl with interest.

'Say, I recognize that accent, young lady. Where you from?'

'My dad's from Rapid City,' said Pearl.

'Is that so?' she smiled. 'Well hell, I was born there too.'

'But I grew up in Hawaii,' added Pearl. 'And we have kind of moved around since. The Marquesas, Tuamoto, Mangareva. Around there, basically.'

'Oh how interesting,' said Trixie, glancing at Sir Henry.

'Very,' agreed Sir Henry, looking at Pearl with interest. 'Well,' he said, clapping his hands together, 'I expect that back in dear old Dragonport it is midnight or something, but here in the Vidla valley it is eight thirty in the morning, and we were just about to have some breakfast. Would you like some eggs, bacon, toast, that sort of thing?'

At the mention of food Tom and Pearl suddenly felt extraordinarily hungry, it seemed like days since they had eaten.

'I'll take that as a yes then,' smiled August, 'come and have a seat.'

Five minutes later Pearl and Tom were sitting sipping tea and listening to a conversation that was so fascinating that it had been a challenge to eat anything at all.

'So you see Tom,' explained Sir Henry, 'over the years we have realized that there are many places from where you can travel from one time to another, just as you have done.'

'It's all to do with magnetics,' said August, 'I won't bore you with the science, but concentrations of iron across the surface of the earth create these hotspots which bend time in a peculiar way. Birds have known all about this for thousands of years, of course. In fact it was one particular "bird" gave us the first clue they existed. Do you remember a certain Australian eagle, by any chance?'

Tom nodded.

'Most extraordinary creature,' added Sir Henry. 'Still around. Turned out to be extremely useful, one way or another.'

'I made this bird,' explained August to Pearl, seeing that she did not understand what they were talking about. 'It was sort of a joke really—it was a mixture of all the biggest birds I could find cobbled together. A quite enormous creature it ended up, almost the size of a glider and not entirely pleasant to look at. Anyway, rather randomly I chose to stuff its head with an old aboriginal dictionary, which, much to my amazement, contained a lost language. The lost language of birds. And being of a wandering frame of mind, and blessed with a decidedly curmudgeonly character, this eagle took itself off on walkabout, and on its many peregrinations it became friendly with the great navigators of the globe: swallows, sheerwaters, arctic terns and albatrosses, and they told him about these time slips.'

'And then he, after a certain amount of cajoling, decided to tell us,' added Sir Henry.

'So, you *all* travel like this?' asked Pearl excitedly. Somehow it was reassuring to know that she wasn't the only one who had slipped through a hole in the air.

'If possible. Though we have had a few accidents, haven't we, my dear?' said August, smiling at Trixie. 'Don't I remember your father telling me something about the famous Dukakis double flip?'

Trixie smiled, a trifle embarrassed. 'That's an old story.'

'But true. Tell them,' smiled August, 'I bet they won't believe it.'

'My father taught me how to fly. And I'm afraid when I was not much older than you I was rather reckless,' she said, looking at Tom and Pearl. 'At fifteen I was a stunt pilot. A barnstormer. I performed in more air shows than I care to remember. I was flying in the Florida keys, during the hurricane season—which I guess was a mistake, thinking back. I did a loop the loop and my harness snapped and I fell out. Tumbled through the air for several thousand feet, and then miraculously, landed back in my seat.'

'Back in the seat of your own plane?' said Tom, not quite believing this was possible. Trixie nodded coolly and lit a cigarette.

'It had happened a few times in the history of aviation.'

'Only once, in point of fact,' smiled Sir Henry, who was also enjoying the story. 'Which is why Trixie is famous.'

'I was way out of control,' she continued, 'the plane was in a nosedive. Just as I was trying to pull out I saw this white gap between the storm clouds. Rather like mist, except it wasn't. I hauled the joystick over, screamed through it and—bang—I found myself in another place entirely.'

'Indeed you did,' smiled Sir Henry. 'I remember it well. It was October, in northern Canada, and the sun was just about to set. I was standing in a bog, waiting for the geese to come in with my gun at the ready when suddenly Trixie burst straight out of a cloud, almost colliding with several thousand birds. Quite an arrival.'

Sir Henry raised his eyebrows and Trixie laughed. 'You've got a very good memory.'

'You can take a girl out of Rapid but you can't take Rapid out of a girl,' he smiled.

'So how did you end up here?' asked Tom.

'Do you remember the Maharajah of Champawander?' asked August. 'He of the sapphire fame?'

'Of course,' said Tom.

'Well we became quite friendly with him years later, and when I told him we were looking for a place that was out of the way, with not too many folk around, he offered this island for nothing. In fact this house used to be his summer residence,' said August. 'And it has a rather curious feature that—'

Sir Henry looked across and in a glance August understood what his old friend meant.

'Of course, silly me.' He smiled and turned to Pearl, and Tom noticed that all three of them were now staring at her intently.

'How can I put it, my dear? We just have to be certain before going any further,' said August delicately. 'Any friend of Tom's is a friend of ours, of course, but nevertheless, we have to be . . . absolutely sure. I hope, Pearl, that you are not offended by my suggestion.'

'No, I'm . . . I'm not offended,' said Pearl slowly, realizing what August meant. 'In fact, in a funny way it kind of brings us round to what we want to ask you. You see, I slipped through a hole in the air like you did,' she said looking up at Trixie. 'I was being chased, you see, and as I was hanging onto a weather balloon I got sucked into this twister . . . '

August glanced across at Tom and he nodded.

'She arrived at Dragonport during a fireworks display.'

'Sounds mighty dangerous,' snorted Sir Henry. 'And who or what was chasing you?'

'Four massive centipedes, and a man named Don Gervase Askary. Whom I think you might know?'

The name hung motionless in the air. It had the desired effect.

'And why was Don Gervase Askary chasing you?' asked August curiously.

Pearl hesitated, she glanced across at Tom.

'I think we should tell them everything,' he said. 'It's the only way.'

Pearl sighed. 'He wanted this,' she said, pulling the battered red notebook out of her pocket and placing it on the table. August looked at the cover.

'For Smoot's Eyes Only?'

'My father's name is Arlo Smoot,' she began, 'he's a radio spy.' She then told them the whole story of what had happened to her, and how she had arrived at Dragonport, and how she had met up with Tom and how they had searched for clues and what they had found. August and Sir Henry listened patiently, until she reached the end.

'Sounds like you two have seriously been through the wringer,' whistled Trixie, 'they must want what that Zumsteen guy found pretty bad.'

August sat flicking through the pages of the notebook thoughtfully.

'Extraordinary that old Nick Zumsteen is involved in all this. Such a curious fellow. What on earth did he find that was so important?'

'Well clearly it was something inside that expedition box,' replied Sir Henry. 'Look at all that paraphernalia to prevent it being stolen. It sounds frankly incredible. Did you know anything about that, August?'

August stared at Smoot's notebook and shook his head.

'Nothing at all. I just gave Oscarine the model, as Nicholas requested, and she must have had the cabinet made up by someone else.'

Sir Henry raised his eyebrows. 'And you had a good rummage around inside it?'

'We did,' said Pearl.

'Anything there?'

'There were some drawers labelled KB, that we couldn't get into. Apart from that,' Pearl shook her head.

'KB,' wondered Sir Henry. 'Ring any bells, August?'

August put down the notebook and frowned.

'That Tithona trip was such a long time ago now. It's all gone a little hazy.'

'Actually, we have got one thing from the expedition box.'

All eyes turned to Tom and he smiled awkwardly, remembering what he had carelessly shoved into his back pocket.

'We have?' said Pearl, staring at him curiously.

'It . . . well, after the guillotine whipped across it became too difficult to put it back,' explained Tom.

'No need to apologize,' said August. 'I doubt very much if Nick Zumsteen will miss it. May we see?'

Carefully Tom withdrew the rubbery, egg-shaped ball from his pocket and placed it on the table. The low sun reflected through the dark ink patterns on the surface into the clear centre.

'I think I remember him buying that,' said Sir Henry, staring at the curious object. 'Can I?'

'Of course.'

Sir Henry picked up the ball and squeezed it. It was strangely malleable and warm to touch.

'What is it made of, some kind of plastic?' asked Trixie.

'Or rubber, perhaps,' suggested Sir Henry, throwing it across to her.

'No, it isn't either of those,' said August thoughtfully. 'As I recall, the lad who found it said it had once been a beetle.'

'A beetle?' repeated Trixie, staring at the ball.

'Exactly. Very curious. I remember thinking so at the time. May I?' August took the ball from Trixie and studied it carefully. Something about it stirred a distant memory. 'I wonder,' he murmured. 'I just wonder if it could be.'

'Could be what?' asked Sir Henry.

'Connected with our particular field of study.'

Sir Henry seemed mystified. 'Really? How?'

August smiled enigmatically, and with the merest glance across to Tom and Pearl indicated that he would rather say no more.

'So . . . do you think there's a slim chance your father and your brother might have escaped, just as you did?' Trixie asked Pearl, politely changing the subject.

Pearl shook her head.

'I just can't see how they could have done.' She took a deep breath. 'I think they have gone, just like Tom's parents.'

'What?' exclaimed Sir Henry, not entirely sure that he had heard correctly. 'Don Gervase Askary has taken Poppy and Sam Scatterhorn as well?'

'We're not *exactly* sure,' said Tom forcefully. 'But . . . Arlo Smoot heard something and wrote it down in his notebook. So, yes, it might be possible.'

'Oh come on Tom,' muttered Pearl, glancing at him across the table. 'It's certain.'

Sir Henry seemed extremely surprised. August turned the ball in his hands thoughtfully.

'And do you believe everything your father has written?' he said with a hint of scepticism. 'Could he be wrong?'

'My dad isn't wrong,' replied Pearl, her voice rising. 'Why would he make it up? It's just what he heard, that's all. Read it if you like,' she said, pointing at the notebook on the table. 'It's all in there.'

Sir Henry sat shaking his head and August frowned. It was a small comfort to Tom that they appeared to have as much difficulty believing this as he did.

'And does your father also record where Don Gervase Askary takes these people?'

Pearl shifted uncomfortably.

'No, not precisely. But there's this place we have heard of called Scarazand. Do you know it?'

Sir Henry raised his eyebrows. 'Scarazand?' he repeated. 'Well, well. Do we know about Scarazand, August?'

August wound his fingers around the ball tightly.

'You'd better hang on to that,' he said, setting the ball down on the table before Tom. Standing up, he stepped out into the brilliant autumn sunlight and paused for a moment, contemplating the silver lake below.

'I think you two are in a bit of a pickle,' he murmured. 'I think you need to know a few things. Important things. Things that might help you.' He turned and glanced at Sir Henry. 'That's what I think.'

'I agree,' replied Sir Henry. 'In which case, Trixie and I might go and do a spot of fishing before lunch.'

August nodded thoughtfully.

'Excellent. Now you two,' he said, turning to Pearl and Tom with a brisk smile, 'let's see if we can't unravel this mystery a little. Follow me.'

CHAPTER 9

TALES OF A HIDDEN WORLD

August led the way through a pair of French doors into the bungalow, which apart from a few maps strewn across a table was sparsely furnished and had a damp, musty smell of a place that was only lived in occasionally. The walls were bare except for a few of Sir Henry's hunting trophies, which eyed them curiously as they passed.

'I have to guard against curious cats,' said August as he reached what appeared to be a small cellar door leading off the hall. Either side of it sat two ferocious-looking mastiffs, stuffed and staring determinedly into space.

'Swamp hounds, from the Mississippi delta,' explained August. 'Originally bred for chasing runaway slaves, but you will be pleased to know that I have softened their natural instincts with a book of jokes. Knock knock?'

'Who's there?' said the hound on the left.

'Interrupting cow,' replied August.

'Interrupting cow wh—'

'Moo!' shouted August.

Both dogs shook their heads and giggled helplessly.

'Never fails,' smiled August, 'the worse the joke the more they seem to love it. Now if you would kindly follow me. Be careful as it might be slippy.'

August opened the door and disappeared down a set of stone steps into the darkness, and Tom and Pearl followed.

'I don't believe anyone knew about this place till Sir Henry and I discovered it,' said August from somewhere down below as he fumbled for a light switch. 'There.'

There was a sound of buzzing electricity and suddenly the whole place lit up, and Tom and Pearl were astonished to find themselves standing at the bottom of a narrow, conical cave. The smooth, curving walls stretched up to a chink of light at the apex, and all around were tiers of shelves with small ladders connecting them together. At first glance it looked like a library, but unlike a library there were no books on the shelves—there were birds, stuffed birds of all shapes and sizes lined up neatly in rows.

'A cave of the most extraordinary proportions, don't you think?' said August, walking over to the central table that was strewn with curious looking bottles of chemicals and odd coloured pieces of glass, as well as bits of beetles scattered about.

'So, what exactly do you do down here?' asked Pearl. 'Are you an inventor?'

'Of a kind,' replied August. 'I'm sure Tom told you that I was once a taxidermist, and I still dabble in that domain, but my creations are really nothing more than an aide-memoire now. My memory is not what it used to be, you see, so these fellows help me out,' he said, indicating the line of rather strange looking birds with large grey heads that stood staring down at them from the first level.

'What are they?' asked Tom.

'Shoebills, from Central Africa,' replied August. 'They paddle about in lakes and eat crabs, hence the massive beak. And they also have very large skulls, which makes them perfect for reference books.'

Pearl and Tom looked nonplussed.

'Thirty-five shoebills, thirty-five volumes of the *Encyclopaedia Britannica*—not forgetting the index,' said August proudly. 'Very useful. Then there's Dendril's *Dictionary of Coleoptera*,' he said pointing at the line of nightjars; 'Kingsley Nitt's study of termites,' he indicated three frogmouths; 'Lamonts's *Entomology*, Dirk Ratt's treatise on magnetic variations, the list goes on and on. I have even committed my own diaries to a few of them. One of the unintentional side effects of living for rather a long time is that I can't remember what happened, say, on the night of twenty-second December 1924.'

'You were dining at the Ritz hotel, in the company of Bucephelus Brem, the Swiss chemist,' chirped a kookaburra, 'who explained his theory of extracting gold from seawater.'

'Of course I was,' smiled August, 'and it's quite possible you know, getting gold that way—but vastly expensive. How about April second 1883?'

'First sparrow stuffed,' trilled a toucan from somewhere high up, 'got six of the best for bunking off school. I do not like school much.'

'That was true enough. Ouch, yes, that was painful, I remember. Not sure I wanted to be reminded of that.'

'Maybe not,' replied the bird, 'but what is done is done. I am merely an extension of you.'

'Of course you are, my friend.' August turned to Tom and Pearl with a mischievous grin on his face. 'Handy, don't you think? Sometimes it almost feels as if I am wandering around inside my own head.'

'Why birds?' asked Tom.

'Well birds can get themselves from A to B, in a hurry, should they need to, which has proved useful in the past. Plus the fact that they speak saves me the bother of having to look something up. If I need to know something I merely ask a question, and the answer comes straight back.'

It all sounded ingenious, and glancing at Pearl Tom could see that she was very impressed.

'So . . . you said you might be able to explain a few things,' she said, bringing August back round to the subject uppermost in her mind. 'Sort things out.'

'Yes,' said August thoughtfully. 'The question is, where to begin. At the beginning I suppose. How much do you know about beetles?'

'Something,' said Tom.

'Something?'

Tom was quite aware that despite his many school holidays spent driving round Europe in a campervan collecting beetles with his parents, compared to August he really knew very little.

'Actually . . . erm . . . maybe not that much.'

'Nothing at all,' admitted Pearl.

'Right,' sighed August. 'Well I'll keep it brief and very simple. As you may know, there are more beetles than any other creature on the planet. They are all small, because they, like all insects, don't have vertebrae. They have nothing to support their weight inside, you see—so their armour does it for them. And this exoskeleton is made of chitin. But I'm sure you learn all this stuff at school,' added August, 'at least I *hope* you do.' Pearl glanced at Tom awkwardly; it was clear she didn't.

'Anyway, millions of years ago, insects and beetles were much, much larger than they are now,' August continued, 'no one is quite sure why. But as you both *do* seem to know, some rather terrifying creatures are evolving back in that direction.'

Pearl nodded grimly: she did not need reminding of those centipedes on the cliff top.

'Precisely. Well they are not only getting larger, unfortunately some of the small ones are living longer as well. Before, they used to spend most of their lives as grubs, and lived as beetles for merely a month or two. Now . . . it's changing. Lengthening even as we speak.'

August glanced at Tom and he felt the colour flood to his cheeks. He knew what August was implying.

'So . . . so you think Don Gervase has taken that bottle and done something with it, to make this happen?'

'It had crossed my mind,' replied August coolly.

Tom felt embarrassed and angry.

'But . . . but how could he? There was no liquid in it. Just a few crystals at the bottom.'

'The crystals create the fumes, and it's those fumes that he wants, isn't it? Had he any sense he might have made some kind of airtight compartment and bred small beetles inside it, so that the gas became a part of them. But that's very difficult, and frankly I'm not sure whether he had that much gumption,' added August. 'You know I even made an antidote to my little potion a few years ago, just in case I ever needed to reverse the effects. Can't remember where I put it now.'

'Black cabinet, second shelf, next to Dr Goatby,' cried a blue jay on the second level.

'Of course, of course,' muttered August, turning round and rummaging around in the cabinet, and returning with a small green bottle.

'There you are, for what it's worth. The antidote to the elixir of life.'

Tom stared at the small green bottle, filled with inky liquid. A tumble of thoughts rushed through his head.

'So we couldn't . . . I mean, it's not worth—'

'Trying to reverse the course of history?' August smiled kindly. 'It is rather too late to stop them now, Tom. You can't destroy billions and billions of creatures. I'm afraid, old bean, Pandora's box is well and truly open.'

Tom could barely conceal his disappointment. In the back of his mind he had always half-hoped, half-dreamt that August Catcher's genius might have been able to reverse the damage he'd done.

'And given that it is, we just have to hope that whatever he intends to do with that gas he fails,' continued August. 'I have to say I am more intrigued about his motives. What does he really want, I wonder?'

'To take over the world?' suggested Tom huffily. 'To breed massive creatures that can wipe human beings from the face of the earth?'

August smiled.

'Of course, in a way you're right. If you had the power, why wouldn't you want to do that? After all, humans are by and large, unpleasant, filthy, highly destructive creatures. But what of it? Beetles existed long before we arrived on this planet, and they will undoubtedly be here long after we have gone. We are already living in the age of beetles.' August pressed his fingers together, thoughtfully. 'No. It strikes me that Don Gervase Askary is raiding the past for what he needs. But *why* he needs it might have nothing to do with us, and everything to do with some future event that we cannot even imagine.'

Pearl and Tom sat in silence for a moment, trying to grasp what August was saying.

'Well we know what he's searching for right now,' said Pearl, 'it's something from Tithona, isn't it? That's why he's kidnapped my dad and Rudy, and that's probably why he's taken them to this Scaraband place—'

'Scarazand,' corrected a shoebill patronizingly, 'Scaraband doesn't exist.'

'Right. Whatever,' she said, somewhat surprised to have been interrupted. 'I suppose you know where that is?'

'Indeed I do,' replied the shoebill, smugly. 'Would you like me to tell you?'

'Here we go, another lecture from volume twenty-one,' complained a shoebill at the far end. 'Nobody ever asks me about zymotic diseases.'

'They might one day,' replied a bird at the other end. 'Ever heard of Anaxagoras? Ever want to?'

'You should try heraldry,' snorted H, dismally. 'I think of what I know and I just want to die of boredom.'

'We should have been jumbled together,' nodded M.

'Yeah right,' agreed Q.

'Yeah, like, like freeform jazz,' said J, 'kind of abstract, totally mashed up and upside down—'

'Quiet up there!' shouted August, and immediately the banter ceased. The shoebill that had walked forward to the railing cleared its throat importantly.

'Shall I begin?'

'If you must,' said August wearily.

The bird ignored the insult and pressed on.

'Scarazand,' it began. 'Scarazand is the name given to the mythical capital of the beetles by the fabled medieval explorer Inigo Marcellus, (1397–1452). He claimed to have visited it on his journey to the centre of the earth. He said that having travelled through the lands of the fabulous dog-headed people, he then navigated through the endless black forests of the east inhabited only by screaming bearded men. At the edge of the forest stretched a labyrinth of colossal proportions. Venturing through one of its many portals he found himself lost in a tangle of tunnels, teeming with weird life, that stretched through time into the bowels of the earth, and when he emerged he found himself—'

'In a richly populated city, formed of a tower, where creatures couth and uncouth walked the streets,' continued August, 'beetles the size of horses, flying dogs, curious spider-headed women, isn't that right?'

The bird seemed a little put out at August's intervention.

'You are correct, sir, but—'

'There is more. I know. Much, much, much more. It's a legend, a fairy story. Did Inigo Marcellus go there? Who knows. Maybe he never even left his bedroom. Maybe he made it all up.'

Tom and Pearl stared at August in confusion.

'So what are you saying, Scarazand doesn't exist? There is no such place?' Pearl looked indignant.

'Of course not my dear,' replied August softly. 'I do very much believe there is such a place called Scarazand, but not on account of Inigo Marcellus. In fact Scarazand has been something of an obsession of mine for quite a while now. I had always known of the legend, of course, and though the unreliable Mr Marcellus was the first, others have followed. He is not alone in describing this place. But what reignited my interest in this old story was when I realized the true nature of Don Gervase Askary and his kind. This set me thinking again. Insect people, time travellers . . . it sounded frankly incredible. Were they from the future, the past, did they act alone or were all these people being controlled by something? I must admit I was struggling, until we found this cave. This place, where you are standing right now, provided me with the key to the whole puzzle.'

August's eyes were twinkling with excitement and Tom and Pearl looked around the tall, smooth walls expecting to see some sort of clue. But there was nothing.

'Erm . . . how did it do that?' asked Tom tentatively.

'It proved to me that millions of years ago, there were not only some very large insects, but also some vast insect colonies too. In fact, this whole island was one of them, a bit like a huge termite mound. And here, in the very centre, precisely where you are standing, was the chamber of the queen. Picture if you can a large blubbery, maggoty thing lying here on the floor. Millions and millions of beetles swarmed around her. They dug out tunnels into the rock, nurtured her eggs, built nurseries for her grubs, dug reservoirs for water, foraged for food, fended off attacks—you name it. And she controlled every single one of them so they acted together like one colossal living organism.'

'How could she do that?' asked Pearl.

August smiled. 'The second piece of evidence. Does either of you have a watch?'

Tom and Pearl shook their heads.

'Never mind,' he sighed, 'I have broken so many I don't suppose another will matter.' Pulling a small fob watch on a chain out of his pocket, he walked over to the far side of the room and crouched down.

'Now if you wouldn't mind getting out of the way,' he said, and set the small watch and chain down on the carpet. Immediately the chain began to uncurl and straighten, as if moved by an invisible hand, then the watch began to swing round and accelerated back towards Tom and Pearl, spinning to a halt in the centre.

'Excellent,' smiled August. 'Now if I could just have it back.'

Tom bent down to pick the fob watch off the carpet, and found it was fixed to the ground.

'So it's magnetic?' he said, pushing on it as hard as he could without success.

'Highly,' said August, walking back across to join them. 'Beneath your feet is a vast concentration of magnetic rock. Now why is this important? For the queen of this colony it was essential, because this was what she used to communicate. Lying on this great lump of metal rock she sent out magnetic pulses which spread far and wide, so that every single beetle heard her.'

'Wow.'

Pearl stared at the floor for a moment, trying to take this in.

'And what were these messages she sent out, do you think?'

'Basic things, I suspect, like all insects. Feed me, give me water, that sort of thing. The queen might have been enormous, but on her own she was little more than an egg producer and a vast amplifier.'

'And did the beetles have any choice?'

'Of course not. She is their queen. They could not think for themselves.'

Tom stared at the table, thinking hard about what August was saying. He was trying his best not to appear stupid.

'So . . . I'm not sure I quite understand how this all connects with Scarazand?'

August smiled.

'Imagine, Tom, if a colony like this one could have existed millions of years ago in the past, is it not possible that there is a much larger one somewhere in the future? A colony of beetles who can not only look after their queen, but also, as we now know, travel back and forth through time, and take many different forms.'

Tom sighed: was that really possible? That Don Gervase and all the rest of them were from some kind of super beetle colony from the future?

'But how do they become people?' asked Pearl. 'Are they like, shapeshifters?'

'Not exactly,' smiled August, 'it's a little more mechanical than that. Have you heard of cark beetles?'

Both Tom and Pearl looked blank.

'No reason why you should. They are parasites, and at the moment barely known to science, but a doctor in remotest Equador told me about them and their rather unusual habits. Cark beetles like to fly by night and lay their tiny eggs in the ear or nose of a sleeping person. Why? you might ask. He did not know, but he noticed that the victims complained of violent headaches, began behaving curiously and always died several months later. I have a theory why this is. I believe that that tiny cark grub burrows its way into its victim's brain, towards some primitive part of the cortex not used for millions of years. The fungus that it releases there activates the cells around it, making them receptive to magnetic pulses from Scarazand.'

'So . . . so what you are saying is that these people's brains have been . . . beetleized?' said Tom, shuddering at the thought.

August nodded grimly.

'I think so. Very unpleasant, isn't it? But there is another type of parasite I have discovered, too. A reproduplid that I have christened the echo beetle. Heard of them, no?'

Pearl shook her head uneasily. This was all so weird she was struggling to believe it.

'Echo beetles copy people. They eat a tiny amount of tissue, a piece of skin or a drop of blood perhaps, that's all it takes. Then they lay an egg, and from that egg comes a grub, and then the grub builds a cocoon and when it eventually hatches, it is not another echo beetle, but an exact copy of their victim. And because they need only the tiniest scrap of their host, echoes can make thousands and thousands of copies of the same person. Sound familiar?'

Tom was silent. He thought back to all those identical men and women he had met, and the vast magnitude of what they were up against was just beginning to dawn on him.

'So what about Don Gervase Askary, and Lotus, how do they fit into all this then?' he said. 'You know I saw him actually turn into a beetle.'

'I do,' murmured August, 'and I confess they puzzle me. I suspect that they belong to some higher order, perhaps elite within Scarazand, who do have the ability to metamorphose at will. I have a theory about that too but,' August checked himself, 'I won't bore you with any more science.'

There was silence for a moment, as Tom and Pearl sat dazzled by all this terrifying information. Pearl took a deep breath. She felt utterly deflated.

'And I guess getting to Scarazand is difficult?'

'Almost certainly, if you believe Inigo Marcellus. What was it again? Beyond the forest of screaming bearded men there was a labyrinth . . . '

'Of colossal proportions. Venturing into one of its many portals he found himself lost in a tangle of tunnels, teaming with weird life that stretched through time into the bowels of the earth,' repeated the shoebill.

'And do you believe that?'

'Finding an entrance would be difficult, certainly,' admitted August, avoiding Pearl's question. 'Could be through a door, a cupboard, down a set of stairs, a hole in the ground—maybe it *is* a labyrinth through time—who knows. They have been very careful to conceal their labours from us.'

Tom said nothing. This whole idea was beginning to sound more and more impossible by the moment. Maybe they were mad to even think of trying to get there. Absently, he stared up at the small chink of light winking high above them.

'But . . . but wait a minute, *wait a minute*, aren't we missing something?' August and Pearl looked at him expectantly. 'If Scarazand is as you say, a massive version of this island, then isn't the easiest way in just to climb down the chimney? Look,' he pointed, 'then you don't have to find a concealed entrance, or go through a labyrinth or anything like that.'

'Very observant, Tom,' nodded August. 'Absolutely, it would be, *if* one could only find it. That was the fundamental weak point at the heart of this colony, and if Scarazand is anything like this place, then of course it will have a chimney leading to the outside world.'

'Why would it?' asked Pearl. 'What's the point, if they have taken all this trouble to be secret?'

'I suspect there is no choice,' replied August. 'I suspect that the queen spends all day booming out magnetic messages and laying eggs, and the result is she gets very, very hot. Her whole chamber is swirling in a mist of unpleasant gases. Some kind of chimney or ventilation shaft would be essential to let it all escape. Out there, somewhere—in a remote desert maybe, or hidden in a mountain range—there is a small hole no wider than a well spewing out poisonous gases. And that is probably the only visible sign of the entire edifice.'

'And you don't have any ideas where that might be?' asked Pearl. 'Or is that a crazy question?'

August looked at Pearl and a flicker of a smile crossed his lips.

'Not crazy at all, my dear. Sir Henry and I spent a long time looking. Not only for that chimney, but also for any other entrance we could find.'

Pearl and Tom turned to August in astonishment.

'So *you* wanted to go to Scarazand?'

'Of course. What person who is interested in such things wouldn't want to go to Scarazand? It has got to be one of the most remarkable places on earth. We would still be looking now if Sir Henry hadn't managed to talk me out of it.'

'Really?'

'Absolutely. And I suppose he was right. It would be extraordinarily dangerous and my interest was purely scientific. I did not have a burning emotional reason to go, like you do: I wasn't prepared to risk everything. But believe me, I would very much have liked to have seen it—if only once.' His voice drifted away. 'Still got all the equipment around somewhere. I suppose you'd like to see it?' He looked across at Tom and Pearl and grinned. 'Now that's a crazy question.'

'Second drawer, grey chest, the key is in the jar!' shouted a golden oriole.

'And which jar would that be?' said August, shambling over to the cabinet.

'The green one on the shelf.'

'Which shelf would that be?'

'The shelf behind you! Behind you!' squawked the birds in

unison. August shook his muddled head above the din. 'It's ridiculous, isn't it? Quite ridiculous. But after a lifetime spent stuffing things inside other things, I just can't seem to kick the habit.'

Following the birds' impatient instructions, August found his way to the grey chest and hauled it up onto the table.

'Now I am not much of an explorer, as you know, Tom, but I did anticipate what might be required,' he said, emptying out a collection of odd objects on to the table. 'Most of it's still here I think.' Tom picked up an ancient looking pair of goggles with almost black lenses. 'Those are compound glasses,' said August. 'My rather feeble attempt to reduce the world to a series of basic colours, to see the world as a beetle does.'

'Do they work?' said Tom, putting them on.

'They certainly have some effect,' said August, 'but as no one really knows how beetles see it is a bit of a guess.'

Tom squinted through the glass: there were vague colours as if in a kaleidoscope, but nothing more.

'They look the part but probably not that useful in truth,' admitted August. 'This, on the other hand, would be.' He held up a thin flask in a leather case and straps, which had a spray nozzle and rubber squeezer attached to the end of it. 'Do you know anything about pheromones?'

'Only what my dad—' Tom stopped and thought better of it. 'Actually, no.'

'Well why should you? But they are fascinating chemicals. Insects use them all the time. In fact certain creatures, like solitary wasps, use them to make themselves invisible to bees. That's what gave me the idea for this stuff.'

'So . . . you have invented a pheromone?' said Tom, taking up the leather flask.

'Indeed. A pheromone that makes one invisible to beetles,' he said. 'I did a few experiments, matched the chemicals, played with them a bit, as you do, and this is what I came up with.'

'And it really works?' asked Pearl, taking the flask from Tom and sniffling the nozzle curiously.

'I think it does. I tried it out on some of the smaller hybrids we came across in Mongolia and they seemed convinced. Could it work on a beetleized person? I am pleased to say I have never had cause to find out.'

Tentatively Pearl gave the rubber ball a squeeze.

'Oh,' she gasped, as a thin film of orange mist spluttered out of the nozzle. The smell was a pungent mixture of almonds and rotten oranges. 'So what would that do?' she said, wrinkling her nose.

'Well, if I was a beetle, your hand would have just disappeared,' said August confidently. 'And if you wanted to disguise yourself completely you would have to spray it all over yourself.'

'And you were seriously going to do that?'

'Something similar. Sir Henry and I had a couple of thin silk ponchos made up, which I impregnated with the stuff, with hoods and visors and what have you. Looked rather like a pair of exotic beekeepers,' he smiled. 'I've got them too, somewhere.'

'And what's that?' said Tom pointing at a small flat wooden box.

'Ah yes,' grinned August, undoing the box and delicately picking out a small white feather. 'That was for luck. Just in case Inigo Marcellus was right about the labyrinth.'

'I knew it! I just knew it!' yelled a tiny voice high up in the shelves. Tom looked up to see a small fluorescent head poke out. 'What a liberty!'

'The night shrike,' grinned August. 'The only fluorescent bird in the world. I rather optimistically hoped to find a beetle and tie this feather to its abdomen, then set it loose in the labyrinth and follow the shining feather all the way back to Scarazand. Slightly mad—but you never know. Might have come in useful. Oh yes, our whole trip was planned out. It would have been quite an adventure.'

'Sounds like it,' said Pearl. 'I'm surprised you let Sir Henry talk you out of it.'

'So was I,' he murmured. 'But in the light of what has happened since he was absolutely right. Things were getting rather hot in Mongolia, to tell you the truth. We had a few close shaves. And of course we never found an entrance, did we? Despite looking all over the world.' August paused a moment, lost in thought.

'But you know it's a curious thing; we never looked in the most obvious place. Which I suppose gives you a distinct advantage.'

'Us?'

Tom and Pearl turned in surprise towards August's ancient wizened face. Somewhere inside the wrinkled nets of skin his eyes sparkled.

'Oh I know what you two are thinking. You want to borrow all this stuff, and why shouldn't you? I would.'

Pearl blushed awkwardly: she hadn't thought it was that easy to read her mind.

'So . . . so where is the most obvious place?' asked Tom tentatively.

'Where your ball came from, of course.'

'What, the Tithona archipelago?'

'Exactly, my dear. The Tithona archipelago, that curious collection of weirdly shaped islands that now alas is under the sea. May I see it again?'

'Erm . . . sure,' said Tom, pulling the ball out of his pocket and handing it to August.

'So odd that I missed it,' he murmured, rotating the ball between his fingers. 'I have to say I completely forgot about this strange find until this morning. But of course I see it now. It makes perfect sense.'

August gazed at the inky patterns, lost in thought, and Tom and Pearl watched him with rising frustration. It was as if he had opened a door to show them the way and then instantly closed it again.

'I'm sorry, I must be really stupid, but I really can't see what that ball has got to do with any of this,' exclaimed Pearl. 'Is it like a lucky charm or something?'

August smiled to himself.

'You see, to you or me, this ball has no value at all, beyond that which we have chosen to give it. It is a curious amulet, a keepsake to ward off evil spirits, nothing more. But to Don Gervase Askary, I suspect that this innocent looking object might give him something greater than anything else in the world.'

Tom stared at the ball in bewilderment.

'And what is that?' he asked.

August paused. He squeezed the clear rubbery surface hard and watched it expand back into shape.

'Power. The power to control every creature in Scarazand and beyond. Perhaps the power to bend the world to his wishes. Limitless power.'

Tom and Pearl stared at the strange, unprepossessing ball in silence. In the long procession of curious facts August had patiently laid before them, this was the strangest of them all.

'Are you serious?'

'Of course. Why shouldn't I be?'

'But how do you know?'

'I don't,' he said looking up at them. 'Remember, I don't *know* anything. It is just what I happen to believe. Shall I explain?'

CHAPTER 10

THE AMULET

Tom and Pearl sat patiently waiting for August to continue. Turning round, he surveyed the room.

'I don't suppose anyone knows what I am looking for?' he said, scratching his head.

'Could they be catalogued under K?' suggested one of the frogmouths. 'I suspect that they are.'

'K? Yes . . . of course, K. Clever girl,' he said approvingly, and the frogmouth beamed as only a frogmouth can. August pulled out a narrow wooden drawer and set it down on the table. Hunting through the compartments he picked out a small object the size of a marble and placed it beside the beetle ball. Side by side, they seemed to be made of the same clear, rubbery material.

'Doesn't have any patterns but it's similar, isn't it?' he said, arching his eyebrows. 'Here, try giving it a squeeze.' Picking up the smaller ball he handed it across to Pearl. 'Strangely warm, oddly tactile? I'd say almost exactly the same.'

'Where's it from?' she asked, holding it up to the light.

'I found it about a metre away from where you're sitting right now,' replied August. 'Lying on the floor of this cave when we first entered it. At first I thought it was a pebble, or a toy even, that someone had left behind. But as I began to piece together the story of this strange place, I realized I couldn't be further from the truth.'

'So . . . what is it?' asked Tom cautiously, not entirely sure he wanted to know the answer.

'The simplest way to describe it would be a ball of thoughts, or instincts. It's a bit like a brain, I suppose.'

'A *brain*?' gasped Pearl, barely able to contain her surprise. 'Whose brain?'

'The brain of the queen beetle that once inhabited this cave,' replied August evenly. 'She has long gone, but this stuff is curiously indestructible.'

Tom and Pearl looked in horror at the anonymous, colourless object.

'But . . . but it's so small,' Tom began, 'I thought you said these queen creatures are huge.'

'They are,' August smiled. 'Big beetle, small brain, does that not tell you anything about them?'

He picked up the clear rubber marble and squeezed it.

'It's that strange milky colour that set me thinking. And the way it feels in your hand. That is the key. How you touch it.'

August looked up to see that Pearl and Tom were entirely lost. He smiled indulgently.

'Do you remember what I told you about the queen sending out messages, using those great pulses of magnetic waves?'

Tom and Pearl nodded.

'Well this little object controls those messages. She is the loudspeaker, and this is the voice, giving the orders. And the strange thing is, this remarkable substance was not always inside the queen.'

'What do you mean—that the queen was born without a brain?' said Tom.

'Almost,' replied August. 'It is a curious fact about the insect world that the more you find out about them, the more alien they seem. In this case it's a bit like a love story with a violent end. Imagine this,' he said, clearing a space on the table and setting down two green beetles side by side. 'In the beginning, there are two beetles, a king and a queen, and they are both the same size. They find a hole in the ground somewhere and begin a colony. And as the colony begins to expand, the queen lies in her chamber becoming larger and larger, producing thousands and thousands of eggs a day, all of which hatch into worker beetles. Soon there are millions of them, each with their own job to do, and the queen has swollen so out of proportion that she no longer looks like a beetle at all,' he said, replacing one small green beetle with a smooth stone the size of an orange.

'So far, so good. You might have guessed this much already. But what of the poor old king, who began the colony with the queen all those years ago? She doesn't need him any more. He's redundant: useless. So what does he do? Something very strange indeed, and I have seen this happen in a colony of tiny fluke beetles out in the rainforests of Papua New Guinea. The king wanders away, looking for dead worker beetles. And when he finds one he picks open their chests and eats a tiny speck of clear, rubbery fungus present at the centre of their bodies. What is this stuff? Nobody knows exactly, but the king becomes addicted to this curious substance, even though he can't digest it. He stores it up in his abdomen, and over time he goes further afield. He searches out dead centipedes, dead flies, dead wasps; any insect carcass he can find that contains this curious clear fungus, until his abdomen becomes swollen to the size of a ball. A ball of what? Memories? Instincts? Thoughts? Maybe all three,' he said, rolling the clear rubbery marble next to the green beetle.

Tom and Pearl stared down at the strange collection of objects on the table. Both of them had an idea where this was leading.

'OK,' said Tom, slowly, 'so how does this ball then become the queen beetle's brain?'

'This is the violent end bit,' grinned August, his eyes twinkling. 'When the king himself comes to die, he returns to the colony, makes his way to the queen's chamber, dragging his heavy abdomen behind him. He can't help himself. And there she eats him, lock, stock, and barrel. But the ball is indigestible, so it stays inside her, just below the surface of her glistening white skin. And here the constant motion of her body massages it this way and that, keeps it warm, and this movement allows her to send much more complex messages through the colony. Instead of just feed me, water me, beetles are now given much more specific instructions and they have no choice but to obey. It is rather like tuning in a radio. What had been a thumping hiss of static and noise suddenly becomes words spoken loud and clear, and at this moment, the colony reaches its zenith. Does this make any sense?'

'I *think* so,' began Tom. 'But does the queen know what she is doing when she squeezes the ball, or is it just an accident?'

'I suspect it is trial and error. Despite her vast size, she is only a beetle, after all. She is not concerned about much beyond her own limited horizons. But in the skilful hands of someone else, like Don Gervase Askary, I'm sure that ball has enormous potential.' August paused thoughtfully. 'Which makes it so powerful. And so dangerous.'

Tom and Pearl stared at the two clear balls sitting next to each other in the middle of the table.

'And you're really sure about this?' asked Tom.

'Not *really* sure. But I have been studying these creatures for rather a long time.' Rummaging around in the drawer he picked out two much smaller balls the size of pearls, and set them down on the table in line with the other two. 'I found those in South America, this one in Turkmenistan, and this, ah yes,' he smiled, 'and I almost clean forgot about this.'

August held up a lump of honey coloured amber and passed it over to Pearl to see. Holding the amber up to the light, she saw trapped inside it a tiny black beetle with a hugely swollen ball-like abdomen.

'A king?' she whispered, squinting at the rubbery substance within the beetle's black form.

'That's right. Odd isn't it?'

Tom scratched his head. He was still not convinced.

'But if there are loads of these beetle balls about, how can you be so sure about Nicholas Zumsteen's? I mean, isn't it possible that the queen of Scarazand has eaten the king already?'

'Possible . . . but I doubt it,' replied August. 'Consider the facts, Tom. Don Gervase Askary is searching high and low for something Nicholas Zumsteen found on the island of Tithona.

Why there? It's a strange little place in the middle of the Pacific ocean. He must know or suspect that it has some connection to Scarazand. Secondly, the boy who found this ball insisted that it was once a beetle, which is more than a coincidence. He said he found it crawling up the wall of a cave, deep underground. We have no reason to disbelieve him. And last but not least, this just feels as if it does something, doesn't it?' he said, picking up the egg-sized ball in his hand and squeezing it. 'Imagine if with the merest flick of your wrist you could send commands booming out to every beetle couth and uncouth, forcing them do exactly whatever you wanted,' he laughed. 'Now *that* would be power.'

Tom and Pearl sat in glum silence, watching August's fingers dance across the ball's decorated surface.

'Maybe that's what you are doing right now,' muttered Tom.

August smiled.

'I very much doubt it. It's bound to be very complicated. But I'll wager good money Don Gervase Askary dreams of holding this ball in his hand and learning its secret language.' August paused thoughtfully. 'Which is why we must make absolutely sure that he never gets anywhere near it.'

August placed the ball carefully on the table and without a word Tom leant forward and stowed it carefully in his pocket. Pearl watched despondently: Tom could tell what she was think-ing, as he felt it too, deep in the pit of his stomach. Suddenly the stakes had been raised: the task ahead seemed more dangerous than ever.

'Well,' said August, clasping his hands together, 'I must confess that all this talking has made me extremely hungry, and I'm almost certain Sir Henry has caught our lunch by now. Shall we?'

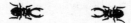

Retreating back up the steps to the house, they walked out onto the sunlit lawn and followed August down a track through the trees. Every so often he stopped to point out the odd curious flower or rare bird, but neither Tom nor Pearl were really listening, they were both too preoccupied by the pressing question of how they were ever going to get to Scarazand now. It seemed virtually impossible.

'Any luck?' shouted August, as they turned a corner.

'Eight!' shouted Trixie, crouching beside a small fire at the water's edge.

'Eight? That's rather good,' smiled August, and led Tom and Pearl down through the beams of sunlight towards the camp, where Trixie was busy threading the small silver fish onto a stick.

'He's getting quite expert at it now,' she said, pointing to Sir Henry standing next to a pool below a waterfall high above, holding what looked like a grey string frisbee attached to a line in his hand.

'Is that a net?' asked Pearl.

'Something like that,' said Trixie. 'Actually it's a spider's web. I picked it up in Papua New Guinea. You'll see.'

They stood watching for a moment as Sir Henry stood motionless on the edge of the pool, his eyes firmly fixed on the rushing water above. Suddenly there was a small silver movement, and a fish leapt out of the water on the far side of the waterfall. In one swift movement Sir Henry flung the grey frisbee looping through the air and in the next instant the small silver fish was enveloped in its twisting form and it splashed down into the water.

'Bravo!' shouted August.

Sir Henry turned round and, seeing Tom and Pearl, he waved.

'One more,' he smiled. 'I'm coming down.'

Five minutes later they were all sitting down beside the camp-fire eating the grilled fish with bread and apricots and scalding cups of hot tea from the kettle.

'So that's really what he's after?' said Sir Henry, blowing on his cup. He had been listening to August patiently explaining his theory about the beetle ball, and why Don Gervase Askary might want it so much.

'To me it makes perfect sense,' said August. 'Without it he has no real mastery of Scarazand at all.'

'And what are the chances of him knowing what it looks like?'

'Slim I'd say. These beetle balls are extremely rare: I've never met anyone who has even heard of such things, let alone seen one. Askary probably hasn't got much clue. He might know it is small, and probably assumes that because it has immense value to him, it has immense value to everyone else, so it's a precious object of some kind. Beyond that—nothing.'

Sir Henry stared at the embers and frowned.

'Maybe we should bury it somewhere, or chuck it into a vol-cano or something like that. Just to make absolutely sure. Get rid of the damn thing.'

'Unless . . . unless there was some way we could learn how to use it ourselves, against him,' suggested Tom. 'Do you think that's possible?'

'I very much doubt it,' snorted Sir Henry. 'Not being beetles, how could we ever know what we were doing?'

There was silence for a moment.

'What do you think, Pearl?' asked Trixie. 'After all, this concerns you as much as anyone.'

Pearl stared at the lake: the bright autumn sun was already starting to fade, and the hillsides were ablaze with gold all around.

'I don't know,' she said at last. 'I was hoping . . . but, I guess that is too dangerous. And it sounds pretty well impossible to get to Scarazand anyways.'

'No no my dear, nothing is impossible,' blustered Sir Henry.

'What do you mean?'

'Well, if what August believes turns out to be true then it is very simple to get to Scarazand. In fact I can't think why we never thought of it before. We simply fly over to Tithona, go up to the crater, find the boy who sold Nicholas the ball and get him to take us down to the cave. Bob's your uncle.'

'But I thought—'

'It's underwater?' Sir Henry seemed confused. 'Obviously it is—now. But I'm talking about flying *back*, before the volcano erupted. We have an old map in the house somewhere and I'm pretty sure Tithona is on it.'

'Oh it is,' said Trixie, 'I've seen it. It's on the greylag shearwater intersection. Entrance 119.'

'119. How interesting,' mused Sir Henry. 'That's through the Shakra Parbat, isn't it?'

Trixie nodded. 'It most certainly is. The meanest of them all,' she added with a grin.

'It's on a magnetic line, you see,' explained Sir Henry, 'not far from here in actual fact. A migrating track for birds that happens to contain various openings into other times. Some are large, and others are, well, slightly smaller.'

Trixie smiled at Sir Henry's careful understatement, and Pearl searched his gaunt, angular face.

'So, you're not joking are you? You really *could* get there?'

Sir Henry shot her a penetrating but not unkindly look.

'You mean, can we take *you* there,' he said. 'And set you off down into some labyrinth, to look for Scarazand by yourselves?' Sir Henry studied their eager faces carefully, and then glanced down at the fire. It was quite clear that was exactly what they meant.

'The thing is, I wonder whether it would be a very irresponsible thing to do. I have never approved of sending people off into impossible situations, and Scarazand sounds like hell on earth. And quite apart from that, I'm just not at all sure you would ever come back again.'

'Well then maybe we should go down there with them,' suggested Trixie, 'help 'em out. Sounds like they could use it.'

Sir Henry considered this for a moment, then glanced across to August sitting at the water's edge. He was contemplating a dragonfly that had come to rest on his finger, and the sunlight shone through his shock of white hair like a halo.

'Once upon a time, that might have been a good idea,' murmured Sir Henry, watching his old friend. 'But not any more, alas. I fear it would all get too complicated.'

Trixie followed his eyes, and understood exactly what he was saying.

'Yes, of course. Silly me.'

They both watched August carefully studying the insect.

'What do you think, August?' said Sir Henry. 'Is a trip to Scarazand courting disaster?'

August blew on the dragonfly and smiled as it danced away across the water.

'In all likelihood, yes. But I'm with Trixie on this one,' he said. 'It is one of my greatest regrets that I never saw that place, and I suspect that now I never will. But I don't see why Tom and Pearl shouldn't go, and I am quite sure that if you and I were younger and more reckless, we would do the same thing. Imagine if it was your mother or your brother, you would raise hell to try and get them out.'

'Absolutely,' agreed Trixie. 'Of course you would.'

Sir Henry flung away the remains of his tea and scratched his moustache.

'I know. That's the conundrum. And what's more, I wouldn't have taken kindly to a pair of old gentlemen who weren't prepared to help.'

He smiled at Tom and Pearl.

'Very well you two, here's the deal. Trixie and I will fly you to Tithona. We will take you up to the crater and set you on your way. And, if August agrees, you are welcome to take everything we have here to help you.'

'Really?' gasped Pearl, her eyes shining with excitement.

'Absolutely,' nodded Sir Henry. 'What say you, August?'

'There wouldn't be much point going without it,' he said, catching another dragonfly and holding it in the palm of his hand. 'Take the ponchos, the pheromone spray, the feather—all the necessary gubbins.'

'Excellent,' smiled Sir Henry. 'But only on one condition.'

'And what's that?'

'You leave that beetle ball here with August for safekeeping.'

Pearl hesitated.

'But wouldn't it—'

'I think that would be essential,' agreed August. 'Just in case something untoward happens. Which would be a shame.'

'Shame being the understatement of the millennium,' said Sir Henry briskly. 'It would be positively cataclysmic. Well?'

Tom did not need any prompting.

'OK,' he said, 'it's a deal.'

Taking the beetle ball out of his pocket he handed it across the fire to Sir Henry, who squeezed the curious object between his fingers before handing it across to August.

'Well done,' he smiled. 'A very wise decision.'

Pearl watched the transaction in silence; she could not hide her disappointment.

'And if we take them, will you be all right here on your own for a bit?' Trixie touched August kindly on the shoulder. 'Only we don't want to abandon you.'

'When you've lived as long as I have, my dear, what's a day or two more?' he grinned, squeezing her hand. 'Though seeing all that gear again made me rather wish I was coming along for the ride. But I don't suppose that's possible, is it?'

Sir Henry smiled and shook his head.

'You're just too damned clever for your own good, old boy. If Don Gervase Askary got hold of you he'd have a field day.'

August sighed ruefully. 'Well, yes. Probably.'

'We won't be long,' said Trixie. 'Promise.'

'Of course. Well, you'd best buzz off then. I expect it's an early start.'

'It will be,' grinned Sir Henry, pleased that everything was settled. 'How about first light tomorrow?'

By the time they had climbed back up the hill the sun had dipped behind the mountains and patches of mist were forming on the glassy surface of the water. Across the lake Tom could see thin plumes of smoke rising up from the villages as the autumn evening stole in.

'Nippy, isn't it?' shuddered August, walking out onto the terrace and handing Tom and Pearl what looked like two blankets with holes in. 'They're called farrans. Quite useful at this time of year.'

'Thanks,' said Pearl, gratefully pulling on the thick woollen garment. Tom could see that she was shivering slightly and he was shivering too.

'I'll see you in a bit,' August said as he scurried back across the lawn. 'Just need to retrieve all those goodies I told you about.'

'Do you want a hand?' Tom called out.

'No thanks,' replied August, and with a wave he disappeared inside.

Tom and Pearl sat down on the grass and watched the mountains turn purple and gold. Soon the curtain of white mist covered the lake and the first stars appeared in the sky.

'So are you excited?' asked Tom.

Pearl did not reply immediately.

'More nervous than excited. I just feel—' She shrugged her shoulders. 'I just wish we had something to offer. Something to trade. It would make it so much easier.'

Tom shook his head in frustration: he found it hard to understand how Pearl could still be thinking like this.

'Pearl, honestly, these are not bargaining people. They get what they want—and that's it. The moment Don Gervase, or Lotus, or any of them found out that the beetle ball was the real thing—if it is—then they'd take it from us by force and kill us.'

'Maybe,' continued Pearl. 'But maybe they wouldn't be able to. Maybe we would be invisible or something like that.'

'Come on Pearl,' snorted Tom, 'remember those giant centipedes you told me about? There's probably much worse things than that in Scarazand.'

'I don't care. I'd just rather have the choice, that's all. In case everything goes wrong. And don't pretend that you haven't thought of that too.'

Tom stared up at the stars feeling thoroughly nettled. Of course he knew that in a way Pearl was right: this whole enterprise was fraught with danger, and perhaps it *was* a crazy idea to go to Scarazand without any kind of security. But was there any choice? He had seen what Don Gervase was capable of with his own eyes, and he knew it would be foolish to underestimate him. Yet at the back of his mind, Tom could not help wondering why he was going to Scarazand at all. For Pearl it was simple: her brother and her father had been taken, she had seen it happen herself. There was no alternative. But for him it was just words on a page that had brought him this far, and those same words were about to lead him down to hell. Supposing everything

Pearl's father had scribbled down was nonsense? Or supposing *his* parents had not been taken at all, and it was some *other* Tom Scatterhorn who had betrayed his family, and this had nothing to do with him? The nagging doubt ate away at his conviction, and that made it all so much harder. Tom stared up at the crescent moon and shivered. Either way, it was too late to turn around now: he couldn't endure the rest of his life not knowing what had happened to them: he had to find out, one way or another. For better or worse. And he had to admit there was something else, too. He couldn't let Pearl do this alone. Not now. That wouldn't be right.

'Going to Scarazand without the beetle ball has got to be better than not going there at all,' he said at last.

Pearl turned to look at him, her beautiful, sunburnt face nothing more than a shadow in the dying light.

'Is it?' she said, searching for some kind of reassurance. 'You really think so?'

'Hey you folks, feeling hungry?'

Tom and Pearl turned to see Trixie at the door.

'Sorry it's so early but we'll be off before dawn. Dinner in five?'

Tom waved and she disappeared back inside.

'Come on,' said Tom, trying to put a brave face on it. 'There's no point being down about it. We're on our way now and that's something.' Getting to his feet stiffly he held out his hand for Pearl. 'Whatever happens—is just going to happen.'

'If you say so,' she sighed, taking Tom's hand and heaving herself up.

'I do. Things always work themselves out somehow. Don't they?'

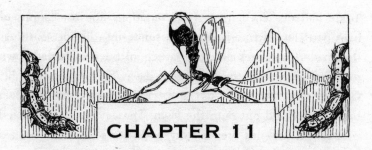

CHAPTER 11

To Tithona

'Wakey wakey.'

Tom opened his eyes sleepily to see the silhouette of August looming over him, holding a steaming mug of tea.

'What time is it?'

'Far far too early,' said August, smiling. 'Just gone three. Sir Henry and Trixie have gone down to the lake to get everything ready, and I think Pearl must be there too.'

Tom blearily gazed over to the small camp bed on the other side of the room where Pearl had slept and saw that it was empty.

'Best get going, old chap.'

Tom fell back on his pillow and rubbed his eyes hard. He had not slept well, his mind racing with everything that August had told them and his anticipation about what the new day might bring. And he had been vaguely aware of floorboards creaking and doors opening as Pearl had got up and paced about: she must have been feeling much the same way.

Pulling on the farran, Tom ran a hand through his tangle of blond hair and thrust his feet into his shoes. Three o'clock was very, very early: why did it have to be that early? Sir Henry and

Trixie had discussed magnetical variations, the oscillations of light particles, thermodynamics in sunbeams, the sort of things that made Tom's eyes glaze over at school, but it all boiled down to shooting through the opening at dawn. So dawn it must be. Gulping down the tea as fast as he could, Tom shambled down the corridor and out onto the lawn. The air was so sharp and cold that it took his breath away, and with a shiver he walked across to the edge of the terrace and looked down. It was a spectacular sight: the lake was shrouded in a thick blanket of mist, above which ragged silver wisps of cloud hung motionless in the moonlight. Not a leaf moved.

'So you're shootin' the Shakra Parbat. That should be interesting.'

The gravelly Australian voice made Tom jump. It seemed to be coming from the tree.

'Hello Tom, me old mucker.'

'Hi,' said Tom, uncertainly. He recognized that voice; he had heard it a long time ago.

'Surprised to see me?' it rasped. 'Nowhere near as surprised as I am to see you. I thought we was off limits out here.'

Looking up Tom saw the silhouette of the vast wandering eagle, perched in the crook of a tree. It looked as strange and angry and awkward as he had remembered it.

'Fraid not,' he smiled.

'Yes. Well just so long as you haven't brought any of them nasties with ya. We don't like them here. Not one little bit. But maybe you do, seein' where you're headed.'

'Scarazand, you mean?'

The eagle harrumphed loudly.

'Don't I just! What a place *that* is!'

'You've been there, then?'

'Can't say that I have,' sniffed the eagle. 'Can't say that I want to. Can't quite see the attraction to be honest. Who in their right mind would want to go down there, and from Tithona of all places! Bloody hell fire.'

'So you don't approve?'

'What I think has nothing to do with it,' growled the bird, studying him carefully in the moonlight. 'You do whatever you got to do. But remember, I have been into the future. I have seen stuff. And I would advise extreme caution.'

'Thanks. I'll bear that in mind,' said Tom, trying hard not to sound sarcastic.

'Don't trust a soul, kiddo,' said the eagle, 'not even—'

'Tom? Is that you?'

Tom turned and spotted August holding a lamp on the edge of the woods.

'We're in something of a hurry, old chap,' he called out anxiously. 'They're waiting.'

'Got to go,' said Tom, looking up at the vast bird. 'Maybe see you again someday.'

'Yeah right,' said the eagle. 'Oh, just one last thing.'

'What is it?' said Tom, who was already halfway back across the moonlit lawn.

'The Shakra Parbat is wider than it looks.'

'Ohh?'

'But not much.'

Tom scampered across the lawn and moments later joined August on the path.

'So you've met G. F. Moore I see,' said August as they walked swiftly down through the silent woods.

'G. F. Moore? Oh. Right. Yes,' said Tom, who had not heard the bird's name before. It seemed an unlikely choice.

'Such a curious creature—a serendipitous accident really. To think where he's been. It's almost beyond imagining.'

Tom nodded. He looked up at the moon moving through the trees.

'He was trying to put me off going.'

'Hmm. Well, it's certainly going to be one hell of a trip,' muttered August. 'Hell perhaps being the appropriate word. But I can't pretend I'm not envious. I can't think of a single scientist alive or dead who wouldn't leap at the chance. Have you got the rucksack?'

'Pearl's got it,' said Tom, remembering that they had argued briefly about who was going to carry it the night before.

'And everything's in it?'

'I double-checked.'

'Good good. Excellent,' nodded August. 'Sorry, I don't want to sound like your mother but it is rather important.'

Tom smiled and said nothing. He was quite certain that if his mother had been here right now she would have done everything possible to *stop* him going, but it was much too late for that now. Still, August's fussing didn't exactly fill him with confidence. Soon the path began to level out and they descended into the thick blanket of mist that had smothered the surface of the lake. The air was so wet Tom could almost feel it brushing past his face.

'August?'

'Yes Tom.'

'Do you . . . do you really honestly think we will find an entrance to Scarazand from those caves?'

It was a question that had haunted Tom's dreams and refused to let him go.

'If that ball was once the king beetle, as I believe it was, then there has to be an entrance down there. It could not have found its way to that remote spot any other way. But there is always an element of uncertainty, isn't there? Wouldn't be much fun if there wasn't,' he winked. 'Oh by the way, when you get up to the crater, see if you can get hold of a jitterjat beetle.'

'A jitterjat beetle?'

'You won't be able to miss them as there are thousands up there. They change colour, a bit like chameleons.'

'Is that for the feather?' said Tom, recalling August's plan.

'Exactly. Well remembered. If you get stuck, tie the feather round its leg then let it go and follow it as best you can.'

They had reached the jetty now, and Tom could just make out the silver plane looming out of the mist.

'Sir Henry will explain everything on the way up to the crater,' said August. 'Oh, and I mustn't forget to give you this.'

August reached into his pocket and pulled out a small silver egg on a chain.

'Very important,' he said, slipping it into Tom's hand.

'What is it?'

'A precaution against the very worst thing that can happen.'

'Which is what?'

'You fall asleep and, through no fault of your own, a cark beetle finds you.'

'Is that possible?' said Tom, looking down at the small object in his palm.

'I'm afraid it is highly likely. Tithona is one of those odd places where . . . well, I don't want to frighten you unnecessarily,' he smiled. 'But you will recall how the cark grub burrows its way into your head, spreading a trail of fungus that beetleizes your brain?'

Tom nodded uneasily: he had forgotten quite how awful this sounded.

'So . . . so what am I meant to do with this?'

'Inside that egg are some grubs. Lapastus grubs, from the Amazonian rainforest. Avoid looking at them if at all possible, as they are disgusting. But they fight fire with fire. They stop the cark's grisly work dead in its tracks. Instantly.'

'So I must—'

'Eat one.'

Tom swallowed hard. This sounded terrible.

'And if Pearl is attacked, you must make her eat one, too.'

'But . . . don't the cark beetles fly at night? How will we know if it happens?'

'You won't,' said August flatly. 'That's the risk, isn't it?'

Tom shivered, and slipped the silver chain round his neck.

'Best of luck, old chum,' he said, taking Tom's hand and shaking it. Tom tried to smile, but found he couldn't. Suddenly he felt very unsure about all of this, and found himself not wanting to let go of August's hand. August Catcher was like some ancient grandfather he had never had.

'Do you think . . . are we completely crazy to do this?' he said, looking up into August's pale, wizened face. His thick white hair was glittering with droplets of water.

'A little,' smiled August kindly. 'But then one has to be sometimes, doesn't one? It's always worth climbing up to the furthest hill to see what's on the other side. Otherwise, how can you ever know?'

'But do you really think we can make it back?'

August stared out into the fog that seemed to be getting lighter every moment.

'If you are careful, there's every chance we'll meet again.'

Their eyes met briefly, and Tom knew there was nothing more to say. He turned and walked swiftly down the jetty to where the small silver plane was waiting.

'Morning, old boy,' said Sir Henry, sitting beside Trixie in the cockpit. There was a large map spread out on his knees. 'Pearl not with you?'

'No. I thought she was with you.'

''Fraid not.' Sir Henry checked his watch anxiously. 'Every second counts on this one and we really can't push it much longer. Where the hell's she got to?'

'There she is,' said Trixie, spotting a small figure running down through the trees.

'Marvellous,' said Sir Henry, watching as Pearl ran out past August onto the jetty, the small green rucksack bouncing against her back. 'Start the engines.'

'Sorry,' said Pearl breathlessly, 'so sorry.'

'Everything all right, my dear?' said Sir Henry. 'No collywobbles at the last minute?'

Pearl shook her head.

'Good good. Climb aboard then you two.'

One after the other Tom and Pearl stepped out onto the float and then clambered up the fuselage and in through the small aluminium door. There were two small green seats in the tiny cabin behind Sir Henry and Trixie, and moments later Tom and Pearl were sitting in them. August stood on the jetty waving, and they waved back.

'That was cutting it pretty fine,' said Tom as the engines began to roar. 'Where have you been?'

'Just getting my stuff together. You know, double-checking. Treble-checking. Making sure,' she said calmly, placing the rucksack on her lap.

Pearl avoided Tom's eyes and he was not sure whether to believe her or not.

'What's that round your neck?' she said, spotting the slender silver chain with the small egg dangling at the end of it. Tom fingered it nervously.

'Oh, well it's . . . sort of protection.'

'I didn't know you were superstitious,' she smiled.

'I'm not,' replied Tom huffily. 'I'll tell you later.'

'OK,' replied Pearl. 'Whatever you say.'

By now the small plane was thundering noisily out onto the lake that was still shrouded in mist.

'Just about to take off now!' shouted Sir Henry above the din.

'What about the mist?' Tom shouted back.

'Can't be helped,' Sir Henry replied. 'Time is rather of the essence this morning. I'm sure no one's out and about at this hour.'

Tom looked out of the window at the still grey surface of the lake spinning past. The pitch of the engine grew higher and higher as the plane accelerated, and the fuselage began to shake. A moment later they were airborne, and Trixie began easing the joystick back towards her.

'Good grief!' yelled Sir Henry suddenly.

In the same instant Trixie flung the plane violently to the right, and Tom was hurled against the window just in time to see a small punt flash past.

'What the hell were they doing there, fishing in the middle of the night!' he cursed. 'Didn't they hear us?'

The plane straightened and Tom turned back. For a second he glimpsed three terrified faces staring up at them, and then hundreds more punts loomed up out of the mist like crocodiles in a swamp . . .

'Forget it,' said Trixie coolly as they broke through the cloud and the picture was gone. 'Nobody died. Onwards and upwards.'

Tom's eyes were fixed on the swirling grey blanket below. It was only for a fraction of a second, but the image burned into his mind like a vision from a nightmare. He was sure they were thin, ratty faces, with large pale eyes and dark lips, and one of them had the lazy, bored look of a cat . . . Taking a deep breath, Tom glanced across at Pearl and found that she was staring at him.

'Take off, huh? Always makes me queasy too.'

Tom nodded breathlessly. Maybe he was imagining things.

'Just thought I saw something down there. Boats all across the lake.'

'Really? I didn't see anything at all. Are you sure?'

'No,' said Tom, sitting back. 'I'm not sure.'

He closed his eyes and rubbed them hard. It must have been

in his head. Ignoring his thundering heart he tried to concentrate on the jumble of grey mountains all around, their steep snowy peaks turning from blue to orange in the first rays of dawn. What kind of strange adventure had they embarked upon? And what had they left behind?

'Next valley,' instructed Sir Henry, studying the map on his knee, 'best approach it from the south side.' He checked his watch. 'The Shakra Parbat is slightly in the shadow as I recall, so that's bought us a few more seconds. Well, I'll be damned,' he said, pointing up out of the windscreen. High above them, silhouetted against the pale dawn sky were four small birds, heading away from the sun.

'Shearwaters I think,' said Trixie, craning forward, 'migrating from Siberia.'

Tom and Pearl watched the tiny specks high up in the vast open sky.

'Incredible how they just know, isn't it?'

'And so do we,' replied Sir Henry. 'Now.'

Trixie lifted the small aeroplane over the ridge and followed its contours down into another hanging valley, deep in grey shadow. There was nothing here but rocks and vast boulders, and at the far end Tom could just make out three thin fingers of rock silhouetted against the skyline.

'There it is,' said Sir Henry, pointing at the smallest of the three pinnacles. 'The Shakra Parbat.'

'Can I take a peek first?'

Sir Henry anxiously checked his watch once more. He didn't seem at all happy.

'You know what that might mean, don't you?'

Trixie nodded.

'Sorry. It's just that it's my first time.'

'Very well,' he blustered impatiently. 'Make it double quick.'

Trixie accelerated hard up the valley and swept up over the top of the three pinnacles. As they banked round, Tom could just make out a chink of daylight breaking through the smallest finger. Sir Henry pointed down at the small triangular gap.

'Rather like the eye of a needle, isn't it?'

'You can say that again.' Trixie exhaled loudly. Even she seemed apprehensive about this. 'What's the tolerance again?'

'Ten centimetres either side, give or take.'

Sunlight was already pouring through the hole, which looked so small a bird might struggle through it.

'Speed?'

'About one hundred and ninety.'

'With an anticlockwise roll?'

'There's no other way. The shape is so awkward, and you will be flying due east, directly into the sun.'

Trixie made a rapid mental calculation.

'Right,' she said determinedly. 'Let's do this thing.'

Sir Henry leaned forward and watched the shadows creeping down the sides of the two large pinnacles, turning them from grey to orange. The sun was rising fast.

'I estimate we have forty-five seconds at the very most. After that it's absolutely no good.'

Trixie did not reply, but opened the throttle and tore back down the valley, banking hard at the other end.

'I think I'm going to be sick,' whispered Pearl above the din, and Tom felt her grip his hand tightly.

'We'll be OK,' he said, hardly believing it himself. 'She's a stunt pilot, remember?'

'Might be an idea to fasten your lapstraps for this bit,' said Sir Henry, turning back to see their ashen faces. 'We have to shoot it at a bit of an angle.'

'Really?' gasped Pearl.

'It's a D shape, so we'll be like that.' He held up his hand vertically.

'Passing one fifty,' said Trixie, levelling the plane and aiming it straight at the rock face. Tom and Pearl scrabbled for their straps and clicked them home.

'I'm really not sure about this,' whispered Pearl.

Sir Henry ignored the rapidly approaching mountain face and peered forward. The flaring sunlight had almost filled the hole, chasing the shadows down the rim . . .

'You're going to have to be very quick or we'll miss it!' he shouted.

'One seventy,' said Trixie holding the joystick directly level. She seemed to be aiming directly at the wall of jagged grey. Suddenly Tom was gripped by panic . . . the triangular shaped hole was way above them to the left . . . couldn't she see it? She was off . . .

'Ten seconds,' said Sir Henry, watching the line of shadow descending, slowly, steadily . . . the beams of light had almost filled the triangle.

'One eighty,' said Trixie, holding her course.

'She's going to miss!' cried Pearl and covered her eyes with her hands.

The engine was screaming now. Tom could not tear his eyes

away from the wall of white and grey rock rushing towards them.

'Steady,' said Sir Henry coolly, glancing forward at the mountainside, then back down at his watch. His raised hand quivered in the air. 'Steady now . . . '

'One ninety.'

Shafts of blinding sunlight burst into the cabin.

'GO!' yelled Sir Henry.

Suddenly Trixie flung the joystick over to the left, violently rolling the plane onto a vertical axis. In that very same instant Tom had a sensation of something grey flashing past the windows as they shot up and sideways through the hole . . .

BANG!

White . . . nothing . . . they were upside down . . . then—

Tom felt himself slam back down into his seat as the aeroplane spun full circle.

'Bravo!' shouted Sir Henry.

'I did it!' shouted Trixie.

'Of course you did!'

Tom breathed again. He opened his eyes. Somehow his arms had locked themselves to the fuselage. Outside the window, strange contorted green islands flashed past, rising up out of the pale green lagoon. Beyond the reef an expanse of black ocean rushed out to meet the sinking sun. It was evening, somewhere in the tropics . . .

'Welcome to the Tithona Archipelago,' said Sir Henry excitedly, glancing out of the window at the brilliant colours all around. 'Still here, thank God. Everyone alive and happy?'

Tom and Pearl smiled weakly as Trixie dipped the seaplane through the strange shaped islands.

'That scared the bejeepers out of me,' gasped Pearl. 'Is it always like that?'

Sir Henry smiled. 'I must confess that Shakra Parbat is the narrowest of them all. Fun though, don't you think?'

'In a way,' replied Tom, who had barely got his breath back.

'Well it must be better than hanging onto a balloon on the rim of a twister,' laughed Sir Henry. 'Now I don't think even Trixie fancies doing that.'

'No sir I do not,' she smiled. 'That's dangerous. Now which is the island we're after?'

'Twelve degrees north, hundred and seventy-seven degrees east,' said Sir Henry, looking down at his map. 'It's an old volcano.'

'Over there?' said Tom, pointing at a thick green lump rising up out of the sea. The shape was very familiar from the model.

'That's the one,' said Sir Henry, following his gaze. 'That's Tithona all right.'

Trixie swung the plane hard over towards the setting sun and they began to skirt around the reef towards the large grey shape, silhouetted against the purple sky. As they drew closer, Tom could see that it was all just as August had made in his model, the steep sides of the mountain were a thick wall of green jungle and he could just make out the roofs of several longhouses poking through the canopy close to the rim of the crater. On the far side there was a jumble of rooftops, and a three-masted schooner out in the bay.

'Tithona town,' said Sir Henry, pointing in the direction of the buildings, 'so it's much better we stay over this side, out of the way. Don't want to draw too much attention to ourselves.'

'Is it dangerous?' asked Tom.

'Just better that we stay incognito, if you know what I mean.'

Staying tight to the steep jungle walls, Trixie brought the aeroplane in low and touched down in a small cove just below a rocky headland. Slowly the noisy propellers clattered to a halt, and Sir Henry flung open the door and jumped down into the shallow turquoise water.

'Perfect,' he said, 'absolutely perfect.'

Taking a rope out of a compartment in the ski he edged the aeroplane up onto the thin crescent of white sand. Tom jumped down gratefully into the shallow water, and looked around. Other than an old wooden crate and the remains of a fishing net, there were no signs that anyone had been here.

'Looks like we'll have this place all to ourselves tonight,' said Sir Henry approvingly. 'Now before that big old sun sets I need to make a quick and rather vital calculation.' Stepping back up into the cockpit he reached for his canvas bag.

'Need a hand?' asked Trixie, who had finished turning off her switches.

'If you don't mind. I find dates rather baffling and August is much better at doing this than me.'

Tom and Pearl watched as the pair of them hurried off down the beach and began measuring the angle of the sun against a compass, then checking it against a book of scribbled mathematical calculations.

'Do you think there's a problem?' asked Tom. Looking down at his hands he noticed they were still quivering.

'I don't know,' said Pearl, wading out into the water. 'Feels good to be back though.'

'Back?'

'This is the Pacific. This is where I live, remember? Sand, coconuts, crabs, mosquitoes, snakes, sandflies, the reef, the heat. This is like home.'

'And beetles?'

'Yep, them too. Even beetles. If I close my eyes and listen to the waves and the birds I can almost believe I am home again and none of this has ever happened.'

Tom watched Pearl standing in the shallows with her eyes closed, smiling. He wished he could do that. Wiping his brow, he turned to face the sunset, which had now transformed into a riot of purple dashes and splashes above a fluorescent orange sea. It really was incredibly hot, there was not even a breath of wind. Everything seemed still somehow, heavy. Even the sea seemed to be moving in slow motion.

'Paradise,' he said, grumpily.

'Hey man, chill,' smiled Pearl. 'You've got to learn to relax.'

'Well would you prefer the good news or the bad news first?'

Night had fallen like a stone, and Tom, Pearl, Trixie, and Sir Henry were sitting round a campfire on the edge of the sand.

'The good news,' said Pearl.

'The good news is that after we have finished this cup of coffee, I should like to get going,' said Sir Henry. 'We can walk by moonlight into town, and at dawn see if we can cadge a lift up to the crater. It's probably better at that time, not so hot, fewer people, that sort of thing.'

Tom nodded. He knew that Sir Henry was by nature impatient, and he didn't want to leave August on his own for too long.

'That's fine by me,' said Tom. 'So what's the bad news?'

'Right. The bad news.'

Sir Henry studied their expectant faces in the firelight. There was no easy way to say this, so he might as well just state the plain facts.

'I'm afraid the day after tomorrow there is going to be a volcanic eruption. It will take place out in the lagoon somewhere, underwater, and every single one of these islands will disappear beneath the waves. Tithona will cease to exist.'

Tom and Pearl gazed at him in astonishment. Tom half-expected Sir Henry to burst out laughing, but he didn't.

'Hard to believe isn't it?' he said. 'But today is the thirteenth of January 1965. I checked it and checked it and rechecked it. And Trixie has checked it too.'

'That I did,' she nodded. 'It's true. Unfortunately.'

'But how,' Tom began, 'I mean, I thought—'

'We lost valuable seconds shooting the Shakra Parbat,' said Sir Henry, wiping the sweat off his face with a handkerchief. 'Every second either side of an opening you lose a year, give or take. I knew it would be close but not quite this close.' For a moment they sat in stunned silence, staring at the flickering embers.

'Puts us in a bit of a pickle, doesn't it?'

'Do you happen to know when the volcano erupts?' asked Pearl timidly. All her good humour had evaporated.

'I have been trying to remember the various accounts. As I recall it happened in stages. On the day before, the tide went out unusually far, then a huge wave came in that swamped everything. This tsunami was caused by some underwater tremor out in the ocean. Then there was a lull, and the following morning the main event happened. The mountain on which the Tithona archipelago is formed collapsed, taking all the islands down with it. I'm sorry to be the bearer of bad tidings, but there it is.'

'And you really think, knowing all that, that we should still go?'

It was Pearl who asked the question, and she was hanging on his every word.

'On balance, yes,' he said, fixing her with his quick eye. 'There's still enough time. August and I devoted many years to looking for entrances to Scarazand and we never found one. You are here, in the right place—I won't say at the right time—but you have everything you need. If you really want to give it a try, then you should go. Definitely. I would. Why not?'

Sir Henry's breezy confidence was breathtaking, and it was infectious, too.

'Very well,' said Pearl, taking a deep breath. 'I'm in. What about you, Tom?'

Tom glanced up from the embers, and found that they were all staring at him intently. He nodded: he couldn't do anything else.

'Excellent,' said Sir Henry, swallowing his coffee and throwing the rest away. 'Then let's get cracking.'

CHAPTER 12

BEFORE THE VOLCANO

Five minutes later Pearl and Tom had kicked out the remains of the fire and stood waiting in the moonlight as Sir Henry secured the plane to a large rock in the shallows.

'Right,' he said, marching purposefully down the beach towards them. 'That won't withstand a tidal wave but it will do for the moment.'

Slipping on his hat, he led the way briskly through the palm trees until they came to a long wide track that had been cut through the jungle.

'East I think,' he muttered, and tore off up the hill. Despite his great age Sir Henry moved with extraordinary agility, and soon Tom and Pearl were panting to keep up. Night had fallen, but if anything the air seemed to have become even hotter, and Tom could feel the heat radiating up off the moonlit track. Wiping the sweat out of his eyes, he tried to take his mind off his raging thirst by watching little white bombs of dust that exploded off the ground with every step. Time really was of the essence now, they all knew it: the journey to Scarazand had turned into a race.

Pausing at the top of the hill, Sir Henry wiped his brow and looked out across the lagoon at the strange animal-shaped islands, shimmering in the hot moonlight.

'Looks beautiful, doesn't it?'

Trixie nodded, breathless at his side.

'Hard to believe it's not going to be here for much longer.'

Turning round, she squinted down at the tin roofs shining just beyond the headland. 'Don't you think we should warn someone?'

Sir Henry shook his head adamantly.

'Always a mistake to interfere,' he said. 'Nothing good ever comes of it. And in this particular case, I think the coming disaster might be doing us all a favour.'

'How do you mean?' panted Pearl.

'Just a few memories coming back,' replied Sir Henry mysteriously, and he left it at that.

'There's a boat out there,' said Tom, pointing at the three tall masts of the schooner he had seen earlier rising up beyond the headland.

'Tithona has always been a popular spot for repairs,' said Sir Henry, 'that's how most of the locals scratch out a living I think. Nothing much else to do if you're surrounded by hundreds of miles of ocean.' And with that he jammed his hat back on his head and marched away down the moonlit track.

An hour later they had reached the edge of the jungle, and the dense black trees gave way to fields and neat avenues of palms.

'Not far to go now,' whispered Sir Henry, stopping to rest against a tree trunk on the edge of the forest. 'Really is extraordinarily hot, isn't it?'

'Unnaturally hot,' agreed Trixie, wiping her neck. 'Too damned hot.'

Tom was so exhausted he could barely nod in agreement, and he noticed that Pearl was equally beat. It had been like marching through a furnace.

'Still, we're making good time.'

They sat in silence for a minute or two, listening to the hiss of the insects. Now they were sitting still, the heat was incredible. Tom could feel his eyelids starting to close, when an abrupt clattering in the trees behind jolted him back awake. Instantly the hissing stopped, and two small monkeys scampered out of the shadows across the moonlit track, protesting loudly.

'What was that?' said Pearl, looking back nervously into the dense black undergrowth. There was a loud screeching sound, and then two more monkeys ran out across the track.

'A snake, perhaps?' suggested Trixie.

'Unlikely,' muttered Sir Henry, listening to the rumpus. Then his expression changed, and rising silently to his feet he padded back down the track towards the sound.

'Aha,' he said with some surprise. 'It's you.'

Tom and Pearl looked back to see Sir Henry standing in the shadows, seemingly in deep discussion with a tree.

'Trixie,' called Sir Henry quietly, and beckoned her to join him.

'Is that what I think it is?' said Pearl, squinting back into the shadows. The large silhouette shifted slightly.

'It is,' nodded Tom, wiping the sweat out of his eyes. 'That's that eagle they were talking about. Must have followed us here.'

'Why would it do that?'

'I don't know,' muttered Tom, but even as he said it troubled thoughts began to tumble through his mind.

'Very well.' Sir Henry nodded abruptly, then turned and hurried back towards them.

'I am afraid there's been a change of plan,' he announced, 'we must leave you.'

'Where are you going?' asked Pearl, taken aback. 'Is something wrong?'

Sir Henry's craggy features looked haunted in the moonlight: even he could not conceal his concern.

'Poor old August is in a spot of bother.'

Suddenly Tom felt a lump rise up in his throat. He pictured the gaunt, frail figure of August standing alone in the mist and those swarms of black punts closing in all around him . . . it was a scene from a nightmare for which he was in some way responsible. He should have said something, trusted his instincts . . . With a thumping heart he raced back down the track to where the great eagle perched in deep shadow.

'What's happened?' he demanded.

The great bird peered down at him angrily.

'Gaff's blown, mate, that's what's happened.'

'Is August,' Tom began, 'I mean, he's . . . they haven't killed him, have they?'

'No, mate, they haven't killed him. Yet.'

'What about his library, the birds—'

'They got away, they always do. And them swamp mutts is quite distracting.'

'So . . . do you know who they were?'

'Same folks as followed you through,' rasped the bird. 'Lotus Askary, plus a fair few of her flunkies. Now isn't that just a coincidence?'

Tom stared at the white dust beneath his feet and kicked it angrily.

'But how could I know? We didn't—'

'I know you didn't know, mate. But every action has a consequence, doesn't it? Intentional or otherwise.'

Tom stared hard at the ground. He felt terrible.

'If I were you, kiddo, I'd watch your travelling companion very closely.'

Tom looked up at the eagle.

'What?'

'I ain't sayin' nothin' more. Stickin' me nose in only causes more grief. Just watch her, mate.'

With a great hop the eagle jumped down onto the track and let out a strange ululating call. There was a twitter in the branches above and a tiny black speck flew down into the moonlight.

'He'll keep an eye out in case things turn nasty,' growled the bird, indicating the swallow dipping up and down the track. 'Which is highly likely. But that's the way the cookie's crumbled, ain't it?'

With a last high call, the eagle began to bound away through the dust flapping its wings hard until it bounced awkwardly into the air.

'I'll be waiting by the plane!' it shouted, and soared up over the trees.

Tom watched it go, his mind racing. Why should he be suspicious of Pearl?

'So you're clear what to do?' said Sir Henry, clapping him on the back. Tom turned to see Sir Henry back to his old confident self.

'I think so. Just get up to that crater as quick as we can.'

'That's right,' he smiled. 'Should be quite straightforward. There's a mine up near the rim, and people go up and down all the time. Now to make life easier for yourselves when you get there, ask in the longhouse for Geronimo.'

'Geronimo?'

'That's it. He chose the name himself and curiously it rather suits him. He's about your age and cocky with it—but he's the one that found the beetle ball. Ask Geronimo nicely and I'm sure he'll take you down into the crater.'

'But isn't the crater like some kind of holy place?' asked Pearl, who had hurried back up the path to join them.

Sir Henry paused a moment.

'Ah. Yes. Quite. I had forgotten that. Right, well you will need some bribes.'

'Take this,' said Trixie, pulling a slim silver cigarette case out of her pocket. 'It's American tobacco but I'm sure they won't mind,' she smiled.

'You're sure?' said Pearl, awkwardly taking the silver case.

'Of course, young lady. It's the least I can do. I have to say I feel a little guilty leaving you in such a rush.'

'Oh lord,' said Sir Henry suddenly, 'and I clean forgot about that ludicrous wizard.'

'Wizard?' repeated Tom, incredulously. 'There's a wizard?'

'Wizard, witchdoctor—"the Mackamack", I think they call him. He's an absolute charlatan who claims he controls access to the crater. Avoid him if you possibly can. But if you can't,' Sir Henry rummaged about in his canvas bag, 'I remember he has a penchant for this stuff.'

Tom looked down at the large bar Sir Henry had thrust into his hand.

'Chocolate?'

'That's it. Which is why all his teeth have fallen out,' he grinned. 'Anyway, we must fly. Good luck.'

'Thanks.'

Trixie stood before them and smiled.

'Hey, don't look so glum,' she said, clasping them both on the shoulder. 'You're a great team and don't you forget it. There's plenty of time for you to do what you've got to do. Plenty of plenty.' And with a wave she ran off after Sir Henry who was already marching swiftly back through the trees. Tom looked after them and felt distinctly uneasy. Were they a great team, really? *Watch her, mate* . . . watch her . . . what did the eagle mean?

'Ready?'

Pearl was looking at him in the moonlight with a determined expression on her face.

'Sure,' said Tom, warily. 'You?'

Pearl nodded and slung the rucksack over her shoulder.

'Let's go find this Geronimo then.'

They fell into single file and began the long hot trudge through the fields. The path zigzagged this way and that, and occasionally Tom glanced up into the jungle walls—but there was nothing really to see, just an impenetrable curtain of blue and black shadows. After half an hour or so, they sat down for a rest under a tree.

'Hot work, huh?' said Pearl, wiping her face. 'Wow, my feet are sore. I reckon they are a different shape to yours,' she said, carefully unlacing Tom's old green trainers and rubbing her toes. Tom felt too tired to say anything, he just lay on his back and closed his eyes. He felt as if he couldn't take another step. Slowly the minutes ticked by.

'Fancy an early breakfast?'

Pearl was squatting over a rock carefully hacking the top off a green coconut with a penknife.

'Where did you find that?' said Tom, watching as Pearl expertly cut away the layers of hard fibrous shell with her knife.

'Over there,' she replied, pointing to the stand of coconut palms in the field with her knife. 'See I may be from the tropics but I'm not completely useless,' she smiled. 'Want to try some coconut water?'

'Yes please,' said Tom, gratefully taking the green ball and pressing it to his lips. For some reason he expected it to taste like coconut milk, but it didn't. The liquid inside was cool and fragrant and delicious.

'Thanks very much,' he said wiping his mouth and handing it back.

'You like it? Rudy and I often have these for breakfast.' Pearl took a long deep drink till the juice dribbled down her chin. Then using the end of the knife she scraped around inside the bowl, shaving slithers of jellylike white meat.

'This is good too,' she said, handing Tom a pile. 'But not everyone bothers to eat it.'

Tom put a slice of the slippery white meat into his mouth. Again, it was not what he expected, but he gobbled it up greedily. Pearl watched Tom squatting on the red earth, eating messily. She laughed.

'My my, I do believe you is turning bush, Tom.'

'I hope so,' he grinned back, and wiped his greasy fingers on his trousers.

Afterwards they sat watching the empty track for a while. Somehow the food had changed everything, and all the troubles and doubts that lay ahead of them were briefly forgotten.

'It seems sort of a shame to go on, doesn't it?' said Pearl, listening to the hissing of the insects all around. 'Wouldn't it be great if my dad and Rudy just walked around the corner right now, and your parents too, and we could all go home.'

Tom stared at the white dust and poked it with a stick.

'But we can't.'

'I know. But I can't say I'm looking forward to going up there,' she said, looking up at the mountain. Tom followed her gaze and in the bright moonlight he could just make out the grey jagged edges of the crater, poking up through the wall of trees. It certainly looked ominous.

'Let's see what those suits August made look like,' he said sitting up onto his haunches.

'What, now?' said Pearl anxiously. 'Do you think we really have time?'

Tom shrugged: the moon was still high in the sky. It seemed like the middle of the night.

'I don't know. But no one's going to give us a lift up there till dawn—are they?'

Pearl didn't seem quite convinced.

'I think we should see if they fit at least. Better to know now rather than later.'

'If you say so.'

Grabbing hold of the small canvas rucksack, Pearl pulled open the drawstring and began to spread out the contents on the track.

'Pheromone spray, glasses to see the world as beetles see it, which may or may not work, box with luminous feather and thread, who knows how useful that will be, and last but not least, these.'

Pearl pulled out two thin packages wrapped in brown grease-proof paper and handed one to Tom. Inside was what looked like a brand new suit of clothes, all neatly folded, made from thin grey silk.

'That is a very strange smell,' said Pearl ripping open the other package and sniffing the curious material that smelt vaguely of butter, almonds, and rotten oranges.

'He must have boiled up a vat of pheromone and dipped these in it.'

'I guess so,' said Tom, who stood up and pulled the poncho over his head. There was a hood with a small visor attached to the back.

'How do I look?' he said, flicking the visor down over his face. The thin floating material was so fine he could see right through it.

'A bit like some weird fireman?' smiled Pearl, who was now wearing her poncho too. 'What about our hands and feet?'

'Maybe that's what the spray is for,' said Tom picking up the small leather bottle. 'But this one's so big, I don't think anyone's going to notice them,' he said pulling his fingers inside the deep sleeves.

'It all seems kind of elaborate doesn't it?' said Pearl, turning round in the moonlight. 'Trying to make ourselves invisible to beetle people, when we don't really know if it's going to work. Supposing it doesn't?'

'I know,' said Tom, pulling down his hood. Pearl was right. Even though he believed that August was capable of inventing anything, it would make sense to try these out. But how? They couldn't walk into Tithona town like this, could they? In the distance he could just see tin rooftops, shining in the moonlight beyond the trees, and somewhere very faintly beneath the noisy stridulation of the insects there was a clear high note.

'Can you hear that?' he said, looking down the road. He could hear it more clearly now. It was a bell ringing in the distance. A church bell.

'Maybe it's Sunday,' said Pearl. 'Maybe there's midnight mass or something.'

And then Tom heard another sound. It sounded like singing. Turning back towards the jungle, he saw something moving up the avenue of palms towards them.

'Hey look.'

It was a bicycle, pedalled by a thin man in a gleaming white shirt wearing a black hat perched on the back of his head. Behind him, riding side-saddle above the back wheel, sat a lady in a white dress with white gloves to match. They looked immaculate, as if they were on their way to church.

'Quick, we'd better hide all this stuff,' said Pearl, quickly gathering all the bits and pieces off the ground and shoving them into the bag. 'Tom give me the poncho.' Tom watched as the bicycle came closer. Suddenly an idea formed in his mind . . .

'Pearl, wait. Keep your poncho on. Come and stand next to me.'

'What?' said Pearl, who had already ruffled it up around her neck. 'Why?'

'Just do it. Quick.'

Pearl obediently walked out of the shadow of the tree and joined Tom standing motionless on the edge of the track. The bicycle was rapidly approaching and she could hear the lady on the back singing softly. And then she understood.

'You don't think?'

'Maybe,' whispered Tom, standing stock still. 'It's one way to find out, isn't it?'

Pearl and Tom stood silently watching the bicycle come closer. The man was concentrating on avoiding the ruts in the track, and it was not until he was almost level with Tom and Pearl that he saw them. At first he looked confused.

'Hi,' said Tom, and waved his hand out from beneath the poncho.

Suddenly his expression changed, and a look of absolute terror crossed his face.

'*Orra!*' he said, and the cigarette fell out of his mouth. '*No cuerpos! No piernas!*'

The woman stopped singing and looked up.

'Aaahh!'

The scream sliced through the hot air and silenced the insects.

Somehow there were the heads and hands of two children floating in the air. One of them had blond hair and he was waving at her.

'*Niños del Diabolo . . . Madre de Dios! Madre de Dios!*'

She crossed herself and began thumping her husband and shouting at him to pedal faster. The man glanced behind him in terror then sprinted away, and in moments they had disappeared around the corner.

'What do you think they said?' asked Tom.

'Devil children,' said Pearl slowly. 'No bodies, no legs.'

Tom took off his poncho and frowned.

'Whoops. You know what that means, don't you?'

Pearl nodded, and looked nervously down the track, now empty in the moonlight.

'Maybe everyone on Tithona is like that,' she said.

'Maybe,' said Tom grimly, bundling the poncho back into the rucksack. Both Sir Henry and August had implied that there was something very wrong with Tithona, and even the eagle didn't sound too enthusiastic. 'But at least we know now, so I suppose that's something. Come on, let's go.'

Slinging the rucksack over his shoulder, they set off down the track once more. The sound of the bell gradually grew louder, and soon the fields gave way to ramshackle corrugated iron huts and painted wooden houses.

'Nervous?' said Tom, slowing a little as they approached.

'Maybe a bit,' admitted Pearl, wiping the sweat out of her eyes. 'OK, maybe more than a bit.'

Tom nodded; he wanted to be reassuring but he couldn't help feeling more than a little trepidation himself.

'All we have to do is get up the crater. Maybe there is a bus up to the village or something. We don't have to talk to anyone much if we don't want to.'

'Sure,' nodded Pearl, grimly.

Soon they were walking into Tithona town, between scruffy tin shacks and shuttered wooden houses decorated with a few rusting metal signs, written in either Spanish or Japanese. At a crossroads they reached what looked like the main street, and found themselves at the bottom of a flight of wide steps leading up to the whitewashed church. Cautiously they walked up the steps and peered in through the open double doors.

'But it's empty,' said Pearl, staring at the bare candlelit interior. 'Where is everyone?'

'All downside now. Lagoon.'

The reedy voice came from the shadows behind them, and turning round Tom saw a spindly Japanese man in a vest labouring over a sewing machine. A dim hurricane lamp hung above his head. He glanced up from his stitching and gave them a friendly nod. Tom and Pearl looked at each other.

'Might as well,' shrugged Tom. They crossed the road and walked down to where he sat on the edge of the moonlight.

'That looks like hard work,' said Pearl politely, watching the thin man carefully pushing the hem through the machine.

'Nobayashi working all night on Sabbath. Nobayashi very bad man,' he grinned toothlessly. 'Nobayashi no care.'

'What's going on?' asked Tom.

'You tourist?' he said, turning over the jacket he was working on. 'Or you zoo people?'

'Zoo people?'

'Zoo people. Ya.'

Mr Nobayashi could see that Tom and Pearl had no idea what he was talking about. He hissed through his teeth then muttered something in his own language.

'Look you!' he said, pointing behind them.

Pearl and Tom turned and were astonished to see two large elephants disappearing into a yard at the far end of the street.

'So there's a zoo here?' said Tom, struggling to understand.

'No no no. Not Tithona zoo. Tokyo zoo. Lion, giraffe, hyena, monkey, elephant, rhinoceros. All coming upside now. Big problem.'

Nobayashi glanced up at them harshly.

'You no see this? Crazy tourist!'

Tom and Pearl were about to ask another question, but the Japanese man waved them away savagely.

'You go see! Go! Go!'

Tom and Pearl got the message and hurried away down a narrow alley towards the lagoon.

'What's the matter with him?' whispered Tom.

'I don't know,' said Pearl. She was both confused and worried now. 'You don't think it's beginning already, do you?'

Reaching the end of the alley Tom and Pearl were met with a most curious sight. There was a small harbour, surrounded by roughly built warehouses and at one end a rickety wooden pier ran out into the lagoon. But there was no water. Instead of the sea, the land sloped down into a glittering expanse of white sand and lumps of black coral that stretched right across to the islands on the far side. Small groups of people stood on what had once been the waterline, looking in disbelief at the strange underwater landscape that had suddenly been revealed. There were old anchors, cannons, rocks, and masses of fish of all shapes and sizes, flapping helplessly in the moonlight. Out in the middle a priest carrying a crucifix led a procession of nuns along the seabed. They were chanting softly.

'It's like someone's just pulled the plug out,' breathed Pearl, watching a conger eel writhing painfully across a forest of coral.

'And that must have been carrying the zoo,' said Tom, pointing to the dark shape of the three-masted schooner, now lying awkwardly on its side at the far end of the harbour. Two long gangways had been hurriedly extended down from its decks, and Tom could hear the shouts of men as they manhandled large wooden crates down towards a waiting truck that had driven out onto the seabed.

'But it's . . . it's all so quick,' she whispered, scarcely able to believe what she was seeing. 'It was only a couple of hours ago this was covered in water.' Pearl looked up anxiously at the full moon, still shining brightly amongst the stars. 'Maybe Sir Henry got his timing wrong.'

Tom turned towards what he thought was east, and stared beyond the reef at the dark line of ocean. Was that a thin sliver of grey light on the horizon? He couldn't tell.

'I think we should get going right now,' he murmured.

'But what about all these people?' said Pearl, watching a group of young boys scrabble down through the coral and start to collect the dying fish into baskets. 'It just seems so cruel to know and not do anything.'

Tom shook his head savagely.

'I know, but you can't think like that. You mustn't,' he insisted. 'Let's get out of this before it's too late.'

Pearl took one last look at the people now thronging down into the lagoon, then turned and chased up the alley after Tom. Reaching the main street, she followed him over to where Nobayashi was sitting, still stitching his jacket.

'Hi,' Tom began with a smile. 'Sorry it's us again. I just have one more question.'

Mr Nobayashi ignored him, and carried on rocking his feet on the treadle, working his way down the seam.

'Could you tell us the best way up to the crater? Is there any-one going up today?'

Nobayashi shook his head.

'No? Maybe there's a bus?'

Nobayashi turned the jacket over. He didn't even bother look-ing up.

'Today Sunday. No bus.'

'Taxi?' asked Pearl.

'No taxi Tithona.'

'How about a truck going up to the mine?'

'Mine finish now.'

'So is there anything?' said Pearl, her voice rising. 'We're in a bit of a hurry you see.'

Nobayashi looked up at them and sneered.

'Why I help you? I seen many you people before. You like Tithona people. No good people!' he shouted, twisting a finger against his temple.

'No . . . no, no, really—we're not like that, not at all,' insisted

Tom, sensing what he meant. 'We're just tourists and we have to go to the crater right now.'

Nobayashi grunted.

'Tithona have one truck left. It belong to mission sisters. Down there, with zoo people,' he waved towards the compound at the far end of the street. 'You ask them. Maybe help you.'

'Thank you, sir. Thank you very much.'

And before Nobayashi had even looked up Tom and Pearl had gone. Running down the road they passed families making their way up twisting tracks into the jungle above. It was obvious from their anxious chatter that they suspected something was going to happen, and they were not the only ones, as when Tom and Pearl neared the compound they heard a weird confusion of growls and squawks, howls and shrieks. Inside the dusty yard all manner of animals paced nervously about inside hastily built stockades and stacks of wooden boxes thumped and growled. Pearl approached the group of Japanese men loitering by the gate.

'Truck coming soon?'

The man chucked his cigarette away. He looked very nervous.

'Five minutes, miss. Maybe more.'

Pearl glanced at Tom anxiously.

'What do you think?'

'Is it going back to the ship?' Tom asked the man.

'No. This time last time. Hyenas, vultures, then finish.'

Tom and Pearl looked at each other.

'It's only five minutes,' she said.

Tom turned back to the sensible people climbing up into the forest above the town, then looked towards the lagoon. The seabed was now swarming with scavengers, and a large group had gathered around the priest and the nuns. They seemed to be conducting a service. Tom swallowed hard: he knew it made sense to wait for the truck, but he could not ignore his pounding heart . . .

'We can't chance it. Let's run. Now. Which way is the road to the crater?'

The man at the gate shrugged his shoulders, but an islander squatting in the dust beside him raised a bony finger back towards the church.

'Crater road,' he said with a flick of his wrist. 'Way up—'

And before he had even finished speaking there was a low rumbling boom . . .

CHAPTER 13

SKIN OF THEIR TEETH

In the face of an impending disaster, it is human nature not to run, but to stop and stare. And so it was that despite everything Tom and Pearl could not help but turn back towards the sound. There, from the far side of the lagoon, a smooth black wall of water was hurtling across the empty seabed towards them, smothering rocks and islands in its path. All around people were starting to scream, but Tom could not take his eyes off the leading edge as it bore down on the priest and his congregation, and all the others who had unwisely ventured out onto the seabed. They turned and stood motionless before the giant black wave like miniature dolls. There was nothing any of them could do.

'Come on Tom! Tom!'

Pearl tugged roughly at his arm, bringing him to his senses. Tearing his eyes away he sprinted after her towards the church. The clamouring of the animals in the compound reached a crescendo behind them and the sound of snapping wood filled the air. Glancing down a side alley Tom saw the wooden shacks beside the harbour crushed like matchsticks and whole buildings began to float away on its crest.

'We're not going to make it!' gasped Pearl as the foaming wall of water crashed across the far end of the street.

'Go up!' shouted Tom, spotting a wooden veranda on the house just ahead. 'The steps!'

Pearl saw them and tore up to the wooden balcony with Tom right behind her. The roar of the wave was deafening now, and suddenly Tom was thrown to the floor as the whole building shook. Dazed, he pulled himself up and glanced back to see a huge zigzag fissure open up in the ground, cutting the street in half. Several houses tumbled into the chasm.

'Oh my god!' screamed Pearl, pointing down the street. 'The animals! They're coming!'

It was a sight so extraordinary that Tom's heart skipped a beat. Charging out of the compound were elephants, giraffes, lions, kangaroos, a white tiger, and dozens of other dark shapes. They were stampeding towards them. Behind them swirled a mass of foaming, churning water, smashing everything in its path. Leading the charge was a rhinoceros, its head down, its eyes wild with fear. On and on they came, this mad menagerie, squawking, roaring, whinnying in a wild, desperate race towards the cliff and certain death . . .

Suddenly Tom recognized this scene: the Scatterhorn Museum, the Zumsteen Collection . . . the deluge, there it was! A living tableau rushing towards him . . .

And then out of a doorway ahead of him Tom saw a man wander out into the moonlit street. His hands were thrust deep into his pockets, and he seemed entirely oblivious to the chaos all around. He stared, fascinated, as the animals stampeded towards the cliff in front of him . . .

'Look out!' shouted Tom.

The man glanced back at Tom standing on the balcony. He was European, with thick black hair and a curious, excited expression. It almost looked as if he was about to burst out laughing, and in that instant Tom knew who he was . . . but the very same moment the rhinoceros careered off the cliff's edge, taking the giraffes, the lions, the bears and lemurs, and every other animal with it, and the wall of water crashed down behind them . . .

'Next house!' screamed Pearl, pulling Tom away violently. Without thinking he followed her, jumping on to the adjacent balcony just as the wood splintered behind him and the structure disintegrated. Pearl darted through the double doors and raced across the upstairs sitting room as the water smashed the glass behind them. She leapt onto the narrow corrugated rooftop of the building behind. Tom just about managed to follow before the whole house began to float away down the street. Breathless, he pulled himself to his feet and glanced back towards the lagoon. The two sides of the vast wave had curled around Tithona town and were now bouncing together as they met in alleyways and corners, demolishing the spindly wooden buildings in their path.

'Come on!' screamed Pearl, who had already bounded across a narrow alley to the next rooftop. Somehow she was much better at this than he was, and Tom did his best to keep up, scrambling over rooftops, jumping over alleys swirling with black water, on and on up the hill until somehow they had got ahead of it.

'Hey look!' he shouted breathlessly, spotting the tailgate of a covered canvas truck sweeping round a corner in front of them.

Pausing for a second, he saw the route it would have to take and realized they could cut it off.

'Follow me!' he shouted, and racing on across a low tin roof he skidded to a halt just as the truck slammed round the corner.

'What are we going to do?' gasped Pearl breathlessly as the truck barrelled up the narrow alley towards them, spraying water everywhere.

'Jump. Onto the roof,' said Tom, crouching ready to spring. Before there was even time to explain, the truck thundered beneath and Tom leapt, slamming hard into the tattered green canvas . . .

Thump!

He felt Pearl landed beside him.

Thump! Then—

Thump! Thump! Thump! Thump! Thump!

What?

Tom raised his head and saw a troupe of squirrel monkeys clinging on all around.

'They've been following us!' shouted Pearl as the monkeys stared at them, terrified. 'Didn't you notice?'

Tom shook his head, he had been so busy trying to keep up and stay alive he hadn't noticed a thing.

'Oh!' shouted Pearl as the truck skidded violently round a corner, slamming into a shed and knocking it over. Before Tom knew where he was his fingers slipped across the canvas and he only just managed to save himself from falling off the back. With his legs dangling over the edge he kicked hard against the flapping side, trying desperately to push himself up again.

'Ow!'

Something pecked at his leg viciously and there was a rip beneath him. Tom managed to swing himself sideways just as three large vultures burst through the canvas hole, squawking loudly. He barely had time to clamber back up onto the roof before there was a rip beside his arm and the pink head of another vulture burst out. The angry bird tore at the canvas with its beak and the next moment it struggled through and fell off the back of the truck.

'Phew.' Tom drew a deep breath and scrabbled forward to where Pearl lay. 'I never expected—' and then he stopped as Pearl's eyes widened and her face froze.

'Oh my goodness . . . Oh my goodness,' she murmured.

Tom turned back to see a black nose followed by a slathering set of teeth emerge through the hole, and the next moment a hyena's head appeared, covered in gashes and blood.

'Oh my good . . . '

The grisly head stared at Pearl and Tom and the troupe of monkeys clinging there, and it was hard to tell who was more terrified. Then suddenly the hyena let out a piercing howl and burst up through the canvas, and was on the point of leaping off the roof when it saw the foaming water racing behind them.

'Quick!' shouted Tom, and daring to turn his back on the creature he shimmied forward and kicking a hole in the canvas roof of the cab he tumbled through. The wild-eyed driver stared at him in disbelief, whereupon a pile of spider monkeys suddenly landed on Tom's lap.

'*Qué pasa?*' he shouted, and the monkeys began leaping around the cab screaming. The driver barely had time to pull them off the steering wheel before the canvas ripped again and Pearl tumbled through.

'*Que diablos está pasando par allá?*'

'Hi. Erm—'

But before Tom could say anything more there was a grunt and a large black nose appeared through the hole just above their heads. The hyena's eyes stared at them menacingly.

'AAHHH!'

Pearl screamed, Tom screamed, the driver screamed and all the monkeys screamed together. The driver slammed his foot on the brake, sending them all thudding against the windscreen, and the next moment the hyena bounced forward off the bonnet and tumbled down into the road. Struggling to its feet it stared at them angrily, then loped off into the shadows. For a moment the driver sat still, too stunned to speak. The two monkeys clinging to his steering wheel started to scream.

'*Fuera!*' he shouted, and threw them out of the window. Revving hard, he accelerated once more, and just as the truck began to gather speed he saw a boy running up the road ahead. The boy turned and waved, and as the truck approached he began to sprint.

'Lemon!' shouted the boy. 'Lemon Gonzales!'

The driver glanced at him and slowed.

'*Para adóne va?*'

Lemon indicated straight up the mountain.

'*Puedo venir?*'

'*Seguro, seguro, entra,*' he said, '*y saca a esos malditos monos de aquí!*'

The boy grinned and leapt up onto the footplate, swinging

himself through the door and squeezing in next to Pearl. The boy was short and wiry, but Tom guessed he was probably far older than he looked, and wore nothing more than a pair of dirty red shorts and a tatty blue T-shirt. Around his neck he had a green stone necklace and his oiled hair was styled into an elaborate quiff.

'Please,' he said in English, and picked a monkey clinging to Pearl like a baby and chucked it out of the window. 'He no like monkey in his truck.'

'Oh, OK,' she said, and moments later every last monkey had gone, and they were hammering up the rough track towards the crater.

Only now, as the roar of the water at last began to recede did Tom realize just what had happened and quite how lucky they had been. Lemon said something in another language to the boy with the quiff, who nodded back.

'He wants to know if you are with the zoo?' he said in a thick accent.

'We were escaping from the water,' said Tom. 'We are tourists.'

'Tourists?' repeated the boy, clearly finding that hard to believe. He translated for Lemon in his own language.

'*Touristica?*'

The driver frowned, then came an explosion of what Tom thought must be abuse that involved a lot of pointing at the large rip in the roof. The boy smiled.

'He is not having a very good day. The wave has destroyed his home and you have wrecked his truck.'

'Sorry,' said Tom guiltily.

'*Lo siento,*' said Pearl.

Lemon rolled his shoulders. So much had happened today that it was difficult to care. Then he muttered something else.

'He is going up to the forest. High ground. In case wave come again. Where do you want to go?'

'Up to the crater,' said Tom. 'Is that where he is going?'

'Yes. This is his way. And my village there too.'

'Oh really?' said Pearl, suddenly interested. 'So could you show us the way up to the crater?'

The boy looked at them and smiled.

'Of course,' he shrugged. 'I am guide also. I speak your language yes? No problem.' He said something fast to Lemon, who nodded in agreement. 'I make good price for you,' continued the boy. 'Your name?'

'Pearl.'

'Tom,' he said, shaking the boy's hand. 'Tom Scatterhorn.'

'Ah. Scatterhorn. Good name,' said the boy. 'I know this name before. Your father, he come here?'

'My . . . my grandfather yes,' replied Tom awkwardly.

'I show him crater, maybe . . . four years ago.' The boy thrust his hand out. 'Geronimo. And this is Lemon, my cousin,' he indicated to the driver.

Pearl and Tom could not stop smiling. This was a truly amazing piece of luck.

'Pleased to meet you, Geronimo,' said Pearl, shaking his hand.

Geronimo grinned, and said something fast to the driver, who nodded back.

'You have smoke?'

'Actually we do,' said Tom reaching into his pocket and finding the slim cigarette case still there. He offered them to

Geronimo who took out two, lit them both, and then passed one across to Lemon who clamped it between his teeth. They both inhaled deeply and filled the cab with blue smoke.

'American,' said Geronimo wisely. 'The best.'

Pearl coughed loudly. 'It's not very good for you to smoke, you know.'

'No this is good. Tithona cigarette no good. This good for chest. I read it on sign!' he laughed.

By now the grey light of dawn had stolen up over the horizon, and through the trees Pearl and Tom could just make out what remained of Tithona town below. Only the white church stood above the water, and the lagoon was filled with debris. Even the ship that had carried the zoo was now lying on its side on the edge of the jungle, as if it had been picked up and flung there by a giant hand.

'Tithona town no more,' said Geronimo, staring down at the mess below. 'All gone.' Tom noticed that he seemed more curious than upset. Lemon said something and Geronimo nodded.

'The gods do this,' he said, translating. 'Too many sick people in Tithona now. This place no good.'

Tom wondered if he meant what he thought he meant, but Geronimo did not elaborate. By now the road had become very steep and they were climbing hard through the jungle. Lemon was all elbows and feet, spinning the truck through the red mud to avoid the potholes and the edges of road that had been washed away. At each corner they whined to a halt to pick up small groups of people sitting at the roadside. All of them had the same wide flat faces as Geronimo and Lemon, and Tom assumed they must be refugees from the town below.

'Everyone coming up to village now,' explained Geronimo as a family hauled themselves into the back. 'Village safe place.'

Lemon shouted something to Geronimo.

'OK,' he said as they accelerated noisily towards the next sharp corner. 'I block-pusher-in.'

'Oh?'

'Very important job,' said Geronimo proudly. 'You'll see.'

Lemon slammed the truck into a low gear and revved hard, trying to get whatever momentum he could, before swinging the wheel round and urging the howling engine up the slide of red mud. The wheels churned and hissed but didn't bite and slowly the truck began to slide backwards towards the precipice.

'*Vamos*, Geronimo,' wheezed Lemon, pumping the accelerator in vain. The scrawny boy leapt out of the cab, seemingly into sheer space, and scrabbled back down to the rear axle, where a large triangular block of wood swung on a rope. In one swift move he unhooked the block and ignoring the flying mud wedged it beneath the spinning tyre. As soon as the wheel found a grip in the mud he removed his block, then leapt up onto the tailgate until the next bend, where he did it again. And so it went on, all the way up the switchbacks, with Geronimo occasionally hauling himself up into the cab for a rest.

'Geronimo good worker—yes?' he gasped, leaning across to take a puff from Lemon's cigarette, which hung limply from his bottom lip. 'Good job me.'

'Do you want a hand?' asked Tom, feeling a little guilty sitting there while Geronimo did all the work. Geronimo shook his head, inhaled hard, and then returned the smouldering cigarette to its rightful place clamped between Lemon's lips.

'No no. You my guest now,' he smiled, and bounded back out into space. After an hour of laborious climbing the track finally levelled out, and they began to work their way through a twisting forest of giant tree ferns and banyan trees.

'We here,' said Lemon at last, and they rattled to a halt in a small clearing.

'Thank you very much, Lemon,' said Pearl. The driver nodded abruptly, and Tom thrust a few more cigarettes into his waiting hand.

'Thanks.'

Gratefully Tom and Pearl climbed out of the cab, stiff and sore from the long bumpy journey up the mountain. For a moment they stood in the cool dark forest clearing, stretching their legs painfully.

'That was some road,' said Pearl, looking over to some thatched huts half hidden in the trees. Already a few small children had gathered on the steps to stare at them.

'It's almost as if nothing had happened, isn't it?' said Tom, watching a woman squatting on the ground pummelling flour, while a few piglets ran around. Geronimo hurried up to talk to some men in tatty shorts and T-shirts who had come out of the forest to meet them, and it was clear from their expressions that he was telling them exactly what had happened. They didn't seem particularly upset. They seemed more interested in Pearl and Tom standing beside the truck.

'I suppose we now have to see this Mackamack guy,' said Pearl, glancing up at the shafts of sunlight shooting down through the trees. 'How long is that going to take, I wonder?'

'I know,' nodded Tom, anxiously. It must be at least mid morning already, and if Sir Henry had been right then how long did they have? The rest of today and tonight, at the most. 'Maybe we can talk nicely to Geronimo and avoid him.'

'My cousins,' smiled Geronimo, walking back towards them.

'Oh,' said Pearl, and smiled up at the men. They looked at her curiously. Taking a comb out of his back pocket Geronimo began tidying up his hair in the wing mirror.

'So will you be able to take us up to the crater?' said Tom.

'You want to go now?'

'If possible. It's just . . . it's quite urgent.'

Geronimo shrugged and thrust his comb in his back pocket.

'OK. What do you want to see? The maze. The carvings, the animals?'

Tom and Pearl looked at each other.

'Actually, Geronimo, it is something else. We need to find a cave.'

Geronimo seemed a little surprised.

'Cave? What cave? There are many caves in crater.'

'It's a cave you know about, Geronimo. A few years ago you found a beetle down there. Shaped like an egg.'

Geronimo raised his eyebrows.

'Sir Henry tell you this?'

Tom nodded.

'He said you decorated it with patterns, then sold it to a man named Nicholas Zumsteen.'

Geronimo said nothing, but it was quite clear that the mention of Zumsteen had made him very uncomfortable.

'Why do you want to go to that cave?' he said suspiciously.

'We just . . . we have to, that's all. As soon as we can.'

Geronimo muttered something to himself in his own language and stared out into the forest. Tom sensed that somehow this unusual request had changed things.

'We're not . . . please, if you think that we are like the people in the town, we're definitely not,' said Pearl falteringly. 'We are different. Sir Henry Scatterhorn sent us here.'

Geronimo did not look entirely convinced.

'What you pay?' he said, without any friendliness. 'Cave is way, way down.'

Tom hurriedly brought out the silver cigarette case Trixie had given them.

'We don't have any money,' he said. 'Just this.'

Geronimo studied the silver case carefully, clicked it open, then snapped it shut and thrust it into his back pocket. He had obviously made his decision.

'Very well. I take you. But we must see the Mackamack on way up.'

'The Mackamack?' said Pearl, pretending she had never heard of him.

'Big man. Only he decide if you can go up there. You pay him too. Yes?'

Tom and Pearl looked at each other.

'But do we really have to see him, Geronimo?' she said. 'It's just, we're in a bit of a hurry that's all.'

Geronimo shook his head adamantly.

'Mackamack give permission, is possible, no permission—not possible.'

Tom and Pearl sensed that they wouldn't be able to change his mind.

'OK,' said Tom, reluctantly. 'If you insist.'

'Is best.'

Geronimo pulled a machete out of the cab, and with Tom and Pearl following led the way up a narrow forest track away from the village. Soon the path grew so narrow that it had all but disappeared, and Geronimo began to idly hack his way round coils of mossy branches, drooping with ferns and orchids.

'So the Mackamack doesn't live in the village?' asked Pearl, twisting through the jungle.

'No no,' said Geronimo. 'He live in special place.'

'And you *definitely* need his permission to go down into the crater?'

Geronimo shook his head and laughed at her persistence.

'If you no see him, he see you. Birds, snakes, monkeys tell him.'

Tom and Pearl stole a glance at each other and carried on. Was Geronimo in league with this wizard? What did he have to gain by them? The deeper they went the less easy Tom felt about any of this, but he knew there was nothing he could do about it, either. Soon the ground began to rise sharply, and Tom caught a glimpse of a clearing through the dense bush ahead. As they drew closer, he saw that the open space contained a tumble-down thatched hut, walled off from the rest of the jungle by a solid phalanx of trees.

'Is this his house?' said Pearl, breathless from the climb. 'Strange—'

'Don't touch!' yelled Geronimo as Pearl was just about to rest her hand on the slim silver trunk.

'What is it?' said Pearl, pulling back in shock.

Geronimo touched the surface of the bark with his blade, indicating the pale, white juice running down the surface.

'This is chongot,' he said. 'Arrow poison tree. Touch the white water and you will swell up like a ball. You no breathe and then you die.'

'OK,' said Pearl, realizing that Geronimo was deadly serious. She took a respectful step back and saw the wall of poison trees extending in a perfect circle in each direction. 'So the Mackamack planted these?'

'Of course.'

'Why?'

'Protection. Against jungle spirits.'

Cautiously they followed Geronimo around the edge of the stockade, and soon came to a narrow gap across which there were a couple of bamboo stakes. In the clearing beyond a tall gaunt man dressed in a pair of tatty denim shorts was squatting over a fire. A long mop of grey-yellow hair was fastened in a topknot on the crown of his head. As soon as he saw the foreigners at the gate he stood up and glowered at them menacingly.

'*Mogethin!*' shouted Geronimo and raised his hand with a cheery wave. The wizard grunted, and looked at Tom and Pearl suspiciously. He shouted out something in his own language to which Geronimo replied. The Mackamack continued to stare at Tom and Pearl, then with an abrupt snap of his fingers beckoned them forward.

'I talk to Mackamack,' whispered Geronimo. 'You say nothing, otherwise he get very angry.'

'Shouldn't we at least say hello?' said Pearl, watching the tall man disappear into his hut and reappear a moment later with what could only have been a dead black octopus hanging limply in his hand. Squatting down beside the fire, he proceeded to hack it to pieces and throw it into the pot.

'No,' said Geronimo firmly. 'I talk to him only.'

Stepping through the bamboo barrier, they made their way into the clearing. Tom and Pearl went over to a tree and sat in its shadow as Geronimo had instructed, while he approached the fire. There was an explosion of words, at which Geronimo sat down humbly and stared at the dirt. He mumbled something in reply, whereupon the Mackamack began giving him some kind of instructions, gesticulating wildly and occasionally glancing over to where Pearl and Tom sat. It was quite clear that Geronimo was terrified of him.

'I hope he likes chocolate,' whispered Tom, watching the intimidating wizard stir his black mess in the pot. 'Otherwise we are in serious trouble.'

'What do you think he is telling him to do?'

Tom shrugged.

'Whatever he wants, by the look of it. I can't quite work it out.'

At length the lecture ended, and Geronimo walked over to them.

'What you have to give him?' he said, without any emotion. Tom could tell instantly that Geronimo hadn't enjoyed his ear-bashing from the Mackamack one little bit.

'It's not that much,' apologized Pearl, fumbling in her bag. 'It's—'

'You bring.'

Scrabbling to their feet they walked over to the fire and sat down opposite the Mackamack, who was now busily stuffing a collection of dried skins and trinkets into his palm leaf bag. His bloodshot eyes swivelled up to meet them, then a torrent of words was directed at Geronimo.

'Show him your gift,' instructed Geronimo.

Awkwardly Pearl withdrew the rather tatty bar of chocolate from her bag, and smoothing out the wrapper as best she could, handed it to Geronimo, who passed it to the Mackamack.

'It's a little damaged I'm afraid.'

The Mackamack stared at the chocolate bar ferociously, and Tom and Pearl half expected him to pick up his spear and hurl it at them in disgust. But he didn't. Instead he sniffed it, tore away the wrapper, and sniffed it again. Suddenly a great toothless smile cracked open his haggard face.

'Chocolate!' he roared, like an excited child.

Tom and Pearl smiled in surprise, and Geronimo grinned too.

'Chocolate!' he shouted again. The transformation was amazing, and suddenly this rather dangerous Stone Age man seemed not half so terrifying after all.

'Chocolate!' he shrieked. 'Chocolate! Chocolate!'

Five minutes later they had retraced their steps through the poisoned stockade and away up the narrow twisting track.

'How you know about chocolate?' said Geronimo, pausing to light a cigarette against a tree. 'Sir Henry tell you this?'

'He did,' said Tom.

'Sir Henry clever man,' smiled Geronimo. 'I like him very much.'

'So you remember them coming here?'

'Oh yes.'

'And Nicholas Zumsteen, you remember him?'

Geronimo said nothing. He exhaled loudly and stared out into the jungle.

'Is Nicholas Zumsteen still here, Geronimo?' asked Tom, remembering that fleeting glimpse of a man he had seen in the street.

'Too many questions for Geronimo,' the boy muttered, and scampered on up the path. Tom and Pearl followed in silence, up and up through the tangle of lianas and ferns. As they climbed higher, vast trees began to extend up out of the canopy, and here and there the bright shapes of huge robber crabs scuttled away into the undergrowth, their powerful pincers poised to snap into the air.

'How much further?' gasped Pearl, as they stood resting against a huge tree root.

'Very close now. Just over top,' said Geronimo, pointing to the ridge above them. 'Nearly nearly. You want drink?'

'You bet.'

Geronimo went over to a narrow stand of bamboo, and taking his machete from his belt hacked down a white and green stick. Then he expertly sliced off the top and bottom, and presented a narrow section to Pearl. To her surprise, it was half-full of water.

'Ancestors give this water. Good water.'

Pearl drank gratefully from the bamboo, and Geronimo then hacked off a section for Tom and one for himself.

'You know a lot about the jungle,' said Tom admiringly.

Geronimo shrugged. 'This no jungle. This garden. I am Karnaka. This my tribe, this my home. My place here, not Tithona town. Here I like. Nobody tell Geronimo what to do up here.'

'Except the Mackamack,' said Tom, looking at him directly. 'Seemed like he was telling you exactly what to do.'

The boy smiled awkwardly.

'You are afraid of him, aren't you, Geronimo?' said Pearl, wiping the sweat off her brow. 'What did he tell you to do?'

'Mackamack very big man,' he said, avoiding their eyes. 'He can make many things happen.'

'Like what?'

Geronimo nodded down towards the sea.

'You mean, like the tidal wave?' spluttered Tom. 'He told you he did that?'

Geronimo said nothing, he just poked the ground with the tip of his machete.

'But surely you don't believe him,' said Pearl. '*Do* you believe him, Geronimo?'

Geronimo stared at the ground angrily. In his tatty red shorts, his tribal necklace and his immaculately oiled teddy-boy haircut, he looked like a strange mixture of the past and the present.

'White men ask too many questions,' he mumbled, and scampered away up the path. Tom and Pearl looked at each other then reluctantly followed. Something felt very wrong about this.

Five minutes later they had reached the rim of the crater, and found themselves staring down at a strange, almost alien landscape. The crater was oval shaped, its steep grey sides dropping down smoothly into a tangle of scrubby trees and bushes sprouting out of the stony floor. At its centre stood a vast jumble of reddish rocks, rising up imperiously above the canopy.

'What are those?' asked Tom, pointing at the red rocks, their smooth forms glinting in the sun.

'Tith's house,' explained Geronimo. 'He make this long time ago.'

'Tith?'

'This is his island. Tithona. First island in world.'

'OK,' said Pearl, realizing what Geronimo was saying. 'So Tith is like, your god?'

'Tith is son of God,' explained Geronimo. 'Like Jesus. But naughty man.'

'Naughty?' smiled Tom. 'What did he do?'

'Tith steals things, makes his father very angry. So he has to hide here, in shape of a beetle.'

'A beetle?'

'Yes Miss Pearl,' said Geronimo seriously. 'Karnaka believe this. Tith's house is old old place.'

'And is this what you think, too?'

'Me?' The scrawny boy looked at them and shrugged his shoulders nonchalantly. 'No matter what Geronimo think. The cave you want to see is on far side. We go now?'

Tom and Pearl nodded. Geronimo led the way down the

steep shale bank and into the tangle of stumpy trees. The moment they stepped into the crater forest Tom noticed that something was different. It wasn't just the absence of creepers and lianas, all coiled around each other like some endless living knot—it was something else. The forest seemed alive with life.

'Oh!' said Pearl suddenly.

A brilliant blue bird, rather like a parrot, clattered noisily onto a branch just in front of her. It was so close that she could almost touch it, but the bird was not in the least bit interested in her, it was far more interested in skewering an insect on the leaf before her eyes.

'It's as if I wasn't here,' she marvelled, watching it go.

'That is right, Miss Pearl,' said Geronimo proudly, 'that is Lorikeet. Very rare bird. Many rare things here. This is Tith's place—no hunting. Only ancestors.'

'Ancestors?' she said, watching a gang of red and green birds clatter through the treetops.

'Yes. Look,' he said, pointing at the ground as a brown beetle scurried past. 'Another,' he said pointing at an iridescent green beetle perched on the leaf of a plant. 'Another,' he said, pointing at a red beetle perched on the red flower of an orchid. As soon as they recognized the shape Tom and Pearl began to see the same beetles everywhere, all brilliantly camouflaged.

'You no see them at first,' he said, walking over to a large white orchid hanging from a branch. 'I show you why.'

Tom and Pearl watched a white beetle scuttling along the edge of the flower towards the black stalk. The instant its feet touched the stalk its colour began to change; and a moment later it was entirely black.

'It's like a chameleon,' marvelled Pearl, watching as the beetle turned green as the stalk met the leaf, then brown as it reached the ground. 'What is the name of this beetle, Geronimo?'

'We call this Tith's beetle. Special beetle. It live for one day only—then die.'

'It only lives for one day?'

Geronimo nodded. 'One year as grub—one day as beetle. Mr Catcher call it jitterjat.'

'The jitterjat beetle.' Tom stole a glance at Pearl. 'That's handy.'

'And so, all these creatures are ancestors?' asked Pearl, looking down at the jewelled beetle, now turning yellow in the sunlight.

'Yes miss. All. We live, we die, we come back as bird, rat, beetle, we all here. And sometimes Tith here too, at night. He walks in the crater.'

'Really?' said Pearl, wondering how this enormous jigsaw might fit together. 'And is Tith like, some kind of enormous beetle?'

'I have never seen Tith,' said Geronimo flatly. 'Only Mackamack see him.'

'Only the Mackamack, eh?' said Tom, raising his eyebrows.

'Yes. He say so,' replied Geronimo. 'Please, this way.'

They moved on down the path until at last they reached the shadow of the red rocks in the centre of the crater. At ground level, they appeared even larger than Tom had estimated, and an ominous quiet hung around them.

'Tith house,' said Geronimo reverentially, pulling out another floppy cigarette and lighting it. 'Very special place. Many years ago Karnaka fortress.'

Tom and Pearl stared up at the flat faces of the rocks in silence. There was something forbidding about these great red shapes looming out of the forest. Between them ran a long narrow pathway just wide enough to squeeze through.

'Many carvings inside. Sir Henry, Mr Catcher, Nicholas Zumsteen all like them very much. But you must be careful.'

'Why is that?' asked Tom.

'Two white boys lost here many years before.'

'White boys?'

'From missionary family. They all come up to see the carvings, the brothers go in and they never come back. Big problem. Family look—they no find. All village come up, they look—they no find. Then soldiers from other islands come, they look—nothing. Boys disappeared. Gone. Some holes go way, way down into mountain. Very dangerous.'

Geronimo exhaled loudly and threw away his cigarette.

'You ready?'

Tom turned to Pearl and saw that her eyes were bright with anticipation. He knew what she was thinking. Here on this strange tropical island was what they had travelled through time and space to find: the entrance to Scarazand. This was it.

'Shall we go in?' he said.

CHAPTER 14

A NECESSARY BETRAYAL

The pathway between the towering red rocks was narrow and silent. Mindful of what Geronimo had said, Tom and Pearl stuck close behind him, their shoulders brushing against the smooth red surfaces as they entered one alley after another, moving deeper and deeper into the maze. It was quite easy to see how someone could get lost in here, as each red boulder looked identical, but Geronimo never hesitated, he knew precisely where he was taking them. At last they emerged through a small tunnel into a long straight alleyway, wider than the rest, that seemed to run the entire length of the maze itself.

'Many carvings here,' said Geronimo, pointing down the avenue. 'You like me show you?'

'Erm . . . OK,' said Pearl, looking up at the smooth red walls on either side that seemed much like every other avenue they had been in. 'Where are they?'

Geronimo glanced up at the sun that was just reappearing from behind a cloud.

'One moment, you see.'

Pulling a small mirror out of his pocket, he rubbed it

hard on his dirty shorts then scampered off down to the far end.

'Watch!' he shouted, angling the small mirror so that it reflected the bright sunlight directly onto the wall. Suddenly what had been a dull red surface was alive with intricate carvings, picked out by the shaft of light.

'You see it?'

Tom smiled and gave a thumbs-up sign. Geronimo waved back and held the mirror steady as Tom and Pearl made their way up the alley towards him, examining the wall.

'It's amazing,' said Pearl, tracing her fingers around the bulging eyes of fish and birds. 'What do you think it means?'

'Must be some kind of story,' said Tom, studying the processions of wild looking men and canoes. 'Hey, there's a jitterjat beetle,' he said, recognizing the shape of the insect carved into the stone.

'And a man, underground. And a volcano,' said Pearl, pointing at what appeared to be a mountain exploding. 'Maybe it's happened before.'

'Maybe.'

'You like it?' asked Geronimo as they reached the far end. 'Story of Tith. And story of Karnaka people. How the world was born. My people make all this, many years ago,' he said proudly. 'It goes long way into the maze. You want me to show you?'

Tom and Pearl glanced at each other awkwardly.

'It's . . . it's really impressive,' said Tom, 'but the thing is, we are in a bit of a hurry.'

'More than a bit, I'm afraid,' added Pearl with a smile.

Geronimo tried not to look disappointed.

'Why you in hurry? What is problem?'

'There is no problem exactly,' Pearl began, and then she thought better of it. 'OK, actually, there is a problem, a very big problem. For all of us. You too, Geronimo.'

'Me?'

Pearl nodded. She took a deep breath. There was no easy way to say this.

'There is going to be an earthquake tomorrow. Tithona is going to sink into the sea.'

Geronimo looked at both of them as if they were mad.

'Tithona?' he snorted. 'I don't believe you. How do you know this?'

'We just do.'

'Sir Henry told us,' explained Tom. 'He knows these things. The wave this morning was only the first step. Tomorrow morning the whole archipelago is going to be destroyed.'

Geronimo shook his head. It made no sense.

'Why should I believe you?'

'He knows, Geronimo, which is why we need to go down to that cave as soon as possible.'

'Mackamack say nothing about this.'

'Well, maybe the Mackamack doesn't know everything. That's possible, isn't it?'

Geronimo furrowed his brow. This was something he clearly found hard to believe.

'Why do you want to go down there? Is the cave safe?'

'No, it's not safe at all,' said Tom. 'We just think that it might lead us somewhere else . . . somewhere beyond this island.'

Geronimo might have been surprised at this news but Tom noticed that he wasn't.

'And you want to go *down* there?'

'Yes.'

'Not coming back?'

'No.'

Geronimo paused and stared at them hard. Once again his friendliness seemed to have evaporated, and he was clearly weighing something up in his mind.

'OK,' he grunted finally. 'I show you cave.'

Turning, he set off at a fast pace through the high red walls and five minutes later they came to a narrow ledge. Beyond it, four large boulders marked out the edge of a wide well that disappeared down into the darkness. Drawing closer to the edge, Tom noticed a set of steps cut into the red rock on the far side.

'Is that the way down?' asked Tom, pointing at the steps across the chasm.

'Yes,' replied Geronimo flatly.

Tom turned to him, but the scrawny boy avoided his eyes. Tom sensed he was hiding something.

'Is it really, Geronimo?'

'Of course.'

'Looks like quite a drop,' said Pearl, peering over the edge into the black hole.

'Down there is many many caves. In old times ancestors go down.'

'So the ancestors went into the mountain?'

Geronimo nodded.

'When the ground shakes, Tith is angry. They go down. Now only Mackamack go down.'

'And what does he do down there?' asked Tom, staring into the chasm.

Geronimo shrugged noncommittally.

'I don't know. It is special place. We go round,' he said, indicating the ledge beyond Pearl. 'You first, I follow.'

Tom looked at the ledge snaking round the rock and back into the maze, then glanced back at Geronimo, who was staring at him with cold, deliberate eyes. Something was not right, Tom could sense it.

'You go,' he said, waving them on.

Tom turned and little by little edged his way round, following Pearl into a dark chamber squeezed between the rocks.

'Are you sure this is right, Geronimo?' said Pearl, looking at the smooth walls all around. 'It's a dead end.'

'Is it?'

Tom and Pearl turned to see Geronimo move cautiously in through the small doorway behind them. Before him, he held the long steel blade of the machete that glinted in the half-light. He seemed both frightened and dangerous, and he was muttering something in his own language.

'Geronimo, what are you doing?'

'We stop here,' he snapped sharply. 'You must stay here now and wait.'

'What are you talking about,' said Tom. 'Wait for what?'

'Mackamack coming soon.'

'The Mackamack?'

Geronimo stalked closer, as if hunting a wild animal, holding his machete outstretched.

'He say you no good people,' he hissed. 'You like people in town. You come to poison our island.'

'Poison your island?' spat Tom. 'How?'

'Make us sick. Up here!' he growled, banging his fist on his forehead.

'We are not like them, Geronimo!' insisted Pearl, edging back towards Tom. 'Really, you must believe us. We are not like them! Can't you see?'

'Then why you want to go down to cave!' he shouted, his eyes bulging.

'We just . . . we have to, Geronimo,' said Pearl, in a quiet, desperate voice. 'I'm sorry. It's . . . we think it will take us . . . somewhere else . . . somewhere where our parents might be. I know it sounds stupid and I don't expect you to understand. But that's just what we have to do, that's all.'

Geronimo shook his head. There was a part of him that wanted to believe her, but the spell of fear the Mackamack had cast was so strong.

'Mackamack say you must stay here. He decide.'

'And just supposing we don't do as you say?' said Tom, glaring back at Geronimo. 'After all, there are two of us and only one of you. How are you going to stop us?'

Geronimo grimaced and tightened his grip on his machete.

'I have knife.'

'And?'

Geronimo seemed more nervous than ever. The blade quivered in his hand.

'I don't want to say—'

'Geronimo!' came a shout, and a shadow crossed the crack of light in the roof.

'Aye!' shouted the boy, then something fast in his own language.

Tom thought he heard the harsh voice of the Mackamack, but there were others with him scrambling up over the rocks somewhere above.

'Who are they?' whispered Pearl.

Tom listened hard—he was sure one of the voices was speaking English.

'It's on a fulcrum apparently,' explained a high, nasal voice. 'Built many years ago. There's a few of them here. Used as prisons.'

'Ingenious,' replied another.

Tom looked at Pearl, his heart was racing now.

'We should go—'

But before they even had a chance to move something flashed across the beam of sunlight and thumped down into the centre of the room. A deep, hollow sound filled the chamber, and Tom looked with horror at the large lump of red rock that had been knocked out of the ceiling and was now standing in the centre of the floor. It was attached to a thick cable of creeper.

'They missed,' gasped Pearl. 'Come on!'

But the moment she began to move the whole floor seemed to wobble precariously.

'Don't move!' shouted Tom above the cracking sound. 'Don't move, it must have knocked something, and . . . '

All three of them stood tensed on the rocking surface, then

suddenly it began to pivot, and before they had a chance to balance it Tom, Pearl, and Geronimo were tipped headfirst down into a narrow well. Earth, dust, and stones tumbled past and they had barely begun to fall before their clothes began tugging at them, slowing their fall.

'Help!' shouted Pearl.

The walls of the well were wet and coated in a thick black substance, like treacle, and as Tom slid down he watched Pearl's hair stretch up high above her head. Seconds later all three of them were in the same predicament, slithering slowly down the glistening black sides of the well, grasping frantically at lumps of moss and rotten roots to halt their descent.

'Three, did he say?'

Two heads were poking forwards into the light high above.

'Indeed, sir. Just three.'

'Very well.'

There was a chink of coins changing hands.

'Mackamack!' shouted Geronimo, followed by a torrent of words in his own language. But there was no reply. The two thin heads reappeared at the hole . . .

'Hmm. Well I suppose one has to admire his animal cunning. He's the local witchdoctor you say?'

'Indeed, sir,' continued the nasal voice. 'Been running his own little fiefdom out here for years. Provides us with a steady supply of converts—from the port down there, mainly. He's Stone Age to the core, and has no real clue what is going on, but he likes his money.'

'So I can see,' sneered the other man. 'And he hasn't seen Nicholas Zumsteen?'

'Apparently not.'

'And do you believe him?'

'I have no reason not to.'

'Very well. Carry on searching. And remember we must be back on the boat by sunset.'

The heads disappeared and Tom, Pearl, and Geronimo were left hanging in silence. Tom had a very strong idea what sort of people these might be, but *who* they were and *how* they got to Tithona was too much to think about right now.

'You OK?'

Pearl was much higher up, clinging on to a twisted branch.

'Fine, almost,' he gulped, twisting his head up to face her. His heels nudged against two tiny indentations in the rock, just deep enough to take his weight.

'Who was that up there? Nicholas Zumsteen?'

'No Zumsteen, miss,' gasped Geronimo, who had somehow managed to brace himself much higher up. 'Those different men. I don't know them.'

'What is this stuff?' spat Tom, sniffing the sweet, sticky surface.

'Some kind of black honey,' said Pearl, struggling to hold her position. 'Tree sap, maybe?'

'Mackamack call this wepotip,' said Geronimo.

'Wepotip?'

'He use for medicine. Healing sick people.'

'Healing sick people?' repeated Tom, bringing his hand close to his face. In the gloom he could just see the silhouette of a small black beetle stuck to his black sticky fingers. It seemed to be eating the strange substance. Then he noticed another on his arm, and another on his shoulder. What kind of beetles were these? They were small, black, nondescript. Then he felt one march up his neck and under his chin, its legs, tickling, scratching . . . with a supreme effort Tom waited until the tiny creature had walked up onto his lips before blowing it away. He drew a deep breath, and tried to ignore the rising sense of panic inside him. These creatures just might have been entirely harmless, but there was every chance they weren't.

'Euch!' gasped Pearl. 'I'm covered in beetles!'

'Me too,' grunted Tom. Looking up towards the dim light of the doorway he could see clouds of insects swirling and descending into the chamber. Maybe it was the smell that attracted them. They had to get out, very quickly—but how? Somehow Tom seemed to have fallen far further than the other two, and it was only his heels that were stopping him sliding further. Glancing up, he saw that Geronimo had managed to detach his legs from the wall and braced them on the other side of the narrow chute. Using his legs as a lever, he was very slowly pushing himself upwards.

'Geronimo's got it!' yelled Tom. 'Try that!'

With immense effort Pearl managed to detach first one leg, then the other, and force them across to the other side of the narrow well. Then with small, driving movements, she pushed her back up through the sticky black slime. Her shoes slithered and her thighs felt as if they were on fire, but somehow it worked.

'I'm doing it!' she cried.

Slowly, painfully, Pearl began to move upwards, but for Tom such movement was much more difficult. Trying again and again, he swung his leg out across the well as far as he dared without losing his balance.

'I can't do it,' he panted, angrily brushing away a beetle from his cheek. 'It's too wide.'

Pearl paused and looked down at him breathlessly.

'I can't reach it.'

'Don't give up!' she shouted. 'We'll get help.' Pearl glanced up at Geronimo who was already almost at the top.

'Geronimo wait! Geronimo!'

Geronimo slithered up over the lip of the well and lay there for a moment panting hard. Then he turned and stared down at Pearl, braced against the wall.

'Tom's stuck. He can't move. You must help me get him out.'

Geronimo wiped the black slime off his face.

'Why must I help you?' he said roughly. 'You poison my island.'

'That's crap!' shouted Pearl desperately. 'You *know* that's not true!'

Geronimo grimaced.

'The Mackamack say—'

'THE MACKAMACK IS AN IDIOT!' she screamed, every syllable trembling with rage. 'He knows you are frightened of him and he has used you, don't you see! He hasn't any magic! He has sold you to those people up there, just like us! We're all in this together!'

Pearl and Tom looked up at the scrawny silhouette of the boy standing at the top of the well.

'Please Geronimo,' panted Pearl, quieter now. 'You *have* to help us.'

Geronimo watched them in silence for a moment, then he disappeared.

'Dammit!' hissed Pearl, her voice shaking. 'Tom, are you all right?'

'Fine,' he said, his voice echoing and distant. 'You go on, get to the top, and see if you can get one of those creeper things. Maybe if you lower it down I can climb up that.'

'OK,' she grimaced. 'I'll try. But you must hold on.'

Tom said nothing, but blew an insect off his shoulder. It was becoming harder and harder to ignore the pain in the back of his legs.

'I'll do my best.'

'Good,' she said and began climbing again in earnest. It was much easier now, as she was spurred on by rage: rage at Geronimo and his misplaced loyalties, rage at the Mackamack, rage at everything that had happened to them on this terrible island. Biting back her tears, Pearl forced herself on and up, on and up, until ten long minutes later she slithered over the lip of the well and lay panting on the earth. She closed her eyes: that was one of the hardest things she had ever done in her life. Pulling herself to her feet, Pearl suddenly remembered the rucksack that had been on her back all this time. It was still intact. Good. Now where? Edging round the side of the rocks, Pearl ran back into the maze and looked about her anxiously. Already the shadows had begun to lengthen and evening was coming on. Somehow she had to get to the trees beyond the boulders, but it all looked the same.

'Geronimo!' she shouted. The insects fell silent. 'Geronimo!'

There was no answer. Pearl felt so angry that she wanted to

scream. If she saw Geronimo again she would kill him with her bare hands: that was certain.

'Geronimo!'

There was nothing. For the first time in a long, long while, hot tears began to prick her eyes as Pearl's anger turned to frustration . . . she would probably never find a way out. The maze was too big, the obstacles too great, and the volcano . . . . tomorrow this would all be gone for ever. Angrily she wiped away the tears. This was all her fault. But she had to do something. And do it quickly. Sprinting down the nearest alley she turned left, then right, then right again. Was this the way? Turning again, she found herself in a long straight alley and suddenly sensed something moving towards her from the shadows at the far end. It was a man carrying a rucksack. She stopped. He hadn't seen her. Should she turn and run? Maybe . . . maybe not. He looked lean and sweaty and there was a boy right behind him . . .

Tom spat again in the darkness. Something large was crawling over his chin. His fingers and feet were so numb that he couldn't feel them at all now, he knew they were there, somewhere in the darkness, but they seemed to belong to someone else. All he could hear was the soft buzzing of insect wings and tinkle of water running far below. In the darkness the sounds seemed almost friendly, like a meadow on a hot summer's afternoon. They lulled Tom's senses, and took his mind off the realization that he was stuck in some kind of trap. How did it work? Maybe the water was a part of it. Maybe he was supposed to be left hanging here as some kind of bait, and then he was supposed to fall down into the water and be washed clean at the end of it. But what was he the bait for? Tom shuddered, and blew another beetle off his chin. He didn't want to think about it. Refused to think about it . . .

And that was becoming easier every moment. The sweet smell, and the soft sound of running water, the darkness . . . it was making him feel drowsy. He was so exhausted after all, why not have a little sleep? Slowly Tom felt his eyelids closing and he began to retreat into the core of himself. He was no longer aware of his fingers losing their grip, nor did he feel his heels relax and slide off the tiny ledge and begin to slip down into the velvet blackness . . . up down, he did not know which was which any more; he did not care. He lay, upright, arms outstretched, completely and utterly asleep.

And had Tom not been so deeply asleep he would have felt the small grey beetle as it scurried across his filthy T-shirt, gently lifting and falling with his every breath. He would have brushed away the small, urgent creature as it clambered up his neck and onto the rim of his ear. He would have been tickled by its tiny legs scurrying down the dish and clambering into the soft darkness of his ear hole, and then he would have tried to scratch it away as it probed deeper into the cavity of his middle ear. He might have even felt the beetle lay its small white egg in those warm, dark depths, before retracing its steps and clambering out again. And later, in the middle of the night, when the tiny grey grub emerged from the egg and began to shuffle blindly further into his middle ear, driven by instinct onwards, he might have felt its tiny teeth burrowing deeper and deeper through the soft cartilage and out into the remotest extremities of his brain, leaving a thin trail of fungus that awakened brain cells lain dormant for thousands and thousands of years . . .

But he didn't.

Instead, Tom was dimly aware of another part of his dream. He was hanging somewhere, and strong arms had lifted him up. Something wet was rubbed over his face and he was carried up through a tree to a platform. It was dark. There was bright moonlight. Was it moonlight? He couldn't tell. It might have been.

CHAPTER 15

MY LIFE AS A BEETLE

'Hello?'

There was silence.

'Hello you.'

'Oh.'

Tom opened his eyes. Somehow the air was black and full of silverish blue lines, moving slowly like tentacles.

'Hello?'

The voice was distant. What was that? Tom looked up at the lines. He was inside them, and it was like a three dimensional grid.

'Is that you?'

But what was that voice? He knew that voice. He closed his eyes again. Then he saw a wave. A red wave, rushing through the darkness towards him, with orange and yellow foam at the top. His first instinct was to hide, but already the wave had reared up like a horse and pulsed right through him, filling his ears with the sound of rushing water. It felt so hot, it tingled . . . but it wasn't frightening somehow . . . the wave was warm and comforting, and he couldn't stop smiling . . . he felt so small before it and it had cradled him like a baby . . . he wanted another one . . .

'Tom . . . you must wake up.'

The urgent voice again. A hand on his shoulder. Something was getting in the way of the next wave . . . he could see it coming . . . the black horizon was turning from orange to yellow . . . here it comes, here—

Suddenly there was a sharp crack on his face.

'Ow!'

Tom opened his eyes, stunned. There before him sat a glistening beetle, its head wrapped in a black cloak. Its beady black eyes stared at him curiously.

'Ahh!'

'Stop it!' shouted the beetle. 'It's me!'

Another smack, this time on the other cheek.

'You?' whispered Tom nervously, as the long black feelers stretched towards him, touching his face. 'W-who are you?'

'You know who I am!'

The beetle stared at him and suddenly it was no longer a beetle. It was Don Gervase Askary, his yellow eyes watching him lazily.

'But . . .'

Then it transformed again, this time into Ern Rainbird, and he threw his head back and laughed . . . and as he laughed his nose grew and his face sprouted hair and he was the mammoth in the museum . . .

'Stop it!' shouted Tom.

'Stop what, you crazy nut!' cackled Uncle Jos. 'This is too much.'

'You've really gone and done it this time,' interrupted his mother, who was suddenly sitting next to Uncle Jos. Her body was a scorpion.

'No, please . . . '

Tom screwed his eyes tight shut to make the nightmare go away. But the silver grid was still there, shimmering. He took a long deep breath, and when he opened them again there was Pearl, anxiously staring at him in the moonlight. There was a man kneeling beside her.

'What happened?' she whispered. 'You've been shouting.'

'I . . . I don't know,' stammered Tom, his face bathed in sweat. 'I think . . . I think something's happened.' For some reason his ear itched, and scratching it violently he found traces of black tree sap on his finger, and the remains of something small and grey.

'What's that?' gasped Pearl, looking down at the remains on Tom's finger.

The man beside her carefully wiped the legs and shell of the creature onto his hand and examined them closely in the moon-light.

'If I am not mistaken, that is the shell of a cark beetle. They are attracted to that tree sap and there are many thousands of them down that hole.'

'A cark beetle?' Pearl's face froze as the realization crept upon her. 'Are you . . . are you quite sure?'

The man nodded grimly. 'Not good at all.'

Pearl looked down at Tom in horror.

'That means . . . does that mean he's been . . . no,' she shook her head, 'no!'

MY LIFE AS A BEETLE

Tom stared at her woozily, then suddenly a ball of hot pain exploded inside his head like a gun going off. Desperately he pressed his hands to his head, the pain was almost unbearable . . . something was happening inside his skull, something he couldn't scratch . . . he wanted to rip it out, tear it away, but how? Panting, he closed his eyes tight shut and saw a pale line spreading along the black horizon. First orange, then yellow, like an elastic string of golden honey . . . here came the next wave, rolling towards him, soft, and warm and comforting . . .

Pearl leant forward and peered at Tom's ear. A thin trace of dried blood was the only evidence of the tiny cark grub's fateful incision.

'But . . . but is there nothing we can do to stop it?' she whispered feverishly.

Tom let the warm wave wash over him, and through the haze of pain he remembered what August had told him that misty morning. Unconsciously, his hand drifted up to his neck and felt the small silver egg hanging there.

'Egg,' he murmured. Pearl watched his fingers fumbling with the small silver object.

'What is it?'

'Inside,' he whispered, 'there's some grubs . . . I think . . . I think I must eat one.' Tom closed his eyes, his head pulsing in agony.

'There's a grub inside that silver egg round your neck?' repeated Pearl urgently. 'And you must eat it?'

Tom nodded weakly.

'Antidote. To the cark beetle.' He blinked hard as the rivulets of sweat ran down his temples. 'August Catcher gave it to me.'

'August Catcher?' repeated the man in the shadows. Suddenly his tone had changed. 'You know August Catcher?'

'We've just been with him . . . '

'Did he tell you what it is?'

Pearl shook her head desperately.

'I didn't know anything about it.'

Something silver on a necklace flashed before Tom's eyes, and instantly turned into a white scorpion, then a worm, then a silver horse, then divided into hundreds of steel knives, jabbing his head . . . Tom screwed his eyes tight shut. He couldn't take much more of this . . . Another sharp slap knocked away the visions and he opened his eyes angrily.

'What are you doing?'

'Be calm Tom,' said the man reassuringly, quickly unscrewing the capsule. 'This is going to help you.'

Tom stared at the silhouette of the man.

'Who are you?'

Pearl gasped. 'Oh my god . . . ' she whispered, covering her face with her hands. 'What . . . what are they?'

'Lapastus grubs,' replied the man urgently.

'But he can't . . . he can't eat that . . . It's too—it's—'

'Be quiet!' ordered the man. 'Now Tom, do you want me to—'

'I'll do it,' grunted Tom, blinking hard. 'Give it to me.'

'Very well,' replied the man, and Tom felt a greasy grub pressed between his fingers. 'But you mustn't look at it.'

Tom felt the creature writhe between his fingers and with his eyes tight shut he brought it up to his mouth. Opening his eyes a fraction he glanced at the grey fat squirming thing with a shaggy blond head.

'Hi Tom,' said his dad, 'you're surely not going to eat me, are you?'

Tom closed his eyes and shook his head.

'Please help me,' he whispered, and brought the struggling creature to his lips.

'I can't help you now, no one can,' said the grub, speaking for itself now. 'You're too far gone, ha-ha! Ha ha! Ha ha ha!'

Tom glanced at it and saw it laughing, its glistening pink lips splitting open. Sweat was pouring down his cheeks now and his fingers were shaking. Another ball of pain burst inside his head and it felt as if someone was forcing hot wires right through his skull . . . August was right, it was just too difficult.

'Tom, you *must* eat it now, do you understand?'

Tom nodded as best he could.

'Do it now!'

But another red wave was coming towards him, faster and faster . . . so soft, so beautiful . . . did he really have to eat this horrible thing? Suddenly Tom thrust the squirming grub into his mouth and felt it on his tongue. He gripped it between his teeth like a nut . . .

Don't think don't think don't think don't—

He bit hard and felt the pulpy body burst, and at once his mouth was full of rubbery, sticky flesh and acid. With every ounce of willpower he swallowed and swallowed . . . and when it was over a water bottle was thrust before him and he gulped and gulped, trying to take the taste away. And then—it was gone. The grub was gone . . . he had done it . . .

'Well done Tom,' whispered the man, 'well done. Now have this, quick,' he said, pressing something dark into his hand. Tom stared hazily at the man, then at the lump of chocolate, and fainted clean away.

Later, Tom woke up. He appeared to be on some sort of platform, high up a tree. Below, the jumble of red boulders spread out before him in the moonlight. Very gingerly he ran his fingers across his head, and he was relieved to find that the great pain inside had gone, and with it the shimmering grid of blue tentacles that had covered everything. Only the faintest pulse remained, like a heartbeat in the distance, and when he closed his eyes, he could still sense that faint red glow on the horizon. Somehow that terrible cark grub must have begun its grisly work. But it had been stopped.

'Tsk-tsk!'

There was a scrabbling and Tom turned to see a small blackfaced monkey trying to prise its way into the rucksack.

'Shoo you. Go away,' hissed a voice.

The monkey glanced up cheekily, then carried on.

'Off!'

A shoe came flying down out of the darkness and it scampered off into the trees.

'Feeling any better?'

Tom looked up at a dark, lean man sitting in a crook of the tree just above him. It was the man who had been here earlier, but only now his visions had gone could Tom really see him. He had slicked-back, black hair and bright, nervous eyes. In the moonlight he reminded Tom of some old-fashioned film star who had been castaway on a desert island.

'Have some more chocolate,' he smiled, and snapping off a generous slab he tossed it down.

'Thanks,' mumbled Tom, enjoying the sweet taste as it flooded through him, making him feel himself once more. The man watched him eat in silence.

'Odd sensation isn't it?' he said at last.

'What is?'

'What you've just been through. The blue lines everywhere, like grids in the air. The shapes changing, and then those big honey-coloured pulses coming at you like waves. Waves that can wash the terrible pain away. It's an odd sensation, don't you think?'

'I suppose,' said Tom, shrugging his shoulders. Now he thought about it, that had been precisely what it was like. 'But . . . but it didn't work, did it? I mean, I'm not . . . I haven't been—'

'Beetleized, for want of a better word?'

The man looked at him closely, then vaulted down onto the platform.

'The lapastus grub contains one of the strongest known poisons in the world. It is used by remote tribes in the Amazon to drive out demons, and shamans eat them to speed their journeys to other worlds . . . it fights poison with poison, fire with fire. All we can hope is that August was right.'

The man squatted down and slipped the chain with the silver egg back around Tom's neck.

'You're a very lucky lad,' he smiled, 'keep this as a memento.'

'So you're—'

'Nick Zumsteen. Well guessed. Geronimo came to fetch me. I was on my way up here to collect my stuff on account of what happened this morning, as I suspected that one wave might not be the end of it. And I am mighty glad I did, given what your friend has told me.'

Tom looked across at where Pearl lay sleeping on the floor, and then rubbed his confused head.

'But I thought . . . I thought Geronimo had—'

'Betrayed you?' Zumsteen smiled. 'He did, but only briefly. He's fiercely loyal to his island, and you can't blame him for doing precisely as the Mackamack says. The man is a despot, who terrifies that tribe with curses and spells and lord knows what else. It was only after he dropped Geronimo into that hell pit that the lad finally saw him for what he was.'

'So he knew about the cark beetles?'

Nicholas Zumsteen shook his head.

'Nor the echo beetles for that matter. There must be thousands of them down there—I've never seen so many. That's where the Mackamack gets them from.'

Vaguely Tom remembered something Geronimo had said in the well that afternoon. But that seemed like almost a lifetime ago.

'And so he uses the beetles . . . to heal people?'

'The Mackamack's the witchdoctor, isn't he? Believe me, Tom, everyone on Tithona is still immensely superstitious. If someone gets ill then the Mackamack is summoned, and out of his little bag of tricks he produces a cark beetle. He puts it in their ear, or up their nose and tells them they will recover. But we know what happens then, don't we? I've explained it all to Geronimo.'

'So he's . . . on our side?'

'I should say so.'

'Then where is he?'

'Well given that the Mackamack used cark beetles to heal Geronimo's father, mother, and two little sisters, he has something of a personal quarrel to sort out. I try not to get involved.'

Tom sat in silence for a moment, trying to take it all in. He felt a twinge of guilt at having judged Geronimo so harshly.

'Pearl has been telling me about all your adventures,' continued Zumsteen, 'and where you're trying to get to, too. Interesting choice of destination.'

'Scarazand?'

Zumsteen smiled curiously, then he laughed.

'You've been down there then?'

'Once upon a time, when I was . . . but I have to be very careful, just like you do, Tom, in what is said and what isn't. There is a lot of gossip about. Idle talk costs lives.'

Tom was not quite sure what he meant.

'So are you saying you *have* been there?'

'Maybe I have, maybe I haven't,' replied Zumsteen, with a trace of irritation. 'It doesn't precisely matter where I have been, rather, where I am going. *That* is what matters.'

Zumsteen turned away and, hauling his rucksack across the floor, began fastening every pocket as tightly as possible. Tom watched him in silence. Whatever Zumsteen was or wasn't, he was certainly enigmatic.

'So you know August then,' asked Tom. 'And Sir Henry?'

'Of course,' he replied. 'We were all here together some years ago on a field expedition. August has a remarkable talent, and I am sure that I will employ him again. In fact, I saw an extraordinary sight only this morning that I would like him to immortalize for me. It was almost biblical.'

Tom smiled to himself: so that *had* been Nicholas Zumsteen in the street. And then he remembered something else: wasn't Nicholas Zumsteen supposed to have perished in the volcano?

'So where are you going now? I mean, to escape what's going to happen tomorrow?'

'There is a boat waiting for me,' he replied coolly. 'Lemon will take me down in the truck. He's waiting already. And thankfully there's not much to carry, as I have already sent most of my bits and pieces back to my wife in England. All that's left up here are the bare essentials.'

As if to emphasize the point, Zumsteen reached into the crook of a branch above and pulled down a pair of revolvers and a box of shells. Breaking each weapon in turn, he filled the chambers then stowed them carefully in his rucksack. Then he stood up and, carefully pulling an orchid off the tree trunk, delved into the deep recess behind and extracted several long flat hessian sacks.

'Whoops-a-daisy.' He laughed nervously as one of the sacks fell over and a cascade of what looked like small white pearls spilled out all over the floor. 'Can't lose any of these little fellas.'

Zumsteen quickly dropped to his knees and began picking up each and every one of them.

'What are they?'

'The fruits of my labours. It's taken me the best part of two years to collect this little lot, which is why,' he carefully popped the last one into the sack, 'I cannot let any go astray.'

'Are they eggs?'

'Something like that,' grinned Zumsteen, 'certainly unique to these little islands and going to be rather important, one day.'

Tom watched with increasing fascination as Nicholas Zumsteen stowed the sacks in his pack, taking great care not to squash them. There was something very strange about this lean, nervous man, and Tom began to wonder if possibly he was . . . one of them.

'So, why did you decide to help us, if you don't mind me asking?'

Zumsteen stood up and hauled the heavy rucksack up onto his back.

'Because,' he puffed, bouncing the weight of the pack across his shoulders, 'you were in serious trouble. And had I not . . . well, I could not let that happen. Believe it or not Tom Scatterhorn, I know that we are going to meet again, you and I.'

'We are?'

'That's right. I travel a bit, just like you do,' he said, making quite sure that Tom understood what he meant. 'And I happen to know that one day, you—' Zumsteen checked himself. 'Let's just say that one good turn deserves another. I wanted to introduce myself. Face to a name, always helps. Plus I know I have a reputation as a harum-scarum fellow, and you may well hear some extraordinary stories about me. Believe them, or not—you decide,' he said, with a hint of a smile. 'But seriously, you and me, Tom, will need each other one day. When that ludicrous upstart becomes too big for his boots and threatens to tip us all into the abyss.' Zumsteen shot him an enquiring look. 'I think you know who I am talking about.'

Tom's mind raced. Could it be . . .

'Don Gervase Askary?' he blurted out.

'Is that what he calls himself these days?' snorted Zumsteen, sitting down on the edge of the platform and swinging his legs out into the air.

'So you know him?'

Zumsteen threw back his head and laughed. He seemed to find this wildly funny.

'Far, far better than you could ever imagine, Tom. Which is why I am going somewhere where he will never catch up with me. Somewhere where there is absolutely nothing. Nothing at all: just snow, rock, and ice.'

'The Antarctic?'

'Or the Arctic,' grinned Zumsteen. 'Better for you, methinks, that you don't know. That way, if anything happens, well, ignorance is bliss, isn't it? *Auf Wiedersehen*.'

Zumsteen turned and slithered down onto the branch below.

'Wait! Please.'

The dark-haired man turned, his head bobbing just above the platform.

'Yes?'

Tom racked his brains, trying to think of all the important things he needed to ask.

'Is there . . . is there any advice you can give us about getting to Scarazand? Anything we should know?'

'Anything you should know?' repeated Zumsteen thoughtfully. 'Hmm. I think you have everything you need in that little bag of yours. Just go down through the caves and then, if you don't mind surprises and oddities and being scared half out of your wits—which I can see you don't—then you will probably be . . . *possibly* be—fine. But even so,' Zumsteen paused a moment and stared at Tom, his pale blue eyes glinting in the moonlight. 'I suppose there is always one question I ask myself before going somewhere dangerous, that you may want to bear in mind.'

'Which is what?' asked Tom, hoping for some nugget of crucial information.

'Is my journey strictly necessary? Good question that,' he said holding Tom's gaze. 'Well is it? Because if it is, I shall be very intrigued to hear all about how you ever managed to . . . anyway,' he smiled knowingly to himself, 'I have said more than enough, and time is of the essence. It is three hours till daybreak, and we all know what will happen then! Goodbye, Tom Scatterhorn. Best of luck.'

And with a wave he was gone. Tom listened as the creepers creaked and rustled below him, and then there was nothing. Nicholas Zumsteen melted away into the jungle, as mysteriously as he had arrived. Tom sat listening to the hiss of the insects, and watching the moonlight shadows. So that was the famous Nicholas Zumsteen, the man who had officially disappeared, and now the man who had saved his life, too. And obviously one day he would expect something in return. But what could that be?

'Pearl, wake up.'

Nothing. Pearl lay fast asleep on a thin piece of matting on the platform, her thick black hair almost obscuring her face. Tom shook her shoulder once more.

'Pearl.'

Pearl opened her eyes sleepily.

'What is it?'

And then she blinked, and looked again at the shadow above her.

'Tom? Tom, you're OK?'

'I think so.' He smiled. 'Still feel a little weird but . . . yeah, fine.'

Pearl sat up and stared at him.

'Really? So it worked?'

Tom nodded. There was still the occasional thrumming of something like an engine in the distance, but other than that, he felt the same as he always did.

'Yes.'

Pearl smiled and the next instant threw her arms around his neck and hugged him tight. Tom felt all the colour rise to his cheeks as his face was engulfed in Pearl's thick black hair.

'Sorry,' she said, pulling away, a trifle embarrassed. 'I'm just so relieved you're OK. I felt so bad that it was you and not me.'

It was all Tom could do to smile back as confused feelings galloped through his brain.

'Could have been either of us,' he mumbled.

'I know, but,' she shrugged her shoulders. 'Well, I'm just really happy.'

For a fraction of a second they sat there smiling at each other, before Tom looked down at the mat, his cheeks on fire. Something had just happened, and he didn't quite understand what.

'We should go,' he said, roughly picking up the rucksack.

'Sure,' nodded Pearl, equally relieved to get back down to the business in hand. She began to lace up her shoes.

'Zumsteen's gone to catch a boat. He wouldn't say where.'

Pearl did not sound surprised.

'He didn't tell me much either,' she said. 'Weird guy, don't you think? I couldn't decide if he was . . . you know, one of them.'

'Me neither,' said Tom, heartened that Pearl had had the same thought. 'But he saved my life.'

'And showed me a short cut down into the caves too,' she said, standing up. 'You remember that place Geronimo showed us with the carvings? Just to the left of it there is a small staircase, and that's the way down.'

'But how are we ever going to find that again?'

Pearl walked forward to the edge of the platform.

'Look down there.'

Tom came forward to where she stood. From this height he could see what looked like fluorescent lines scribbled along the walls of the red boulders, glowing brightly in the moonlight.

'The lines?'

'Jitterjat beetles,' replied Pearl, 'it's some kind of sticky gum that comes off their legs. You can only see it at night.' She pointed to a thick tangle of white fluorescence that concentrated around one small rock near the middle.

'That's the place. Right there.'

Tom stood wondering at the scribble of lines for a moment. It was like looking down at a city at night.

'And did he say if he had ever been down there?'

Pearl shook her head. 'He was kind of mysterious about it, like he was hiding something. Which is how I got to thinking . . . you know.'

Tom nodded resolutely. 'Well I suppose we should trust him. And it doesn't matter now. I doubt we'll meet him again.'

'No. I guess not.'

Sitting down on the edge of the platform, they swung their legs over and, one after the other, slithered down through the long lines of creepers to the forest floor.

'Wow,' panted Tom, as they reached the bottom. 'So he carried me all the way up?'

'With a little help,' she smiled. 'Well hidden, isn't it? That was Zumsteen's secret hideout. No one knew it was there except for Geronimo.'

Pearl led the way back down a tangle of slippery roots winding down into a cave until they reached the back of a small waterfall.

'And through here too?'

'Of course,' replied Pearl, 'it's the only way in. We couldn't leave you behind, could we?'

'I suppose not,' Tom murmured, a little embarrassed at all the trouble he had caused.

'There's a shallow pool beyond, and then we're back in the maze.' Pearl looked at him and smiled. 'Hey you should be grateful.'

'I am, really.'

'Come on then,' she said, and swinging the rucksack round she held it close and stepped through the wall of water.

'It's OK!' she shouted back, and moments later Tom was standing beside her, soaking wet and gasping.

'Cold shower. Lovely.'

'Toughens you up,' she smiled.

'Oh yeah?' he spluttered. 'I'm quite tough enough already, thank you very much.'

Pearl laughed. 'Come on then, Mr Tough Guy.'

Wading out across the shallow pool they entered the maze once more, and following the fluorescent patterns they soon found themselves standing outside the small triangular gap between two boulders.

'I suppose this is it?' said Tom, peering at the thick jumble of glowing lines that stretched down and away into the darkness.

'That's what he said.'

For a moment they both stared at the entrance in silence. Somehow the idea of being here, at the hole that would actually take them down to Scarazand, was unnerving. It had taken them so long to get here, and yet they still had no idea what to expect. Tom switched on his small torch and waved it hopefully into the gloom. The light was so small and pathetic it seemed hardly worth it.

'Oh look, we must catch one of those,' said Pearl, spotting a dark red jitterjat beetle climbing up a red boulder out of the darkness, leaving a dim fluorescent trail in its wake. 'For the feather, remember?'

Tom had almost forgotten August's suggestion.

'OK,' he said, 'have you got something we can put it in?'

Pearl put down the rucksack and rummaged about inside until she found a small paper box.

'Thanks,' said Tom, taking it from her. With a practised hand he silently brought the box up in front of the beetle and delicately flicked it inside with the tip of his finger.

'You've done that before,' said Pearl, impressed.

'Many times,' said Tom, carefully placing the box in his pocket. 'Every school holidays for years and years, in fact.'

'I knew you would come in handy,' grinned Pearl. 'You're the beetle boy.'

'Thanks,' smiled Tom sarcastically.

'I didn't mean it like that.'

'I know.'

Tom turned round and took one last look at the maze and the trees, glowing in the moonlight. He didn't want Pearl to know how nervous he felt. He was anxious about finding his parents, anxious about that distant, barely audible thudding somewhere inside his head, and most of all he was anxious about going down that hole and never coming out again. Taking a deep breath, he drank in all the smells and sounds of the jungle.

'We've really got to get going,' said Pearl, waiting for him on the edge of the darkness.

Tom nodded, and just as he stepped towards her something small and black flashed in front of him and perched on a branch, cheeping noisily. A bird . . . it looked like a swallow. Clearly agitated, the swallow took off and circled Tom's head once more.

'Friend of yours?' asked Pearl, clearly puzzled by the small black speck darting around them. Tom watched it weave and pass again and again: it was obviously trying to tell him something. Could this be the swallow the eagle had sent to keep an eye on him? Just the thought that it might be lifted his heart, and suddenly Tom found he couldn't stop smiling. Maybe everything would be all right after all.

'Ready?' said Pearl.

'Definitely,' Tom replied, and with a broad smile he switched on his torch and edged past her into the darkness. Pearl looked at him in surprise, then back at the swallow, still flitting back and forth twittering. What was it saying? What did it know? Unconsciously she ran her hand across the band of green cotton she had tied just above her skirt and felt for the small shape . . . it was still there. The swallow was watching her.

'Pearl?' said Tom, his voice already distant and echoing in the darkness.

'Coming,' she said, and without a backward glance followed him inside.

CHAPTER 16

INTO THE ABYSS

The wall of darkness was all enveloping.

'Tom?'

Pearl's voice sounded distant but in fact it was very close, and he felt her hand nudge against his fingers and clutch them tightly.

'Sorry, I just can't see anything at all.'

'Neither can I,' he replied, realizing that the weak torch beam barely dented the darkness. 'Let's just go very, very slowly.'

Together they sidestepped down the steps, and then followed the fluorescent lines as they wound around a large boulder. The light from the small opening above had long since disappeared, and the space beyond dropped away into blackness. It could have been a precipice, it could have been flat ground—they could see nothing beyond the glowing trails of fungus on the floor. Only the echoing drips told them that they were in some large chamber underground.

'Oh!'

Pearl flinched as her fingers brushed against something and it fell to the ground, shattering noisily.

'What is it?'

'A skull,' said Tom, shining the dim beam at the delicate ring of an eye socket. 'Looks like some giant rat, or a possum.'

'Yuck!' gasped Pearl. 'What's *that* doing down here?'

'Someone has left it as a marker, look,' said Tom, pointing the beam at more white objects stretching away into the distance. 'I think we should follow them.'

Steeling themselves, they set off once more, cautiously following the ghostly line of skulls that led between boulders and around gullies until at last they reached a high flat rock wall. Here the fluorescent lines stopped: they seemed to disappear straight into it.

'Is this the end?'

'Can't be,' said Tom, squatting down in the dirt. 'No. There's a gap. I can feel it.'

Pearl knelt down and saw that Tom was right. The massive slab tapered to a point, but it did not touch the ground. Somehow it was being held up by a small boulder no larger than a football that was wedged underneath. It was like an enormous guillotine that had been stopped from falling by a pebble. Pearl swallowed nervously.

'Do you think . . . it's really through there?'

'I think it might be,' said Tom, who was lying down now and squinting into the dark slot that did not seem much wider than a letterbox. 'There's another skull on the far side.'

Pearl stared up at the massive black rock towering above them, which suddenly seemed very precarious indeed.

'I don't know,' she faltered, 'supposing we knock it or something, or perhaps it's some kind of trap, like that well.'

Tom looked up at her and in the dim light he could see how frightened she was. Of course, there was every chance she was right: why should anywhere be safe down here?

'OK,' he said. 'We need to see what's inside there. Look for something to burn.'

'Burn? But how? We haven't got any matches,' said Pearl.

'Actually, we have three,' said Tom, pulling the small box out of his pocket. 'Sir Henry gave them to me.'

Pearl groped around in the darkness until her fingers closed around what felt like a walking stick lying on the ground.

'What about this?' she said, holding up the stick that was carved with intricate swirling patterns. 'Seems a bit of a shame, but—'

'It's perfect,' said Tom, taking it and snapping it into small pieces. The wood was bone dry and with one match Tom quickly had a small fire blazing.

'Wow,' gasped Pearl, looking up. The cave was like a cathedral, and the ceiling was festooned with stalactites, all dancing in the flaming light.

'This is *definitely* the right place,' said Tom, stepping back from the slab of black rock. Out of the darkness two large eyes and a nose emerged, carved above the small opening which formed the mouth. The large, wedge-shaped wall was now a huge, screaming face, with its teeth clenched on a gobstopper.

'Looks like the entrance to hell, doesn't it?'

'Hmm. Let's hope not,' breathed Pearl quietly. 'Kind of wish I hadn't seen that.'

Kneeling back down Tom carefully began chucking one lighted stick after another through the narrow slot into the space beyond. They could barely see much of it, but it seemed to be a room. Soon the acrid stench of ammonia drifted back towards them.

'That's a very bad smell,' said Pearl, 'perhaps we should—'

'Ssshh,' said Tom.

They both sat still and listened in silence. High above the crackling wood there was something else. High pitched whistling, or was it screaming?

'That's—'

Tom did not have time to finish his sentence, as the next moment there was a surge of clattering and thudding and suddenly small black shapes began to cannon through the narrow gap, blurring past their heads.

'Bats!' screamed Pearl.

The air was so thick with them that they blocked out the light. Tom lay still, his arms covering his head, as he felt millions of tiny claws and wings brush past his face and hair, blowing it this way and that. The screaming hordes came on and on, driven out by the flames and the smoke until at last, after what seemed like an age, they had all gone. Tom cautiously opened his eyes and in the light of the red embers on the far side he saw that Pearl was shaking.

'Have they gone?' she whispered.

'I think so,' said Tom, feeling a straggler whistle past his face.

Pearl closed her eyes and drew a deep breath.

'I really, really, really do not like bats. Not one little bit.'

'They won't hurt you. Some of them even eat beetles.'

'Oh well, that's OK then,' said Pearl trying to smile. 'They just give me the heebie-jeebies, that's all.'

'I'll go first then?' he said, squinting through the gap to the embers that had almost gone out.

'If you don't mind.'

Tom rolled onto his front, and pressing his cheek flat against the ground wriggled forward into the slot. Cautiously he began to work his way under the rock and around the small stone that was somehow holding the whole thing up. He knew that it was stuck fast, but even so he did his best not to touch it, just in case . . . Squirming and twisting his head finally emerged close to the small pile of smouldering sticks on the far side. His trousers were ripped and elbows rubbed raw in the effort, but he had made it.

'I'm through,' he panted, and, sitting up on his knees, he threw the last stick he had carried with him onto the embers. Blowing on them hard, one meagre white flame leapt to life, and a moment later Pearl had appeared beside him.

'That was cosy,' she gasped. 'I couldn't help thinking that stone had been rolled under there deliberately.'

'I know,' said Tom, finding another stick on the floor and adding it to his fire. 'It's a bit like a gate that's been kept open, isn't it?'

Soon the little white flames were leaping and dancing, and Tom and Pearl could see more of the long narrow chamber they found themselves in. On the ceiling and walls there were carvings, twisting lines of people and monsters, but these were not as interesting as the alcoves that had been cut into the walls.

'Is it a burial chamber, do you think?'

It certainly looked like that. Picking up the longest burning sticks, Tom walked towards the nearest alcove and peered inside.

Underneath the bundle of tattered rags and dusty necklaces he could just make out the yellowing remains of a man, his skin stretched and cracked with age.

'Maybe they are witchdoctors,' he whispered, walking along to the next in line to see another dusty body, wearing an elaborate necklace of feathers round its neck.

'Didn't Geronimo say something about that?' said Pearl, standing next to him. 'He did. Something about ancestors coming down here and making an offering to the volcano.'

Tom looked at the lines of ghoulish, grinning faces and shivered: he couldn't remember all the details.

'Well whoever they are, they've certainly been here a very long time.'

'Except for maybe that one over there.'

Pearl pointed towards a dark shape in an alcove on the far side. 'Seems kind of different, doesn't it?'

Removing another sacred stick from the thin clasping fingers of a witchdoctor, Tom added it to the burning bundle in his hand.

'You're going to get us into serious trouble if you keep doing that, Tom,' whispered Pearl, and she was only half-joking. 'Why don't you use the torch?'

'I prefer to see what's coming,' he replied, sounding a lot braver than he actually felt.

Together they made their way down the hall towards the alcove where the dark shape lay.

'I don't like this one little bit,' whispered Pearl as they drew closer, and peered into the alcove at the dark form. There, lying beneath a fine white film of dust, was the body of a boy, curled up as if he was asleep. His hair was jet black and his skin was a yellowish grey, and he was wearing a ragged collection of old-fashioned clothes. On his feet he wore small black leather boots and around his neck there was a small heart-shaped locket.

'But . . . but he's white,' breathed Pearl, her voice quivering. 'Who is he?'

Taking a deep breath Tom leant over the boy's body and carefully twisted the locket around. There was a small inscription on the back, but it was so faded Tom could only make out two words.

'Dorian Rust.'

'Dorian Rust?' repeated Pearl.

And then beneath the layers of cobwebs Tom noticed the boy's papery hand was gripped around the remains of a notepad and a pencil. Something faint was scribbled on the page. Delicately he pushed aside the cobwebs and began to read.

'So these are my last thoughts. This world is a cruel place, and I pray that the next one may treat me better. I'm going now. November twenty-third, eighteen fifty . . . '

the last digit was buried in the fold of the paper. Tom bent down closer, almost touching the body.

'Nine.'

Suddenly there was a loud creak and the boy rolled onto his back.

'Ahh!!'

Tom and Pearl screamed and leapt in the air.

The boy had now changed position. Tom and Pearl stood tensed, waiting, expecting . . . nothing. Nothing at all. The torso lay on its back, detached from the arms and legs, entirely still.

'Wow.' Pearl breathed a loud sigh of relief. 'I thought for a moment . . .'

'Me too,' whispered Tom, his heart galloping. Stepping forward he instantly saw the reason why the torso had moved. The chest was split open, and there was nothing inside. No bones, no organs, nothing. Dorian Rust was nothing more than a thin shell of papery skin.

'That's . . . how is that possible?' said Pearl, gaping at the empty black cavity.

Tom did not reply, but a tumble of ideas began to cascade through his mind; he had seen something like this before . . . Don Gervase Askary, his daughter Lotus, hadn't they also left shells like this when they had turned back into beetles? Tom shuddered: they had . . . he knew it.

'Maybe they're all like this,' he said quietly, looking back along the lines of bodies. 'Maybe that is what happens down here. They change somehow.'

'Change into what?' said Pearl.

'Beetles.'

Pearl stared at him as if he was crazy.

'Beetles? But I thought that cark beetles infected your brain, or echo beetles copied you. How could a beetle be living inside . . . inside the skin of another person?'

Tom looked down at the body of the young boy. It did seem incredible, like something from a nightmare, but a nightmare that had already come true.

'Perhaps there is . . . another type, like a parasite, that lives inside you somehow, and then, when it wants to, it hatches out . . .'

'Really?' said Pearl, hardly able to believe what Tom was saying. 'You're serious aren't you?'

'I've seen it happen,' said Tom with a shiver. 'To Don Gervase Askary.'

Pearl shook her head in horror. 'That's disgusting.'

'I know,' nodded Tom grimly. 'It was.'

'So . . . if these people have changed into beetles somehow, then where have they gone?'

'Maybe where we're going,' he said, walking around the chamber looking for an exit. There was nothing obvious, and then Tom realized that the end wall was obscured by a pyramid of red sand. At the top of the heap there was a small gap.

'Look!' said Pearl suddenly, pointing to the far side of the heap. 'There's another one.'

Tom walked swiftly to where she stood and saw the body lying sprawled on the floor. His heart quickened: the old-fashioned clothes were identical, the dark hair, the pale yellowed skin . . .

'It's those twins who got lost, isn't it?' she said in a faltering voice. 'The two boys Geronimo told us about. The missionary's children.'

Pearl was right. Two boys, lost in the maze many years ago . . . this is where they had ended up. Trapped in this cave . . .

'What a terrible place to die,' she said quietly.

Moving closer, Tom noticed that this boy was lying at an unusual angle. His body was twisted, and his arms were outstretched, just as if he had thrown something with both hands. Tom turned back to the gap they had crawled through: it seemed to line up. Suddenly a thought crossed his mind.

'Do you think he was the one who rolled that stone under the rock?'

Pearl glanced over at the doorway, then back to the body.

'Looks like he's just thrown something, doesn't he?'

'But why would he do that?'

Tom shrugged his shoulders.

'Maybe they were trapped inside here. Maybe they triggered something by accident, and sand was rolling in and that great slab of stone was coming down and he rolled the stone underneath it so that they could get out.'

Pearl paused to think about this.

'So, why didn't they, then? He looks like he was killed somehow.'

Tom considered the twisted body of the boy and he had to admit Pearl was right. There was a riddle here, some terrible event that had lain undiscovered for all this time. Nervously, he bent forward and read a name in the collar of the boy's shirt.

'Caleb Rust.'

'Dorian and Caleb Rust. The lost boys who turned into beetles.'

For a moment they stood in silence, contemplating the two dead brothers.

'Doesn't make you feel good, does it?' said Pearl.

Tom shook his head.

'Not one little bit.'

'We should get going. Before this place disappears.'

'It's up there I reckon,' he said, indicating the small gap at the top of the sand heap. 'And I think it's time to put those ponchos on. Just in case this is where it begins.'

Pearl nodded seriously, and without a word unfastened the straps of the rucksack and pulled out the two thin silk ponchos, still in their greaseproof paper. She handed one to Tom and they pulled them on quickly and in silence. Tom was pleased to find that despite everything they had been through, these curious costumes still smelt vaguely of butter and almonds and rotten oranges. Whatever chemicals August Catcher had impregnated them with were still there.

'Is everything else OK?' he asked, pushing the hood back and rolling up his sleeves.

Pearl nodded. 'It's all there, except the jitterjat beetle, which is in your pocket.'

Tom had almost forgotten about that.

'Let's get up there first before we try it,' he said, looking up at the heap. 'Just in case I make a mistake.'

Pearl glanced at him anxiously.

'Well it's possible, isn't it?'

The pile of sand was not very high, but climbing up it was surprisingly difficult, and by the time they reached the top Tom and Pearl were panting hard. Scraping away the top of the pile, Tom widened the hole and, crawling through, they found themselves on a small stone ledge, beyond which was a short stone bridge that led to an archway cut into a cliff face.

'The entrance, perhaps?' he puffed.

Delving into his pocket Tom brought out the small cardboard box and Pearl handed him the thin wooden case.

'This always sounded a bit crazy to me,' she whispered, watching as Tom carefully lifted the small white feather out of its case and held it in his hand. Its fluorescence shone so brilliantly that it lit up their faces.

'How are you going to attach that to the beetle?'

'It's not as difficult as it sounds,' said Tom, taking out the small piece of thread. 'My dad was always mucking around with things like this. Measuring the strength of insects, watching where they flew, that sort of thing. All we need is . . . '

Tom stopped.

'What?'

He looked down at the feather crossly.

'It has to be still while I tie the feather on, otherwise it might just fly away.'

Pearl thought for a moment. 'Do you think it likes mango?'

'Maybe,' scowled Tom, annoyed with himself that he hadn't thought of this before.

Pearl opened a small pocket at the front of the rucksack and pulled out several large red fruits. 'Zumsteen didn't want them,' she said, quickly snapping out a penknife and cutting out a square. 'How do you think we should do it?'

'Mush it up a bit,' instructed Tom nervously.

Pearl placed the lump of wet fruit on the stone and did as she was told, as Tom gently slid the lid open and coaxed the purple-backed jitterjat out of its box.

'Come on,' he said, gently prodding its back. The jitterjat hesitated a moment, then scurried forward, its colour instantly changing to blend in with the dark stone. Cautiously it approached the mango's pulpy surface, walked round it a couple of times, then began to eat.

'That was lucky,' breathed Tom, with relief. Skilfully he made a small slipknot and slid it around one of the beetle's back legs, gently pulling it tight. The other end he attached to the feather. The beetle was so preoccupied with its meal it didn't even notice.

'And now?' said Pearl, impressed by Tom's quick work.

'I think we should carry it across that bridge, then let it go,' said Tom, hastily slipping the box back into the rucksack and slinging it over his shoulder. 'August said they had some kind of homing instinct, so hopefully it will take us in the right direction. The sooner the better.'

Carefully Tom scooped up the creature and the glowing feather in his hands, and crossed the small stone bridge to the opening in the rock on the other side.

'Right,' he said, holding out his cupped hands. 'The moment of truth.'

Slowly opening his fingers he let the jitterjat sit in his palm. It was exactly the same colour as his skin.

'Doesn't seem to want to go anywhere,' whispered Pearl, watching the beetle twitching. 'Maybe we are still too far away.'

'I don't think so,' said Tom, 'look.'

The jitterjat's antennae vibrated slowly, rhythmically, as if listening to a great beating heart.

'It's finding its bearings,' he whispered. 'Orientating itself.'

Tom closed his eyes, and he was unnerved to find that he could feel it too, a very distant pulse, thudding heavily. He strained to listen: was that his own heart, or something else?

'Tom!'

The voice slammed through Tom's thoughts and he blinked quickly.

'What? What is it?'

'It's off! It's gone!'

There was the jitterjat beetle, trailing the luminous feather behind it like a tiny light bulb, flying away down the dark rock passage ahead. Pearl stared at him curiously.

'Are you OK?'

'Yes. I'm fine. Fine no problem,' he mumbled, 'sorry, just . . . you're right let's go.'

Tom marched off down the passage, avoiding her eyes.

The jitterjat beetle was not a fast flier, but it was very determined. Keeping up a brisk walking pace, it flew upright, turning left into another rock passage, then right again, then left.

'Seems to know exactly where it's going,' whispered Pearl. 'That's good, isn't it?'

Tom did not reply, but he had a growing sense of how the jitterjat beetle was navigating through this dark warren. As they went on the throbbing in his head seemed to become steadily louder, and the jitterjat kept turning towards the sound. Suddenly the luminous feather wafted up and out of sight.

'Quick!'

Tom sprinted on to the corner—and stopped himself only just in time. Now he could see why the beetle had disappeared: they were standing on the edge of a cliff. Attached to the lip was a narrow walkway, made of white stone, which arched away into the darkness. Above, beyond, below, and as far as the eye could see were a myriad other white walkways, all identical, that snaked off in every direction. It looked like a vast tangle of string.

'What is this?' gasped Pearl.

Tom shook his head. He had a strong sense that this place, whatever it was, was not on the island of Tithona. It was the beginning of somewhere else, connected only by that slender walkway, and that was all. This cliff was where the world he knew ended, and another world began.

'But who . . . who built all this?' wondered Pearl in astonishment. 'Beetles?'

'Maybe,' breathed Tom.

Maybe this was the labyrinth that the old medieval explorer had talked about. Maybe this was how they travelled through time, down these pathways. And maybe the reason why there were so many of them was because each one led to a different time, a different place . . . so where did they all begin— Scarazand? Tom's thoughts exploded in a thousand different directions at once, but before he could follow any of them he spotted the luminous feather drifting out into the tangle of walkways.

'The jitterjat,' he said, 'come on, before we lose it.'

Running out onto the narrow stone bridge they set off in pursuit of the beetle. The jitterjat flew slowly, but in a direct line, and Tom and Pearl soon found that keeping up with it was very difficult: they had to keep jumping down onto lower levels, doubling back on themselves and looping round just to keep going in the same direction. It was like trying to climb through a giant tangle of spaghetti. As they hurried along Tom tried to explain to Pearl what he was thinking.

'But *why* did they bother to build all this, that's what I can't understand. Why do they want to go to loads of different times? What was the point?'

It was a good question, and Tom could not immediately think of an answer.

'Maybe they are like termites,' he said breathlessly. 'They don't *know* why. They just keep building and building and building. It's their instinct.'

'It must have taken them millions of years,' she said, marvelling at the sheer scale of the undertaking.

'Or maybe there's millions of them,' replied Tom uneasily. 'Billions even.'

'This way,' panted Pearl, leading Tom up a long looping path arcing over a great void. The jitterjat was now flying along just below them on the left hand side.

'Funny, isn't it, how it's somehow navigating through all this. Do you trust it?'

Tom nodded; he was trying to ignore the steady beating in his head. It was like a pulse now; he could feel it, every beat . . .

'Oh!'

Pearl stopped dead, and stared up at the underside of the walkway just above them.

'What is it?' hissed Tom, but no sooner had the words left him than he had seen it too. There, motionless against the stone and well camouflaged, hung a large white insect, rather like a woodlouse with tentacles, except that it must have been as long as a car. It was busily rubbing white liquid oozing from its mouth across a gap between two stones, repairing the hole. Soon more and more of these creatures began to appear, starting and stopping in jerky movements, working their way through the tangle of walkways, gluing this, mending that.

'Maintenance gang,' whispered Pearl, watching in fascination, and then suddenly there was a scratching sound behind as one of the large white creatures came beetling up towards them. Pearl stared at it, ashen-faced.

'Erm . . . Tom, what—'

'Down,' he whispered quickly, 'it can't see us remember.'

Dropping to the floor beneath their ponchos they waited as the insect approached. Reaching Pearl first, it probed her blindly, then Tom heard a muffled squeal as its wiry tentacles picked her up and threw her onto its back.

'Pearl?'

There was no answer, but the very next moment two busy antennae danced across him.

'Ow!' he shouted, as the creature hoisted him up and slammed him down next to her.

'You OK?' she whispered.

'I think so,' he said breathlessly. Clinging on to the knobbly shell Tom dared to lift his head and look out. The creature was moving at speed down the stone walkway, and he was relieved to see the luminous feather drifting far ahead in the same direction.

'Must have picked us up for a reason,' whispered Tom. 'If it's a builder then it's going to—'

'Use us to build with?' suggested Pearl, helpfully. Suddenly the creature crossed over to another pathway and stopped abruptly. The tentacles whipped back and before Tom knew what was happening it had picked him up.

'Hey!' he shouted as it tried to cover his head and feet with white glue oozing from its mouth. 'Stop!'

But the great creature seemed to be both deaf and blind. In the next instant Tom found himself being thrust head-first into a crack between two rocks on the underside of the path where a stone block had fallen out.

'Ow!'

Tom was not a good fit. He was taken out, turned round and wedged in backwards, then sideways.

'Get off!' he shouted, struggling in the insect's grip. 'Get—'

And at that moment the creature lost interest its awkward rock, and with a loud squeak tossed Tom out into the darkness.

'NO!'

Thump! Two large claws caught him, punching the air out of his chest, and before Tom knew what was happening he was flung onto the back of another, much larger creature, trundling along in the same direction. All around him were rocks and boulders, and Tom could only think that it was like being in the back of a truck, except the truck was another large white beetle . . .

'Leave me go! LEAVE ME GO I SAID!'

There was Pearl high above, being mercilessly squashed and jumbled about as the blind builder tried to ram her into the hole.

'I AM NOT A ROCK!' she yelled, and finally the insect decided to believe her. Giving up, it scurried on, complaining noisily, and the next moment threw her out into the darkness.

'Ow!'

The lumbering truck-like creature plucked her out of the air and unceremoniously hurled her back onto the pile of boulders next to Tom.

'Ow! That really hurt.'

'You OK?'

'No I'm not,' she said crossly, rubbing her sore head.

'Sorry,' he said. 'Looks like we're with the rejects.'

Catching his breath, Tom crawled across the boulders and searched the tangle of walkways for the jitterjat. Where was it? Left, right . . . he couldn't see it anywhere. Tom's heart quickened: if they got lost now they'd never find the way out of this labyrinth . . .

'There it is!' he said suddenly, spotting the tiny shining feather floating directly beneath them. It was turning towards a narrow column of rock that rose like a tree through the tangle.

'There what is?'

'The jitterjat,' he gasped, struggling to his feet. 'We've got to get off this thing right now. It's going down into that—'

But at that moment Tom's foot slipped and there was an angry hiss beneath him.

'What—'

Suddenly the large pile of boulders on which they lay rose up as one and marched straight down the long bony back of the great insect, taking Tom and Pearl with them. The moment the boulders touched the stone walkway they scattered in all directions, squeaking noisily.

'But . . . but they're all . . . beetles?' gasped Pearl as she tumbled to the ground.

Tom watched the weird, rock-like creatures escape in silence. What strange, alien world was this? He closed his eyes and felt that thudding inside his head growing more insistent now: rising and falling, pulsing in waves. It must be some kind of aftershock . . . He mustn't tell her. He must ignore it. Pretend it wasn't there somehow.

'The jitterjat,' he muttered grimly, seeing the feather glide in through the stone entrance just below. 'We'd better go.'

Swinging his legs over the edge of the stone walkway, Tom dropped down onto the pathway beneath and helped Pearl after him. They trotted on in silence, following the luminous feather through into the dark rock passage. There was a gathering noise somewhere up ahead.

'Do you think . . . could this be it?' whispered Pearl anxiously.

'It's got to be,' said Tom, as the roaring, clattering, sizzling sounds grew louder and louder. The jitterjat accelerated and they quickened their pace, following the glowing feather until it turned a corner and flew straight towards a circle of bright light. They hesitated for a moment: the chaotic din was coming from somewhere out in the light beyond: it sounded like a great factory, or a machine in motion.

Pearl closed her eyes and took a deep breath—she felt she didn't want to walk another step.

'Come on,' whispered Tom, and ignoring the dark pulses inside him he began to edge forward. Steeling herself, Pearl followed after him, until at last they reached the tunnel's end, and peered out . . .

CHAPTER 17

SCARAZAND

The jitterjat beetle hovered for a moment in mid air, its purple body iridescent in the light.

'Whump!'

Something hard and heavy flashed before them and in an instant the beetle was gone. All that was left was the luminous white feather, floating down gracefully into the chasm.

'What was that?' gasped Pearl.

Tom dropped the visor of his poncho and edged out as far as he dared.

'That was that,' he said softly.

Pearl craned forward and, looking up, saw the centipede, as high as a house, hanging off the wall directly above them. Its pale brown eyes stared blankly, apparently unable to see her. Quickly she withdrew into the safety of the hole, her heart racing. Painful memories were flooding back.

'Do you remember, do you remember I told you—'

Tom touched her arm and pressed his fingers to his lips.

'Look down there,' he whispered.

Pearl steeled herself, and peered over the edge of the hole once more. For a moment she could do nothing more than stare in dumbfounded silence. The hole in which they crouched was one of millions cut into the walls of a vast, spherical cave. At the centre stood a thick column of black rock, rising up like a skyscraper out of a deep chasm far below, and as it rose higher it grew narrower and narrower, tapering to a fine point where it met the ceiling high above. This too was honeycombed with holes that hung like black stars. The whole, vast cave was lit up by luminous bellied insects the size of airships that drifted slowly around the central column.

'Scarazand,' she whispered. 'Hardly seems real, does it?'

Tom nodded, and his gaze was drawn down to the fizzing, clattering noises far below.

'Look,' he said excitedly, 'look at those bridges.'

All around the great stone column, spindle-thin causeways stretched across the chasm and connected to the cave walls, and marching across these precarious-looking structures were all manner of insects great and small. Large armoured creatures, nose to tail like trucks, long necked lolloping things like giraffes, and some that seemed to be walking backwards or even upside down.

'Oh!' Pearl gasped. 'Look, look in the middle of that big bridge.'

Tom scrutinized the weird collection of life teeming across what looked like the central causeway and he was equally astonished.

'People?' he whispered, not quite believing that it could be true.

There was a group of men, looking vaguely like monks in long grey capes and small black hats, making their way through the swirling tide of insects.

'Prisoners, perhaps?' suggested Pearl.

But there were no guards or chains that Tom could see: they didn't particularly look like prisoners.

'Maybe they are coming in from the future.'

'Or going out to the past,' Pearl replied, spotting others moving in the opposite direction.

Either way, seeing humans in this alien place was strangely comforting, and as Tom studied the rock itself he could make out windows, balconies, battlements—there even seemed to be something like a cathedral at the top. Scarazand was like a vast, vertical beetle's nest, with a higgledy-piggledy town clinging on to its upper reaches. And somewhere deep inside it, there was Pearl's father and brother, Oscarine Zumsteen, and maybe even his own parents too . . . maybe . . .

'Come on then,' he said with a determined expression, 'let's head for that main bridge.'

Drawing the long grey ponchos carefully around them and lowering their visors, Tom and Pearl crept out of the hole and followed a steep, craggy path down the side of the sphere towards the wide causeway.

'See, we're invisible,' whispered Tom, glancing back up at the great brown centipede hanging above them, its black jaws drooling.

'Thank goodness for that,' shuddered Pearl, spying more of them scattered around the walls of the cave, snapping viciously at anything that moved.

Soon they reached the level of the main causeway and joined the chaos. All around them insects were streaming out towards holes in the sphere, while an equal number were emerging, just as Tom and Pearl had done, to make their way down to the causeway. Dodging around a pack of vicious looking termites, Tom and Pearl drifted in behind a large cow-like creature ambling towards the great gates.

'Stay close,' murmured Tom, as they passed between two vast rhinoceros beetles the size of tanks that appeared to be guarding the causeway. Their flanks were daubed with crudely painted black and gold flags, and beside them stood groups of soldiers, identical young men with narrow, shaven heads and bored, yellow eyes. Tom hunched his shoulders deep into his poncho as they passed right under their noses.

'Scary, huh?' whispered Pearl as soon as they were out of earshot. 'What are all these soldiers doing?'

'I don't know,' whispered Tom nervously, spotting more of them standing at intervals along the causeway. He had little idea what Scarazand might be like, but he certainly had not expected anything like this: it was like a military state. Halfway across, Tom and Pearl fell in behind a group of tourists, hard-bitten women and men dressed in what looked like green plastic blankets. Their leader strode ahead, holding aloft a long luminous stick with an eye stuck on the end of it, which might have once belonged to some gigantic snail.

'See Scarazand an' die . . . tha's what 'e said, ain't it?' marvelled one man, staring up at the vast edifice rising before him.

'I's never ever believin' I'd get to this golden place,' clucked a round woman. 'Ya see the size of 'em bujangas?'

'Not in all my livingness!' rasped her friend, glancing back in awe at the two vast rhinoceros beetles.

'Hail, hail, the revolushy!' yelled a wizened character at the front, jabbing his bony arm into the air.

'They says tis even betterin' than t'was before.'

'Course tis. Now t'em blazzards in the Chamber is done way with. Most certain.'

'An' to think they 'ad us over a bleedin' barrel for thousand score years.'

'Pilgrims! Pilgrims!' screeched the leader as they reached the far end of the bridge, stopping beneath the watchful eye of two more vast bujangas, upon which another gang of soldiers sat.

'You is about to enter Scarazand, city of dreams. Be a-doffin' of yous 'ats an' salutin' to yous glorious noo leada!'

Instantly the group uncovered their bony heads and stared up at what looked like a large waxy scroll that had been fastened to the wall of black rock beyond the gate. Out of the surface materialized an enormous, familiar face. Instantly Tom felt the blood chill in his heart. The large, milky green eyes blinked once and stared down with a bored expression.

'Welcome, good comrades and pilgrims, welcome to you all,' the voice boomed, and the small mouth split open to reveal a set of cracked and yellow teeth.

'Oh!' squealed a man, and threw himself to the ground before the image. The eyes blinked lazily once more.

'It's him,' whispered Pearl in a trembling terrified voice. 'It's—'

'Sshh!'

A beaky-nosed tourist turned round and he was about to launch into an angry tirade when he was surprised to find nobody there. Nobody that *he* could see, anyway.

'You have come from far and wide to visit Scarazand,' boomed the enormous head of Don Gervase Askary. 'It is the centre of our new world, and I guarantee you will not be disappointed. Enjoy its many delights, feel for yourselves the heartbeat of our glorious Queen. Let it nourish your hearts, inspire your minds, and send you back to wherever you came from, to live out whatever portion of your tiny lives you have left, with renewed faith in our noble cause.'

'Amen!' shouted the tourists.

'All hail our glorious revolution!' boomed the head.

'All hail! All hail! The glorious revolution!' shouted the tourists at the tops of their voices.

Don Gervase smiled, then disappeared.

'I can't believe it . . . ' murmured the thin man, crawling to his feet. 'I've actually seen him . . . seen *him*.'

'Ain't 'ee just the bee'snees?' crooned the small fat woman.

'And so 'tractive!' tittered her friend.

'This way, comrades!' shouted the leader, forcing his way through the moving tide of creatures. 'No dawderlin' now, as you don't want to find yourselves somewhere you shouldn't. Scarazandy security is tightest in the known world!'

He pointed up at a round spiked beetle clinging to the wall. It had a dull red carapace and large pink eyes the size of saucers. 'You dig me?'

The two ladies in front of Tom and Pearl nodded vigorously, then looked across the street at a pair of very tall hooded men standing on the corner. The men held red bombardier beetles on leashes, and the tatty crests on their helmets bore the same spiked beetle insignia.

'Skrolls,' whispered one to the other breathlessly.

'Skrolls?'

'Secret Police, innit?'

'Oh my!'

With a frightened titter the two ladies scurried away up a nar-row alley to catch up with the rest of their party. Tom and Pearl stared at the Skrolls. They moved with terrifying slowness, and their angular grey faces seemed to be made from charred wood.

'I never thought,' whispered Pearl, 'I had no idea that he was like . . . so powerful.'

'Me neither,' shuddered Tom, watching the large red bom-bardier beetles straining and snapping at the heels of the passers by. Of course it stood to reason that Don Gervase would have a secret police—he must have spies everywhere. How else could he control this vast edifice except through fear?

'Sounds like he has led some kind of revolt against the Chamber, whoever they were, and taken over,' said Pearl watch-ing the endless stream of beetles. There were literally thousands of them passing every moment, some the size of horses, some no bigger than cats endlessly scrabbling in and out of the alleyways that led straight into the rock. 'But how do you think he man-aged it, against all this lot?'

'Maybe there was some massive beetle battle somewhere, in the future,' suggested Tom.

'Perhaps,' Pearl continued. 'I guess he must have promised them something pretty big in return for storming this place.'

Tom said nothing. He had a terrible feeling that he knew what that something was; it was the elixir, the extraordinary potion invented by August Catcher which he had used to preserve his exhibits in the Scatterhorn Museum. Wasn't that what the bee-tles wanted more than anything else? Wasn't that what Don

Gervase had hunted through time and space to find, the secret of eternal life, the potion that could extend their short lives, and maybe even make them immortal? Pearl was probably right: he probably *had* used this promise to gather a vast army and storm Scarazand.

'Come on,' Tom whispered harshly; he had seen more than enough. 'Let's follow those tourists and find out where they keep the prisoners.'

Shrinking deep into their wafting silk ponchos, Tom and Pearl cautiously made their way up past the pair of Skrolls and on into the narrow cobbled alley. Up here there were barely any insects, but a thronging mass of people, most of whom were duplicates of each other: pairs of ratty-faced doctors in long black coats, straggling groups of moon-eyed tourists and dark-skinned witch-doctors with curious beetles perched like parrots on their shoulders. The shops that lined the narrow winding street were doing a brisk business, selling curious trinkets of every description. There were black models of Scarazand, made from '100 per cent rock an' beetle spit', tattered gold and black flags and armbands, 'genuine worn in the battle of Callaboose', and wizened old street traders hawking trays of roughly cut busts of Don Gervase.

'Have your piece of him, have your piece!' called one, who was missing a leg and wore a strange helmet perched on the back of his head. 'Prove you's true comrades of the revolution! Show yer 'legiance to the leada!'

Don Gervase was everywhere: and it was not only the trinkets. On every wall there were blank, waxy posters that frequently lit up with his large oval face accompanied by his voice booming a slogan. 'Strength in numbers', 'One heartbeat, one blood', 'Long life for a new age'. The images and sounds flashed through the crowds, and everywhere there were those pink-eyed beetles, watching . . .

'Hooley Brothers: General Outfitters and Directionists,' read Pearl, looking through a window into what might have been a chemist's or a pet shop. 'Lost? Confused? Don't be! Ask the Pros!' was scrawled across the door.

'Shall we?' she whispered.

Tom peered in the window—it seemed safe enough.

'Let's just go in and see,' he said. 'Maybe they don't have those beetle spies everywhere.'

The small interior was stuffed with boxes containing beetles of all colours, giant flies, and hundreds of small wooden drawers.

'Fast and slow, long haul, sprints, challengin' navigations, 'culiar environs, all voyages through the labyrinth catered for, gents,' explained a small man with a walrus moustache to three fresh-faced identical young men with ginger hair, gawping across the counter. 'Now where is it you young fellas gotta goo?'

One of the three drew out a scrap of paper and struggled to read the words.

'Tim . . . buc . . . too, fourteen . . . ninety . . . too?'

'Timbuctoo, 1492, that I can dew,' wheezed the man, 'you got that, Nige?'

Another man at the back with an even larger walrus moustache raised his hand and consulted a battered book.

'My brother, he's havin' a butchers for ye,' he grinned. 'What you on, lads, amulet squad?'

'Cark spreading, Mr Hooley, sir.'

'Carkin', eh?'

'Snackatit 341!' shouted Nige, squinting at the page.

'Snackatit 341.' Hooley whistled loudly. 'Now there's a super beaut.'

With a hook he fished down a small wooden box and shook out a case containing a yellowish cocoon.

'Due to hatch tomorrow this one,' said Hooley, placing it before them on the counter. 'Red and yella coloured wings, nice flyer, not too fast. Snackatit is quality breed. Accurate to within five exits, that.'

'Five exits?' repeated the second young man, somewhat taken aback. 'But we daren't make a mistake. It's forbidden.'

'Is that a fact?' rasped Hooley, his moustache bristling. 'Listen sonny. This here Snackatit likes sand, see. Sahara sand. Follows the vibrations. But there's an awful lot of that Sahara sand, 'en't there? Now, you's sayin' get me to Timbuktu, and I'm sayin' yes, *maybe* Timbuktu, but possibly Timbucthree, or even Timbucfour!' Hooley chuckled, pleased with his own little joke. 'I ain't makin' no guarantees where's yous gonna emerge, cos the labyrinth, s'endless, innit? An' it's still being built. You seen all them holes out there?'

The three young men looked very confused.

'But . . . don't you have anything more accurate, like a map?' said one.

'A map? A map?' Hooley guffawed loudly, and so did Nige at the back. Their moustaches wobbled like squirrels. 'What, was you born yesterday?'

'That's right,' said the first young man. 'How did you know?'

Hooley raised his eyebrows and shook his head.

'Listen lads, Snackatit 341 is best you're gonna get round here,' he rasped. 'Now what else—eye-nacks, thrumma juice?'

'Erm . . .'

Hooley delved under the counter and brought out three boxes and opened them up. Inside appeared to be three sets of yellowish green contact lenses.

'Eye-nacks,' said Hooley, laying them out. 'Latest style. One hundred per cent glasswing construction. Tinted same colour as our glorious leader,' he winked.

'What are they for?'

'Recognizing each other. It's a fashion thing mainly, but we sell a lot of these. Helps keen whippersnappers like yerselves recognize each other out in the big bad world. Judge a person by the colour of his eyes an' you're halfway there.'

The young men looked down at the yellowy lenses doubtfully.

'But . . . are we really allowed to have the same colour as . . . as the glorious—'

'Course you is! There's been a new directive, in't there, Nige?'

''S right,' snorted Nige from the back of the shop. 'New directive.'

'Look,' hissed Hooley, pointing up at the ceiling to where a pink-eyed beetle hung in the centre, watching everything. 'Would I sell you boys something that ain't official?'

The three young men swallowed hard.

'And the thrumma juice?'

Hooley smiled and produced three small black bottles made of moulded beetle armour.

'Thrumma juice. Keeps you thrummin', don't it? It's what we call in the trade "a perpetuator". What's your span?'

One of the lads lifted up his sleeve and showed the small blue number tattooed under his elbow.

'Twenty days, ten hours.'

Hooley nodded sagely.

'Well, with this here thrumma juice, "a subtle concoction of pupae sweat, ground caddis tails, and Scarazand gold pulp",' he said, reading the label, 'you are lookin' at, say, another *seven* whole hours of life.'

The lads' faces lit up.

'Seven whole hours!' they all chimed together. 'That's incredible.'

'So it is,' growled Hooley, 'and until things change around here and we get a *proper* bit of *longevity*—'

'All hail to our glorious leader!' interrupted Nige loudly from the back.

'All hail! All hail!' shouted the three young men in concert.

'Indeed,' added Hooley, glancing warily up at the large pink-eyed beetle on the ceiling. 'Not that I am wishin' to belittle the great sacrifices of the many millions out on the plains of Callaboose—'

'They died that we may live! They died that we may live!' chanted the young men, automatically.

'Precisely lads, precisely. And until you *do* live a little longer, this here thrumma juice is the best a beetle person can get. Nine crockits the lot,' said Hooley abruptly. 'Take it or leave it.'

Tom and Pearl watched the young men pay up excitedly and with a nervous glance at the beetle above quickly followed them out into the street.

'Wow,' whispered Pearl, as soon as they were back amongst the crowds. 'So those boys were echoes, because they were identical, right?'

Tom nodded; they certainly looked that way.

'Going out to spread cark beetles, infecting people. Poisoning their brains. Making them want to come back to this place.'

'Surfer dudes?' said Pearl, watching a group of bleach-blond backpackers shamble past in shorts and flip-flops. 'My dad looks a bit like that.' She paused for a moment. 'So, do you really think they're all—'

'Makes sense doesn't it?' shrugged Tom. 'That's how they knew how to find this place. Everyone in Scarazand must be, except for us.'

Pearl took a deep breath: suddenly the immensity of their task seemed truly daunting.

'We need to ask someone where the jail is.'

Tom nodded grimly, and spotted another pink-eyed beetle clinging to the wall opposite. That was going to be a lot more difficult than it seemed.

'Tickets for the show! Tickets buy or sell, anyone need tickets!' screamed a small man with a twisted, beetle-like body as he dodged through the crowd. He wore a ragged greatcoat tied up with a rope, and a faded cap, and his head was so flattened that he looked more like a praying mantis than a person.

'What's on?' asked Tom, falling in behind him.

'Tonight's show?' squawked the strange little character without turning round. 'Demon dog racing, bujanga bangers, a skinnynip ballet, and a terrifyin' new creation straight from the cocoon gardens, my friend. The very first appearance of the—'
He turned round to find that he was alone.

'Havin' a good chat with yerself down there, are we, mantis man?' laughed a shaven headed soldier, sneering down at the creature.

'Ha-ha, very—'

'Half-breed,' spat his mate, cuffing the little man hard over the head. 'What a disgusting mess. I'm surprised they let you survive the revolution.'

The mantis man steeled himself.

'Now just look here, sonny,' he began, jabbing a finger at the tattered black and gold ribbon on his coat. 'I'm a front line infantry shock troop, first out the trench, me! Just cos I ain't too pretty don't—'

The mantis man stopped abruptly as a Skroll loomed over the top of him.

'Pass,' it whispered, and a strange smell of sulphur oozed from its mouth. The soldiers grinned.

'Pass?'

The mantis man gulped, then pulled off his cap and delved inside it.

'I . . . it's here somewhere, mate, honest.' He laughed awkwardly. 'Stone me—where've I put it . . . '

The Skroll extended a withered, blackened hand from its long tattered cape.

'Pass,' it hissed again.

'Ow,' howled mantis man as the red-eyed bombardier beetle pecked hard at his twisted legs. 'Call it off now, won't cha mista?'

The hooded figure stared down at him impassively.

'What, no pass, half-breed?' said the soldier. 'Tsk, tsk. You's very much in the wrong place.'

'Better go back down to the underworld and get it, scum,' sneered his mate, and with a brutal kick sent the mantis man flying.

'Why you—' But the mantis man thought better of it and slunk away, rubbing his misshapen body. Pearl glared angrily at the soldier, who looked straight through her.

'Come on,' whispered Tom, pulling her away, 'let's not get into this.'

At the top of the alley the road divided. Most of the tourists and pilgrims seemed to be heading on up the hill towards the muffled roars of what sounded like a stadium.

'Up there, maybe?' said Tom, looking around for a signpost.

'Doesn't exactly sound like a jail, does it?' said Pearl, listening to the cheers. 'We've just got to ask someone, somehow.'

Tom nodded, it was the only logical thing to do.

'The problem is, how? We are invisible.'

Pearl watched the strange procession of people and insects moving back and forth in frustration.

'But *everyone* looks different here. Do you think they will really notice if we took these cloaks off?'

'Definitely,' Tom replied, spotting another large red beetle with bulging pink eyes clinging to the corner of a building. 'I bet the moment those things see an intruder we are going to be in serious trouble.'

'Well what do *you* suggest?' she hissed crossly. Irritated now, Pearl turned to face down the hill and saw a dark man in a sandy red cloak slam the door of a small narrow shop and walk off. 'Amulets bought and sold', read the dirty sign above the door. Amulets . . . *amulets* . . .

'That's the place,' she whispered, staring at the tumbledown building.

'Amulets?' read Tom, nonplussed. 'Why amulets?'

Pearl did not reply, but slipped across the street between two giraffe-sized insects and darted through the door. The interior was dark and empty, and smelt vaguely of old books.

'Pearl, what—'

'Ssh,' she whispered, pointing to a small, pear-shaped man dozing quietly behind the counter. On his bulbous head he wore a thick woolly hat and on his lap was something very much like a fat grey cat—except it wasn't, it was a fat grey caterpillar, and it appeared to be dozing too. Around the walls were shelves and jars crammed with amulets of all shapes and sizes. Taking a quick look up Pearl pulled off her poncho and rolled it into a ball. Tom stared at her in horror.

'It's the only way,' she said simply. 'We have to risk it.'

Tom shook his head, and glanced up into the gloomy rafters. Was there a pink-eyed beetle lurking up there? He couldn't be sure.

'You're insane,' he muttered angrily, but the next moment he too had taken off his poncho.

'Hello, and welcome.'

Tom and Pearl almost jumped out of their skins as the familiar voice rumbled behind them. They turned to see the face of Don Gervase emerging from a piece of waxy paper stuck to the wall.

'Can you imagine all your wildest dreams coming true? Can you? Well this could be your lucky day. Chose an amulet, any amulet. Come on, comrades, don't be shy. Bring it to the ministry and try your luck. Remember, I will grant the person who finds the winning amulet anything in my power. Anything at all. Good luck . . . '

The head smiled and faded back into the waxy paper.

'Ahh.'

There was a snuffling from behind the counter as the sleeping man woke up and stared at Tom and Pearl with bleary eyes.

'Come come, Huffkin,' he said, shifting the dozy caterpillar onto the counter. Even awake the small man looked very tired.

'Hi,' said Pearl, approaching the counter with a winning smile. 'We've just arrived at Scarazand and we don't quite know what to do.'

The man rubbed his nose and appeared somewhat surprised.

'Arrived? Where from?'

'Erm . . . Tithona.'

The man stared at the children curiously, then shrugged his shoulders.

'Never heard of it. Well?'

'Actually,' said Tom quickly, 'actually, we were wondering if you could help us. We are looking for the jail.'

The man blinked. 'The jail? Young comrade, you are mistaken. This is not the jail.'

'I know *this*—'

'I take it you can read?' interrupted the man, his reedy voice growing irritated. 'This is an amulet shop. AM-YOU-LET. You come in here because you haven't got one, and therefore you have to buy one. From me. Got it?'

'We *have* to buy one?'

'All new visitors to Scarazand must register their amulets at the Ministry. There are no exceptions to this new directive.'

'So, do you mean *everyone*'s looking for amulets?'

The man stared at Tom suspiciously.

'I'm surprised you haven't heard. Have you not received your directives?'

'Erm . . . ' Tom felt the colour rise in his cheeks. 'Well—'

'We were born yesterday,' explained Pearl with a smile. 'That's why we don't know anything. In fact we don't really know why our glorious leader wants this amulet at all.'

The shopkeeper continued to stare at them. He was convinced there was something peculiar about these two: they looked very strange and they asked far too many questions.

'Do *you* know why he wants it?' asked Pearl, innocently.

'Ha!' He snorted loudly. 'Your youth may excuse your ignorance, young lady, but that is a very unwise question to ask—or even think. Treason talk.'

'It's something to do with controlling the queen, isn't it?' she said, pressing the point.

The shopkeeper's face turned grey and he shot a fearful glance at the ceiling. Obviously there was a spy beetle skulking up there in the shadows. Tom wondered what she was driving at.

'That is simply rubbish. C-c-codswallop,' blustered the little man, 'our glorious leader does not rely on mere trinkets—'

'So it is then?' persisted Pearl.

'Wild, wild speculation, I . . . you'd better leave,' insisted the shopkeeper angrily. 'This shop is now closed.'

'Pearl?'

'One more thing,' she said, ignoring Tom.

'Out!' commanded the man, tottering round the counter and marching towards them purposefully.

'Do you know what the right amulet looks like?'

The shopkeeper's eyes bulged; he seemed as if he was about to explode.

'I mean, you must have some idea, having seen so many.'

'Get out!' he shrieked. 'Get out before I call—'

Pearl calmly put her hand inside her waistband.

'Is it like this?'

Tom glanced down at the object in her palm and his mouth fell open. For a moment he was too shocked to speak.

'Sorry Tom,' she said apologetically. 'I had to take it.'

The shopkeeper peered at the clear ball, decorated with swirling black patterns. In an instant his mood had entirely changed. Glancing up at the ceiling he pushed Tom and Pearl roughly around the corner behind a large pile of boxes next to a small oval window.

'Where did you find that?' he said abruptly. 'I mean, comrade, please show me your most interesting amulet again.' He smiled, weirdly. 'Please?'

Pearl stared at the shopkeeper hard: he looked like a peculiar garden gnome and she had no reason to trust him, but it was clear that something had excited his curiosity.

'Only if you can tell us if it's the real thing.'

The man grunted in irritation. 'Only the Ministry have authority to do that, missy.'

'What makes you so interested in it, then?'

The man shrugged his shoulders, feigning indifference. 'Just curious. Have you . . . err, tried to use it?'

'How could we have done that?' demanded Tom angrily. 'It's just some trinket we bought in a market.'

'Where it comes from is immaterial,' said the shopkeeper with an oily smirk. He was refusing to be drawn off the scent.

'Do *you* know how to use it?' asked Pearl.

'That is restricted knowledge,' he replied, evasively. 'I have merely . . . heard the rumours.'

Pearl stared at the little man hard: he seemed to be telling the truth.

'Very well then, show us how you think it's done,' she said harshly, placing the ball in his small hand. The shopkeeper stifled a grin—then held it up to the light.

'Could be a fake of course. Plenty of them about,' he muttered, peering through the dark patterns into the clear interior. He stroked the surface very carefully.

'So you've never used it, you say?'

Pearl shook her head. Tom noticed there was a hungry gleam in the man's eye now.

'And there was no case or jewelled casket or anything to protect it?'

'Why, should there be?'

The shopkeeper seemed vaguely disappointed, but nevertheless held the ball lightly in one hand and screwed his eyes tight shut. Then with his other hand he began to minutely massage its surface, barely moving his fingers at all.

'What are you asking it to do?' said Pearl.

The little man ignored her and kept his fingers playing across its surface in a circular pattern . . . and before Tom knew it there was a great rumbling in his head. Closing his eyes, he saw an angry red wave coming up over the black horizon and accelerate towards him in a noisy hissing rush, a jumble of words and screams . . .

'Ow!'

Tom shook his head angrily and forced his eyes open. His brain felt as if it was on fire.

'That really hurt.'

Taking a deep breath, he saw Pearl staring out of the window, wide-eyed.

'Out there,' she whispered in a low, astonished voice. 'Look.'

Tom glanced through the dirty window at the crowded street: it was like watching a film running backwards. Every single person, insect, and half-breed was moving very slowly in reverse. Tom turned back to the shopkeeper, who seemed to have gone into a kind of trance. His large woolly hat was bobbing up and down.

'He's . . . he's doing that, isn't he?' whispered Pearl, watching the man's gnarled thumb moving around the edge of the ball, barely touching it. The decorated surface seemed to be humming . . . The shopkeeper exhaled deeply, then gently began to roll his head on his shoulders. After a moment all the people in the street began to do the same. This time Tom was ready for it, and through sheer force of will managed to ignore the red wave as it pulsed right through him. There could be no doubt that this was the right amulet now. He stared down at the beetle ball furiously: how had they managed to bring the most powerful object in the world right into the heart of Scarazand?

'We have got to get out of here,' he grunted, pulling on his grey poncho and flipping up the hood.

'I'm sorry,' said Pearl, hastily doing the same. 'Really I am, Tom, but I knew you what you would say. Don't you see it's all we've got?'

Tom was so angry he couldn't see anything at all.

'Look, now we know it's the one let's take it up to the Ministry straight away and declare it.'

'Fine,' snorted Tom tersely, 'and what then? Ask Don Gervase Askary to release our families in return? Are you insane?'

'I—'

But Pearl never finished her sentence as at that moment the door banged open.

'Scurf!' shouted a familiar voice. 'Would you mind telling me precisely what is going on?'

Tom just had time to pull the visor over his face as he glimpsed a black ponytail bobbing between the boxes. The shopkeeper snapped out of his trance and blinked wildly.

'Scurf!'

The next moment Lotus Askary stood before them. The sight that met her was so strange she was momentarily lost for words. There was the diminutive Mr Scurf, cowering in the corner, cupping his hands. Suddenly his hands were knocked upwards by some unseen force, and a plastic ball flew up into the air, seemingly of its own accord. And then the ball vanished. And at the very same moment, Lotus glimpsed the face of a frightened girl, hovering in mid-air.

'You?' she said, certain she had seen that face before. 'Who are you?'

But before she knew it the girl had disappeared too . . .

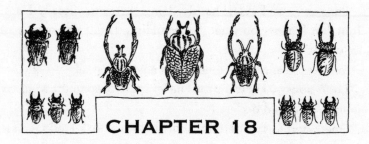

CHAPTER 18

THE LOWEST OF THE LOW

Tom and Pearl dived behind a pile of boxes as two looming Skrolls swept past them into the shop, their red-eyed bombardier beetles straining at the leash.

'Please, not Huffkin!'

There was a muffled yelp and the caterpillar was no more.

'What is going on, Scurf!' yelled Lotus. 'What was that you were playing with just now?'

Scurf howled. 'I . . . these . . . two carks, I think they were . . . asking too many questions . . . they had an amulet, it—'

'What amulet did they have, Scurf?' she spat.

'I-I don't know,' he stammered, 'please, my lady, I had never seen such a thing before . . . '

Lotus glared around the room.

'And you are telling me that they've disappeared?'

Scurf stared at the floor and nodded.

'Poor Huffkin,' he said quietly, looking down at the mess that was the caterpillar.

'Search this place,' ordered Lotus, and the two Skrolls set to work. Scurf watched in silence as the red bombardiers began to systematically ransack the shop, tipping over every shelf and throwing out every drawer.

'You were promoted up here, weren't you, Scurf?' said Lotus, picking up a small blue figurine.

'That's c-c-correct, my lady,' he stammered, 'from gang master mining detail, level 2469.'

'Level 2469.' Lotus tossed the figure nonchalantly to the floor, smashing it. 'Well, well,' she smirked, 'the underside of the underworld: the lowest of the low. I thought you looked odd.'

'That's right, my lady,' quivered Scurf. 'Only duplication and city jail below that.'

Lotus walked up to Scurf and whispered very quietly in his ear.

'And that is precisely where you shall be returning, if you don't provide some answers very, very soon. Do I make myself clear?'

Scurf nodded in terror.

'I want to see that ball—and those two cark converts—at the Ministry. Imminently.'

Lotus turned on her heel and strode out of the door.

'Come on,' whispered Tom, and pulling Pearl by the hand he followed close behind Lotus, sliding out just before the door slammed shut. Out in the street, a small crowd had gathered around a strange contraption that looked like an enormous hollow egg, harnessed to two gleaming white insects. There was a gasp as Lotus appeared from the shop in her white cape and stepped inside, and another when the whole surface of the egg began to flicker and blur, as the beating of thousands of golden moths' wings lifted the entire machine off the ground. Lotus flicked the reins nonchalantly and the two spiky creatures reared to life then galloped away up the hill.

'It was her,' gasped a man, 'really it was.'

'They're calling her the white goddess now,' gawped another.

'I never thought, in all my puff, I'd see such—'

'Move along there!' shouted a soldier. 'All those for the Ministry up to the left: to the stadium, up to the right!'

Tom and Pearl threaded their way through the crowd and dipped into an alleyway.

'That was Lotus Askary, wasn't it?' whispered Pearl as soon as they were alone.

'Yup,' said Tom, tersely. He was still boiling with anger about the ball.

'The last time I saw her was the night I was blown off the cliff,' said Pearl. They were both silent for a moment.

'Listen, I'm sorry, Tom, I really am. I was only trying to do the best. But the way I see it, we have a chance now. We can get them out, my dad, Rudy, your parents too. And us.'

Tom glared furiously down the street. He was not convinced.

'But OK, if you're so sure that Don Gervase should never get hold of it, fine—let's take it down to that bridge and chuck it into the chasm.' Pearl stared at him indignantly. 'It's gone for ever, then, isn't it? Is that what you want?'

Tom knotted his brow and said nothing.

'You see?' she said, her voice rising uncontrollably. 'You *know* there's no point throwing it away. We've got it, so we should use it. We should take it up to the Ministry right now.'

'No,' said Tom firmly. 'Not now. That should be the last resort. Only when there is no other alternative.'

Pearl shrugged in exasperation.

'So, what are you proposing?'

'I think we should go down to the jail and the duplication place, now we know where they are. We should look down there first, see if we can find them.'

'And if we do?'

'Then we should try to find a way out.'

'And if we get caught?'

'Then . . . then we should propose a swap. The beetle ball for our parents, as a last resort.'

'I thought you didn't approve of swaps,' said Pearl sarcastically, 'I thought these people didn't do swaps.'

Tom shook his head.

'You just don't get it, do you? We can't give Don Gervase Askary even more power than he has already. We can't do that. He's evil,' he said angrily. 'He's . . . if he could control that ball, use it properly, then . . . you have no idea what it feels like.'

Pearl stared at him petulantly, but she could tell from his grim expression that Tom was not about to change his mind.

'Very well,' she huffed, 'it's a plan. Let's do it. And I suppose I don't really have a choice in the matter anyway.'

'Not really,' said Tom, shoving the beetle ball deeper into his trouser pocket. He was the one who had knocked it out of Scurf's hand and caught it, and he was glad of that. It was his responsibility now. 'Let's go down to level 2469, wherever that is.'

Making their way down a series of side alleys and steps, Tom and Pearl navigated back through the tide of insects and people until they reached the great gates once more.

'That way?' suggested Tom, pointing towards a great tunnel into which most of the curiously shaped beetles were disappearing.

'OK,' nodded Pearl. 'As long as it's down. Level 2469 sounds like somewhere very near the bottom of the heap.'

Falling in behind a long train of bulbous green beetles, they entered the tunnel. Soon it began to spiral downwards, and as it did so the air became gradually hotter and wetter. Unlike the chaos of the causeways above, here the beetles streamed in orderly lines, up to the right, down to the left. There was precious little sound save for the constant clattering of spiky legs and the rubbing of armour. Across the domed ceiling, flat, crab-like creatures moved slowly from one side to the other, their shells caked with brilliantly luminous fungus that cast a sickly greenish twilight over this alien world.

'Get it . . . get it, half-breed! Who the 'ell they thinks they is? They've only taken over five minutes ago! Bet they've never even been darn 'ere to the engine room! No no, not brave enough to do that, is they?'

Tom searched around for the familiar voice and spotted a flattened triangular head bobbing through the crowd ahead of them.

'We's the geezers who took it at Callaboose!' ranted the mantis man, raising his fist at a soldier standing guard in a doorway. 'That's right, mate! Not you squealers!'

'We could ask him the way,' whispered Tom, trying not to lose sight of the misshapen figure limping along. 'He's going to know isn't he? Probably just come straight out of jail himself.'

Pearl nodded.

'Beetles led by clones, innit? Beetles led by clones!' he shouted as one of the guards waded into the stream and made a lunge at him.

'Gotta be quicka than that, sonny Jim!' he chuckled, rolling under the belly of a fat insect and darting in through a doorway. 'Ha-ha! Can't catch the manty man!'

Tom and Pearl scrambled after him, and found themselves in a large room full of shallow rock chambers that each contained an egg. Here and there parties of brown beetles scurried about, painstakingly turning each egg over, but neither they nor their overseer noticed the little man as he jumped up onto a balcony and slid down a pole to the next level, where there was more of the same.

'Wow, he's fast,' panted Pearl, struggling to keep up. The mantis man may have had one leg considerably shorter than the other, but he lolloped along at tremendous speed. Tom glanced down at the tiers of identical egg chambers stretching down as far as he could see, but instead of continuing his descent the mantis man dodged through an arch over which the number forty was written, and suddenly he was hauling himself across a rope bridge that stretched across a deep, steaming chasm. On either side thousands of blue beetles were busy milking racks of swollen white ants clinging to the wet walls.

'I like milk and I'm half-crazy, I like ants' legs dipped in gravy,' sang the little man to himself. 'Live to work, lads, live to work!'

It was all so alien and strange, but Tom and Pearl barely had time to even glance at it before the mantis man darted into a tunnel on the far side, turned right and slid down another banister into a different area entirely. Here gangs of beetles were feeding lumps of rock to each other, chewing them up and spitting them out as a kind of white cement.

'Hello,' panted Tom, rolling up his sleeves and pulling down his hood as he drew level with the mantis man. 'Hi.'

The mantis man glanced up and he was shocked to see the face of a boy and a girl and two sets of arms and feet dodging through the beetles beside him.

'Gawd I thought I was bad—look at the state of yous!' he growled. 'You ain't even connected together!'

He spat roughly on the ground. 'They did that to ya, did they?'

'Yeah, that's right,' panted Tom.

The mantis man grunted and muttered something to himself.

'Goin' back darn, are yer?'

'Level 2469,' said Pearl. 'City jail and . . . '

'Duplication,' he rasped. 'Goin' that ways meself. Brother's a jailer, need a new pass don't I? Cus they don't take kindly to undersiders like yous and me up there no more. Which ways you goin?'

'Erm,' Tom faltered, 'which way you going?'

'I don't fancy walkin'. This is forty-one, innit?'

'That's right,' said Pearl, trying to sound convincing.

'Looks like we's best catch a beam on a swiggy, then. You on for that?'

Pearl and Tom did not understand the jargon but both nodded violently.

'Dig it,' growled the mantis man. 'I know of a hole through pulping and the nurseries. Follow us, ladies.'

Ducking into a side tunnel, mantis man danced down some steps and into yet another huge steaming wet chamber, this time filled to the ceiling with brown logs that were stacked, sliced and chewed up by thousands of large black weevils.

'Pulping?' whispered Tom, watching workers force beetles to vomit up huge lumps of wood pulp, which they rolled away down chutes.

'Correct,' said the mantis man, 'pulping pulping pulping, all day long. Cos the poor little blighters gotta eat something, ain't they?' With a cackle he hobbled straight through an archway and out onto a long wide balcony. Beyond and above stretched layers and layers of pens filled with grubs of all shapes and sizes rolling around in heaps of the brown mush.

'This is a seriously weird place,' whispered Pearl, staring about her wide-eyed. 'It's like one giant, living machine.'

'I know,' whispered Tom. The scale of Scarazand and everything in it was truly breathtaking; it was as if they had shrunk and found themselves in some weird insect universe in which people played a small and almost irrelevant part. Was this the past, or was this the future? Tom had no idea: but it was real all right, the deep nagging thud in his brain told him that . . .

'There's one!' yelled the mantis man, as something bright flashed past the hole at the end of the corridor. He hurried on and leapt up onto the ledge, with Tom and Pearl hard on his heels.

'Oh!' she gasped, and grabbed Tom's arm. It was a dizzying sight. There before them was a wide, circular lift shaft, extending hundreds of metres in each direction. Running up and down it were luminous cages swinging off huge black cables, carrying people, eggs, beetles, cocoons, Skrolls, and all manner of other creatures. Some cages moved astonishingly fast, others were painfully slow, and all were powered by vast cogs of various sizes suspended across the chasm. At first sight these massive wheels appeared to be part of some giant bicycle, or a clock, but looking closer Tom realized they were formed by huge grey beetles, their spiky backs interlocking with each other like teeth, marching endlessly around stone discs.

'Ready?' rasped the mantis man, craning his neck out of the hole. 'Good fast VIP swiggy coming down now, straight from the Ministry.'

Pearl glanced at him nervously.

'Erm . . . so what, we're going to jump onto the roof?'

'That's it missy. Now you ain't going to fall apart cos you ain't properly connected, are ya?'

'No,' she gulped. 'I just—'

Suddenly there was a rush of air and something flashed before them.

'Jump!' screeched the mantis man.

Tom and Pearl leapt into space and somehow landed with a thud on the luminous roof of the cage which wobbled as it flew down.

'Most delicately done,' smiled the half-breed, sitting up nonchalantly. 'This is the way to go down to the underside. Ridin' on the roof of the nobs. Hobo stylin'!' he cackled to himself. Tom and Pearl could barely manage a smile as they lay clinging on to whatever they could, hardly daring to move a muscle as the wind rushed in their ears and the floors flashed past at terrifying speed. Three hundred . . . five hundred . . . eight hundred . . . Tom hauled himself onto his elbows and squinted over the lip of the cage as far as he dared . . . below was a black chasm, nothing more. Only the air was changing: it seemed to be becoming warmer and wetter, and there was a strong smell of sulphur . . .

'Two thousan', nearly us,' shouted the mantis man, climbing to his feet. The lift was slowing now. Somewhere below them there was the sound of boiling water.

'How do we get off?' asked Pearl.

'Same way we got on, Miss Discombobulate,' he grinned. 'But don't hang about, cos they check the roof of these VIP swiggys for the likes of yous and I.'

There was a sudden juddering as the lift came to a rapid halt beneath them.

'Just the two is it, sir?' said a muffled voice inside the cage below.

'That's correct. And don't delay as it's tonight.'

'Very good, sir.'

The cage swung to a stop and the men stepped out.

'Quick,' whispered mantis man, and he leapt onto the rock face, climbed up a short way and burrowed into a hole. Tom and Pearl followed suit, and turned round just in time to see three long, oily-grey tentacles emerge from the wall further down and feel around the sides and the roof of the cage.

'Better luck next time mate!' spat the half-breed.

'What was that?' breathed Pearl, staring at the tentacles slithering back into a hole just below them.

'Believe me, Miss Diss, yous do not wanna know. Come on, jail's this way.'

The mantis man made his way to the door and poked his head out into the tunnel, quickly checking right and left.

'Looks clear enough,' he muttered cautiously. 'You discombobs hear anything?'

Tom and Pearl looked in either direction and listened. Unlike anywhere else in Scarazand, this tunnel was silent, dark, and apparently completely empty.

'Looks OK to me,' whispered Tom, noticing that the walls were caked in some glistening substance. 'Why, is there a problem?'

'If you can't hear nothing, and I can't hear nothing, then nothing's the problem, dig it?'

Mantis man hopped out of the hole and hobbling around the puddles darted in through another archway and down a short spiral staircase, at the bottom of which was a large wooden door.

'This is where me brother works,' he said, 'official jail entrance. Yous an' me have just taken the back route, hence the caution.'

Opening the door, Tom and Pearl followed the mantis man into a long, low guardroom, jostling with people. Somewhere at the far end there was a noisy argument going on.

'But how's he supposed to know the rules! He's only 'rived this morning?'

A distraught woman stood at the head of a party of tourists, all wearing yellow plastic jackets. In front of her sat a large, fat man with waxy skin. He had a small cap perched on the back of his bald head, and on his forehead two stubby pink antennae wriggled wetly. Surrounding him were a collection of irregular shaped half-breeds, wearing approximations of a black uniform.

'Mr Winston,' grunted mantis man, bowing low. He was clearly in awe of this monstrous jailer. Mr Winston nodded briefly and popped a small glistening ball into his mouth from a bowl on the table beside him. It might have been a grape, but it looked much more like a snail's eye.

'This is Scarazand, lady,' rumbled Mr Winston, chewing hard. 'Rules is sent from the glorious leader—who received them direct from the Queen, and Queen's rules is rules for all. No exceptions.'

The woman was distraught.

'But . . . he's an old man, absent minded, that's all—he just wandered off . . . he didn't know it was an 'atchery, lord knows he didn't.'

The fat jailer shrugged.

'How longs you gonna keep him in for, then?' demanded her mate.

Mr Winston consulted a large grey book beside him and began to read.

'Trespassing into hatchery 389d, without a pass, falling into jelly vat and displacing egg in said hatchery, causing egg to roll out into busy corridor, resulting in destruction of said egg, *and* causing an unpleasant mess . . . ' He held the book up to his face. 'Punishment at head jailer's discretion? Hmm.' He rubbed his chin and his antennae twitched. 'What shall we say then . . . life?'

'Life?'

'With no visits.'

The woman swooned.

'Hard but fair,' crooned the chorus of half-breeds around him. 'Hard but fair.'

The woman was dragged away by her gang of friends, who scowled hard at the grinning jailers.

"'Ere, look what the cat's dragged in!' squawked a half-breed, nudging Mr Winston. The gang stared in amazement as the mantis man walked forward trailing Tom and Pearl in his wake.

'Awright Scuzz, Natzy, Fizzer, Mr Winston, sir.'

'By all the beetles on the backside of Beelzebub, what is *they*?' rasped Mr Winston, staring at the heads and arms and feet of the two children that did not seem to be connected to each other.

'Discombobs,' said mantis man proudly. 'New breed. S'periment gone horrible I reckons. Found 'em up on level 41. Thought yous like to see 'em.'

The jailers stared in silence.

'Do they speak?'

'We do, Mr Winston, sir,' said Pearl, smiling nervously. One of the half-breeds took a step back in fear. 'We're the new cannon fodder. Harder to hit see, nothing in the middle.'

'That's right,' said Tom, marvelling at Pearl's ingenuity. 'Nothing inside,' he said, pointing to his invisible chest.

Mr Winston scratched his head.

'Well I'll be—' he wheezed. 'How do they do it?'

'Miraculous,' chimed Natzy, squinting forward. 'Discombobs— eh?'

'So what brings you strange looking messes down 'ere?' enquired Mr Winston. There was a moment of awkward silence, as Tom and Pearl thought quickly. It was obvious that now they had been revealed there was no way into the jail without some kind of bluff.

'We've come to check the register,' said Pearl coolly. 'We're looking for runaways.'

'Runaways?' Mr Winston let out a surprisingly high-pitched titter. 'I take it you know what guards this place, Miss Discombob. There is no runaways here. None that have *survived* at any rate.'

Scuzz and Fizzer twitched with glee.

'Be that as it may, we are looking, and we will find them,' Pearl continued, her voice hardening. 'We want to check your register. Now.'

There was silence for a moment and Mr Winston bristled visibly. It was clear that no one told him what to do down here.

'Who are you?'

Tom glanced at Pearl, then up at the ceiling. Hanging in the darkness was another red shadow, with blank, staring eyes . . . too bad. In an instant he ripped off his poncho and stood before them. Pearl stared at him in horror.

'We're agents,' he said, staring directly at Mr Winston.

The fat man's pink antennae twitched.

'Agents? *Agents?*'

Suddenly he started to titter wildly.

'Correct,' barked Pearl, instantly removing her poncho. 'Agents of Don Gervase Askary. We work for the Ministry, and we are hunting down enemies of the Revolution,' she said, singling out the mantis man. 'Particularly those intent on stirring up dissent.' The half-breed's mouth fell open and even the jailers seemed momentarily taken aback. They sat gawping at Tom and Pearl while Mr Winston glared at them in surly silence. He swallowed his eyeball noisily: it seemed the ruse had worked.

'The register, Mr Winston, if you please.'

The large man flicked his head angrily and two half-breeds scurried off, returning with an enormous black book between them that they hefted onto the desk. Opening the book in the middle, Tom could see that it was covered in tightly packed, minute writing.

'Do you have names of these "runaways"?' grunted Mr Winston, heaving his huge frame over to the register.

Pearl and Tom looked at each other quickly.

'Smoot,' Pearl began, 'Arlo and Rudy Smoot. Rudy is . . . six.'

'Age is of no concern, Miss Diss. If they've been in here their names will be in the register.'

Mr Winston swung what appeared to be a large anglepoise lamp over the top of the book and thumped it hard with his fist.

'Smoot,' he ordered.

Tom and Pearl watched wide-eyed as eight thin spider's legs uncurled from the bottom of the lamp and stood on the page.

'Smoot!' bellowed Mr Winston once more, and popped another wet eye into his mouth.

The spider's legs began to flick through the pages, so fast that they rattled, then stopped abruptly and traced down to a line in the middle. Mr Winston bent forward and squinted at the tiny writing.

'Arlo Smoot . . . Rudy Smoot.'

'Are they here?' asked Pearl, her voice trembling.

'No longer. They've been discharged. Level ten order.'

Pearl gasped: she stared at him in disbelief.

'So . . . level ten order? What does that mean?'

Mr Winston rolled the eye around on his tongue and peered at her suspiciously.

'I take it you're familiar with the Revolution Games?'

'We are,' said Tom quickly.

Mr Winston nodded, knowingly.

'Well then.'

'Level ten can mean duplication, boss,' added Scuzz, peering over Mr Winston's shoulder.

'True enough. Might be across the way there. We is connected, see.'

'Duplication? You mean to be—'

'Killed and duplicated, or duplicated then killed, yes.'

Pearl stared blindly at the register. She was trying immensely hard to keep a straight face, but her cheeks were burning and tears began to well up in her eyes.

'Any others?'

'Sam and Poppy Scatterhorn,' said Tom nervously.

'Scatterhorn.'

The spider's legs blurred through the pages, and Tom prayed that his parents' names would not be in the register.

'No Scatterhorns,' thundered Mr Winston.

Tom gasped; his heart began to gallop.

'No Scatterhorns? Are you sure?'

'Positive.'

Tom swallowed hard: was it possible that his instinct had been right all along?

'Maybe he did make a mistake, after all,' said Pearl in a quiet, sad voice.

'And there's no chance they might be here without you know-ing?'

Mr Winston stared at him with ill-concealed contempt.

'Listen, young sir,' he spat, 'there's one way into this jail and it is right past my nose. If you is an undesirable, or an enemy of the revolution, you will go through that door, and I will make sure that is where you stay. Get it? Now what about the rest of these runaways?'

Tom's mind was swirling with emotions, he wanted to laugh and shout out loud—but Pearl was utterly dejected. She could do nothing more than stare at the floor, confused and miserable.

'More names!' demanded Mr Winston, his antennae flickering impatiently.

'Erm . . . August Catcher?' said Tom quickly.

'Not here,' said Mr Winston as soon as the spider had finished flicking. Tom did his best to conceal a small smile: they must have got back just in time.

'Oscarine Zumsteen?'

The spider's legs spun.

'Hmm, curious. Was here—removed, pending duplication request. Is that the lot?'

Pearl looked at Tom desperately, and he could tell what she was thinking.

'We need to see duplication,' he said firmly to Mr Winston. 'To make quite sure. How do we get to duplication from here?'

'Into the main hall, through the ninth door on the left. I take it you have a pass?'

'We do,' replied Tom.

Mr Winston looked at Pearl who nodded weakly.

'Cos you won't get in without it. Bobulated or discombobulated,' he snarled.

'Why is that?' asked Tom. Mr Winston's antennae wriggled suspiciously. 'I mean . . . erm, what I mean is, what level of security do you have around duplication to prevent runaways escaping?'

'Witchit warren, ain't it? Now I take it even you *proper* folks way up there in the Ministry have heard of witchits?' added Mr Winston, sarcastically.

'We have. Excellent,' said Tom with a smile. 'Thank you. Now if you would kindly let us in?'

'Just as you wish,' sneered Mr Winston, popping another eye into his mouth and biting it. With a glance he indicated to Fizzer to unlock the large wooden door behind them. The rest of the crew watched in fascinated silence as Tom and Pearl slipped on the ponchos once more, their bodies melting away into the air.

'Sir, miss,' said Mr Winston, reaching for his hat and offering an excuse for a salute. The door clanged shut behind them, accompanied by the sound of a heavy lock turning.

For a moment there was silence, and they thought they were alone. Then a vast luminous crab crawled out of its hole, lighting up the cavern, and the walls erupted with shouts and banging.

'Oh my lord,' breathed Pearl, looking up. All around the walls were people suspended in small wooden coffins up to their necks, with small holes for their arms. Most were so old and thin and hairy that it was hard to tell whether they were men or women, or even whether they were alive at all. They looked like grubs, hanging there.

'To think Dad and Rudy were in this place,' whispered Pearl in horror.

'Well they're not here any more,' said Tom determinedly. 'Come on.'

Ignoring the stench and the clamouring all around, Tom and Pearl crossed the circular stone hall and counted their way round to the ninth doorway and stared at it. The door looked just like any ordinary wooden door: there was nothing special about it.

'Best just go through,' said Tom steeling himself. Opening it, he found a wide, empty tunnel, a little like a tube line, similar to that they had crossed with mantis man earlier.

'It must be just across there,' said Tom, noticing the small wooden door on the opposite side. Pearl nodded, and looked up and down the tunnel. The walls were covered with a glistening substance, and it was curiously silent.

'So this is part of the witchit warren?'

'Reckon so.'

They listened, and still there was nothing. Just silence.

'I wonder what's so terrifying about them?' Pearl said.

'Come on,' said Tom, and without a further thought they scampered over the puddles to the far side and slipped through the door. For a moment they crouched against a dark stone wall, waiting, listening. But there was nothing.

'They're going to be on to us soon, you know,' whispered Tom, remembering that pink-eyed beetle on the guardroom ceiling.

'I know,' shuddered Pearl. 'And I'm really not certain about this. Supposing there are hundreds of Rudys, or hundreds of my dads, what then?'

Tom had no answer to that.

'They're probably not here,' he said, as carelessly as he could manage. 'Mr Winston didn't sound convinced.'

Stepping out of the shadows Tom and Pearl cautiously made their way forward and looked out. They were standing on the lip of a shallow stone dish, some twenty metres wide, that was one of hundreds stretching up and down in interlocking stacks. The stacks were arranged in a semicircle, and on the surface of each dish lay orderly rows of grey, lozenge shaped cocoons arranged in concentric patterns. Some cocoons were the size of men, others were no larger than babies, and picking their way amongst them were great black spiders, ridden by Skrolls, engaged in careful work. Some were painstakingly unwrapping the bodies inside and carrying them away, while others were adding more grubs to the pattern and wrapping them up in silk. It was like an enormous, grisly factory.

'We're never going to find them,' sighed Pearl despairingly, 'it will take us days to search this place.'

Tom stared grimly at the layers and layers of dishes stretching down into the darkness. She was right—there must be thousands of duplicants here.

'Maybe, if all of these cocoons are copies, the originals are kept somewhere separate.'

'Like a morgue, you mean?'

Pearl bit her lip angrily and tears welled up in her eyes: it was almost too much to bear. Tom craned forward and looked down. Two levels below them he could just see the edge of a glistening black dome, set back from the stacks, and around its entrance there was a mass of activity. Gangs of small beetles scurried in and out, carrying what looked like grubs that they loaded onto the backs of waiting spiders.

'Maybe that's the place,' whispered Tom, spotting groups of

Skrolls loitering either side of the entrance. 'Shall we have a look?'

Pearl leaned over his shoulder and saw that he was right.

'OK,' she muttered, with no enthusiasm. Tom turned back to her and saw a great sadness in her eyes.

'Pearl I bet they aren't there, they won't be.'

Pearl said nothing. She seemed resigned.

'But, we've got to know . . . haven't we? We might be so close. We can't stop now.'

Pearl stared at the dome and drew a deep breath.

'I just don't want to find them, that's all.'

'You won't.'

'What makes you so sure?'

'I'm not. But I'm hoping. And that's something, isn't it?'

Reluctantly, Pearl followed Tom out onto the bowl. Moving carefully through the lines of tightly packed cocoons, they made their way to a narrow spiral staircase cut into a rock pillar and descended two levels down to the black dome. Drawing closer, they could just glimpse through the open doorway the outline of a person wrapped up in filaments of silk.

'You might be right,' whispered Pearl, shivering a little. Avoiding the Skrolls prowling around the door, they slipped inside and found themselves in a large circular room. At first sight it looked something like a library, with aisles and shelves radiating out from the centre: but there were no books here— only corpses. Darting into the nearest aisle marked M, they stole down the long avenue, peering in at the racks of bodies lying there. Tom stopped beside what appeared to be a medieval knight and brushed the dust off the label.

'Inigo Marcellus,' he read quietly. 'Italian explorer. Entry: glacier, Hindu Kush, 1337. Used: education and deception, Italian renaissance.'

Tom studied the angular, weather-beaten face beneath the grey silk. Inigo Marcellus . . . the name was somehow familiar, and then he remembered: he was the man who had written the first account of Scarazand.

'Elisa Martin, Scottish weaver,' whispered Pearl, standing before the body of a beautiful woman further down. 'Entry: bog on St Kilda, 1799. Used: New York hospital doctor. Cark distribution.' Pearl stared at the face of Elisa Martin. It was dusty and white, but there was still a ruddy glow in her cheeks.

'She doesn't look dead somehow,' she whispered. Pearl walked on, peering in at each face in turn. 'None of them do. It's like . . . like they are sleeping.'

'My god, it's Shadrack and Skink!' Tom blurted out, forgetting where he was.

'Who are they?' breathed Pearl, moving next to him.

'Copies of this man: "Dr Pierre Gaspard, poisoner. Entry: Forest of Ardennes 1891. Used: elixir search."' Tom stared at the small, bony-faced man with straggly black hair pressed to his temples and a frayed swallowtail coat. 'There were thousands of him. Thousands and thousands.'

Tom and Pearl gazed at the thin white man in silence. This place answered many questions, but there were still a great deal more to be answered. Working their way down through the alphabet, they passed the bodies of postmen lost on moors, fugitives in forests, children who had fallen down wells, chimneysweeps stuck in chimneys, until they came to the letter

S. Gingerly Tom led the way up the aisle, and his heart began to thump in his temples: despite everything Mr Winston had told him, he could barely bring himself up to the spot where Scatterhorn should be. With a lump in his throat he looked into the rack, and there was nothing there. Of course there wasn't. Taking a deep breath, he moved down to Smoot.

'Can you see them?' whispered Pearl softly, standing some distance away. She was unable to walk any closer. Tom peered into the rack and saw an empty space where the bodies had been. There was a note.

'Arlo Smoot,' it read, 'radio spy. Captured, the Marquesas Islands, 2009. Interrogated.' And underneath, scrawled in red was written, 'Original removed. RG.' Below was a smaller space where Rudy should have been. The label simply said, 'Removed'.

Tom turned and looked at Pearl. Even through the gauze of her visor he could tell that she was trembling.

'Well?'

'They've gone. They've taken them away.'

Pearl stood motionless.

'So, but . . . what does that mean?'

'I don't know. Maybe they are somewhere else in Scarazand. And they could be still alive. It's possible.'

Pearl said nothing. Cautiously she walked forward and read the label for herself. Not quite understanding it the first time, she read it again.

'You just have to believe it, Pearl.'

'In that case, we must trade the beetle ball,' she said simply. 'There is no other choice. We don't know really how to use it and we can't search this place for ever. So we must take it up to the Ministry and trade it for them. Maybe save their lives.'

Tom said nothing. He could feel the round ball pressing gently against his pocket. He wanted to think of something that might dissuade her, but right now he couldn't.

'You would do the same thing, wouldn't you, Tom?' she said, her pale blue eyes searching his. Tom stared down at the label awkwardly, trying to imagine his own parents' names written on it. He could feel Pearl's gaze burning into him.

'I don't know . . . if I was completely certain, maybe . . . ' He shook his head. 'But I just—'

At that moment there was a high shout and a clatter of footsteps and hundreds of men burst into the room.

CHAPTER 19

SPIDERS, WITCHITS, AND A GROOT SLANG

Tom and Pearl just had time to scrabble into the adjacent aisle before a group of soldiers burst in upon them, thrashing this way and that with swords and spikes.

'Now for the sake of my sanity be *careful* with them things,' wheezed Mr Winston, tottering behind the line of men cutting their way through the empty air, evidently hoping they were going to hit something they couldn't see. 'These is most precious and I'm not havin' this little break-in turn out tragic for us all.'

'Quick,' hissed Tom, and they dodged around into the next aisle, only to find another line of men slashing their way towards them, and another in the aisle after that. Half-running, half-crouching, they doubled back and sprinted across to the far side of the library, bursting down towards the letter Z just as a scrabbling sound met them from the from end of the aisle . . .

'Oh . . .'

Pearl tried to speak, but her voice was barely more than a breath. Edging backwards, they watched in fascinated horror as a large spider emerged around the corner with a Skroll on its back. The hooded man grunted something, then dug his spurs hard into the spider's hairy flanks, whereupon the creature produced a large ball of glistening goo from its mouth, spun it out between its front legs and began to march forward, swinging the blob rhythmically through the air, faster and faster and faster till it became a dizzying blur. It took every ounce of effort for Tom to tear his eyes away from the weird creature and glance behind, only to see a line of men scything up the aisle towards them. What to do? They were caught in a trap . . . unless—

'In there?' whispered Pearl desperately: she had seen it too.

The next instant they leapt up onto the rack and slithered into the small space behind the man lying there, wrapped in faded silk. Tom flattened himself against the rack as the spider thundered past, and as he did so a glint of something silver caught his eye on the rack below. It was a bangle, engraved with curious patterns; familiar, somehow . . . and then he looked up to the face that owned it . . .

'Oscarine Zumsteen,' he whispered to himself. There she was, lying placidly beneath him, dressed in the same yellow mackintosh as she had worn in the café. That was probably only last week, but it seemed like light years ago now. Was she dead? He couldn't tell. Had she managed to keep her promise not to tell them anything? Something in her pleased expression suggested that she had.

'It's gone.'

Pearl's voice brought Tom back to his senses.

'Tom, they've all gone. Let's go.'

Slithering out of their hiding place, Tom and Pearl crept down to the end of the aisle after the great creature and peered out.

'Oh my lord.'

There were two more spiders, parked like monstrous trucks across the entrance. Before them stood a line of Skrolls watching the aisles. And in front of them a very nervous Mr Winston paced about menacingly. There was no way through there. No way at all. Could there be another exit? Given the nature of this place it was unlikely, and they both knew it: that must be the reason why they had blocked it up . . .

Think Tom, think . . . something clever.

Racking his brains, Tom glanced at the spider and its hooded rider, now spinning their way down the adjacent aisle. The Skroll sat astride its hairy head, his long black cloak flapping aimlessly across the spiders flanks.

'I've got it,' he whispered suddenly. 'We could hide under that Skroll's cloak.'

Pearl's eyes widened. 'Are you nuts? How?'

'Climb on from the back. Look, it's so long he won't notice.'

'He will,' hissed Pearl, 'how could he not? But . . . '

Out of the corner of her eye she spotted a large monk lying beneath wisps of silk on the rack. Maybe it was not such a bad idea after all . . .

'How strong are you?' she said urgently.

Tom did not understand.

'Well . . . I—'

'Could you lift me up on your shoulders? For about half a minute, say?'

Tom shrugged. 'Maybe, just about, I think.'

'Good,' she said, breathlessly. 'Come on you crazy cat.'

And so it was that less than a minute later the spider reached the end of the aisle and it felt a thump on its back—two thumps to be precise. The Skroll was so busy coaxing the great creature to turn towards the door that he didn't see another hooded Skroll rise up behind him, and when he did he showed no surprise. He grunted something, but the tall thin Skroll just stared straight ahead, its hands folded inside its cape. Moments later Mr Winston dodged out of the way of the great creature and the two spiders blocking the door reversed awkwardly to let it pass.

'Not much further,' whispered Pearl.

Tom clenched his teeth, trying to balance her weight on his shoulders above him. He couldn't see a thing, but he could feel the spider begin to walk down the slope.

'Now!' hissed Pearl, and in an instant Tom dropped gratefully to his knees and they both tumbled off the back behind a line of cocoons. For a moment they lay there panting, not daring to move a muscle. The Skroll glanced back at the chaos around the door and showed no surprise he was on his own. Cracking his whip, he urged the creature up and away across the field of cocoons.

'I can't believe we just did that,' said Tom, breathing hard. 'They're obviously more stupid than they look.'

'I know,' replied Pearl, her eyes shining. 'Exciting though, wasn't it?'

For the first time in a long, long while Tom realized that she was smiling.

'So you're feeling better now?'

Pearl grinned. 'You bet. That was audacious.'

Leaving the monk's cowl tucked beneath a long grey cocoon, Tom and Pearl pulled down their hoods and threaded their way back to the spiral staircase that led up to the level they had entered from.

'Do you think that's our best exit?' whispered Pearl, looking at the small door in the shadows on the far side of the bowl.

'I don't know,' breathed Tom, 'didn't they lock the guardroom door behind us?'

Pearl nodded, she had quite forgotten about that.

'What about going straight on up?'

They peered out at the hexagonal pattern of bowls that stretched on and on above them.

'It's going to be a really long way. Unless we can—' Tom stopped and stared down. Below them, a large black spider pulled out the black monks' cowl from its hiding place and turned it over curiously. The Skroll rider barked out an order, whereupon it obediently passed the cloak up for him to see.

'That was unfortunate,' whispered Pearl.

The Skroll let out a high-pitched scream, bringing a gang of soldiers racing out of the dome, followed by Mr Winston himself. One look at the black cowl told him all he needed to know.

'They're out!' he bellowed, his head turning purple. 'Them discombobs is out! Fan out and find 'em! Smartish!'

Without even a glance back Tom and Pearl dashed out across the bowl.

'Natzy, Fizzer, git up to that connectin' door!' yelled Mr Winston, his antennae wiggling wildly as he puffed over to the staircase. The two half-breeds tore on ahead and, reaching the top, they spotted parts of Tom and Pearl vaulting over the cocoons.

'Discombobs! Over there!' screamed Fizzer, as a large spider clambered down onto the bowl. 'The door in the middle, mate!'

Another spider scurried across from the far side and its Skroll rider drove his heels hard into its flanks. On it came at speed.

'We're not going to make it,' panted Pearl, as the rushing black forms closed in on them like a pair of combine harvesters.

'Yes we are!' shouted Tom.

Don't look at them, he told himself, just get out of that door. His arms ached as he vaulted cocoon after cocoon after cocoon, three more lines . . . two more . . . one . . . Tom flung himself at the door, dragged it open a fraction and tumbled through. The next second Pearl somersaulted over the top of him, and he rammed the bolt shut.

Thud! Then—thud thud thud . . . the spiders, Skrolls, and jailers clattered into it: then—silence. Tom and Pearl lay motionless, fighting for breath.

'You gonna follow them?' panted Fizzer on the other side of the door.

'No bleedin' way. Not through there.'

The handle twisted and rattled above them.

'They's locked it in any case.'

'Get through, did they?' panted Mr Winston, his small feet tottering up behind.

'That they did sir.'

There was a pause.

'And the jail door's locked on t'other side?'

'Yes boss.'

Mr Winston grunted.

'Shame. Ahh well. Witchits'll 'ave them, then. 'S good as dead now.'

'That's right, boss. Good as dead.'

The voices faded, and Tom and Pearl picked themselves up.

'He's right,' said Tom, trying the door on the other side of the tunnel that led back into the jail. 'It's locked.'

'I don't fancy the sound of these witchit-things at all,' said Pearl, dusting herself down. 'Do you think they'll be able to see us?'

'They'll certainly see me,' replied Tom grumpily. All that was left of his thin grey poncho was hanging in tatters round his neck.

'Must have ripped off as I dived through the door.'

Pearl smiled.

'You'll look really discombobulated now.'

'Very funny,' he said, trying to raise a smile but he couldn't. He looked down the long tunnel towards the grey lights in the distance.

'Maybe we can find one of those little interconnecting tunnels that will take us to the lift shaft. I reckon those are the only ways out.'

'OK,' shrugged Pearl, glancing in both directions. 'It all looks pretty similar to me.'

Together they set off down the long wide tunnel. Unlike anywhere else in Scarazand, this place was completely quiet and completely empty, and the closer they got to the lights, the more oppressive the silence became.

'I'm not sure about this,' said Pearl, whispering for no apparent reason. 'It feels like something's going to happen, doesn't it?'

Tom nodded uneasily: he noticed that all the way along the

rough stone walls and ceiling were coated with a glistening liquid, as if something wet and sticky had been dragged past them. Soon they reached the dim fluorescent crabs and the tunnel began to curve away to the right.

'Wait,' whispered Pearl, stopping dead in her tracks. 'What was that?'

'What?' said Tom, who found that he was whispering too.

There was a faint rumbling in the distance.

'Can't you hear it?'

Tom looked down at the puddle at his feet, and he could just make out the black surface of the water rippling. The rumbling was getting louder. The water was beginning to vibrate. Something was coming towards them from beyond the lights . . . something big, coming fast. It sounded like a rocket.

'We must hide,' said Tom urgently, glancing around at the rock walls.

'Hide where? There is nowhere.'

Tom cursed under his breath. Pearl was right, there *was* nowhere . . . then he noticed that the uneven surface of the walls had created shadows that the glistening liquid had not touched. Could that be because—

'Come on!' he shouted, sprinting back towards a narrow slither of dry wall. If they squeezed in tight then . . .

'Oh no . . . oh my, oh—'

'What? What is it?'

Pearl let out a strange high-pitched squeak and pointed. Tom turned . . . For a fraction of a second he saw it. Something grey and white, like a maggot the size of a train, wriggling towards them at terrific speed . . .

The next instant he grabbed Pearl and pulled her into the rock shadow, squeezing in next to her just as the roaring, sweating, slithering thing cannoned past and disappeared around the corner. A rumble, and then . . . nothing. For a moment, Tom and Pearl stood pressed to the wall, too shocked to speak.

'Witchit . . . ' mumbled Pearl, her voice tiny and scared. 'This is the witchit warren, so that must be . . . a witchit.'

Tom touched the wall beside him: it was glistening brightly and smelt of sulphur.

'But . . . but the size of it, how could anything grow that big?' He stared down the empty tunnel. 'Imagine what it's going to turn into.'

'I know,' muttered Pearl. 'And I don't want to meet another.'

They pressed on, more urgently now, until they reached more grey crabs, their luminous shells glowing dimly. Both of them scanned the walls and the ceiling for any kind of opening.

'Ha!'

'What is it?' said Pearl as Tom sprinted towards a small pile of rubble beyond the lights. There, halfway up the wall was a small hole.

'Do you think that's safe?' said Pearl, watching Tom levering himself up into the narrow opening. It was a chute that wound vertically upwards in a spiral.

'It looks OK. And a witchit wouldn't fit in here. So that's got to be good.'

Pearl hesitated. 'Supposing something else does?'

'I think that's a risk we should take,' said Tom, grimly. 'We'll be killed down there. Come on.'

Helping Pearl up after him, he crawled up the narrow spiral.

Several turns later, they emerged into the wall of another long, wide, horizontal tunnel, and this too was covered in the same sticky, glistening substance.

'It must be some kind of worker's entrance connecting different levels of the warren together,' whispered Tom, scanning the other side for the next opening. Sure enough, about twenty metres away he spotted another dark hole.

'Ready?'

Pearl stared at the opening and took a deep breath. 'As I'll ever be.'

'Let's go.'

Stealing out into the wide tunnel, they looked in both directions. It was quite dark. There was no sound, no vibrations . . .

'Run,' Tom whispered.

But it was almost too late. The slithering witchit came on in a rush, from behind them this time, and without any warning. Tom almost felt those long wet feelers grab him as he threw himself after Pearl into the dark opening.

'Oh!'

Pearl was somewhere ahead of him in the darkness, but before he could stop his feet slipped on the polished stone and he tumbled forward. He was vaguely aware of Pearl ahead of him as he began to accelerate, winding faster and faster down the spiral chute until they both shot out of the roof of another large tunnel onto a pile of damp brown wood pulp.

'Wow,' gasped Pearl, 'that must be the food—'

And then she turned round. There was another witchit, stationary this time, gobbling excitedly through the pulp. The moment it saw them it stopped chewing.

Whump!

The great wet mouth lunged but Tom and Pearl just managed to tumble down the back of the pile and sprint away, darting into the next opening. This one did curl upwards, but no more than a few metres before . . .

Whoosh!

They hovered on the edge as the witchit hurled past them in the other direction.

'I—'

Whoosh!

Another went by, chasing the first.

'This is—'

Ssshum!

A third squealed past, chasing the other two.

'Madness,' gasped Pearl as they dashed across to the next entrance.

'I know,' replied Tom, breathing so hard he could barely speak. The witchit warren was one of the most terrifying places he had ever been, and after the adventures of the last few days, that was saying something. They had to find a way out.

'Up?' he panted.

Pearl nodded grimly, and they began to climb up the next rough spiral. After a couple of turns it levelled off and divided, one way leading to a set of steps that curled up, the other, straight ahead into the darkness.

'They're very young, you see—infants really.'

Tom and Pearl froze in the darkness. Footsteps began clattering down the steps towards them . . .

'One has to think of them as unruly children, or puppies.'

There was a ripple of polite laughter. More footsteps, a group of people coming down . . .

'That's right, General. Rather large puppies. Full of fun and completely incapable of controlling themselves.'

Tom and Pearl did not wait to hear any more, but dashed down the dark passage and round a corner. Suddenly they stopped. At the far end there were lights and shadows dancing on the rock.

'What's that?' whispered Pearl, as they drew closer. There ahead of them was another wide horizontal tunnel, but it was different somehow. They could hear distant clanking, rushing sounds . . .

'The lift!' cried Tom out loud. That was it—they must be near it . . . perhaps those people they had just heard had got off. Yes! It must be. Scarcely daring to believe they might have accidentally found a way out of the warren, Tom and Pearl quickened their pace to the end. The rushing sounds were growing louder and louder.

'Feeling brave?' breathed Pearl.

They listened hard.

'It's got to be, hasn't it?'

Tom nodded, and with great care pressed his face to the rock and edged out towards the sound.

'That's it.'

'Is it there?' asked Pearl nervously. Tom nodded; he couldn't stop smiling. Thirty metres away there was a large opening onto the vast central shaft, alive with lights and cables and cages whizzing up and down. They had made it. They were safe. All they had to do was jump on the roof of one of those swiggy things travelling up, and then . . .

And then Tom became aware of something tugging at his hair.

'Ow,' he said, as the tugging became more insistent. 'Ow! Ow, ow, ow, stop—'

And before he knew it he had been led out into the large tunnel on tiptoes and hurled to the floor. Instantly Tom leapt to his feet, whipped around . . . and his heart skipped a beat. The witchit filled the entire tunnel directly behind him. Its grey feelers examined his face and his body, then ripped a piece of his poncho off his neck and stuffed it into its black blubbery mouth. The creature chewed thoughtfully, then decided to help itself to more. Tom stood, frozen in fear, as the witchit's feelers wrapped themselves around him and began to drag him towards it . . .

'Stop! Just you stop that! This instant!'

Pearl strode out into the tunnel, her eyes blazing. The witchit was so surprised that it did as it was told. Then it extended its feelers towards her.

'Oh no you don't!' she shouted, brushing them aside. 'You are a very naughty witchit—yes you are! Bad witchit! Naughty witchit!' Pearl flung her arm out. 'You go home!'

The vast glistening creature seemed so surprised that it released Tom. Then, mimicking Pearl, it flung out a feeler and knocked her over.

'How dare you do that!' she screamed. 'How dare you! Go back! Back!'

The witchit closed its eyes and shuffled backwards. Tom stared at Pearl in amazement and saw that she was both surprised and terrified. Somehow it was working: the vast blubbery grub was cowering like a whipped dog.

'Sit!' she screamed. 'Stay there!'

Incredibly, the witchit stayed. Carefully they began to edge backwards towards the end of the tunnel. Then the witchit noticed them moving and shuffled forward.

'I said stay, Witchit!'

The creature cowered—but crept forward anyway, wanting to play. This was a good game. Tom glanced behind him, the end of the tunnel was not far now, they could be there in seconds . . . but supposing there wasn't a lift?

The witchit became bolder and cheekily extending a feeler ripped a chunk of Pearl's poncho away and stuffed it in its mouth.

'Bad boy!' shouted Pearl, but with less conviction now, as they had almost reached the edge of the tunnel.

'Going up. Hold on everyone!'

The voice was followed by a clanking sound below . . .

'Quick, one's coming,' whispered Tom, and ripping away the tattered remains of his poncho he flung it before the witchit then turned and ran. Pearl did the same, and moments later they stood teetering on the edge of the great chasm. The luminous roof of the cage accelerated up towards them.

'Hurry up,' gasped Pearl, stealing a terrified glance back at the witchit, which had almost finished munching through her poncho. 'Quick quick quick quick!'

The witchit looked up at them and its mouth oozed. It wasn't going to let the rest of this delicious meal get away. Certainly not. It gurgled excitedly, then bunched, ready to spring . . .

'Oh my goodness,' whispered Pearl. 'Oh my—'

'Jump!' shouted Tom, grabbing her hand.

The witchit rocketed forward, its mouth gaping.

BANG!

The roof of the lift rushed up to meet them, knocking the wind from their chests, and in the same instant oily white feelers slithered and grasped at the cage, slowing it down violently. But the witchit was unable to hold on, and the next moment the cage sprang up out of its slippery grasp.

'Yes, we do have a little trouble with them wee beasties from time to time,' droned a matter-of-fact voice beneath them, 'they have even been known to take a whole swiggy on occasion.'

'W-what, you mean eat them?' enquired a nervous passenger.

'Oh yes. Cage, cables, cogs—the lot. They'll eat anything.'

The lift accelerated upwards, faster and faster, until the rushing of air was deafening. Tom and Pearl lay flat on the top, holding on to whatever they could as the numbers flashed past . . . One thousand five hundred . . . nine hundred . . . five hundred . . . two hundred . . . fifty . . . the lift was slowing now, twenty-one . . . eleven . . . six, five, four . . . the lift thundered to a halt.

'All change, gentlemen, this is as far as you go. Take the passage to your right and you can walk the rest of the way from there.'

The door slammed open and the passengers stepped out beneath them. Carefully Tom and Pearl pulled themselves to their feet, a little bruised and battered after their ride. Below, the chasm stretched away into darkness, and above there was all the living machinery of the lifts, wheels of spiky beetles marching and spinning in different directions. This must be the top. Then a stone hatch lifted in the rock right next to them to reveal a small tunnel.

'I said, all change, gentlemen!' shouted the same voice. 'That means you too!' The lift began to tip and shake. 'Get off my swiggy!'

Tom and Pearl had no choice but to do as the man said.

'I guess this is it,' whispered Pearl quickly as they stepped across and crouched in the opening. 'They can see us now, so we'd best be straight. You've still got the ball, haven't you?'

Tom felt the bulge in his pocket and nodded: the beetle ball was still there.

'I'll get rid of this,' he said, swinging the small rucksack off his back.

'But keep that little bottle of pheromone spray.'

'Why?'

'You never know,' she shrugged. 'If there's a chance, you could get away.'

'Me?' he said, delving inside and pulling out the small leather bottle with its rubber puffer. 'Why don't you take it?'

Pearl looked at Tom hard. 'That's very big of you, Tom, but I'd rather swap it for the beetle ball. This is my show now, isn't it?'

Tom shook his head. Despite everything that had happened, he still had serious doubts about this.

'OK,' he began, 'just as long as you—'

'All right let's be having you!'

Suddenly two long wiry tentacles lashed themselves around their legs, and Tom just had time to throw the rucksack out into the void before they were both dragged into the dark chute and thumped down mercilessly onto a hard floor.

'Ach. Painful. I betcha that hurt, man.'

Tom opened his eyes dizzily and looked up at the ceiling. Something like a giant black horseshoe crab clung to the rocks above, silently rolling its long tentacles back into its body.

'Ye could at least put some pulp there or summat like that,' continued the singsong Scottish voice. 'That's what happens to me every time, laddie. Every single time.'

Painfully Tom crawled to his feet, rubbing his sore back. That floor was very hard indeed. Glancing around, he saw they were in a cell. In one corner sat a little half-breed, not unlike the mantis man, wearing a tam-o'-shanter and a large pair of boots.

'Aye-aye boss,' he twittered, as Tom caught his eye.

'Ouch.' Slowly Pearl pulled herself to her knees.

'See?' said the small man, pointing at her indignantly. 'This ain't correct. You can't treat us like—'

'Shut it, McMaggot. Since when has anyone cared what you miserable apologies think?'

Tom peered through the bars and saw a line of three pale women, sitting behind a long desk. They were all identical, and dressed in identical grey uniforms. They looked severe and tired and very bored.

'Name?' shouted one.

'Tom Scatterhorn.'

'Spell that.'

'T-O—'

'Not that, hobo. The other bit,' ordered the woman in the middle.

Tom took a deep breath and he was about to begin again when he noticed a team of small green beetles dragging a piece of paper across what looked like a large flat printing press. The

paper was crawling with tiny black ants busily arranging themselves into patterns. Somehow they had already formed the
word 'Tom'.

'Scatterhorn,' said Tom watching the ants working feverishly.
'S-C-A-T-T-E—' Tom broke off and stared in amazement at the
paper. Not only were the ants making his name as he said it, they
had formed a square above and inside it they were starting to
draw his portrait.

'Yes, it's "a machine", hobo; whoopee,' droned the woman at
the end. 'And yes, these are predictive ants, connected to the
central information system at the Ministry. We're not all living in
the Stone Age, comrade. Get on with it.'

Tom finished spelling his name, unable to take his eyes off the
living document appearing on the paper.

'And your excuse for riding lift 386b without a pass, to floor
four of the Ministry for Control, section twelve, room 921, is?'

'Erm . . . '

'We want to see Don Gervase Askary,' said Pearl, now standing
beside Tom, rubbing her bruises. 'We have something for him.'

The women squinted at her with something approaching
interest.

'Are you drunk?'

The ants then formed the words, 'travelling with lunatic companion'.

'No she's not, but she's right,' said Tom, glancing up from the
ants. 'We need to see him in person. Immediately.'

The ants paused, as if waiting to receive something, then
quickly made the words 'alien to Scarazand . . . traveller . . . cark
convert, Tithona, 1965.'

'What?' gasped Tom, staring at the ants' writing. How could they know that?

'Special interest,' continued the ants, moving into capitals. 'INFORM IMMEDIATELY.'

'And you are?' asked the woman on the end with a sneer.

'Pearl Smoot.'

The green beetles grabbed the edges of the paper and dragged it across, revealing another piece underneath, upon which a new set of ants began to swarm.

'Pearl Smoot, eh?'

She glanced at the other two and raised her eyebrows.

'Smootie-tootie.'

'That's right,' continued Pearl uneasily. 'Why, does Smoot mean anything to you?'

'The Smootster,' said the woman in the middle, and the other two sniggered.

'Why are you laughing?' asked Pearl, her voice rising.

'Ignore them,' whispered Tom. 'Look at that.'

The ants were beginning to form words beneath her portrait: 'alien to Scarazand . . . cark convert, Tithona 1965.'

Pearl read the words, her eyes widening. Somehow the Ministry believed that *both* of them had been infected by cark beetles on Tithona . . .

'But—'

'That's brilliant—really,' whispered Tom as quietly as he dared, 'it means we've got a chance. We could get out.'

The ants paused, then went on at speed: 'possible radio spy relation . . . wanted alive or dead . . . if captured, INFORM GLORIOUS LEADER IMMEDIATELY'.

'You think so?' she gulped, reading the words.

'Definitely.'

'Right!' barked the woman in the centre. 'What class of hobo have we here. Groot Slang!' she bawled. The huge armoured creature hanging from the ceiling shuffled across and the beetles on the table scattered, leaving the ants standing motionless.

'Commit.'

The Groot Slang brought down its tail like a clenched fist, and with two fast punches it printed the ants flat onto the paper. The beetles then returned and dragged the pages across for the women to read. The moment they picked them up their expressions changed.

'Does . . . does he read the predictive ants bulletins?' gulped one, not quite believing what was written there.

'All the time.'

'They've got replicators in every room in the palace.'

'And we committed, so he will know.'

The women stared at the papers anxiously, their faces turning even greyer than before.

'But . . . but supposing he doesn't?' dithered the woman on the end. 'It says here we must inform, so we must go up and—'

'Unless he comes down,' interrupted the middle woman. They were all sweating now. 'We must tidy up, we must—'

'Do nothing of the sort, ladies,' rumbled a deep voice from the doorway.

'Oh my . . . '

The three women gasped and struggled to their feet. In strode a very tall, narrow man, dressed in a jet-black velvet suit. He had a large domed head, yellowish skin, milky green eyes and very small feet. He looked both elegant and quite hideous at the same time. The woman on the end took one look at him and crumpled back into her chair.

'Please, stay seated everyone,' he said, grinning wolfishly. 'This is not an inspection. I merely glanced at the bulletin and I wanted to say hello. In person.'

Tom stared at Don Gervase Askary with ill-concealed disgust, but he couldn't help feeling the cold fear that had seeped into the room. Even Pearl took an involuntary step backwards.

'It's been a long time, Tom,' he said, flashing a brief smile. 'I was wondering when you would arrive. But how extraordinary that you should be *here* of all places.' Ceremoniously Don Gervase stepped forward and unlocked the cell door. 'What *have* you been doing?'

'We . . . we wanted to come up to the Ministry to see you, and err . . . well, we somehow got lost on the way up,' stumbled Tom, rapidly remembering his role.

'Indeed you did,' he grinned. 'Well do be careful. We have a few rules about getting lost in Scarazand, as you might have discovered to your cost,' he said, glancing at the three ladies, who had almost recovered their composure. They bowed their heads and stared at the table in terror.

'We will. Sorry,' mumbled Tom.

'Don't be sorry,' he replied silkily, 'I merely wanted to welcome you to my earthy world.'

Tom was momentarily taken aback by Don Gervase's courteous behaviour, it was the very last thing he expected: but he knew that Don Gervase could not be trusted one iota . . . unless he truly believed they were now cark beetles.

'And a warm welcome to you, Miss Smoot,' said Don Gervase, studying her face closely. Was this the daughter? He couldn't be sure. It had been so dark on that clifftop and he had only seen her for a brief moment . . . Taking her hand he pressed it as she walked out through the cell door. Pearl looked as if she had shaken hands with a viper, and kept her eyes fixed firmly on the floor. McMaggot the half-breed sat motionless in the corner of the cell, his mouth hanging open in amazement.

'Here . . . here, your honour, what about me?'

Don Gervase turned and stared at the small, misshapen man who suddenly jumped to his feet and bowed low.

'I's with them too, see.'

Don Gervase's milky green eyes bored into him.

'An' I fought at Callaboose an' all,' he said proudly, pointing at his cap. 'Up the glorious revolution!' and he gave a half-hearted salute. 'An' all that.'

There was a chilling silence. Don Gervase's eyes flickered.

'Good fighter, are you?'

'O yes sire, I mean err . . . your gloriousness. No one comes near McMaggot without a toasting,' he said, dancing from one foot to the other and throwing a few hopeful punches. Don Gervase stared at the man, then turned coldly to the three women still quivering at the table.

'Send him up. Let them see him fight.'

McMaggot instantly stopped his routine and gulped loudly. He looked as if he had just been sentenced to death. Perhaps, thought Tom, he had.

'Now you two,' said Don Gervase with a menacing smile, 'please, come with me.'

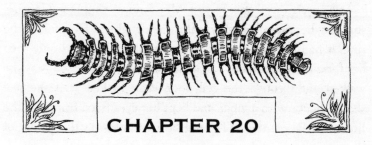

CHAPTER 20

UTOPIA

The three identical women watched in astonishment as Don
Gervase led Tom and Pearl out of the guardroom and down a
short corridor. In the darkness Tom touched Pearl's arm and,
catching her eye, brought his finger to his lips.

'Don't ask him yet,' he whispered as loud as he dared.

'Why not?'

'Let's just see where he's taking us first. If we play along we
might be able to get away.'

That seemed highly unlikely, but even Pearl was forced
to admit that when actually faced with the cold, ruthless
power of Don Gervase everything felt much more difficult.
They followed the tall man in silence, and around the corner
they were met with an extraordinary sight. There before
them was a small gleaming cage, shaped rather like a sedan
chair, inside a large wheel. It was resting on what appeared
to be squadrons of large black woodlice, rolled up into balls,
and there were thousands of others waiting on the rim. The
whole contraption was balanced on a very steep diagonal
track.

'My little capriccio,' grinned Don Gervase, holding open the door. 'A private lift that I designed myself. You like it?'

'Remarkable,' said Tom as they stepped inside.

Don Gervase beamed, evidently pleased with his invention.

'One of the many miracles of Scarazand is that there is never any shortage of labour,' he boomed, and banged on the roof with his fist. The machine began to move upwards, and Tom was dimly aware that the hundreds of black woodlice were scurrying over the roof, rolling themselves into balls and wheeling the carriage along, then scurrying over the roof again in an endless pattern.

'Well isn't this fun,' said Don Gervase, breaking the awkward silence. 'You are probably curious to know where we are going?'

Tom and Pearl nodded.

'How could mere cark converts who have come on a pilgrimage to Scarazand possibly interest the glorious . . . my good self?'

'That's right,' said Tom, doing his best humour him. 'That is exactly what we were wondering.'

'Of course it is,' grinned Don Gervase. 'Well Tom, we have more than a little in common, you and I.'

'We do?'

'Indeed. We share a mutual interest in something rather important. I should like to show it to you.' He smiled, dangerously. 'And you too, Miss Smoot. You intrigue me.'

Pearl felt his milky eyes bore into her and she shifted uncomfortably.

'Actually,' she began, 'actually we have something to show you too,' she said, ignoring Tom pressing hard on her foot.

'Oh? Is it a present?'

'Kind of.'

'How thoughtful of you,' he murmured, 'I adore presents from the lower . . . converts such as yourself. A leader can never have enough gifts,' he grinned. 'How convenient this all is.'

The awkward silence descended once more and the track began to spiral up around a rock column, passing up through a series of rooms and corridors.

'This is the inside of the Ministry,' explained Don Gervase. 'I like to see exactly what is going on.' They sped up through egg rooms, kitchens and state offices, filled with small bespectacled workers wearing a black and gold insignia on their armbands. The moment the curious lift appeared they leapt to attention and bowed their heads. Soldiers saluted, Skrolls bared their bony black heads and Don Gervase smiled and waved back.

'And here the Chamber used to meet before our glorious revolution,' he boomed as they swept up through a large hall that looked something like a cathedral. It was empty save for huge posters of Don Gervase hanging from the rafters, and massive banners of gold and black.

'What happened to them?' asked Tom, with as much absent curiosity as he could manage.

'They and their armies were defeated in battle. On the great plain of Callaboose. Millions upon millions were slain that day, a carpet of death stretched as far as the eye could see.' Don Gervase grinned at the thought. 'You may have seen souvenirs from that great battle for sale down in the town, even met some of the survivors. In fact, you're looking at one right now.'

Tom glanced up at Don Gervase uncertainly. His tongue flickered between his cracked yellow teeth.

'Oh yes, Tom, much has happened since we last met. This is a brave new world, as you will discover. Aha, here we are.'

The chair came to a halt at the top of the spiral and Don Gervase hopped out, disappearing through a narrow stone archway. Tom and Pearl found themselves in a series of dimly lit, empty rooms, all made of the same black stone and intricately carved.

'The revolutionary palace,' boomed Don Gervase as he clattered down a wide staircase. 'Impressive, no?'

Tom and Pearl peered through the gloom at curious machines, half-mechanical, half-insect, that buzzed and flickered in every corner. They were the only objects here.

'This way,' called Don Gervase, his short quick footsteps echoing across the hall. They followed him through a wooden door and were surprised to find themselves in what might have been the library of a grand country house. Unlike the rest of the palace, this room had a strangely homely feel about it. The walls were panelled, books and maps were strewn everywhere and a large Persian carpet stretched out across the floor. There was even a marble fireplace with a fire roaring in the grate.

'The only naked flame in Scarazand,' said Don Gervase, marching up to it and eagerly warming his fingers. 'We have to be very careful with fire down here you see, very careful indeed. A lot of highly flammable materials about.'

Pearl nodded politely, and made a quick mental note of this vulnerability. Tom noticed that in amongst the maps and military paraphernalia there was a divan in a corner with a rough grey blanket thrown over it. He wondered if Don Gervase was even sleeping in here as well.

'You recognize this room, don't you, Tom?' said Don Gervase, greedily warming himself.

Tom was sure that he did.

'Is it . . . the study from Catcher Hall?' he said, not quite sure how that could be possible.

'Correct,' smiled Don Gervase. 'I became rather attached to it during my stay there, so I decided to liberate it, shall we say. A memento of the beginning of my rise to great office.'

Tom tried to recognize anything in the room, and his eye was drawn to a small wooden toy standing on the mantelpiece. It was the figure of a miner, with one arm missing and half its hat knocked off. It looked like a very old, well-loved toy, and seemed a curious object for Don Gervase to have in here.

'So, I am sure that you must be burning with questions to ask me,' said the glorious leader, turning around from the fire.

'Erm . . . actually—'

'How I planned our glorious revolution, perhaps?' interrupted Don Gervase. 'What is the purpose of my great project? Of course, as young converts these thoughts must be uppermost in your mind. Well sit down, and I shall tell you.' Don Gervase stared at them as they stood motionless in the room.

'Didn't you say you had—'

'Sit,' he hissed. 'Please.'

Tom and Pearl obediently sat down on the narrow sofa and waited. Don Gervase cleared his throat and composed himself. Something told Tom that this might take rather a long time.

'I won't begin at the beginning, as that is too tedious,' he droned, as he began pacing the length of the bookcase. 'But you should be aware that the hidden world of Scarazand has existed for many millennia. Here we stand beyond time, outside it, which is why insects from the past, present, and future throng through our gates every day. Some are very small, such as those you might be familiar with, while others are considerably larger. These creatures are from other ages, times when insects, not humans, were masters of the world. You may find this surprising.' He turned towards them and smiled. 'You may ask yourself, how can such creatures be real? Well, let me tell you this, young comrades, there is far more that you don't know about insects than you do. Just because a giant centipede did not have the misfortune to become caught in some swamp and fossilized, does not mean it never existed.'

Tom and Pearl stole a glance at each other and wondered where all this was leading.

'Now,' continued Don Gervase, 'what is my great project of which you, through the good offices of a cark beetle, have both become part? I shall tell you. It is the creation of a new world order, nothing more, nothing less. The washing away of everything you know: all that scrabbling and squalor, filth and greed; washing away all the nastiness of the human race and replacing it with something sharper, cleaner, better. A world without choices, where everything is already decided. Imagine that. Exciting, no?'

Don Gervase paused, allowing these words to sink in.

'It sounds great,' said Tom, with little enthusiasm.

'It *is* great,' smiled Don Gervase. 'And you have the privilege of being chosen as foot soldiers of the great new project. You can feel the Supreme Being pulsing through your minds, can you not?'

Tom nodded.

'She is reminding you of what you are now. Up here,' he droned, tapping his temple with a long finger. 'She is your new country, new family, everything. You will defend her to the death. In fact,' he grinned, 'you won't be able to help yourselves. It is your instinct.'

Tom stared at the carpet and shuddered: was that his instinct as well?

'And is she going to tell us what to do?' he asked.

'Not directly,' continued Don Gervase. 'The Supreme Being is concerned mainly with her own personal well-being. All the rest, the governance of Scarazand, the organization of the great project, she has entrusted it to me. All you need to know is that the Ministry's directives bear the Queen's seal of approval. So as new converts you will be given a duty and sent out into the world. It will be cark conversion, most likely. Cark beetles are most active at night, and there is not a man, woman, or child alive on earth who does not sleep. And the sleep of reason produces monsters, as someone said.' Don Gervase grinned, and permitted himself a little chuckle. 'You will find ways to distribute them, and you will know that your short but glorious lives have been well spent.'

Tom and Pearl sat in silence, wondering how long this pretence was going to go on.

'But why do you want to do this?' she said.

'Why?'

Don Gervase's large yellow eyes held Pearl's like a magnet, but she did not flinch. Perhaps she should have done.

'What a very curious question for a young convert to ask her leader, why?'

'Is it like some big experiment or something? Why do you hate people so much?'

Don Gervase laughed wildly.

'My own deep-seated hatred does not come into it, Miss Smoot. Of course, I would happily wipe the human race from the face of the earth, with good reason,' he said, staring at the small wooden figure on the mantelpiece in front of him. 'But even I, leader of the glorious revolution, am a servant. The Queen is the source of all power at Scarazand. I merely listen to her desires, then act accordingly.'

Tom stared at Don Gervase in wonder: did he really expect them to believe all this nonsense? Maybe millions of others did.

'So what do you do, pray to the Queen and she tells you what to do?' he said.

Don Gervase smiled patronizingly.

'Not quite, comrade. I . . . interpret . . . look through the glass, darkly. It is far too complex for your young minds to understand. But, Tom, it is my fervent hope that one day she will communicate with each and every one of us. Directly.'

He paused to stare at the fire, and both Tom and Pearl knew precisely what Don Gervase was talking about.

'We heard a rumour about an amulet or something,' said Pearl nonchalantly, 'down in the town.'

Don Gervase raised his eyebrows but did not bother to reply.

'And some guy called Nicholas Zumsteen, we heard about him, too.'

There was silence. The name seemed to have a curious effect on Don Gervase: he seemed to grow visibly colder.

'And just what do you know about Nicholas Zumsteen?' he replied, icily.

'Not much. Just some gossip that he found something you want, that's all.'

Don Gervase twitched: was it possible that this girl knew something he didn't? Highly unlikely, in view of what had happened, but still, since he could not be entirely sure . . .

'I should warn you, Miss Smoot, that as a new convert, everything you know now belongs to the glorious revolution. All secrets will be discovered, whether you like it or not,' he murmured, holding Pearl's gaze. 'But, as you are up here, and in a considerably privileged position compared to the rest of the riff-raff in Scarazand, I shall be frank. Nicholas Zumsteen, as he likes to call himself, was once a good comrade, and a loyal servant to the cause. In fact,' he paused a moment, and stared out of the window at the luminous globes floating in the cave beyond, 'in another life, when we were young, like you, we were . . . close. Very close indeed; we had to be. Read each other's thoughts, almost . . . ' Don Gervase's voice had descended to a whisper, and Tom struggled to hear what he was saying.

'As youngsters we were outsiders in an alien world. Being different bound us together, and we made many extraordinary journeys and discovered many things. In fact, he was the one who first discovered the humble cark beetle, deep in the forests of Erebus. But that was a long, long time ago now.'

Don Gervase gazed up at the sea of glittering holes above, lost in his own memories. He seemed almost wistful. Tom waited patiently for him to continue, and as he did so a strange and curious idea started to form in his mind. He thought back to that cavern on Tithona, and those two brothers lost in the maze . . . could it be? Was that possible?

'But, when the time came for action, I am afraid this man you know as Nicholas Zumsteen revealed his true colours,' he continued, turning back to the fire and flicking a log into it with his toe. 'He turned against our glorious cause. I might have forgiven him, had he admitted his treason. But he didn't. Instead, he did something very foolish. He took it upon himself to escape—not through the labyrinth, but by exploiting our only weak spot, our one vulnerability. And in doing so, placed the whole future of Scarazand at risk.' Don Gervase's fingers twisted behind his back like eels. He seemed to be trying to control his temper. 'He is a traitor,' he growled. 'An enemy of the glorious revolution. There is none greater. And despite his capacity for disguise, he will find no hiding place: he knows that. I will personally hunt him down.'

Pearl and Tom glanced at each other and said nothing. There was nothing to say. But in the uneasy silence that strange idea kept ricocheting around Tom's mind. Could it really be that Don Gervase and Nicholas Zumsteen were brothers? Had they both become beetles many years ago, but somehow managed to inhabit people like parasites? Maybe . . .

'Quite how or why I have told you all this I can't imagine,' barked Don Gervase, pulling himself together. 'It was not the reason I brought you here.' Rubbing his hands together, he stalked across to a small panelled door in the corner of the room.

'As I mentioned, I have something to show you. And I guarantee that you in particular will find it interesting, Tom.' Don Gervase grinned, and seemed to have quite recovered his good humour. 'It is the crown jewels of our work at Scarazand.' Tom smiled awkwardly, wondering whether he meant what he thought he meant.

'Come come, no dawdling.'

Opening the small door, Don Gervase bent low and stepped into what appeared to be a giant oily bubble. The ceiling was caked in luminous fungus.

'In the middle, comrades, that's it.'

Balancing on the small platform, Pearl and Tom stood side by side and watched in amazement as black feelers swiftly sealed the gap around the door, and they began to move gently upwards.

'We're . . . we're underwater?' murmured Pearl, watching a large yellow nymph kicking past in the gloom.

'Of course we are,' rumbled Don Gervase. 'I had this vertical tank especially constructed and filled, which was laborious, even by the standards of Scarazand. Every drop of water you see was carried up here on the back of a beetle, and these bubble spiders have been bred especially for this purpose.'

Tom and Pearl stared down at the black shape propelling them upwards, then spotted more of them, swimming around lines of luminous globes tethered together in a grid.

'The regulation of air is vitally important to this work. Nothing could be achieved without it,' droned Don Gervase as they drew closer. Tom had a feeling he knew what this extraordinary experiment was all about, and he hoped despite himself that he would be proved wrong.

'Where it all began,' said Don Gervase proudly, as they came up level with the smallest bubble, no larger than a football. 'The cornerstone of the glorious revolution.'

Tom peered inside the luminous bubble and he felt the blood

drain from his face. It was just as August Catcher had told them it would be.

'I take it you have not forgotten about that little blue bottle you so kindly gave me, have you, Tom?'

Tom could do nothing but gape at the blue bottle from August Catcher's workshop. The bottle that had once contained his extraordinary elixir.

'You may have wondered quite how I was going to make use of it. After all, it was empty, and the dregs inside produce only the smallest amount of gas. But I don't need much. Particularly if that gas has the power to immortalize, animate, prolong life, as you know it can. Given the very brief lifespan of the beetle, that is of enormous importance. Which is why so many rose up and followed me. I had found the key.'

Tom did not know what to say. He realized that as a convert he should appear to be delighted, but he just could not bring himself to do it.

'So how does it work?' he asked, with no enthusiasm.

'The seeds of every great project are always small. In this case I am using oil beetles,' said Don Gervase, pointing to the tiny black specks crawling around the bubble. 'The air the oil beetles breathe in that bubble is heavily suffused with the vapour emanating from that blue bottle. So the beetles hatch, walk about a bit, maybe fly, mate, die, whereupon more are born. And so it goes on, and in sixty generations August Catcher's elixir has become a part of them.'

'And then?'

'Then these oil beetles are bred with other beetles, a little larger than themselves, and after a number of generations it becomes a part of them too. And so it will go on. Gradually I am moving up the orders, from simple to complex, until one day traces of that elixir will exist inside each and every creature in Scarazand, and the last great obstacle that has blocked our path for thousands of years will be removed.'

The spider began to swim across the rows of bubbles, and Tom and Pearl marvelled at the strange underwater laboratory in silence. So this was Don Gervase's dream, to create billions of immortal beetles of all shapes and sizes loyal to Scarazand, which he could then control . . . but only if he found that beetle ball. No wonder he was so desperate to get his hands on it.

'What about cark beetles, and those echoes, too: have you tried breeding the elixir into them?' asked Pearl, watching the tiny grubs.

'Indeed I have, comrade, but these beetles have so far proved remarkably complex, despite their size.' Don Gervase's lips cracked into a mean smile. 'Unfortunately, Miss Smoot, you will never enjoy a long and fruitful life just as I do.'

'So you used it on yourself, then?' snorted Tom, trying hard to conceal his simmering anger. Somehow he knew that he was responsible for all this.

'Actually Tom, I didn't need to. Some of us, the *very* select few, can shift and change *ad infinitum*. But the privileges of the highest orders do not concern foot soldiers such as yourselves,' he grinned.

'How long have we got?' asked Tom uneasily.

'Two months, three at the most: the lifespan of the cark beetle,' replied Don Gervase. 'So you must make sure you use your time well. Beginning now.'

Don Gervase stamped on the floor and they descended swiftly back towards the door. Tom watched the spider deftly fastening the sides of the bubble to the wall in glum silence. He knew that he had not been completely converted, but how much damage had that cark beetle done? Was three months really all the time he had left? He closed his eyes and listened: that distant pulse was still there, beating somewhere at the back of his skull . . .

'To work, comrades,' said Don Gervase as soon as the spider had finished, and led them out through the study and onto a long balcony overlooking the great cave. With an abrupt snap of his fingers he signalled for the large Skroll lurking in the doorway at the far end to come forward.

'This man will take you back to the Ministry where you will receive your instructions,' he said sharply. Now that they had ceased to be a useful audience, whatever friendliness Don Gervase may have shown them had evaporated. The Skroll drew closer and Pearl glanced at Tom: this was the moment.

'Yes,' she insisted, 'before it's too late.'

Don Gervase turned back to them in irritation.

'Erm . . . glorious leader,' she began, not quite sure if this was the right form of address. 'Before we go, there is something we would like to show you,' she said boldly.

Don Gervase stared at the girl impatiently; then he remembered.

'Ah yes. You have a present for me.'

'Yes well it's more than that really. It's . . . you see it's—'

Pearl never finished her sentence, because at that moment a small blue form darted between her and Don Gervase, so close she could feel its wings beating. She gasped as it flew back, almost touching her face.

'What is that?' she cried.

'It's . . . it's a—'

'Swallow,' growled Don Gervase, his eyes narrowing as the bird bombed the girl again and again, then alighted on a stone pinnacle, twittering noisily.

'But how did it get in here?' gasped Tom. 'Through the labyrinth?'

'Obviously not, comrade,' spat the glorious leader. He glowered at the bird, which was just out of reach. Its very presence seemed to be mocking him. 'There is another entrance, an old entrance, formed thousands of years ago. It is well guarded, but clearly not well enough.'

Tom stared at the swallow and his heart began to race. With the greatest difficulty he stifled a smile. Instinctively he knew where it had come from, and who had sent it . . .

'That bird will be the last ever visitor to Scarazand,' muttered Don Gervase, and turning his back he stared sullenly over the railing. 'Once again, I shall have to see to it myself.'

'Erm—'

'You may leave now.'

'But the present—'

'No more presents,' he said sharply, waving them away.

'But you must—'

'Go.'

'It's the amulet,' Pearl blurted out desperately. 'The one you are looking for. The amulet. We found it.'

Don Gervase turned round and stared at her icily.

'Young comrade, I have millions of amulets.'

'I realize that but—'

'But what, precisely?' Don Gervase loomed forward. 'You know Miss Smoot, you really ask a lot of questions for a cark convert. Far, far, *far* too many questions.' He bent down low and scrutinized her. She was ill-mannered and wild-looking, just like her father, but rather beautiful nevertheless. Pearl flinched as he ran his long cold fingers down her cheek. 'You must remember your place, comrade,' he whispered dangerously.

'Take these two to the Ministry, amulet detection room twelve,' he commanded the Skroll, 'then issue them with their life mission, and see to it that they leave Scarazand immediately.'

'No! Absolutely not!'

Lotus Askary stood breathless in a doorway behind them. Her cheeks were flushed and she had obviously been running.

'Lotus?'

Don Gervase seemed surprised to see her.

'Don't trust these people,' she panted. 'They are not what we think they are.'

'What?'

Lotus stood aside, and two sorry figures were thrust out onto the balcony by a pair of Skrolls. Tom and Pearl recognized them immediately; it was Scurf, the owner of the amulet shop, and Mr Winston, the jailer.

'Is this them, Scurf?' she barked.

The terrified little shopkeeper kept his eyes firmly fixed on the ground. He dared not look Don Gervase in the face.

'Look at them when I tell you!' she yelled, and cracked him hard across the back with a white whip. Scurf glanced up.

'Y-y-yes, my lady,' he stammered. 'They was them that was in my shop. In bits.'

'And you, fat man?' she said, poking Mr Winston forward. 'Are these the two you let into the jail? Who then walked through the duplication chambers into the echo library unchallenged, and then—*escaped*?'

Don Gervase bristled visibly. Mr Winston's bald, oily head was running with sweat. His eyes slid in their direction.

'They said they worked for the Ministry,' he blabbered, his antennae twitching. 'Sometimes I could see 'em sometimes I couldn't. I thought they were discombobs, or summat.'

'Discombobs?' spat Don Gervase. 'Would someone kindly explain exactly what is going on?'

'What is going on,' said Lotus, her voice swelling with self-righteous zeal, 'is that these two snivelling miscreants have been up and down Scarazand, hiding beneath some kind of material that makes them invisible. Evidently they have been searching for something. Or someone.'

Don Gervase stared at Tom and Pearl, barely comprehending. 'Is this true?'

Pearl and Tom kept their eyes fixed to the ground. How could they deny it?

'But why would two converts want to make themselves invisible?'

'Because they are *not* converts,' insisted Lotus. 'Or at least we cannot be certain. There is a doubt.'

Don Gervase's eyes widened.

'What precisely do you mean?'

'The man who claimed their conversion is a witchdoctor. He

has since proved to be unreliable. He used a boy named Geronimo to help him, but we have since learned that this boy had connections with . . . with . . . ' Lotus cleared her throat, it seemed that even she did not want to mention the name. 'Nicholas Zumsteen.'

Don Gervase frowned and said nothing. Then he turned and stared down at the thin causeways far below, thronging with insects great and small.

'So you are telling me that these two children found an entrance to the labyrinth somehow, navigated it somehow, and crossed over into Scarazand undetected?'

There was silence. Don Gervase twisted his fingers into a knot; he did not even bother turning round.

'Furthermore,' he continued, 'they have broken into one of the most tightly controlled floors in Scarazand, searched it, then come up here into the very heart of the revolution, where they have . . . I have . . . ' Don Gervase was finding it very difficult to control his temper. He leant forward and dug his fingers into the stone railing, crushing it. 'Is that what you are saying?'

'Yes,' replied Tom. 'That is what we have done.'

Scurf and Mr Winston stared at Tom, their mouths hanging open. Don Gervase turned towards the boy, his face blotching with rage.

'And do you really expect me to *believe* that?'

'We do,' said Pearl, realizing that this was her last chance. 'We did find a way down here, and we have been looking for my brother and my dad. We tried to find them, but we couldn't. So now we came up here to make you an offer, if they are still alive.'

Don Gervase stared at the girl as if she was insane.

'An offer?'

'That's right. You say you will promise anything to the person who finds the amulet you've been looking for. Well, we've found it. And if you let Arlo Smoot, my dad, and Rudy, my brother, go free, we will give it to you.'

Don Gervase shook his head and grinned. And then his grin turned into a chuckle, and his chuckle became a long, wild, gale of hysterical laughter.

'What's so funny?'

'Such innocence, such brave innocence,' he said, wiping his eyes. 'So charming.'

Pearl felt all the colour rush to her cheeks. Her heart started racing.

'What . . . what do you mean?'

'I do not "make offers". I do not "trade". I do not "honour my promises". Do you really think I could have risen so far if I had? How naive you are. And you, Tom Scatterhorn. I thought you had more gumption. There is no question of you ever leaving Scarazand now. Show me your feeble trade.' He clicked his fingers impatiently. 'Give it. I want to see it.'

Pearl looked at Tom desperately. Despite everything, she still clung on to the feeble hope that this might work; that seeing it might change his mind somehow.

'Please,' she begged.

Lotus and the Skrolls and Don Gervase all stared at Tom expectantly.

'Come on!' snapped the glorious leader.

He had no choice. They were surrounded. This was it.

'Very well,' Tom said, delving into his pocket. 'Here, take it, it's yours.'

Don Gervase looked down at the object in his palm and raised his eyebrows. Pearl gasped, then stared at Tom uncomprehendingly.

'W-w-wait,' she stumbled. 'No! Wait a minute, but no, that's not—'

'Your trade?' interrupted Don Gervase, holding up a round red stone with a face carved into it.

Pearl glanced at Tom and with the merest movement of his eyes he indicated the bird twittering above them. She did not understand . . .

'Erm . . . but no, no, it—'

'Scurf,' hissed Lotus, sensing the confusion, 'is that it?'

The shopkeeper gulped in terror.

'Answer correctly if you value what little is left of your life. Was that the amulet these people escaped with from your shop?'

Scurf knitted his brow; suddenly he was very muddled.

'I'm sorry, my lady, but do you mean—'

'Answer correctly you idiot man!' she yelled. 'These are the fugitives that were in your shop, correct?'

'Yes, my lady.'

'They left your shop with an amulet, correct?'

'Yes, my lady.'

'Did they take *that* amulet out of your shop?'

Scurf was so terrified and bewildered that he couldn't bring himself to look at Lotus glowering down at him. He squinted at the red stone face in Don Gervase's hand.

'Yes. Yes, yes they did take *that* amulet from the shop, my lady. Only—'

'Right,' said Lotus triumphantly.

Scurf was so cowed that he daren't say any more. Pearl glanced at Tom and his eyes told her to keep silent. The swallow was still cheeping agitatedly above them.

'Good,' boomed Don Gervase impatiently. 'This has gone on far too long. Take this trinket away and send them down to jail.'

'Jail?' Lotus stared at him incredulously. 'Jail? Do you realize where they have been? Others have died for less!'

Don Gervase paused for a moment, appreciating what Lotus was saying.

'Very well, Lotus. Your vindictiveness is admirable. It will have to be something else.'

Lotus grunted approvingly, and the glorious leader turned towards the glittering cave, thinking hard. Something unusual was required . . . Suddenly he had an idea.

'What about giving them a sporting chance?'

'Meaning what?'

'As an aperitif before the main event.'

Lotus looked at him, and then a thin, unpleasant smile spread across her face.

'So—'

'Absolutely. It's tonight isn't it? And bearing in mind who is taking part, I think that would be something of a spectacle, don't you?'

'Ingenious,' said Lotus with a giggle.

'Good,' he smiled. 'At last we agree about something.'

Scurf and Mr Winston, sensing that their luck had changed, began grinning inanely.

'What are you talking about?' demanded Pearl. 'What's going on?'

Don Gervase stared down at her with icy curiosity.

'Young lady, your short lives have just become a good deal shorter. Save whatever greatness you might have achieved in life for your death.'

He snapped his fingers and instantly the two hooded Skrolls held Tom and Pearl in a vice-like grip.

'Take them up,' he barked. 'Take them up to the arena.'

CHAPTER 21

LUPOSERPSIS MAXIMUS

At first glance it appeared to be some kind of holding area beneath a stage. Tom and Pearl had been forced up several steep flights of steps, passing a series of dimly lit cages filled with men and half-breeds of all shapes and sizes. Some sat astride ungainly-looking insects, others wore remnants of military clothing tied around their misshapen bodies. All of them seemed very nervous as the roar of the crowds rang down from above.

'Ignore this rabble,' sneered Don Gervase, leading the way to a circular platform that was connected to the ceiling. 'They are nothing but cannon fodder. And they know it.'

The assorted cannon fodder watched in surly silence as the Skrolls shoved Tom and Pearl roughly onto the platform and Don Gervase clapped his hands sharply.

'Gord! Where is that old fool?'

A sturdy, grey-faced figure shambled out of the darkness wearing a collection of wicker baskets strung about him on leather belts.

'Your grace?' croaked the old man, hardly daring to look up. Tom's eyes widened as he noticed that Gord's heavy coat was crawling with shining black insects, and he had a pile of thin red worms coiled around his hat.

'I have an addition to tonight's performance.'

'An addition, your grace?'

'Yes. These two will begin the proceedings.'

'And the other prisoners?'

'They will follow on. Or maybe they will join them, I haven't decided. Now bind them together. A milliwig on each wrist, I think.'

'Just one wrist, your grace?'

'Yes yes, get on with it,' snapped Don Gervase impatiently.

'Very good, your grace.'

Tom and Pearl had their arms held out, and the old man undid a basket around his waist and pulled out a thin, writhing millipede the size of a small eel.

'Oh!' gasped Pearl, as Gord shook it off his hand into her hair, whereupon it darted down and coiled itself around her neck. She closed her eyes, expecting the worst . . .

'Don't worry, Miss Smoot,' smiled Don Gervase, enjoying her discomfort. 'It's not you it wants to kill.'

Opening another basket Gord placed a second milliwig on Tom's back, but barely had it coiled itself around his throat before it spotted the other milliwig.

'Euch!' grimaced Tom, as the creature tore down his outstretched arm. The milliwig around Pearl's neck rushed down to meet it, and the next moment they had clamped around each other: legs, bodies, jaws entwined in a solid knot, handcuffing Pearl and Tom together.

'It's a test of strength, you see,' explained Don Gervase. 'Once two male milliwigs have joined in battle they will never let go until one of them dies. Rather appropriate don't you think?'

There was a moment's pause, and another roar filtered down from above.

'So what's going to happen to us up there?' demanded Tom, fiercely trying to ignore the writhing knot that now bound them together.

'That is entirely up to you,' replied Don Gervase smoothly. 'I have to see how the new breeds perform, test them somehow, and for that purpose I need adversaries. The crowds adore it, of course. I had planned to start the proceedings with two worthless prisoners, but you will be so much better. If you *have* been converted, then listen to the pulses inside your head. Who knows—they might even help you, but I doubt it. If not, then your annihilation will offer a wonderful spectacle.' He grinned. 'So either way, you will have done something useful.'

Pearl shook her head in disgust.

'You're so sick.'

There was a collective gasp and the room fell instantly silent. Don Gervase cocked his head, he wasn't sure if he had heard correctly. Pearl stared down at Don Gervase with outright contempt.

'This whole glorious revolution is sham—isn't it? Fiddling around in your little fish tank upstairs, claiming you have found the secret of eternal life, pretending you have the authority of the Queen—Ha! That's a good one! You have no idea what she's thinking; you can't control her any more than any of us in this room!' Pearl was shouting now, and every syllable trembled with rage. 'That's why you are so desperate to find the amulet, isn't it—before they find you out!'

Pearl swallowed hard, her eyes filling with hot, angry tears. 'You think you're some great leader, but you're a nothing. An impostor, and a bully—nothing more. A fake.'

The silence in the room was deafening. All eyes were on Don Gervase. It was clear that the assembled half-breeds fully expected him to step up and kill the girl there and then. But for some reason, he didn't. He simply wound his long fingers into a knot and cleared his throat. Lotus watched him nervously.

'I think,' he growled, 'I think I shall not grace that little outburst with so much as a reply, so far is it from the truth.' He glared around the room, dangerously. 'Instead, you may like to know about your adversary. You have, I believe, seen the bombardier beetle?'

Tom and Pearl said nothing: she was still shaking with rage. 'Well tonight you will be the first adversaries, or should I say, victims, of its big brother. Luposerpsis Maximus. The wolfskidder beetle.'

There was a nervous silence.

'What do you think about that?'

Tom shrugged his shoulders.

'Not a lot.'

'Not a lot?'

'Yeah. I quite like bombardier beetles.'

There was a suppressed snigger at the back, which Don Gervase silenced with a glare. If anything, Tom's calculated insolence seemed to offend him almost as much as Pearl's outburst, but once again, somehow he managed to bottle his fury.

'Don't presume to play games with me, Tom Scatterhorn,' he murmured darkly. 'I need not remind you of your predicament. Gord,' he barked, and the old man juddered to attention. 'Take them up, then wait for my signal.'

Gord bowed so deeply that the red worms dripping from his hat almost touched the floor.

'As you say, your grace.'

Don Gervase shot them one final, withering glance, then turned on his heel and swept out of the room, swiftly followed by Lotus and the Skrolls. The old man leapt up onto the circular platform and barked a command, whereupon a team of large yellow ants appeared carrying long poles. Slotting them into a ring of holes beneath the rim of the platform, they each took up their position.

'Wheel right!' screeched Gord. The ants bent their weight to the poles and began to push and slowly the platform started to revolve upwards, turning on a massive screw and lifting the roof above it. Beneath the knot of milliwigs Pearl gripped Tom's hand tightly as the noise erupted above them.

'Break a leg!' shouted one of the half-breeds in the cage.

'Yeah, stick 'em where it hurts!' shouted another.

'Remember they's all terrifyin' lookin' but dead stupid really!'

The chorus of advice continued as the platform rose up, and moments later Tom and Pearl found themselves standing in the arena of a large stadium, close to the pinnacle of Scarazand. The whole edifice was built around the rock column that extended right up to the cave roof above, and the roar that greeted their arrival was fantastic.

'I'm really sorry I got you into all this,' whispered Pearl, glancing at the legs, carapaces, and broken remains of beetles scattered in the dirt all around.

'You didn't,' said Tom, trying to ignore his heart thumping in his temples. 'I came because I wanted to. We both got in and we're both going to get out of this place together, somehow.'

'That doesn't make me feel better.'

A roar swept around the stands as Don Gervase, Lotus, and their entourage took their seats in a large box at the centre. The glorious leader waved absently and sat down.

'Right you two—off!' wheezed Gord, thrusting Tom and Pearl off the platform. Lifting a loose plank he shouted a command to the waiting ants below. Immediately the lift began to screw back into the floor, whereupon Gord ceremoniously began searching their pockets. The crowd cheered as out onto the dirt went Tom's penknife, the small leather bottle of pheromone spray, and then, at last, the beetle ball, wedged in Tom's back pocket.

'Oh look, he's brought his ball with him,' squawked Gord, holding it up to show the crowd. 'Come to play football have yer, sonny!' and he punted it away into the dust. The crowd howled and Don Gervase smiled, but his eyes followed the odd rubbery ball as it rolled to a halt beneath him. This was a little unexpected, why was the boy carrying that? Gord danced across to a small ladder hanging off the stone column and waited beneath a large horn. He looked across at the royal box expectantly and the crowd hushed. All eyes turned from the old man to Don Gervase.

'Dad?'

Lotus nudged Don Gervase, who was still staring at the ball lying in the dust. He could see patterns on it. It was probably nothing, just a toy. Anyway, he was searching for something quite different. Something precious, not any old rubber ball . . .

'Dad? Can they begin?' Lotus stared at him impatiently. 'Dad, what are you doing—'

'Yes, yes,' he said, and nodded briefly at Gord, who blew a deep penetrating blast on the horn.

'I guess this is it,' whispered Pearl, as the crowd fell silent. Two large doors were rolled aside and something began to rumble forward out of the darkness. It was a team of powerful black beetles, drawing a large grey cocoon behind them. A ripple of anticipation swept through the stands.

'Ladies and gentlemen,' boomed the announcer through a large trumpet as the great cocoon was hauled out into the centre of the arena. 'Before we begin tonight's show: a re-enactment of the battle of Callaboose, where our glorious leader led us to victory . . . '

There was a pause to allow the crowd to shout in unison, 'All hail our glorious leader!'

' . . . we have a surprise for you,' the announcer continued. 'A new design, straight from the hatchery.' The walls of faces craned forward excitedly.

'For the first time in Scarazand—he's black, he's bad, and he's the beast, he's the wolfskidder beetle!'

Thunderous applause met the announcement, and all eyes turned towards the large grey cocoon. What extraordinary, hideous creature was hiding inside? The crowd did not have to wait long to find out. Gord shuffled across to the dark entrance, grabbed a long spike and shuffled back again.

'You ready for this!' he howled. 'You ready?' The crowds

cheered and Gord tipped his hat and did a little pirouette: he was obviously enjoying his moment in the sun.

'Well let the fun begin!'

Taking aim, Gord hurled the spike with surprising force straight into the cocoon. The point stuck hard and juddered, whereupon the old man skittered to the safety of the entrance. There was a collective gasp as the cocoon began to swell and split.

'Quick,' whispered Tom, 'the spray and the ball.'

Carefully they began to edge sideways towards the small bottle lying in the dirt until they were right in front of it.

'Trip me up,' whispered Tom.

'Why—'

'Just do it,' he hissed.

'Ha ha! Look! They can't even walk proper!' shouted a man as Tom and Pearl tumbled to the ground. A ripple of laughter rang round the stadium and suddenly all eyes were on them once more. Awkwardly they got to their feet to howls of derision.

'Thanks,' whispered Tom, slipping the small spray bottle into his pocket with his free hand.

'Arm yourselves, you idiots, it's gettin' out!' shouted a woman.

Tom and Pearl turned round and their eyes widened as long, spiky legs began to force their way out of the cocoon, followed by a gleaming black carapace. It was enormous.

'Arm yerselves! Arm yerselves!' chanted the crowd. 'We want a proper contest!'

Tom glanced back to where the beetle ball lay in the dirt: it was directly beneath Don Gervase. There was no time to get it now. And what good would it do them, anyway?

'Erm . . . maybe arming ourselves would be a good idea,' breathed Pearl, watching as the spiky wolfskidder sloughed off the remains of the cocoon with its leg. The creature turned round, its small red eyes dully inspecting the new world it found itself in. It seemed to be made of polished black steel and it was the size of a truck.

'There's a shield, over there!' yelled Pearl, and pulling Tom over to a large round piece of chitin lying in the dirt she picked it up.

'What about a spear,' breathed Tom, moving back towards a long black spike that had once been a mandible. 'We need—'

'Wait!' shouted Pearl, tripping up over the shield and dragging Tom to the ground.

'We're stuck together remember,' she hissed crossly, hauling herself to her feet, 'you can't just run off!'

'Sorry,' said Tom, 'it's just that there's—'

'I can see that,' interrupted Pearl. 'Here, help me with this.'

Taking one side of the shield each, they shuffled across to where the spike lay, then Tom bent down to pick it up. The dull-eyed wolfskidder watched the object with four legs scurrying underneath it. To its simple mind, anything that moved was worth attacking. So it did.

There was a gasp from the crowd as the wolfskidder raised its barbed mandibles and careered across the arena towards them at terrifying speed.

'Oh my God . . . it's, erm, what-' Pearl grabbed Tom's arm as the insect approached. Tom stood up as long as he dared, then hurled the spike at the rushing creature. Suddenly a jet of hot reddish liquid shot out of the wolfskidder's side, knocking it away as if it were a twig. The crowd screamed with pleasure and instantly Tom dropped behind the shield next to Pearl.

'It shoots hot acid,' he trembled, 'I forgot they could do that.'
Pearl looked terrified.

'What are we going to do?'

'Crawl under that one?' gulped Tom, indicating another broken carapace lying a couple of metres away.

'OK.'

Without a moment's thought Pearl and Tom threw themselves towards the carapace, and scurried under it just as the air behind them ripped with the sound of splintering. The crowd cheered, and Tom glanced back to see their chitin shield fractured into a thousand pieces. The wolfskidder foraged past them, probing.

'We've got to get rid of these milliwigs somehow,' he grimaced, tugging hard at the knotted creatures around his wrist. 'We can't do anything like this.'

'Here,' said Pearl, pulling Tom's penknife out of her pocket, 'let me try.'

'You picked it up?'

'Of course I did,' she whispered, 'I dropped the shield remember? How else was I going to get it?'

Tom gasped at her ingenuity and watched as Pearl began hacking viciously with the blade. But it was as if the milliwigs were made of wire. Just then there was a loud clang on the carapace above them.

'There they are! Under there!' screamed the man who had cast the stone. Another clang and the carapace wobbled and fell over. Instantly Tom and Pearl scrabbled to their feet: and the wolfskidder saw them. Movement. It charged. There was nothing for it but to run.

'Go left!' screamed Pearl, pulling Tom away around the stone column.

'Right!' he shouted back as they dipped behind a carcass.

The crowd howled with delight as Tom and Pearl ducked and darted through the debris with the wolfskidder firing shot after shot of scalding red liquid right behind them, smashing everything in its path.

'We've got to use the spray, or get to that beetle ball—something!' shouted Pearl above the din.

'Look!' panted Tom, sprinting hard, 'the milliwigs, they're moving!' Pearl glanced at the living knot locking their wrists together and saw that Tom was right. The gap between them had lengthened slightly. Maybe all the tugging and wrenching was having some effect . . .

'I've got an idea,' screamed Tom, seeing two broken pieces of carapace ahead of them. 'Let's get behind those.'

'But we can't stop, it will—'

The next moment Tom dived down into the dust, dragging Pearl with him.

'Are you crazy,' she panted, 'it's seen us, it'll—'

'I know,' trembled Tom, frantically pulling the small spray bottle from his pocket, 'I just can't think what else to do.'

Quickly he sprayed Pearl's arm up to the elbow, then his own.

'It senses movement, then fires at it. Maybe it will do this job for us.'

Tom slithered across to the adjacent piece of chitin and, hiding behind it, stretched out his arm.

'Pull!' he shouted. Pearl did as she was told, and the milliwigs began to writhe around each other. 'When it fires, pick up that carapace and run behind the wolfskidder,' he instructed, 'I'll do the same.'

Whatever Pearl said was drowned out by the roar of the crowd, watching the wolfskidder stalk the two pieces of debris.

'Move you idiots! It's seen you!' they screamed.

Inside the giant beetle's simple mind it saw two motionless objects. In the air between them was a black lump, writhing and coiling. Movement . . . it fired. A ferocious blast of hot acid knocked Tom and Pearl backwards—but they were free. What remained of the milliwigs hung in melted shreds around their wrists.

'Run round!' screamed Tom. Instantly the wolfskidder became even more bewildered as the two pieces of debris suddenly sprouted legs and ran behind it in opposite directions. It reversed awkwardly, firing first at one, then the other, then rotated again and fired again, missing them both. It was quite unable to decide which to chase.

'Keep going!' shouted Tom as they ran round and round the great beast, whose shots became more and more erratic, cannoning up into the stands and showering the spectators with scalding red liquid.

'Rubbish!' shouted a woman.

'Too easy!' screamed another. 'This wolfskidder's crap!'

Suddenly the atmosphere changed, and loud hissing and booing began to echo around the stadium. Tom and Pearl skittered away to the far side of the stone column but the wolfskidder did not follow, it kept hunting behind itself, shooting at anything and nothing, misfiring like a broken toy. The booing and whistling reached a crescendo and Don Gervase looked very uncomfortable indeed. Lotus glared up at the stands furiously.

'This dissent should not be tolerated, you know. Stop them.'

Don Gervase stood up abruptly and nodded at Gord, still hovering at the dark entrance. The old man bowed low, then barked a command back into the darkness. There was a heavy creak, and another circle in the floor of the arena began to turn. Lotus was beside herself.

'What are you doing?' she demanded. 'You can't bring more up, it will just make it easier!'

Don Gervase ignored her, and settling back into his seat he twined his fingers into a knot.

'Do you want us to be humiliated?'

'Of course not!' he snapped. 'I guarantee this will *not* make it easier. Quite the contrary, in fact.'

Slowly the screw began to rise, and the crowd quietened a little, curious to see who would appear next. The wolfskidder noticed it, and abandoned its hopeless hunting. Lotus craned forwards, and so did Tom, and so did Pearl, too . . .

'A stroke of genius, don't you think?' smirked Don Gervase.

Lotus watched as the two figures were hustled off the platform by a bombardier beetle nipping at their ankles. Her cat-like face split into a smile. Suddenly Pearl ran forward.

'Dad!' she screamed. 'Dad!'

At first the man did not appear to hear her, but the boy did.

'Pearl!'

'Rudy!'

'Oh my god, it's you!'

Entirely forgetting the arena, the wolfskidder, and the watching audience, Pearl sprinted across the arena and threw herself into their arms, hugging them tight.

'Dad! Dad, it's me! Pearl!'

'Oh, hi sweetie,' said Arlo absently, 'I guess it's you, isn't it?'

Pearl stepped back and stared at him.

'Dad? Are you OK?'

Something was not right; she could feel it.

'I guess I am. Yeah. Sure. Why not?'

'They took him away. Those alien dudes took him away. He only came back last night,' said Rudy, staring nervously up at the crowds and the ceiling of the glittering cave above. 'Where are we?'

'They took him away? Really?'

Pearl's bright blue eyes searched her father's crumpled face. He looked more dishevelled than ever.

'You the rescue squad, huh?' said Arlo absently, glancing across at Tom who was watching them.

'Wow, what's *that*?'

Rudy pointed at the vast wolfskidder on the other side of the arena watching them curiously. The sight of something new brought it to its senses. It started to move forward . . .

'That is something extremely dangerous,' breathed Pearl, nervously watching the wolfskidder advance. 'And you are going to have to run as fast as you can very, very soon.'

'Run? Oh OK. Whatever,' said Arlo Smoot absently. 'Let's go, man.'

'What's it going to do?' whispered Rudy, staring in horror at the oncoming creature.

Before Pearl had a chance to reply the red bombardier scurried towards the wolfskidder and began firing thin jets of liquid at its head. A wave of derision swept through the stadium: it was like watching a mouse firing a water pistol at an elephant. Suddenly a line of red-hot acid exploded from the wolfskidder's flank and hit the bombardier squarely between the thorax and abdomen, cutting it neatly in two. The crowd screamed and began baying for blood.

'Ow!' shouted Rudy, as a stone hit him on the back.

Then another hit Pearl. Then another.

'Run! Run! Run! Run!' The chorus rang around the stands, and soon they were being pelted from all directions . . .

'This should be interesting,' smirked Don Gervase, watching the Smoots huddled together before the oncoming beast. 'Who is going to save whom? Will the weakest be sacrificed?'

Suddenly the Smoots bolted, Pearl dragging Rudy with Arlo bringing up the rear, and the wolfskidder galloped after them, firing left and right. Tom crawled out of his hiding place and quickly took in the scene. They weren't going to last long . . . seconds at the most . . . His eyes blazed furiously, what could he do?

Think, Tom, think . . . if only—

Tom saw the rickety steps hanging off the stone column leading up to where the horn hung. Suddenly he had an idea. It was mad, but so mad it just might work.

'Pearl!' he shouted. 'Pearl!'

She glanced across at him wildly, the shots of hot liquid cannoning down all around them.

'To the ladder!' he screamed. 'Lead it under the ladder!'

She nodded uncomprehendingly and sprinted round the far

side of the arena, dragging Arlo and Rudy as best she could. The crowd were noisy now, cheering as each shot got closer and closer.

'Come on Dad!' shouted Pearl, dragging Arlo who was struggling to keep up.

Everyone ignored Tom, who leapt to his feet and, dodging through the debris, hared across to the stone column and clambered up the small rickety ladder. Breathless, he saw Pearl racing around the bend towards him. On came the wolfskidder, thundering behind . . . surely it was only a matter of seconds now . . . Don Gervase leant forward and the crowd screamed . . . Tom hung off the ladder as the vast creature barrelled towards him. Could it see him? It was too late now. With his heart thumping in his temples Tom chose his spot behind the wolfskidder's head, and the next moment he jumped . . .

BANG!

He hit the carapace so hard he almost bounced off it, but the beetle did not even notice. Left, right, left . . . its flanks lit up with jets of scalding liquid.

Don Gervase leapt to his feet incredulously.

'What is that boy doing?' he shouted, as the wolfskidder disappeared around the far side of the column. Clinging on to the galloping creature, Tom reached forward and with one hand squirted the little bottle of pheromone liquid first into one beady red eye, then the other. The wolfskidder kept on, but somehow the movement it sought was no longer all there, just fractured parts. And then suddenly its prey disappeared. The great beast skidded to a halt, sending Tom flying forward over its spiky head onto one black barbed mandible, then crashing down into the dirt. Suddenly the crowd hushed: surely it would kill him now, it must. Tom lay panting on the ground, then slowly, and with the utmost care he pushed himself up and swivelled to face the vast creature. If he was going to die now, he wanted to see it coming . . .

The excitement was palpable: how could the boy run? He was right under its nose. Tom's heart was beating so fast he could scarcely think, but with every scrap of self-control he made himself as still as a statue, staring into those dull red eyes. The wolfskidder shook its head: it sensed there was something directly in front of it, but where? It let off a couple of aimless shots to the right and left. Nothing. Then it began to back away. A ripple went around the stadium, what was it going to do? It looked as if it was about to charge . . . why didn't the boy run? Pearl, Arlo, and Rudy stood watching, open-mouthed—and Don Gervase and Lotus were on their feet watching too. Either this Tom Scatterhorn was very brave, or very mad, or possibly both. Tom sat motionless, he could hear nothing, see nothing more than those two dull red eyes . . . he was concentrating so hard it was as if he had gone out of himself somehow, and that the boy sitting in the dust was someone else . . . A stone landed beside him and bounced away. He didn't flinch. Then another: to the left. The wolfskidder saw it. Movement . . . instantly it charged forward and fired salvo after salvo at the stone, sending it cannoning into the debris beyond. Tom threw himself to the ground as the wolfskidder galloped right over him, firing wildly, following the trail of its own destruction with more destruction. It did not even see the Smoots standing pressed to the stone column.

'Like a dog with a ball,' seethed Don Gervase, watching the wolfskidder rampaging round the arena, chasing the bags and stones and hats raining down from the stands to the delight of the crowds. This was not what he had had in mind at all. With an impatient nod he signalled to Gord that the main event should begin. Gord barked another order into the darkness, then scurried across to the horn and let out a deep and penetrating blast.

'Ladies and gentlemen,' boomed the announcer, 'and now we give you a faithful recreation of the great battle of Callaboose!'

A dozen circles on the arena floor began revolving upwards, revealing gangs of grim-faced half-breeds armed with swords, men on beetleback carrying spikes and chariots pulled by centipedes.

'The forces of the Chamber!' shouted the announcer. There was a loud booing and hissing, and spectators began to pelt them with stones.

'And the forces of our glorious leader!'

Out through the dark entrance poured phalanx after phalanx of magnificent brown beetles, powerful and shining, accompanied by narrow-faced soldiers bearing black and gold standards and armed Skrolls leading hundreds of angry red bombardier beetles. The crowd roared as the soldiers and hooded men waved to the stands.

'This is going to be really, really crazy,' gasped Tom as he joined the Smoots pressed against the stone column. 'You OK?'

'I think so. Dad?'

Arlo turned round. He seemed weirdly relaxed.

'Yeah?'

'Are we OK?' asked Pearl.

'No problem,' he said, watching the forces massing all around them. 'I'm chilled.'

'Chilled?' Pearl shook her head in exasperation: it was quite obvious that something had happened to her father and from now on she would have to take command. 'Thanks for what you did back then,' she said, turning to Tom. 'Really.'

'Oh, it's nothing.'

'You saved our bacon,' she smiled, 'as you might say.'

'Yeah,' breathed Rudy, looking up at Tom in admiration. 'That was like awesome.'

Tom shrugged, a little embarrassed.

'You would have done the same thing I'm sure.'

'What, my sister?' gasped Rudy. 'You've got to be kidding.'

Pearl laughed. 'Thanks bro',' she grinned, ruffling his hair. 'Now let's find a way out of this.'

But finding a way out of this was easier said than done. Tom had half-expected there to be a blast from the horn to signal the start of the battle, but when he looked back at the arena it had already started. Everywhere tightly packed waves of beetles swarmed down upon the motley gangs of half-breeds and men, slicing at them with long mandibles and skewering them with their horns, who defended and parried as best they could. In amongst the chaos the wolfskidder crashed this way and that, squirting all and sundry, and beneath its legs the swarm of red bombardier beetles sank their teeth into anything that moved.

'Now remember, ladies and gentlemen,' boomed the announcer above the din, 'battles are dangerous! Take care in the front row!'

'Take care? That's why we're bleedin' here, innit!' screamed a woman, dodging out of the way of a flying leg and pelting a half-breed with stones.

'Stick together fellas,' screamed a familiar voice at the head of a roughly formed square, around which wave after wave of brown beetles were breaking. 'Just like we did in the real thing!'

Tom looked across and saw little McMaggot, their fellow prisoner, wielding a broken mandible.

'Yeah but we was on the other side then!' screamed his mate, knocking a beetle away. 'And we won!'

'That's freedom for you, laddie!' McMaggot yelled back. 'You get to do it all over and over again!'

Tom and the Smoots stood huddled beside the central column, dodging the flying armour slamming into the stone all around them.

'We've got to get that beetle ball back, you know,' gasped Pearl above the din. 'He can't have it now. No way.'

'I know.' Tom nodded grimly, staring into the mayhem. 'I'll go.'

'Not without me you won't,' said Pearl.

'Me neither,' added Rudy. 'I'm sticking with you.'

There was nothing else for it.

'Come on then!' shouted Tom, and dived into the battle.

'But—'

Pearl picked up Rudy, covered his eyes and ran.

'Is that really a good idea?' mumbled Arlo, watching them disappear into the chaos. 'Oh OK,' he said absently, and shambled in after them.

Don Gervase stared down into the arena, in which there was

no longer any semblance of lines or sides, just a wild jumble of creatures fighting each other, hand to hand.

'Do you think they will survive?' said Lotus, enjoying the battle.

'I very much doubt it,' he replied. 'Few are left standing at the end of these affairs. And if by some accident they are, they will certainly not get away,' he added, slyly. 'That is taken care of.'

Lotus smirked, but she did not quite understand. Don Gervase craned forward and stared at the spot just below him where that curious ball had fallen. Amazingly it was still there in the dust, half-hidden now beneath an upturned carcass. For some reason that clear rubber ball intrigued him, he could not think why . . .

'I can see it!'

Tom crashed down behind some debris, panting hard. Somehow they had made it this far. Pearl thumped down next to him and spotted it too, glittering in the dust just beyond. Suddenly a gang of red bombardier beetles scrabbled over the top of them, biting viciously.

'Ow!' screamed Rudy.

'Get off!' roared Tom, kicking them roughly aside. Ignoring the chaos, Pearl began to crawl out through the legs of the battling men and insects towards the ball. Don Gervase recognized her instantly, then Tom, and then the Smoots too, hiding amid the debris just beneath him. How intriguing: why on earth would they risk life and limb to retrieve that ball? It looked like a toy—probably a sentimental keepsake that boy happened to have in his pocket. A present from his mother perhaps . . . unless, *unless* . . . Don Gervase's eyes widened and he almost choked at his own stupidity. Unless the girl had been telling the truth! And that Scatterhorn boy had deceived him: was that possible? His eyes narrowed as he watched the girl snatch the ball out of the dust: of course it was—of course it was! But what of The Chamber, their scrolls and traditions and libraries of ancient texts? Hadn't they all told him that this amulet would be something unique, highly prized—probably encased for its own protection? He watched the boy beat off another pair of bombardiers with his bare hands and drag the girl back to safety. No . . . no . . . they were wrong—all of them . . . quite wrong—these idiot children proved it. His lips parted excitedly: there it was, the secret key to his revolution, so close! He would stop this charade immediately—prise it from them before—

'Here, what's that?' shouted a man in the crowd. Spectators were turning round, craning upwards towards the roof of the cave.

'What is it?'

There was something out there, getting closer . . . a noise?

'Listen up lads, listen up!' shouted McMaggot to the battered remains of his square. The bloodied, misshapen men ignored the din of the raging battle and stared up into the vast cave. What *was* that sound?

Pearl raised her head out of the dust and she heard it too. A droning. Getting louder . . .

'It's an engine,' she whispered, 'isn't it?'

'Bloody hell . . . bloody hell! Here comes the bleedin' cavalry!' shouted a half-breed. The spectators looked up above the stadium and suddenly began cheering wildly.

'It's a proper show this, innit! Proper show!' they screamed.

Don Gervase stood up, oblivious to the din, his face a picture of scandalized incomprehension. There, circling around the rim of stands just above him were a swallow, an eagle, and two biplanes. He was utterly speechless. And so was Tom, lying there in the dirt.

'Isn't that Sir Henry Scatterhorn?' gasped Pearl, hardly daring to believe it.

CHAPTER 22

BARNSTORMING

And Pearl was right. It *was* Sir Henry in one plane, and Trixie in another, and the Australian eagle following on behind. Tom stared up in amazement, watching the two planes circling beneath the great dome of the cave, just beyond the jaws of the vast snapping centipedes.

'But how could they have found the entrance?' said Pearl, still not sure whether to believe if it was real or not.

'Must have been that swallow, maybe it showed them the way in somehow—hey, look!' shouted Tom, pointing to a tiny black speck darting across the stands, 'there it is.'

Pearl spotted the bird and her heart began to soar. Suddenly there might be a way out of this.

'Rudy, we're going to get out!' she shouted joyfully, picking him up out of the dust and hugging him tight. 'We're saved!'

The small boy looked up at the biplanes circling around the great rock tower. They were almost inside the stadium now.

'But do they *know* we are down here?' he said doubtfully. 'And like, how are we going to jump into a moving plane?'

All around the battle was raging fiercely and the crowd were screaming louder than ever: to them these new arrivals were part of the show. The two biplanes banked steeply, then dived down low over the chaos. Tom scrambled to his feet.

'They must be looking for us!' he shouted. 'Here! Over here!'

The crowd screamed and Don Gervase could barely contain himself as they roared right past his nose.

'The mimicwings,' he spat above the din, 'where are they?'

'Ready, as ever, my lord,' growled a particularly tall Skroll lurking behind him.

'Release them.'

'All of them, sire?'

'All of them. This charade has gone far enough.'

The hooded man slid away into the shadows, and Don Gervase was forced to watch as the planes came round yet again. This time he could quite clearly see Sir Henry Scatterhorn piloting one plane, a red-haired woman piloting the other, *and* that infernal bird. This was really adding insult to injury.

'I thought you had dealt with these people!'

Lotus shifted uneasily as Don Gervase's sallow features turned white with anger.

'I had dealt with them!' she protested. 'I-I located their hideaway, searched it, burned it—'

'But you didn't kill them?'

Lotus scowled at him petulantly.

'How was I to know they would find a way in here—'

'There's always some excuse, isn't there, Lotus? Always some reason why you seem incapable of doing the simplest thing. Well?'

Lotus seethed, but said nothing.

'I must say I am rapidly tiring of these little scenes,' he muttered menacingly. 'Go,' he barked, waving her away. 'Guard all causeways, watch all exits, then wait for my command. Do *not* fail.'

Lotus turned on her heel and strode off without a word.

Don Gervase shook his head: would he ever be able to trust anyone to do anything? It seemed not. Staring down into the chaos still raging below him he searched for that Scatterhorn boy, and those Smoot people, but they seemed to have disappeared into the fray. Never mind . . . they wouldn't get far . . . and neither would those intruders once the mimicwings appeared.

'Come on come on,' he hissed impatiently, scanning the ceiling of the vast cave, 'where are you . . . '

Tom and Pearl had somehow managed to drag Rudy and Arlo back through the battle and took shelter beside the stone column.

'Tom!' hollered a familiar voice. 'Where the blazes are you? Tom, mate!'

Stepping out from the wall Tom narrowly missed being decapitated by a piece of flying armour and looked up to see the Australian eagle banking towards him.

'Here!' he shouted. 'Over here!'

'Dang it there you are . . . Wo!' The eagle twisted sharply to avoid a hot jet of red acid from the wolfskidder thundering round the corner. 'I hate bloody battles!'

'What shall we do?' Tom cried.

The eagle turned again and swept in as low as he dared.

'There ain't no chance in hell we can pick you folks out of

this—it's too durned difficult and no mistake. Can yer—' The
eagle ducked, dodging a flying carapace that shot up into the air.
'Can you get yerselves down to one of them spindly bridges
round the back?'

'Erm . . . ' Tom thought quickly.

'Reckon that's about the only place for it.'

'You can really pick us up?' shouted Pearl.

'We'll have to,' rasped the eagle, 'won't we?'

Suddenly the air was alive with buzzing and whistling and
there was a gasp of astonishment from the crowd. The eagle
glanced up to the lip of the stadium, which had somehow
fallen into dark shadow. The hissing was growing louder and
louder . . .

'Gadzook-a-rama,' it breathed, momentarily stunned by what
it had seen. 'Get yourselves down to one of them causeways fast
as you can!' And in an instant the eagle was gone.

The crowd hushed as the dark shadow crept on around the
stadium.

'What is it?' whispered Pearl, craning around the stone column. 'Some kind of swarm?'

It was some kind of swarm, but it was unlike any kind of
swarm Tom had seen before. It was like a moving carpet in the
air, made up of insects the size of small birds. The carpet shim-
mered and rippled as the millions of creatures beat their wings
in unison, and as they flew down into the stadium they formed
a vertical surface . . . and then something extraordinary happened: the insects instantly rearranged themselves to form a pattern . . . The crowd gasped, as the next moment the head of Don
Gervase had appeared, as if hanging on a huge poster in the air.

'All hail our glorious leader! All hail!'

The chanting rang round and round the stadium, and before it had finished the mimicwings had changed again: their surface was now a mirror of the other side of the stadium. And as the two biplanes circled into view, they reflected them too . . .

Pearl's mouth fell open in astonishment.

'How . . . but how do they do that? Who is controlling them?'

'Must be instinct,' breathed Tom, marvelling at the living mirror. 'Don Gervase can't make them do that. It must be the Queen. They must be defending her.'

The two small planes turned in a tight circle in front of the mirror, which suddenly fractured and charged at them in a great hissing mass. Banking steeply to avoid the swarm, Sir Henry and Trixie looped round and almost found themselves in the stands once more, but the moment they had done so the stand suddenly dissolved . . .

'Good sport this, sire,' grinned a thickset general at Don Gervase's side.

'Marvellous idea to add a dogfight. Just the ticket,' gushed another.

The crowd were screaming with excitement and Don Gervase concealed his anger with something like a smile, watching the mimicwings rapidly reforming into a mirror that wrapped itself around the stone column.

'They're deliberately confusing them,' said Tom as the biplanes roared past, their wingtips barely above the raging battle, 'disorientating them so they can't find a way out.'

It was true. The moving mirror formed and reformed whichever way they turned, and powering into a vertical climb,

Sir Henry suddenly found himself apparently diving straight towards the battle raging in the arena beneath him. Faces, insects, dirt rushed up to meet him as he went up, or was it down? At the last moment he pulled out.

'We've *got* to help them,' whispered Pearl, her heart racing. 'They're going to crash, aren't they?'

They watched in rising panic as the mimicwings formed a lid over the top of the stadium and slowly began to descend. Tom racked his brains for inspiration.

'The beetle ball,' he said suddenly. 'Maybe we can disrupt them somehow.'

Pearl glanced at him.

'You could try what Scurf did in the shop. That did something, didn't it?'

Pearl stared at the ball in her hand anxiously. She swallowed hard.

'I don't know . . . I'm not sure how . . . what if he realizes, then he'd know for certain, wouldn't he?'

She glanced up through the chaos towards the box where Don Gervase stood watching the aerial combat. There was an unpleasant smirk on his face as the mirrored ceiling decended lower and lower, the two biplanes buzzing this way and that like angry wasps in a jar . . . Sir Henry and Trixie were obviously completely confused: up, down, left, right—it was all the same . . .

'Pearl, you have to try,' hissed Tom forcefully. 'I can't do it, but I can tell you if it's working or not, so you *have* to do it.' Looking up, he could almost see his own reflection now. 'Before it's too late.'

Pearl took a deep breath. She realized there was no alternative. 'OK.'

Taking a deep breath, Pearl crouched down behind an upturned carapace and held the ball in the palm of her hand. Ignoring the shouts and fighting all around, she tried to remember what it was that Scurf had done.

'What about you?' she said suddenly.

'Forget about me,' said Tom harshly, crouching beside her. 'Whatever happens—happens. Just do it.'

Pearl looked down at the ball and concentrated. Placing her index finger on the surface she began to run round and round it in concentric circles, pressing its soft surface as she did so. Tom watched her finger passing rhythmically across the dark patterns.

'Maybe go forwards, then backwards, jumble it up a bit,' he suggested.

Pearl tried that, then switched to a slower rhythm. She glanced at him hopefully.

'Is anything happening?'

Tom shook his head. He could feel nothing. Another piece of debris smashed into the stone wall just above them, and a gang of red bombardier beetles skittered over their hiding place.

'I think . . . maybe I'm too tense, I'm pressing it too hard. If you squeeze it and push it nothing seems to happen.' Pearl was struggling to control her rising panic: there was a real fear in her eyes now, fear that she might fail.

'Try to think of something as you do it,' whispered Tom, watching her finger bumping over the inky patterns. 'Maybe if you have a picture in your head it will be easier.'

'OK,' breathed Pearl. Closing her eyes, she tried as hard as she could to ignore the chaos raging all around her. Another black beetle galloped past, then stopped and shoved its head in towards them.

'Go away!' shouted Tom, lashing out at its shiny mandibles with his foot. Pearl saw none of this: her eyes were closed . . . suddenly an image came into her mind and she held on to it as tightly as she could, imagining it in all its detail . . . She was breathing steadily, deeply, and Tom watched as her finger began to trace infinitesimal patterns across the clear surface, making a figure of eight. Rudy looked up to Tom and he put his finger to his lips, silencing the question. Crouching under another piece of debris just beyond them was Arlo Smoot, and his furtive eyes were watching her too.

Pearl almost seemed to be in a trance now and the ball began to hum . . . Tom closed his eyes expectantly . . . he could feel something coming, sense it, a rumbling . . . there! There it was, the red wave, racing angrily towards him across the dark horizon . . . its crest foaming orange and gold . . .

'Ahh!'

Tom yelped with pain as an electric shock pulsed across his forehead.

'Tom!' shouted Rudy.

But Tom heard nothing: suddenly he was thrown onto his back . . . another violent jolt and he was instantly flipped onto his front.

'Is he . . . is he OK?' stammered Rudy, watching Tom shaking in the dirt.

'It's working,' grimaced Tom, spitting between his clenched

teeth. 'Do that again.' Pearl glanced down at Tom wild-eyed; he was obviously in extreme pain.

'Are you sure—'

'DO IT!' he shouted.

Pearl concentrated once more, holding that picture in her mind and making that figure of eight with her finger, pressing so lightly on the soft slippery surface. After a moment, the ball began to hum once more, and this time Pearl kept going . . .

Suddenly the crowd began to scream.

'Wow!' said Rudy, staring up, open-mouthed. 'Wow!'

'What is it?' whispered Pearl, not daring to look. She kept her finger moving up and round, up and round, in a lazy figure of eight . . .

'It's . . . it's like a snake, a massive green snake.'

Rudy was right, the mirror had suddenly shattered into fragments and reformed itself into a vast writhing python turning in a long lazy pattern stretching right across the roof of the stadium. And the audience seemed to be shaking and twisting too . . .

'A figure of eight!' yelled Rudy, pointing up excitedly.

Pearl smiled breathlessly and told herself not to: it was working! She was sending a message to the Queen and the Queen was broadcasting it back, directing the insects. She was so powerful they could not resist.

'What about the planes?'

Rudy watched as the two aircraft shot out between the serpent's writhing coils, followed by the bird and the eagle.

'They've escaped. Straight through.'

'Really?'

'Definitely. They've gone.'

Pearl stopped abruptly and looked up. There was the vast ser-pent, hanging motionless in the air, then it shattered and reformed itself as a mirror.

'Wow,' she gasped, not quite daring to believe it. Somehow she had managed to send just one message, however clumsily she had done it, and that cloud of mirror-winged insects had formed the image in her mind. She stared down in wonder at the beetle ball in her hand. She was almost too afraid to touch it now. Imagine what someone who knew how to use it properly could do . . .

'That was one cool trick, kid,' said Arlo, scrabbling through the dirt to where they lay. 'So you made them do that?'

'I guess . . . yes, I did,' said Pearl, her face shining with the effort of concentrating so hard.

Arlo stared at her with a curious glint in his eye.

'So *you* told those insects to make that snake,' asked Rudy, 'and *you* made Tom wriggle around?'

'She did,' muttered Tom sitting up and rubbing his sore head. His whole body was still tingling. Arlo seemed mesmer-ized by the beetle ball in Pearl's hand: his mind was slowly focusing, grasping the significance of the object; clearly he was impressed . . . and he was not the only one: up in the stands Don Gervase had spotted the little group, huddling beside the stone column. His eyes were burning with anger, greed, and desire . . . he had all the proof he needed now . . . how unbelievably stupid they were to have brought it right here to the heart of Scarazand, and then they even had the audacity to use it . . . Tom and Pearl felt the heat of his gaze upon them and turned round. There he was, the glorious leader, smiling his bored smile, his milky eyes shining with delight . . .

'Quick,' murmured Tom, 'let's get out of this place.'

He did not bother to look back as Don Gervase vaulted down a level and scurried away, but dragged Pearl and her family back into the thick of the battle. Dodging this way and that, they made for the dark entrance where the squadrons of black beetles had emerged, but soon saw that reinforcements were still being thrown into the arena.

'We can't go through there,' gasped Pearl as a phalanx of yellow scorpions dashed out of the entrance like racing cars.

'Damn right you can't!' screamed a half-breed on the corner of a square, duelling with a large brown beetle. 'You lookin' to get out?'

'That's right,' shouted Tom above the din.

'Only *one* way out of this, mate. Death,' he rasped, savagely slashing the beetle's mandible in half. 'Or back down a screw lift if you can grab it. Look, they's still bringin' 'em dollywhips up.' He pointed with his sword across to where a man astride an ungainly blue insect had just taken wing. It looked something like a giant crane fly.

'Courage of lions, but they ain't got a hope in hell out here.'

Tom and Pearl watched as the rider urged it round in a slow circle and aimed his lance at the rampaging wolfskidder. With one shot the giant beetle cut them down mercilessly, and the crowd roared as the man and dollywhip collapsed into the battle.

'Thanks!' shouted Tom as another wave of green beetles broke against the square. Leaving the half-breed to it, they dodged back through duelling creatures towards the screw lift. Already it had sunk back into the arena floor and had started rotating up once more, with another blue dollywhip ready for the fray. There was the rider, perched on the gangly insect with his visor down and lance ready.

'As soon as it flies off—jump on,' instructed Tom. 'We'll have to be fast.'

Pearl and Rudy nodded. Up and up it twisted, and the moment the dollywhip's slender legs reached the level of the arena the rider dug his heels hard into its flanks.

'Come on you crazy flying heap of whatever you are, let's go get him!' shouted the rider. 'Giddy-up!'

But the ungainly blue insect took one look at the chaos all around and decided it was going precisely nowhere.

'Mush!' shouted the rider, kicking hard. 'Mush!'

Tom gave the reluctant dollywhip a hefty slap on the abdomen, whereupon it lurched upwards over the arena, almost sending its rider flying. The next moment they all jumped onto the vacant platform that was already beginning to rotate back down into the ground.

'Hey thanks, you guys!' shouted the rider, turning back, and for a second he saw Tom, Pearl, Rudy, and Arlo revolving down on the screw lift. He seemed stunned.

'Hey!' he shouted, throwing up his visor to get a better look. 'Hey wait!' But already the lift had disappeared into the ground.

For Tom and Pearl the battle was already behind them and there were new dangers to focus the mind. Spinning down fast into the holding pens they found themselves surrounded by lines of dollywhips waiting to be sent up. Soldiers and Skrolls prowled amongst them, fastening saddles and distributing lances.

'That way,' whispered Tom, spotting a doorway in the corner, and before anyone could stop them they leapt off the platform and scrambled away through the forest of spindly legs towards the far side of the room.

'Oi you!' screamed a guard, watching them slip through the exit. 'That's restricted access, that is! You can't go in there! Oi!'

A shrill blast of a whistle followed them down the stone corridor. They were all running now, even Arlo, as a gang of guards and Skrolls scrambled after them. Tom could not remember much about their descent, it was an endless race down dim staircases, across gantries, through dark tunnels inside the honeycombed rock of Scarazand. They never caught a glimpse of their pursuers, but their shouts were always close behind. At last Pearl ducked into an alcove overlooking one of the hatcheries and they stopped.

'How far down are we now, do you think?' she panted, listening to the footsteps of the guards clattering somewhere above. 'We must be on the level of those bridges by now.'

'I don't know,' nodded Tom breathlessly, 'feels like we're right in the middle somehow. We need to get out to street level and see.'

Arlo leant against a rock wheezing loudly.

'I know this place,' he said, taking in the rock tunnels leading off in all directions. 'I recognize it. Definitely. I've been here before.'

'No you haven't, Dad,' frowned Rudy. 'Not with me you haven't.'

'I was taken here *without* you, kid,' said Arlo confidently, 'most certainly. Absolutely so. If we go right, down those steps, there's a long curving corridor to the end. It's kinda restricted, but at the far end we're into a narrow alley at the bottom of the town.'

Rudy, Tom, and Pearl stared at Arlo in astonishment: suddenly he seemed to have recovered his senses.

'And that's right next to one of them little causeways on the opposite side to the main entrance,' he added. 'Which is good. Because that's where we want to go, isn't it?'

'It is,' began Pearl, 'but Dad, how can you be so certain? This all looks the same to me.'

'But I am certain, Pearl,' repeated Arlo. 'Most certain. Like I said, I have been here before. Definitely.'

Arlo smiled, but there was a weird look in his eye, something odd . . . Pearl hesitated.

'Y'all believe me, don't you?'

'Course we believe you, Dad,' smiled Rudy with relief. 'Come on Pearl, Dad's been here before. He knows the way out, so let's go.'

'OK,' said Pearl with some reluctance. 'Whatever you say.'

Arlo was already up and moving fast down the steps.

'Hurry up, you guys, there's a race on, remember?' he said as Rudy scampered after him. 'We've got to get through this super quick.'

'He could be right you know,' whispered Tom, and they trotted down into the dark curving corridor and followed along behind.

'Come on, guys, come on,' hustled Arlo, 'this is a totally dangerous place. We shouldn't be in here at all.'

'What's so dangerous about it, Dad?' panted Rudy, struggling to keep up.

'It's just totally dangerous. Totally. Can't you feel it?'

'Feel what?'

'The noises, man. The static,' replied Arlo, rubbing his hand over his crumpled face. 'Like white noise—everywhere. Can't you feel it?'

Rudy shook his head. He felt nothing: just very tired and hungry, and he really wished his dad would lighten up.

'Wow. What's down there?'

Tom stopped suddenly and stared into a small tapering side tunnel halfway down the corridor. The end was wreathed in thin smoke rising upwards. It looked like a window onto a vast chamber, and the smell of sulphur drifting towards him made his eyes water.

'What is it?' whispered Pearl, putting her sleeve over her mouth.

'Bad idea, man. Very bad idea,' muttered Arlo, shaking his head apprehensively, 'that is completely out of bounds. Come away, dude. Right now.'

'Why?' asked Rudy.

'Bad karma. Totally off the map. Not allowed. No way.'

Tom stared at the steam rising, and he had a feeling he knew what was at the end of this tunnel. It was something August Catcher had told them about but had never seen, something that perhaps no person had ever seen. Ignoring Arlo's protestations, he hoisted himself up into the shaft and began to crawl towards the light. Holding an arm over his face he drew closer, shielding himself from the pungent acid smell that was now almost overpowering.

'Man oh man, any second they are coming. Any second,' muttered Arlo, fretting in the corridor. 'God my head hurts.'

'What is it, Tom?' asked Pearl, watching anxiously as he neared the end. Tom stopped and peered over the edge of the ledge down into the steam. For a moment, he said nothing, as no words could describe what lay below. It was like a scene from outer space. Tom turned back.

'You should see this,' he mumbled, clutching his mouth. The pungent steam was making his throat burn and he could barely speak.

'No no, you shouldn't! Not at all,' instructed Arlo, tearing at his hair, 'definitely not. Rudy, you stay right where you are, little man.'

A moment later Pearl had crawled up next to him, and tentatively she too peered over the precipice. A hundred metres below lay a glistening white form, shrouded in sulphurous steam. It was the size and shape of a submarine, and all across its flanks thousands of worker beetles scurried this way and that, massaging its skin, oiling it, and rolling a steady stream of eggs away into the darkness.

'So there she is,' whispered Pearl at last. 'At the very centre. August was right.'

'He was.'

There she lay, the Queen beetle, the Supreme Being, the secret beating heart of Scarazand. She was the strangest sight they had ever seen.

'And where do you think that leads?' said Pearl, craning up the tall chimney to the tiny speck of light at the top.

Tom shook his head. He was trying to ignore the hammering of the Queen's heartbeat inside his skull, but he couldn't shake it off. He was so close now, far too close for comfort.

'Must have been built to let all this gas out,' he gasped. 'The only place where Scarazand is in direct contact with the earth. The only place where there is no labyrinth to protect it.'

'The one weak spot,' marvelled Pearl, 'the most vulnerable . . .'

And even as she said those words she realized she had heard them before . . . and so had Tom.

'You don't think—'

'I do,' said Tom. 'That is where Zumsteen escaped. He climbed right up there. Makes sense, doesn't it?'

Tom stared up at the smooth rock sides of the chimney tapering to a tiny chink of light. That must have been quite a climb, but Zumsteen had looked fit enough. Where did it come out? Was it at the top of a mountain somewhere, maybe it was in the middle of a desert; after all it didn't have to be very big, it probably looked like nothing from above. Wherever it was, it must be somewhere completely inaccessible to have survived discovery for thousands of years. Only Nicholas Zumsteen could know, thought Tom, and that was why Don Gervase wanted to find him. Controlling the Queen was one thing: but protecting her was quite another.

'Hey look.'

Tom's thoughts were interrupted by a huge pulse ringing through his skull, and shaking his head dizzily he saw Pearl holding the beetle ball in her hand. Its clear centre was glowing white and fading, glowing white and fading, and the patterns on its surface appeared to swirl and dance . . .

'Don't touch it,' croaked Tom, who could almost feel the air around him vibrating with energy. It was the same rhythm as the pulses in his head. One command now and he felt that his brain would explode.

'Look down there,' whispered Pearl, her eyes widening, 'she's doing the same thing.'

Tom glanced at the vast Queen below, and beneath her sticky, glistening surface he saw black veins glowing and fading in the same rhythm.

'It's like they are two parts of the same.'

'They are,' gasped Tom, 'this little ball is the brain, that massive insect is the voice, the king and queen of the colony, together.' He closed his eyes and rubbed them. His head hurt so much now he could hardly think. 'We've really got to go,' he murmured. 'It is getting too much.'

Slithering back down the shaft, Tom jumped into the corridor to find Rudy waiting for him.

'Where's Dad?' asked Pearl, slipping down beside him.

'Oh, he's waiting by the door,' said Rudy, pointing down the corridor.

'Why?'

'He said he couldn't stand the noise. Said it was bothering him. I didn't know what he was talking about.'

Pearl looked down to where Arlo stood hovering in the shadows.

'Can you hear anything?' she asked.

Tom nodded. 'In the distance,' he lied. 'Pulses. Massive pulses.'

Pearl shook her head crossly: something was not right at all.

'Come on, Rudy,' she murmured, and taking his hand they hurried down to where Arlo stood pacing up and down beside the small wooden door.

'Seen what you wanted?' he asked Tom sharply.

'We did.'

Arlo rubbed a hand across his crumpled face. He seemed in pain.

'So we go?'

'Of course, Dad,' said Pearl with a smile. 'You're the boss. We'll follow you.'

Arlo grunted, and opened the door onto the street. It was just as he had predicted, they were at the bottom of a narrow alley that twisted up around the rock. Tom gulped in the air greedily: and closing his eyes he was relieved to find that the thudding in his brain had receded to just a dull, distant hum. It had gone— for now. Thank goodness for that. But when he opened them again his pulse began to quicken: unlike the other side of Scarazand, this street was strangely empty, and all the shops were shuttered up. It was like a ghost town.

'Where is everyone?' said Tom, unnerved by the silence.

'This way, people,' muttered Arlo, hurrying down through an ancient archway.

They followed him round the corner to where a narrow stone causeway no wider than a cart stretched out across the chasm. Beyond was the dark wall of the cave, honeycombed with holes and gangways that continued right up into the glittering dome above. Only the occasional cheer from the stadium and the distant roar of the aeroplanes broke the silence. Arlo shuffled straight out onto the causeway, with Rudy at his side.

'Come on!' shouted Rudy. 'Before they see us!'

Pearl hesitated. 'What do you think?' she said. 'Is it safe? Feels . . . odd.'

'I know,' replied Tom: it did not quite make sense. Somehow this was all just too easy. He could hear the engines getting louder, and looking up he spotted two black specks flying round the edge of a large floating luminous globe and diving down towards them.

'I think we've got to risk it,' he said quickly. 'Otherwise they'll never know we've made it. Come on.'

Together they raced out onto the empty causeway as the aeroplanes drew closer. Rudy began jumping up and down and waving frantically.

'Here!' he shouted. 'Down here!'

Moments later Tom and Pearl were at his side, shouting and waving too. Immediately one biplane dipped down towards them, and Sir Henry roared past, waving.

'He's seen us he's seen us!' shouted Rudy excitedly, as Trixie followed through. They watched the planes turn high above, then down came the eagle.

'You folks OK?' it bellowed, dipping over the causeway. 'Excellent. Most excellent. Now listen up, because here's the plan. It's not difficult, just involves a bit of clever timing. First things first: get yourselves up—'

But the eagle's explanation was drowned out by the blast of a horn splitting the air all around them. Tom glanced back at Scarazand and his heart skipped a beat. There was a black tide of hooded Skrolls advancing towards them at a run, their lances raised. And from the other end, hundreds more poured out of the holes in the cave wall and onto the narrow causeway.

'Oh . . . jeepers,' whispered Pearl, grasping Rudy tightly to her. On they came, like a black swarm, their boots clattering on the stone, and Tom could see the unmistakable figure of Don Gervase at the head of one column, and Lotus the other.

'Don't be foolish, folks, whatever you do; we'll find a way out of this!' shouted the eagle, and dived away into the darkness.

The two columns converged and slowed, and the rows of hooded men lowered their lances menacingly. The small, terrified group shrank back before the flashing wall of spikes and Don Gervase strode forward. There was a horrible, satisfied smirk on his face.

'Well, well, well. Tom Scatterhorn, Pearl Smoot, Rudy Smoot and even old Arlo, caught escaping *yet* again. There is a certain déjà vu about all of this, isn't there?'

The small party stared at him angrily and said nothing.

'And not even a cunning plan to get out? I'm very disappointed.'

'You'll not have it, never,' snarled Pearl bravely.

'Is that so?'

'Yeah, come any closer and my dad'll punch your nose in,' squeaked Rudy. 'He will you know!'

Don Gervase grinned wolfishly at the small boy, and reaching down, pinched him on the cheek.

'Touch him again and I'll kill you,' muttered Tom darkly, sparks of anger dancing in his eyes. Don Gervase appeared mildly surprised, whereupon Lotus stepped forward, stretching her fingers lazily. It seemed that she was about to execute some crazy karate kick. She looked to Don Gervase expectantly.

'Shall I?'

'*Un momentino*, Lotus,' replied Don Gervase, his voice dropping to a dangerous growl. 'First, I should like to see how Arlo Smoot intends to defend his family this time. Arlo? Are you really going to punch my nose in? Arlo?'

CHAPTER 23

THE SLEEP OF REASON

'Well Arlo, we are waiting.'

A sardonic smile spread across Don Gervase's face as Arlo Smoot rubbed his crumpled features. He looked very awkward indeed.

'Well?'

'Don't listen to it, Dad, just hit him,' snarled Rudy.

Arlo stared at Don Gervase dully, then back at the floor.

'Go on!'

Suddenly Arlo Smoot snapped: but not in the way Rudy expected. He turned and stood menacingly before Pearl.

'You'd better hand it over,' he said curtly.

Pearl stared at him in amazement.

'What?'

'Give him what he wants, otherwise I will throw you over this parapet right now.'

Rudy stared open-mouthed at his father.

'But Dad, I thought—'

'NOW!' he screamed, so loud and high and downright

terrifying that Rudy edged away. Pearl looked into his face, searching for something that wasn't there.

'D-Dad?' she stammered, pressing back against the parapet, 'Dad . . . you're not well . . . something's happened to you . . . Dad—'

'Give. Me. The. Ball!' he hissed, his eyes narrowing.

'I'd do what he said if I were you,' added Don Gervase with a smirk. 'He does not make idle threats.'

Suddenly and without quite knowing why, Tom sprang forward and slammed into Arlo Smoot's chest, knocking him so hard that he tumbled back and his head smacked hideously on the stone. In a flash Tom was on his feet again, tensed and quivering. Pearl and Rudy stared at him wide-eyed.

'But—'

'That's not your father,' he said hoarsely, as Arlo lay groaning on the causeway. 'Don't believe it. It's someone else.'

The hooded Skrolls crowded forward, their lances lowered ready to strike . . .

'Wait!' barked Don Gervase sharply, staying their advance with his hand. 'Wait, comrades, please.'

He looked down at the groaning man, then back at Tom. Don Gervase seemed vaguely disappointed, but also, vaguely impressed. With a wry smile he turned to face Pearl once more.

'Of course, Miss Smoot, Tom is right. That man is not your father, he merely looks like him,' he said evenly. 'Your real father is here.' With a snap of his fingers the wall of Skrolls parted and another man walked forward.

'Pearl? Rudy? Is that you?'

The voice was familiar, and so was the face. Arlo Smoot,

grizzled, differently dressed, but with the same crumpled demeanour. He looked as if he had just got out of bed.

'Dad?' said Rudy, uncertainly.

'That's right, it's me,' the man replied. 'Can't you tell?'

Pearl stared at the man in confusion: he certainly looked exactly like her father, but then so did the man on the floor.

'Not really,' she replied frostily. 'Where have you been?'

'Oh, just around. Hey, I've been looking for you guys,' he blustered, 'and now I've found you. Boy, what a relief.'

Pearl and Rudy stared at the man suspiciously: Tom could tell what they were thinking.

'So what do *you* think I should do with the beetle ball?'

Don Gervase turned to Arlo; he also seemed genuinely curious. The man squirmed uncomfortably.

'Well Dad, what should I do?'

Still Arlo would not look her in the face. Pearl was glowering at him now.

'Well?'

'Honey, that thing is way too dangerous to carry around,' he smiled, shambling forward. 'Jeez, it's so powerful, and dangerous. I think it would be best if you gave it to me. For safekeeping, you know.' He held out his hand. 'Come on, Pearly, give it to Popsicle.'

There was silence. Pearl cocked her head, not quite believing what she had just heard.

'What did you say?'

Arlo stood grinning at her inanely.

'I said honey, give it to Popsicle.'

Something snapped inside her: and it was Pearl's turn to surprise.

'OK,' she shrugged, and in an instant she had grabbed the man's outstretched hand and wrenched it towards her, stepping sideways as she did so.

'Hey!' he shouted. 'Hey! But—'

But the next moment Pearl had shoved him over the parapet and he was gone.

Rudy's mouth fell open in shock. He was stunned.

'Pearl, that might have been our dad!'

'Don't be ridiculous!' she yelled, and turned angrily to face Don Gervase. 'What is this, some kind of freak show?'

Don Gervase was surprised by her spirit, but only mildly.

'Yes, well some are more convincing than others,' he admitted. 'But you may rest assured that this is just a selection,' he said, and with a snap of his fingers another Arlo Smoot appeared behind him, then another and another, and another after that—all identical. Pearl and Rudy shrank back from the line of men now standing behind Don Gervase.

'And of course there are many, many more. Which is your real father? All of them, or one, and does it even matter? They only have one purpose in their short life and that is to extract that beetle ball from you, young lady. And they will.'

Don Gervase approached her menacingly.

'So why don't you save them the trouble and give it to me? And if you do, well I can promise you safe passage out of Scarazand, provided you assure me you won't come back. Ever.'

Don Gervase's milky green eyes bored into her, and Pearl

gripped Rudy even tighter. She stared at the prickling wall of spikes all around.

'Do you really mean it?' she said, her voice small and quavering.

'Of course I mean it,' he said silkily. 'You don't want to be involved in all this. My quarrel is not with you, or young Rudy. Give me the ball and you can go free, and remember this whole episode as an amusing adventure, nothing more.'

Pearl was trembling: she was beginning to crumble, Don Gervase could sense it. Tom looked from one to the other, then his eyes widened as Pearl took the ball out of her pocket.

'No,' he hissed, shaking his head vigorously, 'don't, Pearl. Don't do it.'

Don Gervase ignored him, and kept his eyes firmly on hers. The merest hint of a smile played on his lips. There it was, the amulet he needed above all others, right here in Scarazand, how convenient . . .

'But what are you going to do with it?' she asked softly, turning it over and over in her hand. 'Aren't you going to use it to kill people?'

'Don't be silly. Why would I want to kill people?'

'Because you hate them.'

The grin fixed upon Don Gervase's face: he sensed his spell was fading.

'I do not hate all people, and neither do I want to kill all people,' he continued reasonably. 'This is simply about government. I am a leader, my people require me to lead them. Without it they are like lost sheep. I am their shepherd, I need to show them the way.'

Pearl stared up at Don Gervase and felt his honeyed words and huge green eyes drawing her in once more. Instinctively she wanted to kick against them, but it was so difficult to deny . . .

'But . . . but shouldn't they think for themselves?'

Don Gervase shook his head sadly.

'Alas, they cannot. It is both their tragedy and their strength. They are not like us, you see. That is why I must guide them. With that ball,' he added pointedly. 'Which frankly, my dear, will become your death warrant if you do not hand it over. Take a look around: your options are decidedly limited, are they not?'

Pearl glanced at the lines of spikes surrounding them, then back at Tom, who shook his head obstinately. He could imagine all too easily what was running through her mind, as against his better judgement he had given Don Gervase that small bottle of elixir. But somehow a spark of hope still spluttered inside him: there *was* another way out of this. But Pearl couldn't see it.

'Believe me, Miss Smoot, it is the only way. All exits have been sealed,' added Don Gervase as the sound of the two biplanes droned somewhere beneath them. 'These aerial intruders may through sheer luck have stumbled upon an ancient entrance to Scarazand, but they will certainly never find the way out again. That has been closed—permanently.'

The engine grew louder. It sounded as if one of the planes was climbing up the chasm towards the causeway . . .

'And if I chucked it down there?' she said, her fingers tightening on the ball.

'Then obviously I would descend into the chasm and retrieve it,' smirked Don Gervase. 'And you would suffer the consequences. Which would be peculiarly unpleasant. Particularly for young Rudy.'

Suddenly Pearl seemed to have made up her mind. The thudding engine was growing louder and louder beneath them, turning into a roar . . .

'Very well,' she said. 'Take it, I don't care.'

She unclenched her fist and opened her hand. Don Gervase grinned insanely.

'I knew you would see sense.'

He leant forward, his fingers outstretched . . . and at that moment something very peculiar happened.

'No!' screamed Rudy, thumping Pearl's hand as hard as he dared, sending the ball flying up into the air. At the same instant, Sir Henry's biplane appeared from beneath the parapet, and seemed to almost hang in the air as it looped just above their heads. The engine stalled, and Don Gervase watched in total amazement as the small rubbery ball was caught on the rim of the empty passenger seat.

'Jump!' shouted Sir Henry, hanging upside down in his straps, but a second later he was plummeting down into the chasm once more and the engine roared back to life.

'Jump and we'll catch ya!' came another shout as the great eagle swept over the parapet and wheeled around.

Don Gervase's skin turned from yellow to beetroot; he was so angry he could barely speak. He turned on Pearl, ready to kill her with his bare hands. She stared at him in terror.

'T-t-that was . . . erm . . . an . . . an accident,' she stammered, pressing back against the parapet wall, her hands grasping Rudy's shoulders.

'An accident?' he said, his voice thick with rage. 'What kind of an accident do you call that?'

The Skrolls began to crush forward, their lances bristling and jabbing.

'Come on!' shouted Tom, and the next moment he jumped off the causeway into dark space. A second later Pearl threw Rudy after him and she was standing alone on the parapet, the spikes thrusting towards her . . . and at that moment their extraordinary good fortune was undone . . . The engine roared and suddenly Sir Henry reappeared upside down, hanging at the top of his second loop.

'Jump!' he shouted again, unaware of his precious cargo bobbling and rolling along the inside rim of the fuselage behind him. 'Jump in!'

Don Gervase watched open-mouthed as the clear ball teetered on the very lip, then—it tumbled out . . .

And at the same moment Pearl leapt off the parapet and threw herself headfirst into the passenger seat.

'I've got it!' screamed Lotus, snatching the ball out of the air hungrily as the plane roared away beneath them.

'Is that so?' rasped a voice, and there was a rush of wings as Lotus was plucked off the causeway as lightly as a rag doll.

'You ain't havin' that, missy!' screeched the vast eagle. 'No bleedin' way!' Holding her twisting, kicking, fighting body in one vast yellow talon the bird somehow managed to stay airborne and grabbed at her clenched fist.

'You'll have to kill me first!' she screamed, kicking the eagle's head so hard that feathers flew out.

'I'll take great pleasure in that,' it replied, prising her hand open. Lotus kicked and fought even harder and stretching up her legs wound them around the eagle's neck. She began squeezing for all she was worth.

'Git off!' cried the great bird, desperately pecking at her this way and that. 'Off I said!'

But Lotus locked her legs even tighter, and Don Gervase watched powerlessly as the bird and the girl began to tumble down into the chasm, a thrashing bundle of legs and wings and talons and fists. Faster and faster they fell, Lotus clamped like a vice around the eagle's neck, her body pecked to pieces, her hand still grasping the ball.

'You'll kill us both!' roared the thrashing eagle.

Lotus had a wild look in her eye.

'I don't think so,' she grinned, 'you have no idea, do you?'

'Give me that damn thing and I'll let you go!'

Lotus laughed madly.

'I think your little friend needs your help!' she shouted as they flashed past something massive on the wall of the chasm. The eagle glanced back.

'Holy smoke!' it yelled, and with one last desperate kick punched its yellow talons into Lotus's body above . . .

'GETTHEHELLARTOFVIT!'

But suddenly there was nothing there . . . just air and strips of clothing and an empty, lacerated shell of the girl hanging round his neck . . . somewhere above was a large green beetle, flying upwards towards the causeway . . .

'Help!'

The cry wrenched the great bird to its senses. Steadying its fall,

471

the eagle spread its vast wings and began to climb hard towards the dark shape hanging from the cliff high above.

Tom was trying desperately not to look up. He had witnessed something of the chaos above him: he had seen Pearl leap bravely into Sir Henry's passenger seat, he had seen Trixie cleverly accelerate and catch Rudy on her upper wing and help him safely inside. But his own fall had been broken by a large, glistening ball of glue that had shot out from the wall of rock and stuck to his legs and chest. He had bounced once, twice, as if on the end of a bungee, and then steadied to a halt, dangling upside down against the cliff-face. And now he was being hauled swiftly upwards. All he could see of the massive bolas spider in its hole above him were its two short white legs either side of its red jaws, winding him in. Ignoring his galloping heartbeat Tom tried to think what, if anything, he could do. Did bolas spiders immobilize their prey with poison then eat it, or was he about to be swallowed whole and dissolved into soup in its stomach? He couldn't remember, it was too terrible to contemplate.

'Tom!'

Tom turned to see the eagle soaring up towards him.

'Oh this is not good, mate, not good at all,' snorted the bird, anxiously watching the enormous arachnid reeling Tom in. The sight of the eagle made the spider pull even faster.

'Can you move?'

'Barely,' he whispered. 'Just my arms.'

'Dang it kiddo, just grab hold of whatever you can!'

The great bird wheeled out into the chasm, cursing to itself. 'Never come between a monster and its meat. Always a mistake. Bloody hell fire. Hold on down there!' it hollered.

Tom twisted round to face the rock bumping past him and searched feverishly for anything to slow the spider's progress . . . there, he wedged in his fingers into a narrow crevice and felt the glue above him start to stretch . . . his shoulders burned and his fingers ached as he held on, but the spider felt him resist and one powerful yank jerked him upwards—it was just so strong . . .

Whump!

There was an angry hiss and a scream.

'He ain't yer breakfast, mate! No he ain't!'

Tom glanced up at a furious blur of legs and wings and feathers. Great balls of glue splattered past him.

'Git back into that hole with yer, yer big ugly brute!'

Tom felt his legs slacken, and the next moment the top half of his body swung down like a pendulum and he found himself hanging off the wet rock face by the slenderest of ledges. Tom was so surprised that his fingers danced across the slippery edge.

'I—I can't hold,' he gasped, his legs kicking helplessly inside the glue. 'I'm going to—it's—'

Too late, his fingers slipped off and he was gone, dropping like a stone, head-first into the dark chasm. Its inky depths rushed up to meet him, faster, faster, so fast that the wind burned . . .

'Easy, tiger!'

Two great talons curled around his waist, slowing him.

'There ain't no exit down there!'

Tom was thrown up; spinning helplessly in the void . . .

WHUMP!

Down he came onto the eagle's back and those vast soft wings enveloped him.

'OK mate?'

'Just about,' trembled Tom, recovering his breath inside that wide raft of feathers. 'Thanks.'

'Looks like we've got a bit of catching up to do—hold on!'

The eagle soared upwards towards the far side of the rock where the two small biplanes were circling. As soon as Rudy and Pearl saw the bird they waved wildly, and Tom waved back. He was very, very pleased to see them, but Sir Henry looked concerned. He pointed towards the wall of the cave, and then at his watch.

'Dang it,' muttered the bird. 'Out of time. That puts the kibosh on that idea.'

'What's the matter?'

'Ah . . . I dropped something,' it said, angrily scanning the thronging mass of creatures crossing the causeways below. 'Probably never find it now, anyways. Needle in a bleedin' haystack. Dang and blast.'

The eagle slid away and fell in behind the two small biplanes heading around Scarazand to the far side of the great cave. Tom was just wondering what it was that the eagle had dropped when he heard a loud twittering behind him.

'Hey mate!'

The eagle watched the swallow diving past and let out a strange ululating call. The swallow twittered back noisily.

'Damn right he is,' replied the eagle, and made another strange sound.

'What's it saying?'

'Three things. First, we've got to get out of here right now before it's too late. Second, you's one lucky fella; and third, I'm a bloody nong for dropping that ball.'

'The ball?' Tom's heart began to quicken. 'You mean—'

'That's right mate, the one and only bloody beetle ball, that's what. Lotus Askary pulled a fast one and got the better of me. Too bad, but there it is.'

Tom looked helplessly at the great rock column of Scarazand crawling with insects and men and every kind of creature: but there was nothing he or anyone else could do now.

'All right all right, I've got the message, strewth!' rasped the eagle as the swallow continued chattering in its ear. 'I tell yer, Tom, they's good blokes but they do like to lay it on with a trowel.'

The eagle accelerated, the swallow followed, and soon they were lined up behind the two biplanes and diving hard towards the curving wall of the cave.

'Which one's the exit?' shouted Tom, watching the honey-combed wall of rock rush towards them.

'They all is!' the bird shouted back.

'All?'

'It's not what you think! Look at it!'

Tom's eyes watered in the rushing air, but he could just make out three shimmering reflections amongst the holes ahead . . . two aeroplanes and a bird, closing fast . . . the swarm of mimic-wings: they had formed a vast mirror to block the entrance to the tunnel.

'So . . . so we going through them?' he shouted.

'No choice!' yelled the bird. 'Hang on to yer hat!'

Tom flung his arms around the great bird's neck as they

cannoned towards the mirror . . . closer . . . closer . . . suddenly there was a loud rushing sound as a million insects fled and Sir Henry's biplane tore a hole in the mirror and accelerated into the dark tunnel beyond. The mimicwings hardly had time to reform themselves before Trixie smashed through, ripping another hole higher up. A second later Tom closed his eyes as they swept in after her with the swallow just behind, so close that he felt the beat of the mimicwings on his face. He opened his eyes and gasped: suddenly they were flying through a series of narrow caves, twisting round columns of stone, diving sharply through gaps, a giddy blur of rock and stalactites and water, and all the while those two small lamps on the planes kept just ahead . . . Tom was concentrating so hard on keeping his balance he barely had a chance to steal a glance behind him, but he knew that something was coming, he could sense it, a hissing, rushing sound was growing louder every second. The mimic-wings . . . they must have reformed, and they were gaining.

'Not far!' shouted the eagle as Tom bounced this way and that. It had heard the hissing too. Accelerating hard, they cannoned into a long straight and Tom glimpsed a chink of light just ahead. That must be it, the exit, and there seemed to be trees, tall trees all around . . . but when he turned round his heart leapt into his throat. The throbbing ball of silver mimicwings was right behind them now, shaped like the nose of a rocket, pushing harder and harder. Don't look, Tom told himself, just hang on. They were flying so fast now he felt sick. The hiss of a billion wings screamed louder, almost touching them now . . . but those trees were getting closer every second, lining the sides and the walls and the roof of the cave . . . trees? Roof? But—

'Ever run a gauntlet?' screeched the eagle.

Tom did not reply; he really did think he was going to be sick. They weren't trees at all, but brown centipedes as high as houses, hanging, waiting, their gaping black jaws outstretched . . .

He pressed his head into the feathers and suddenly they were amongst them, a blur of red eyes, coiling legs and wet teeth snapping just centimetres away . . . left, right they weaved between the huge coiling bodies that grabbed and lunged. At one point the eagle swung violently upside down and Tom found himself hanging off its neck. Glancing back, he saw that the swarm of mimicwings was being decimated. On they came, like a silver blurring ball, but it was just too large to avoid the centipedes' thrashing attacks, and millions upon millions were being swiped out of the air in a feeding frenzy. The dark air of the cave glittered with countless wings and bodies as the carnage unfolded, but still the mimicwings came on and on, chasing and harrying them to the end, obeying some last, desperate order . . .

'Just in time!' shouted the eagle. 'Looks like my mate was right!'

Tom faced forward just in time to see Sir Henry shoot into the narrow chink of light, followed by Trixie. The next moment they too were sweeping over a large heap of rocks where teams of beetles were heaving one stone on top of another—and they had almost reached the top. It wouldn't be long before this ancient entrance to Scarazand was closed completely. With one final burst the eagle soared over the top of the pile and straight through the gap into the white light . . . the blinding bright light of the world beyond. Tom was shaking uncontrollably, he couldn't help it. Somehow, against all the odds, they had done it. They had escaped. Looking down, he saw the sea. A wave of sheer relief welled up and broke over him, and his eyes filled up with tears. They were safe.

A short while later, the eagle clattered to a halt on a crescent of white sand where the two planes had landed and were waiting for them. They were on a small atoll, and across the dark sea stood the large, cone-shaped mountain from which they had come.

'Is that Tithona?' asked Tom.

'No,' replied the eagle, 'but you're not a million miles away. They all look the same around here. Matey-boy spotted the hole,' he said, indicating the tiny swallow cheeping in a bush. 'Those blokes have known about it for a long, long time. But you'll appreciate it's kind of a dangerous place to visit, if you're a bird.'

Carefully the eagle lifted Tom off its back and set him down on the white sand.

'Thanks,' said Tom, 'for everything.' And he really meant it.

'No worries,' the bird replied, cocking its great head. 'Just sorry I couldn't get that damn ball back. But there you go.'

Rudy and Pearl came running up the beach towards them, and the eagle tactfully retreated into the shadows. Rudy watched, fascinated, as the odd-looking raptor climbed awkwardly up onto a branch next to the swallow. Then he squinted down at Tom lying flat on the beach.

'Hey Tom, what happened to you?'

Tom looked at his legs in embarrassment. The whole lower half of his body was still encased in a vast blob of clear glue.

'Erm . . . well, there was this spider, quite a big one, and it lassoed me with this gluey stuff, and,' he shrugged helplessly, 'I'm stuck.'

Rudy giggled, and Tom couldn't help laughing either; somehow now that they had left Scarazand this seemed ridiculous.

'So what are you going to do?'

'I think seawater should sort it out,' smiled Pearl, and with a wink at Rudy they grabbed Tom by the arms and ignoring his protests dragged him down the beach into the water. And sure enough, Pearl was right, the glue began to dissolve. Thrashing around in the shallows Tom managed to free himself, then did his best to drag Rudy and Pearl into the water too. Sir Henry and Trixie walked up from the aeroplanes to watch the three of them chasing each other around and laughing.

'Good to see them having some fun again,' said Sir Henry with a smile.

'God knows they deserve it,' said Trixie. 'That was quite the tightest spot I've ever been in.'

Sir Henry nodded in agreement.

'And I'm awful glad August wasn't with us,' she added. 'Can you imagine? His nerves would be shot to pieces.'

'No place for old men—eh?' smiled Sir Henry ruefully. He watched the fun for a moment, then ambled across to where the eagle perched in the shadows. A short conversation told him all he needed to know. With a gloomy expression he returned to her side.

'Lost, is it?'

'Inevitably,' muttered Sir Henry: he couldn't hide his disappointment. 'I insisted they didn't take it.'

Trixie said nothing for a moment.

'But you can't really blame her, can you? She was desperate. It was a calculated risk.' She glanced at his stern expression and smiled. 'Come on, I bet if you were in her shoes you'd have done the same thing.'

'I know,' he sighed. 'No point being angry now. It's done. And we all came out alive, so that's something.'

'Not *quite* all of us,' corrected Trixie, watching as Rudy and Pearl threw Tom backwards into the water. Sir Henry's eyes narrowed, he could see what she meant.

'Well, indeed. Yes, that is a conundrum. What are we going to do with them?'

Trixie did not reply, as her eye was caught by a strange silhouette coming over the waves towards them from the direction of the island.

'Good grief,' muttered Sir Henry, who had seen it too. It appeared to be a lopsided hang-glider, with whirring wings, and it was trailing a tangle of thin, crumpled legs behind it. On the creature's back sat a man, wearing an odd collection of battered armour, urging it on for all it's worth.

'A dollywhip!' shouted Pearl, pointing in astonishment at the spindly blue insect, half-flying, half-staggering over the waves towards them.

'There's a girl! You can do it! You can do it!' shouted the man, his legs flapping against the dollywhip's flanks. 'Nearly there!'

With one last final, heroic effort the exhausted insect crashed down into the shallows and lay there panting, utterly spent.

'Good girl!' wheezed the man, equally exhausted, and he flopped down into the water.

For a moment there was silence. Nobody moved.

'Who . . . is that?' said Tom, watching the man lying in the shallows, breathing heavily.

'And how did he get past those centipedes?' whispered Pearl. The man took off his battered helmet and threw it away carelessly, then hauled himself to his feet.

'Do you think he's come to chase us?' said Rudy timidly.

The man began to wade through the water towards them, a dark silhouette against the brilliant white sand. He was limping slightly, but there was something familiar about him . . .

'Hello?' said Sir Henry, walking forward. 'Can I help you?'

The man stopped before him and pushed the mop of wet hair out of his face. He looked shattered.

'Yes sir, you most certainly can. In fact I'm relying on it, seein' as my transport's collapsed.'

'Dad!' Rudy gasped, and started forward towards the dark figure.

'Rudy! You stop right there!' shouted Pearl, so fiercely that the small boy did exactly what he was told.

'We don't know who he is,' she said quietly. 'He may be another one, remember?'

The man hesitated and found them suddenly staring at him suspiciously. Instantly the atmosphere had changed.

'Who are you?' said Trixie, walking forward to confront the dishevelled stranger.

'Well ma'am, my name is Arlo Smoot. And you may find it hard to believe this, but those two are my kids. And frankly I never thought I'd see them again,' he said looking at Pearl and Rudy, who stared back at him menacingly.

'And you have come out through the tunnel from Scarazand?'

'That's right, ma'am. I saw you's escaping, an' I guess hell wasn't hot enough for me either, so I followed your lead,' he smiled. 'Thank you.'

Pearl shook her head; she wasn't convinced.

'How did you get past those centipedes?' she demanded. 'How come they didn't eat you?'

'Well, Pearl sweetheart, by the time me and Tonto came through it looked like they'd eaten about a billion of somethin' else and didn't fancy a dessert course,' he said, pointing back at the collapsed dollywhip. 'So I suppose I should thank you for that too.'

Rudy was looking at the man differently now, and his hostility was beginning to melt.

'Where did they take you when they separated us, Dad?'

'I can't tell you, Rudy. I have no idea,' Arlo replied. 'You remember it was a tunnel, right? And it was dark. Well after that I went way down to some place full of eggs, then someone hit me over the head and I was out. Next thing I knew, I woke up in a cage with all these other guys. We were told we would be riding these crazy insects for some show, and that we were definitely going to die. But hey, that was cool, because it would please the glorious leader,' he paused and grinned. 'So, I guess I decided to get the hell out of Dodge.'

Arlo Smoot stood staring at them all and held out his hands. 'Is that OK for yer?'

Rudy began to smile: it was OK for him.

'What's the square root of eighty-nine?' said Pearl.

'What?' laughed Arlo. 'Come on Pearl, what is this, the Spanish Inquisition?'

'Kind of,' she replied, only half-joking. 'OK then, fifty-three?'

'Fifty-three?'

'Why is three hundred and thirty special?'

'But—'

'And what is Schrödinger's cat?'

'Stop, stop, stop,' said Arlo holding up his hand. 'Pearl you know as well as I do that eighty-nine and fifty-three are both prime numbers, three hundred and thirty metres per second is the speed of sound, and as for Schrödinger's cat—do you think I have forgotten the first proof of quantum mechanics? Jeepers creepers, come on!'

That was enough. The next moment she ran forward and hugged him tight, and Rudy clung on to them both. It was a moment they had all waited for, for a long, long time.

'Said I'd find you, didn't I?' said Arlo, choking back his tears. 'Said I'd find you.'

Pearl shook her head in relief. She had never been so pleased to see him.

'You are one crazy man, Dad. One crazy man.'

Arlo patted her on the back, then saw Tom standing watching them. Tom smiled awkwardly, suddenly feeling that he was in some way intruding, but Arlo grinned and walked forward.

'I guess I need an introduction.'

'Oh yes, Dad,' said Rudy, excitedly, 'this is Tom.'

'Hi Tom,' said Arlo, shaking his hand.

'Tom Scatterhorn,' added Pearl. Arlo stared at the boy: his name was somehow familiar.

'Don't I know you from somewhere?'

'The book, Dad. Your notebook, remember?'

Arlo did remember. It was all starting to come back now, that whole bizarre story he had listened to over the airwaves.

'Tom Scatterhorn. Right. Tom Scatterhorn.'

'Tom was looking for his parents too. But we didn't find them. They weren't there.'

'Oh.'

Now that Arlo remembered the story he seemed a little surprised.

'Looks like you made a mistake, Dad.'

'Is that possible?' asked Tom. 'Do you make mistakes?'

Arlo studied the boy. He was tall for his age, and his dark, almost black eyes questioned him from beneath a mop of blond hair. It was a look so intense that it could almost have been frightening.

'Hell yes!' he shrugged breezily. 'I can't be right about everything. It's a big old world out there,' he smiled. 'What do I know?'

Tom seemed visibly relieved, and so did Arlo.

'Tom has done some pretty cool stuff, Dad,' said Rudy proudly, 'like psyching out a wolfskidder beetle and jumping on its back and spraying potions in its eyes and stuff like that. You know, cool stuff.'

Tom smiled at Rudy, a little embarrassed.

'That's not quite true, I never—'

'He has, actually,' said Pearl, enjoying Tom's discomfort. 'And much more besides. I'd never have gone down to Scarazand on my own. No way.'

Arlo looked at Tom.

'OK,' he said, beaming in admiration. 'Sounds like you're a bit of a hero.'

Tom shrugged awkwardly and smiled like an idiot. 'It's nothing. We both . . . '

But he never finished what he was attempting to say, as Arlo clasped him to him and hugged him hard.

'Thanks, kid.'

Tom felt the colour flood up to his cheeks: all this emotion, it was almost too much. Pearl and Rudy laughed as Tom was squeezed so tightly his feet lifted off the ground.

'I'm not sure Tom does all-American Smootster-hugs, Dad,' said Pearl.

'Well, there's a first time for everything,' chuckled Arlo, finally letting him go.

Tom grinned; actually it felt really nice.

'Erm . . . maybe you'd like to meet my great-great-great-uncle?' was all he could say, then somehow wished he hadn't.

'Sure,' said Arlo. 'It would be an honour.'

CHAPTER 24

AN EYE FOR AN EYE

After all the introductions and the explanations, suddenly everyone felt painfully hungry. Tom could not remember the last time he had even seen food, let alone eaten anything. With this in mind, Sir Henry and Trixie set out onto the reef with their spear guns, Pearl and Rudy went foraging in the woods, while Arlo and Tom busied themselves with a fire. Tom noticed that Arlo seemed keen to avoid any further discussion about his parents, preferring instead to swap stories about the extraordinary world of Scarazand. Soon Sir Henry and Trixie reappeared with half a dozen red snapper, Pearl and Rudy marched triumphantly out of the woods with armfuls of mangoes and pawpaw, and in no time at all they were sitting down to a feast washed down with clear coconut juice. At the end of it all Sir Henry marched across to his biplane and produced a surprise, a large bar of dark chocolate.

'For emergencies only!' he smiled, cracking off chunks and handing it round. 'But I think we've earned this.'

They sat munching it, staring at the flames in contented silence. The sun was setting now, and the white crescent of sand had turned into a dazzling pattern of blue and gold.

'Nearly time to go,' said Trixie, watching the bank of purple clouds building on the horizon. The occasional flash of lightning burst into the black sea.

'Are you sure you can squeeze us all in?' asked Arlo.

'Of course,' she smiled. 'And you're quite sure about going home?'

'Absolutely. That's right, isn't it, kids?'

Rudy nodded, but Pearl looked less certain.

'It is,' she said, 'but only on one condition.'

'A condition?'

'You never spy on those beetle people ever again.'

'Honey, you know I don't do rules,' he blustered. 'I'm not a suit. It's not in my genetic make up. In fact it's physically impossible. I can't even for one moment consider—' He glanced across to see that Pearl was deadly serious. 'Ah, hell's bells.'

'You promise?'

'OK. I promise.'

'Not even secretly?'

'Not even.'

Pearl held his gaze, and he hers.

'All right, it's a deal,' she said, winking at Tom. 'But there's another condition.'

'Oh is there now? Don't push your luck, missy,' snorted Arlo.

'You promise to take us over to England to see Tom and the Scatterhorn Museum someday.'

'Yeah!' shouted Rudy. 'The Scatterhorn Museum!' He paused. 'What is it?'

Arlo laughed, and so did they.

'It's a little museum over in England, that I founded over a hundred years ago. And it is really rather good, though I say so myself,' smiled Sir Henry.

'Do I have a choice?' asked Arlo.

'Not really,' grinned Pearl.

'OK. Whatever. You're on.'

Rudy whooped and ran around the fire, sending sparks flying.

'And you, Tom?' said Sir Henry. 'Do you want to go back to sunny Dragonport, old chum?'

Tom stared into the embers. Somehow, despite all the dangers, the idea of going back to his normal life seemed so boring and flat. It felt like having to go back to school.

'I'd like to see my mum and dad again,' he replied, which was about the only thing he could think of. 'So I suppose so.'

Sir Henry smiled kindly.

'I think you've got plenty to look forward to, old boy. Now that Mr Askary has got precisely what he wants I doubt he will ever darken your door again. Get on with your life is my advice. Forget all about him.'

Tom stared out at the billowing clouds piling up on the horizon: somehow he doubted that was possible.

'We really should go, you know,' said Trixie, standing up.

'Yes, you should. We all should,' said Sir Henry as the lightning flashed once more. 'There'll be plenty of openings in that little lot.'

'So we're going through a time hole?' asked Rudy excitedly.

'We most certainly are, kid,' replied Trixie, kicking out the embers. 'Shooting the gap between the thunder and lightning at full throttle. Maybe with a little twist, maybe a roll. You'll like it.'

Rudy beamed and Arlo stared up at the towering black clouds apprehensively.

'Isn't that dangerous?'

'After what you've just been through? Piece of cake Arlo,' grinned Sir Henry, glancing over to where the dollywhip lay floating in the shallows. It had finally given up the ghost.

'Actually, it rides better than it looks,' said Arlo.

'Evidently,' he smiled, 'I'll remember that next time I meet one.'

He turned and led the way over to the two biplanes parked side by side at the end of the beach. Arlo helped Rudy up onto a wing, then squeezed into the passenger seat beside him.

'See ya kid,' said Trixie, giving Tom a hug. 'Been a real pleasure meeting you at long last. You take good care of yourself now.'

'I will.'

'And don't whatever you do give them darn beetle people anything.'

'I won't,' grinned Tom, as she clambered up into the front and began to strap on her helmet.

'Bye then.'

Tom turned to see Pearl standing in the shallows. She had taken off her shoes.

'Bye.'

'I don't suppose you want these back?'

Tom looked at the old green trainers in her hand and shook his head sheepishly.

'Not really,' he said. 'You keep them.'

'Thanks.'

They stood awkwardly for a moment, not quite knowing what to say. They had been through so much together, it was hard to believe that they were both going back to their own normal lives.

'I really meant it, you know, what I said back then. I'd never have been brave enough to do this without you.'

Tom shrugged. 'Well I was looking for my parents, too. It was something we both had to do, wasn't it?'

'I guess.'

There was silence once more. The sun was just edging over the horizon now, and the sea was turning milky green. Lightning flashed insistently inside the black clouds behind them.

'I hope you find them.'

Tom nodded, and her pale blue eyes held his.

'You will, you know. My dad made a mistake, that's all.'

'I know.'

'So, I'll be in touch,' she said. 'I'll write.'

'Me too.'

'Come on Pearl!' shouted Arlo.

'Bye then, Tom,' she said, and with a small smile climbed up onto the wing. Then suddenly she thought better of it, and turning back, flung her arms around Tom and kissed him hard.

'Sorry,' she said, her cheeks turning crimson, 'just . . . had to do that.'

And then she climbed up into the plane.

'Woo!' shouted Rudy merrily. 'Did you see *that*!'

Tom stood in a daze as the engine started, his cheeks ablaze. That was just about the most exciting thing that had ever

AN EYE FOR AN EYE

happened to him. He was dimly aware of Pearl waving, and he
waved back, and suddenly the plane was trundling away down
the beach, gathering speed, and then it was up, off and banking
away towards the great purple mass of cloud.

'Looks like you've made a fan there,' laughed Sir Henry, patting Tom on the shoulder as he walked over to his plane. 'Gutsy
girl. Not afraid of anything. Always the best sort.'

Hauling himself up into the cockpit, he merrily slipped on his
helmet and goggles, and Tom walked round the wing beside him.
His cheeks were still on fire, but he had just about come back
down to his senses.

'So, you're going to join August?'

'I certainly am, old bean. If I can find him.'

'Where is he?'

'South. Somewhere about as far south as it is possible to go
without falling off the bottom of the world. He's been doing
some sleuthing you see, using old Arlo's notebook. Reckons
that's where we'll find old Nicholas Zumsteen.'

'Oh,' Tom nodded. He vaguely remembered Zumsteen saying
something about that, but he had been careful not to say exactly
where.

'Why are you looking for him?'

Sir Henry flicked a couple of switches pensively.

'August has a notion that he might be up to something. But
whether we can get any sense out of him . . . can't say I'm opti-
mistic. Zumsteen's a wild one, make no mistake, an absolute hell
raiser. His allegiances are . . . well, muddled, to say the least. Who
knows which side he's on, or what he wants.'

'What do you mean?'

Sir Henry stared at the last rays of the sun flaring gold on the horizon. Tom wondered whether he was going to confirm what he thought about Nicholas Zumsteen. Pulling on his helmet, he strapped it up tight.

'Didn't want to frighten the horses earlier, old boy, but this is not over yet. Not by a long shot. In fact, I am afraid that it's only just begun. I predict there are going to be some serious consequences to all of this. Seriously serious consequences.' Sir Henry fixed Tom with his quick eye. 'Our friend Mr Askary now holds all the cards, doesn't he? All of them. And it will take something, or someone, rather extraordinary to stop what has been set in motion.'

He pressed the starter motor, and the engine clattered to life.

'Is there anything I can do?' shouted Tom above the roar of the engine.

Sir Henry shook his head. 'Just keep calm and carry on!' he shouted. 'What will be will be, as they say. And when the time comes, who knows?'

Sir Henry carefully let off the brakes and the plane slowly began to accelerate down the beach. He raised his hand and waved.

'*Au revoir*, Tom!'

Tom stood alone on the empty beach, watching the biplane until it was a just a black speck melting into the purple clouds. He knew that Sir Henry was right, this *had* only just begun ... and for him, perhaps it would never end, as somewhere deep inside his brain there was now a part of him that was beetle. And what did that really mean? That his life would be short, or that some part of him would always be under the control of Don

Gervase Askary? Tom felt a cold knot of fear close around his heart: suddenly he felt more alone than ever.

'Ready to go, number three?'

There was the great eagle, shuffling awkwardly in the shadows at the edge of the sand.

'Only, you didn't seem so keen earlier.'

'No,' admitted Tom. He smiled. 'But I'm ready now.'

'Thought you might be,' rasped the bird. 'Party's over, ain't it?'

The bird bent down stiffly and Tom slid onto its giant back. The warm feathers felt strangely comforting, and in a few ungainly steps and a flap of its massive wings they were airborne.

'So you know the way?'

'Not *the* way, cos there's crinkles and crankles everywhere, particularly in tropical storms. Which is where my mate comes in,' it said, as the swallow dived ahead of them, cheeping noisily. 'He can spot the angles.'

The eagle ascended higher and higher, and soon the atoll was just a small white ring surrounded by the dark ocean. Night was coming on fast, and slipping over the top of the heavy grey rain they swung through a gap in the clouds into a completely different landscape. Here everything was a tumbling, pillowy mass of purple and deep blue. Occasionally there was a fearful bang and the whole prospect lit up from within.

'There's one!' shouted the bird, nodding to the left. Already the swallow was diving down fast, and Tom craned forward as much as he dared. There was another ominous rumble of thunder, and in the split second of lightning he saw something spinning below . . . red skyscrapers, glittering glass domes . . . an airborne city at night . . . The swallow swept up again twittering about the eagle's head.

'Wrong time wrong place, mate!' he shouted. 'Close but no cigar!'

Tom barely had time to wonder what that strange world was before the swallow darted on, skimming over cliffs and ridges into the heart of the storm. The thunderclaps and lightning were bursting left and right, above, below; Tom pressed himself into the eagle's neck and prayed they wouldn't be next.

'He's got it!' shouted the bird. Tom raised his head as high as he dared and saw the black speck dropping like an arrow, and the next second they were diving after it at colossal speed. The wind screamed and they shot straight into the wall of air . . .

BANG!

A flash of white light—and then . . . streetlights . . . cranes . . . the dark estuary below . . . Dragonport.

'Now that's what I call a welcome committee!' yelled the bird.

Below them a carnival was in full swing, there were stalls and bands and people everywhere. The end of the Dragonport festival, thought Tom, his heart still galloping. That had been so exciting he wanted to go and do it again.

'Well I'll be blowed, look who it is!' said the bird, falling in behind a small red motorbike and sidecar weaving drunkenly down the road. There were Jos and Melba, and even from up here Tom could hear them singing.

'Reckon they're going home, mate. Shall I drop you back at the museum, like in the good old days?'

Tom nodded. 'Why not?'

Slowly, silently, they glided down over the wet rooftops and swept around the turrets of the Scatterhorn Museum before clattering to a halt on the roof above Tom's old window. Slithering off the bird's back, Tom nudged the frame with his foot and found that with a little persuasion it opened just enough for him to slip inside.

'Right Tom, me old mucker,' declared the bird, 'looks like we're done.'

'Looks like we are,' replied Tom, smiling up at its permanently angry face. 'So where are you going now?'

'Walkabout,' it growled. 'But first I'm in dire need of a repairist. Have you seen the state of this?' it said, turning in an ungainly circle on the roof.

Tom grinned: on reflection the great bird did look even more motley than ever. Half the feathers were missing from its head, its grey feathered ruff was hanging off its neck and one of its wings was full of holes.

'Now don't you giggle, mate, it's a touchy subject. Tusslin' with weird creatures is doin' nothin' for me vanity.'

'OK,' said Tom, stifling a smile. 'Will you be back?'

'Well that all depends, doesn't it?'

'On what?'

The bird fixed him with its quick yellow eye.

'I ain't one to blab, but put it this way: we ain't seen the last of each other, you an' me.'

Tom nodded ruefully; somehow he had expected the eagle to say that.

'I just wish,' he began, 'I wish I could do something more. I just feel so . . . I dunno.'

Helpless was the word Tom was searching for, but he didn't
care to admit it.

The eagle shrugged.

'Just be yourself, mate. What more can you do? No point getting yer knickers in a twist about it. Yes all right, we've lost a few
battles, but when it comes to the crunch, you an' me's gonna be
there, ain't we?'

'Are we?'

'Course we are! We's survivors, mate. Lucky. Born sunny side
up and no mistake.'

Tom wished he could share the eagle's optimism, but somehow he couldn't.

'Remember where I've been,' it rasped enigmatically, and let
out a long, strange call. The black speck of the swallow darted
out of the darkness. 'And look after that crazy head of yours,' it
added with a wink, and clattered away.

Tom watched the great bird soar out over the estuary: what
was it talking about, did it know what had happened to him?
Perhaps it did, it had been to the future after all . . . Flinging himself onto his musty old bed in the corner, Tom pulled the rough
blanket over him and stared up at the peeling wallpaper. He felt
strangely empty now it was all over, but also angry that it
wasn't. Life was definitely not going to be the same again, how
could it be? This strange world had invaded his world, he was
connected to it now—inside. A cark beetle lived for three
months only . . . Tom shuddered; was that really all the time he
had left? And then there was the small matter of Arlo Smoot's
notebook. Try as he might, he had been unable to believe Arlo
when he said he had got it wrong about his parents. Arlo was

496

only trying to be nice, to make him feel better; he knew it. And that could only mean one thing: if Tom hadn't betrayed them yet, then somehow he was going to betray them in the future . . . It wasn't cold, but the stark realization of this crept up over him like frost. Bundling himself up into a shivering ball, Tom turned to face the wall. He closed his eyes: to his immense relief, there was no red wave, no pulse, just plain, empty darkness. Sighing deeply, he fell asleep.

''Allo?'

Silence.

'Anyone up there?'

Tom opened his eyes groggily to see clouds scudding across a brilliant blue sky. The wind was blowing the threadbare curtains this way and that.

'No?'

Ern Rainbird was thumping around below, obviously starting his morning round. Tom turned over and tried to go back to sleep but found he couldn't. What day was it? He rubbed his face wearily. If last night was the end of the Dragonport festival, that meant today must be the last day of the summer holidays. Tomorrow he was going back to school. His parents were coming to pick him up today. And after everything he had been through, he certainly couldn't wait to see them. As long as they *were* coming back . . . They must be. He'd better get up. Hauling himself stiffly out of bed, Tom made his way over to the door and found it wouldn't open. Pulling at it, he could hear a padlock rattling on the other side. Of course, it was locked: Ern

Rainbird had closed it up after Pearl's break in. How annoying. He would have to go all the way round. Taking a deep breath, Tom pushed open the window, and a minute later he was standing outside the front entrance in the windy street. Wearily, he leant against the heavy oak door, feeling as if he had done enough clambering and jumping to last a lifetime.

'Gordon Bennett!'

Ern Rainbird was standing in the centre of the main hall, staring at Tom in astonishment. 'You nearly frightened the living daylights out of me then.'

'Hi,' said Tom, just about managing a smile. Ern stared at him curiously.

'Been away, have you, son?'

'Something like that.'

Ern's freckled, bony face glowered with obvious disapproval.

'Nice trip?'

Tom was just awake enough to remember that Ern Rainbird was not to be trusted. Not one little bit.

'Yes, as it happens.'

Ern whistled through his teeth.

'Well your parents are due back this morning so I suppose you've got yer cover story sorted. Cos I sure as hell don't know what to tell 'em. Where you's bin gallivantin' is not my concern.'

Tom felt a wave of excitement rush through him. 'Thanks.'

Ern grunted and went back to his floorsweeping.

'Do you know what time they're expected?'

'First thing, so yer uncle said. Hence yours truly is here at sparrow's fart getting this place tiptop and Bristol fashion,' he spat.

'Some of us have to work for a livin', y'know.' Ern stopped and nodded towards the dark office door. 'Yer post's in there by the way—not that you'll want it, mind. Bills, bills, bills.' Ern cackled to himself, and brushed his way into the gloom.

Tom scratched his head and wondered what to do. The excitement of seeing his parents so soon was tempered by the prospect of having to spend an hour listening to Ern Rainbird's long list of whinges, and he decided to take himself off into the office until they arrived. Wandering around the African diorama, Tom carefully closed the door and saw the large pile of brown envelopes neatly stacked up on the desk. Idly he rummaged through the pile, until he came to a large brown envelope that said 'private and confidential' on the front, covered in exotic South American stamps. It looked vaguely official, but something about that writing was familiar . . . Carefully Tom opened the envelope and pulled out an old-fashioned bill. It was headed *'Bogie and Khan, chemicals, lead, and rope suppliers,'* and the price was $71. Bogie and Khan? But there was writing on the back: long, spidery, familiar writing . . .

'August,' breathed Tom, and his heart quickened. Hungrily he began to read.

My dear Tom,
Apologies for the curious stationery: a bill from Bogie and Khan is probably the very last thing you were expecting, but they have very kindly been putting me up, and disguise is the order of the day. As you have probably heard by now, after you all left I received a visitation from a horde of very unpleasant characters, led by that

veritable banshee Lotus Askary, who succeeded in burning the house down.

Luckily that was all; my library was untouched—it flew away in the nick of time, and with the timely arrival of Sir Henry and Trixie I was spirited away too, to a place just about as far south as it is possible to go without falling off the bottom of the world. I'm afraid I can't be more specific, for reasons you will fully appreciate, but while twiddling my thumbs in this godforsaken place I have been reminded of something rather important.

A certain bird has informed me that the Scatterhorn Museum has recently acquired some rather dramatic tableaux from Hellkiss Hall. This, of course, is not news to you, but it is to me. You see, I happen to know that one of them, a terrifically vulgar scene entitled 'The Deluge' has been tampered with. During its long years of exile in Hellkiss Hall it was 'restored' by a bunch of so called 'taxidermists', who knew about as much about the business as a shoal of fish.

Dear old Oscarine Zumsteen warned me something was up, so I made a surreptitious call while they had it in pieces, and of course she was right. These so called restorers had placed a 'gift' inside it—I recognized it immediately. I suspect it was intended as a surprise for the master of the house, should he ever return—and I confess this annoyed me considerably. So after a little careful calculation, I waited till they were done, then rather cheekily added some calling cards of my own. Hidden inside some wood pulp—'within' their gift, so to speak. I'm sorry to be so *obscure, but I wouldn't want someone to read this and give the game away. The long and the short of it is that my calling cards are due to hatch at nine twenty-one a.m. on the first of September. Theirs, I suspect, will be marginally before. Thought you might like to know, as even though mine have been in there for nigh on seventeen years, their arrival is likely to be very precise indeed. I hope this vaguely makes sense—Good luck!*

    Yours affectionately,

    August Catcher

Tom stared at the spidery handwriting, trying to take it all in. It sounded as if there was some kind of parasite hidden inside The Deluge, and those so-called restorers were working for Don Gervase, laying a trap for Nicholas Zumsteen. Then something that Lotus had said floated up out of his memory, something about The Deluge being an interesting surprise . . . could this be what she had meant? Possibly, but what was so significant about the first of September? Tom glanced at the clock on the wall and swallowed hard. He hadn't realized, but today *was* the first of September. And it was almost nine'o clock. In twenty minutes, something was going to happen . . .

Throwing down the letter, he strode anxiously out into the dark hall. He could hear footsteps and a voice filtering down from the East Wing: it sounded like someone giving a tour. Maybe it was Uncle Jos, showing someone around, perhaps it was even his mum and dad and they had arrived already . . . yes, maybe . . . Tom hurried across to the stairs and leapt up the steps two at a time.

'Hello?' he called out, passing the tiger crouching in its alcove and sweeping around the balcony towards the far end.

'Unc—'

Click!

The sharp sound pierced the gloom. Tom stopped dead in his tracks and looked down towards the door.

'Ern?'

Tom's voice echoed away into the heavy silence. That sounded very much like the lock on the front door turning. It sounded as if Ern had locked them in. Why would he do that? Something strange was going on here . . . Steeling himself, Tom walked on to the entrance to the East Wing and peered around the corner. There were the tableaux of the Hellkiss Collection standing motionless in the half-light. At the far end he could make out the tumbling mass of animals plunging down the cliff. Seeing The Deluge again, Tom was struck by how realistic it now looked. Every detail of the animals' wild stampede was vividly precise: it was almost like a photograph of the real thing.

'Hello?'

There was no reply. Tom's heart began to gallop: where had they gone?

'Uncle Jos?'

Silence.

'Mum? Da—'

Suddenly Tom felt as if he had been hit over the head by a hammer. He was thrown to the floor, dazed, and before he had a chance to stand up again another burst of energy slammed him over onto his back. Tom fought for breath, his whole body tingling as pulses of electricity thumped through him, one after another. The air had turned black.

'Come here,' hissed a voice, burning in his head. 'HERE!' it screamed.

Tom writhed and skidded on his back across the floor, until he was lying directly beneath the plunging black rhinoceros.

'That's better.'

Tom fought the pain and forced himself to open his eyes. The room was spinning, throbbing with every pulse, and leaning nonchalantly against the rhino was the dim silhouette of a very tall, narrow man with a dome-like head and yellowish skin. In one hand he held the beetle ball between his fingers.

'Remarkable,' said Don Gervase to himself, 'so accurate. I must be getting better at this.'

'What . . . what do you want?' gasped Tom.

Don Gervase stared at him in disgust.

'Did you really think you could get away with it, you and your brave little band of friends and their amateur heroics? What fun it must have been. What an adventure! All the way to Scarazand—and back again. Do you have any idea who you are dealing with?'

Don Gervase's finger caressed the ball, and another iron pulse slammed through Tom, burning his head inside. He curled up like a baby, trying to hide from the pain.

'Oh yes,' he smirked, 'I know that my little cark beetle has done its damage, not nearly enough perhaps, but it will suffice. I know what you are feeling now, boy, because there is a part of you that is like me.'

Don Gervase glowered at Tom quivering on the floor beneath

him. Such a shame he couldn't kill him right now and be done with it, but for a few minutes longer he needed him alive.

'Get up,' he shrieked. 'Up I said!'

Tom was shaking uncontrollably as he staggered to his feet. Despite his jangling nerves he was thinking desperately, thinking of a way out. Don Gervase glared at him in silence.

'I want to know something,' he said quietly. 'You will answer truthfully, if you value your life. Do you understand?'

Tom said nothing, his eyes fixed on the ball twisting in Don Gervase's fingers.

'It has come to my attention that you did indeed meet Nicholas Zumsteen on the island of Tithona. Is this true?'

Tom shrugged his shoulders.

'Well it is. A certain Geronimo da Piedad has confirmed it. We have him, by the way, and with a little persuasion he has told us many things. He has helped us significantly.'

'Then why are you asking me?' grunted Tom belligerently.

Don Gervase's voice dropped even lower.

'Careful, boy. Do not provoke me.' He paused, dangerously. 'You saw Zumsteen packing his rucksack. What did he put in it?'

'I don't know!' snorted Tom, amazed by the question. 'Loads of things.'

'Like what? Think carefully.'

Tom desperately tried to remember back to the night in the tree house, and what it might be that Don Gervase wanted to know . . . could he lie? He could try . . .

'Pistols.'

'And? What else?'

'Food, telescope, mosquito net, I don't know, just stuff—'

Don Gervase's fingers stroked the ball minutely, and suddenly Tom felt a roar of pain behind his eyes, and the room swam once more.

'Think harder,' said Don Gervase absently.

'Pills . . . ' mumbled Tom, his mouth somehow moving without him, 'sacks of white pills . . . like eggs . . . like pearls.'

Don Gervase smiled. 'Good. Interesting. Better. And how many of these white pearls were there?'

Tom covered his head in his hands, trying to find a way out. Hot wires seemed to be passing right through his skull.

'I don't know. Hundreds maybe. Please . . . stop this.'

Don Gervase ignored him. 'And did he tell you where he was taking this little hoard?'

Tom began to shake his head, but already there was nothing he could do . . . the pain was too much.

'South . . . ' he murmured, 'somewhere they can't get you . . . ice . . . snow . . . '

'The Antarctic, is that what he said?' demanded Don Gervase. Tom mumbled incoherently.

'IS IT!' he screamed.

Another pulse hit Tom and he crumpled back down onto the floor. The walls of darkness were closing in now. Sweat poured down his cheeks.

'I think so. I don't know.'

Don Gervase glared at the boy viciously: he seemed to be telling the truth. How could he fight against it? The pain and noise would be more than anyone could stand. A fully converted cark beetle would be dead by now.

'Very well, boy, I believe you,' he said with a smirk. 'Thank you for being so accommodating.'

Tom opened his eyes groggily. He was vaguely aware of Don Gervase standing before the vast tumble of animals of the Hellkiss tableaux.

'Really remarkable, isn't it?' he grinned. 'I can't help but admire Catcher's genius, despite everything. Shame that it will soon be no longer.' He glanced at his watch impatiently, then back at Tom lying spread-eagled on the floor. A cruel smile spread across his lips. 'Seventeen minutes past nine. Do you know what day it is today?'

Tom nodded thickly.

'It is the first of September. My birthday. And it is also Nicholas Zumsteen's birthday, too. What a coincidence. Now, many years ago I had hoped he might be having a little party in Hellkiss Hall to celebrate. This was going to be my present to him. A little gift, from his long lost bro—' Don Gervase checked himself, then grinned, wolfishly. Ah, what did it matter what the boy knew? He was as good as dead already.

'You will have to receive it instead. Which pleases me some-what: all our efforts have not been entirely in vain.'

He bent down to examine the boy who had given him so much trouble, his yellow eyes bulging with spite.

'No schoolboy bravery is going to save you this time, Tom Scatterhorn,' he whispered. 'Goodbye.'

Tom lay spread-eagled on the floor, listening to Don Gervase's sharp footsteps clattering out of the gallery behind him. He breathed slowly, deeply, and the waves of pain and noise began to recede into the distance. Tom was sure he had never felt such agony in his life, and never wanted to again, ever. Opening his eyes, he stared dizzily at the tumble of animals plunging down towards him. The whole construction seemed to be quivering, trembling almost . . . Tom blinked hard, and forced himself up onto his elbows, trying to focus . . . it *was* moving, he wasn't imagining it—the whole tableaux was starting to sway like a tree . . .

SNAP! Snap-snap-snap!

Tom's heart leapt in his throat as suddenly the massive grey body of the rhinoceros burst open, revealing straw and stuffing underneath, and its charging head began ripping apart . . .

'CRACK!'

The rhinoceros split in two, and the next moment every lion and hyena and giraffe and lemur and bear and parrot and snake came tumbling out of the air and smashing to the floor. Bang bang bang bang . . . the rolling thunder echoed around the gallery, and Tom lay transfixed, his mouth wide open. There, in place of the rhinoceros, stood a large, red, oily creature, staring at him with beady grey eyes. It was something like a beetle, with short serrated mandibles and a jagged horn. Before he could stop himself Tom began violently pushing back with his feet, trying to get away, and the hideous creature sensed his movement. Instantly Tom froze, his heart drumming a crazy rhythm in his temples. That was a big, big mistake—but it was already too late. The creature dashed forward and loomed over him menacingly. Tom gasped as he saw its small red jaws, grinding this way and that between its black lips. Lowering its great jagged horn, the beetle poked at him roughly, shunting him along the floor. Then it bent its head and peered at him curiously. Closer and closer it came, until he could feel its short antennae brushing his cheek, smell its oily flesh . . . Tom closed his eyes: this was it, this was—

Somewhere far away, two men on a dogsledge swept into a snowbound valley.

'Halloo!' shouted the driver, and hauled on the reins, bringing the dogs to a panting halt.

'Is that it?' he said.

The other man pulled down his thick fur hood and studied the scene. Everything in the valley was silent and still, the snow sparkling in the moonlight. Out in the centre, on what appeared to be a frozen lake, the silhouette of a ship lay on its side. Something like a vast frozen seasnake coiled around it, binding it to the ice.

'I'd say so,' said the man on the sledge grimly, his breath steaming in the cold night air. 'Now then,' he puffed, delving deep into his fur coat and pulling out a brass fob watch. 'Regarding that other matter, if I've got my timings right, I predict it will all start happening . . . ' he squinted at the pale watchface in the moonlight. 'Very shortly indeed.'

The second hand was moving up towards the hour.

'Five, four, three, two . . .

Tom stared at one large grey eye centimetres from his own. He could see its ridges and contours, all the weird detail of the beetle's spiky, alien head . . . he was waiting for it to attack . . .

waiting, waiting . . . and then, quite suddenly, the beetle appeared to freeze solid. It just stopped moving.

Somewhere down below, the door rattled, then a key scraped in the lock.

'Tom, we're back!' shouted a familiar voice. 'Tom?'

But Tom was transfixed: he could not speak—he could barely move. Everywhere above him the shining red armour was starting to swell and stretch and snap. Tom gasped: it was like looking down a microscope at some strange metamorphosis as the beetle, like the rhinoceros before it, began to break apart. Sliding away on his back he saw one of the beetle's eyes pop out and quite suddenly a long yellow insect emerged from the socket. It was a cicada. Then another, and another, and then the other eye popped open and more began to appear, crawling through the gap and flying up and away into the gallery.

'Tom, is that you?'

The footsteps were coming closer.

'Hello! Tom? Where are you?'

Tom's mother appeared at the doorway and stopped dead. Her mouth fell open in astonishment.

'What . . . what on earth is that?'

Splits appeared in the shiny red carapace, and streams of cicadas were fluttering away in all directions.

'It's called "The Deluge". A biblical scene of high drama, and quite without doubt the fanciest piece of taxidermy ever made,' wheezed Jos, puffing up the stairs behind her. 'Breathtaking, isn't it? Absolutely, completely—'

Jos stopped in mid-sentence.

The Deluge was no longer. Before the great dark wave lay a

heap of animals, strewn across the floor. At the centre, where the rhinoceros had once stood, there was a vast and quite hideous red beetle. And it was hollow. Out of its eyes and head and shell streams of yellow cicadas were escaping, filling the gallery like confetti. The air was so thick with them that the noise was deafening. Jos could do nothing more than squeak helplessly.

'*Magicicada septendecim*. Well, well, that is a surprise,' said the gaunt blond man who had followed them in. 'What have you been up to?'

Tom pulled himself to his feet and turned around. It was his parents, and he had never been so happy to see them.

The man on the dogsledge flipped the glass back over his watch, and slipped it inside his furs.

'Do you think it really worked?'

'When has it not, August old bean?' replied Sir Henry, patting him on the back. 'Come on, let's see where that rapscallion Nick Zumsteen has got to.'

And with a crack of his whip, he drove the sledge down the moonlit valley towards the frozen ship . . .

Photo credit: Chloe Stewart

Henry Chancellor has spent many years of his life making documentary films, which have taken him all over the world, meeting some very peculiar people in some very peculiar places. Some of these films have won awards. He has also written a couple of factual books: *Colditz: The Definitive History,* (based on his Channel Four series) and *James Bond: the Man and his World*. *The Hidden World* is the second book in his Tom Scatterhorn trilogy. He lives in Suffolk with his wife, three children, two cats, and several other animals.

FIND OUT HOW TOM'S ADVENTURES BEGAN IN

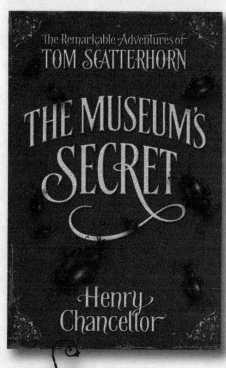

The Remarkable Adventures of
TOM SCATTERHORN

THE MUSEUM'S SECRET

Henry Chancellor